Charles Wallace French

Abraham Lincoln, the Liberator

A Biographical Sketch

Charles Wallace French

Abraham Lincoln, the Liberator
A Biographical Sketch

ISBN/EAN: 9783337099046

Printed in Europe, USA, Canada, Australia, Japan

Cover: Foto ©Raphael Reischuk / pixelio.de

More available books at **www.hansebooks.com**

ABRAHAM LINCOLN

The Liberator

A BIOGRAPHICAL SKETCH

"Lincoln, the man who freed the slave"

BY

CHARLES WALLACE FRENCH

~~~~~~~~~

FUNK & WAGNALLS
NEW YORK

LONDON   TORONTO
1891

PREFACE.

BIOGRAPHICAL writings in general may be divided into two distinct classes. The first, which may be called the objective class, is made up of those works which regard the individual as only a factor in the world's progress. They narrate more or less faithfully the important events in his life, and trace their connection with, and influence upon, the life and thought of the age. Thus the life of the individual becomes a chapter in universal history. Such works may have great historic value but if they go no further they lack the essential element of true biography.

The works of the second, or subjective class, deal no less carefully with facts and environments not as finalities, but as manifestations of character. Through the deed they seek to know the doer and to trace his moral and intellectual growth. The writer studies the life of the individual as closely as the botanist studies the development of a strange plant, and for the same purpose. The scientist cares little for the leaves and flowers, simply as leaves and flowers, but rather as exponents of the life and habits of the plant. So the true biographer would read a man's character in his deeds, calling attention to its weaknesses that other men may be warned, and exalting its virtues that they may excite the emulation of mankind.

The career of Lincoln is so closely interwoven with the great events that make up the nation's history in the most critical period of its existence, that the temptation is strong to dwell more upon his deeds and

environments, than upon himself. Therefore, many
of his biographies fall within the first class, notably
the larger and more pretentious works, which are but
little more than histories in which the great President
figures as the principal hero.

On the other hand, his personality was so unique and
attractive that it forces itself into prominence even in
histories of the period. Probably no character in
history offers a more tempting field for research, and
yet few are more difficult to comprehend. Previous
to his election to the Presidency, no one believed him
to be possessed of the elements of greatness, and during his whole life he had few if any friends who fully
appreciated his character. Many of his acts were
misunderstood and his most intimate friends sometimes distrusted him. It is not strange, then, that his
biographies are too often one-sided and inaccurate.
Indeed, it is doubtful if it is possible even yet, to make
a complete and just analysis of his many-sided character. It is much easier to relate what he said and
did, than to correctly describe the man himself as he
was.

It is probable that generations may pass before his
true biography can be written. Certain it is that sufficient time must pass to dim the memory of the great
events of the Civil War, and to obscure the bright
light in which they stand to-day. Events lessen in
importance as they recede into the past, but great
characters shine the brighter as the ages roll on.

Meantime, the character of Lincoln must be regarded as one of the most precious possessions of the
American people, precious not only as a cherished
memory, but also as a living power, influencing life

and character to-day no less strongly than when he was yet alive.

The multiplication of his biographies, then, cannot be deplored since each one must present his life from a different, and, to some extent, novel point of view ; and each new book must add to the great circle of readers and help to extend an influence which is as beneficent as it is powerful.

The historic field has been so thoroughly searched that few new facts can be procured. The material has been practically exhausted and the most enterprising biographer can only hope to present familiar facts in a new form and with different lights and shadows.

The author has no excuse for adding this simple work to the long list of biographies already in existence beyond that of a deep reverence and love for the great man, "who, though dead, yet speaketh." And if a single reader shall obtain a truer appreciation of his character, and a deeper love for the country whose altar was stained with the blood of so noble a sacrifice, the effort will not have been made in vain.

CHICAGO, *January* 30, 1891.

CONTENTS.

vii

ABRAHAM LINCOLN.

CHAPTER I.

THE attention of an observer, who stands upon the seashore, and surveys the changing surface of the deep, is not attracted so much by the mighty mass of waters spread out before him, as by the waves which lift their crests high in the air, as if to assert their individuality and power, and then dash themselves upon the beach in the vain attempt to burst through the barriers which confine them.

So, in studying the history of past ages, the attention of the student is not attracted by the masses of the people, who have inhabited the earth during any given period, but rather by the individuals, who, by their genius, heroism or devotion to principle, have towered above the dead level of humanity and performed deeds or perpetuated institutions of which the memory and influence have become immortal. It is such men as these who, by directing the giant forces of society, government and religion, have made history. Thus all history must be, to a large extent, biographical, for it is the record of the thoughts and deeds, not of the many, but of the few who have played the principal parts in the great drama of life.

There are many men who have secured renown by their achievements, but comparatively few have been so fortunate as to have their names linked with the triumph of a great principle over opposing forces.

There are multitudes of great generals, who have conquered empires, or conducted glorious military campaigns. The annals of time teem with the names of statesmen and philosophers who have formed and directed governments and institutions, or opened up hidden treasures of knowledge. But the number is small of those who have been instrumental in instituting great moral or political reforms. Yet there are some names that always suggest the great movements with which they are connected and with which they have become almost synonymous. Thus the history of religious reform centres around the lives of such men as Luther, Huss, Wickliffe and Wesley; while Cromwell, Mirabeau and Washington are always identified with the cause of popular freedom against tyranny and oppression. And no less intimately are the names of Wilberforce, Alexander and Lincoln identified with the cause of. personal liberty.

The careers of most of these men have passed into the domain of history, and it is possible to estimate their character and influence, unbiased by the glamor of their achievements or the sentiment inspired by their personality in those who came into contact with them. But this is not true of Lincoln. The generation, which witnessed his deeds, has not passed off the stage, and there are men still living who have clasped his hand and felt the charm of his presence. Future generations may arrive at a true estimate of his character, but those who have lived in the same century with him can never do so.

An observer at the base of a mountain can see the rocks, trees and precipices and note the solidity and ruggedness of the great mass, but in order to form a just estimate of its symmetry and majesty, he must take his position at a distance so great as to render the minor details invisible.

So it is with any man who has achieved a history for himself. Those who stand within the circle of his life are too near to take the measure of his character and influence.

It matters little what shall be the verdict of history in the case of Abraham Lincoln. Whether it shall rank him as the foremost American and the peer of the world's greatest men, or only as a patient, faithful toiler, who was suddenly raised to a position of high responsibility, and who triumphed over the difficulties of the place by hard common-sense and painstaking industry, but not by the brilliancy of genius, which is commonly considered to be the essence of such success. The great fact must still be recognized that he saved the country from a peril that threatened her very existence ; and that he inspired and encouraged a burdened people, in the midst of a terrible civil war, by his own indomitable energy and unwavering faith in ultimate success. Whatever future ages may say, the American people will always regard him as a national benefactor, and will inscribe his name high up beside that of Washington, the two heroes whom a grateful country most delights to honor.

When the Romans conquered Britain, they both

established a military supremacy over it and also introduced their own manners and customs, locating colonies, founding cities and leaving the impress of their civilization upon the lives and character of the native inhabitants.

Among their many prosperous colonies was one which they called Lin Colonia, located in the fertile country between the River Humber and the Wash. This old Roman colony has developed into a prosperous county, the largest, save one, in England. But its name, Lincoln, is to-day the only reminder of its ancient founders.

While it is easy to ascertain the origin of the name, it is impossible to trace the lineage of the modern Lincoln family back to it. Yet it is certain that the great war President was descended from one of the sturdy, Lincolnshire families, who have done so much to develop the English character of to-day.

In 1638, or thereabouts, one Samuel Lincoln emigrated with his family from the county of Norfolk, Eng., to Massachusetts, where he settled in the little town of Hingham. From this pioneer settler in the new world the various Lincoln families, scattered over the country, are probably descended. These early Lincolns were a devout people and earnest students of the Bible. For a number of generations their children were named after some of the Old Testament heroes, many of them bearing such names as Mordecai, Abraham, Isaac and Jacob.

Samuel's eldest son, Mordecai, removed to New Jersey and thence to Pennsylvania, where he accumulated a large property. Upon his death one of his sons, John, received, as his share of the inheritance, an estate in Virginia, to which he removed, where he developed into a prosperous planter, and was blessed with a large family of children.

At this time but little was known of the imperial domain which stretched out in an unbroken wilderness of prairies, forests and mountains from the Alleghanies to the Pacific. A few venturous pioneers had entered the wilderness, where attracted by the fertility of the soil and the boundless resources of the country, they had formed small settlements. The lives they led were laborious and full of danger, for they were compelled to contend not only with want and hardship, but also with the savages who roamed about in large numbers.

The career of Daniel Boone had just begun in Kentucky, and it is probable that he was a personal friend of the Lincolns, and that, induced by his glowing descriptions of that land of promise, Abraham, John's eldest son, with his wife and five children, decided to emigrate to a place where it was possible to obtain a great estate for a nominal price. He soon selected a location in Mercer County, and pre-empted a claim, afterwards, at various times, securing possession of tracts of land, which amounted in all to 1,800 acres. He thus obtained a splendid estate, which, with its fertile valleys and thickly wooded hill-sides, would have enriched his descendants could they have retained possession of it.

The labor of clearing the land and rendering it fit for cultivation was great. A heavy growth of trees, obstructed by dense undergrowth, covered much of the ground, all of which must be cut away and burned, and the land thoroughly worked before seed could be sown and harvest gathered. Nor were these natural difficulties the only ones that assailed the pioneers. The blue grass regions were among the most highly prized hunting-grounds of the Indians, and different tribes were continually contending for their possession. Hence they regarded the whites with savage hatred, who were striving to dispossess them of their lands.

The settlers were thus compelled to be constantly upon the alert. The rifle and the spade were inseparable companions, where every stump might conceal a savage foe, or every unwary move bring a tomahawk hurtling through the air, thrown with unerring aim. Courage and persistence of purpose alone could enable men to overcome such difficulties and labor on in the almost hopeless attempt to convert the wilderness into productive farms and prosperous communities. Many men were overwhelmed by their discouraging surroundings, and, not possessing the requisite means to return to their former homes, settled back into a wretched existence, doing just enough to keep the wolf, real and figurative, from the door, fretting and repining throughout their miserable lives at the fate that had brought so much evil upon them. This class increased in numbers with increasing population, and came to bear about the same relation to society, as the "poor whites" of later days. Into this class of unfortunates many of the descendants of the well-to-do Lincoln family relapsed.

Aside from a number of wandering hunters and trappers, but few people had entered the country up to this time ; but now a migratory instinct seemed to seize the families along the borders, and large num-

bers entered " the dark and bloody grounds," to settle there permanently. Yet the settlements were
widely separated, and communication was difficult
between them.

The Lincolns built a rude log-cabin in the midst
of a clearing, upon or near the site of the present city
of Louisville, and began their exhaustive labors of
taming the wilderness and gaining a living from it.
A few years afterwards, while at work with his sons
a short distance from the house, Mr. Lincoln was shot
and instantly killed by an Indian, who had been hidden in the bushes. When Mordecai, the eldest son,
saw his father fall, he ran to the house, seized his rifle,
and shot the Indian while he was attempting to scalp
the dead man, aiming at a medal on his breast. Thus
the head of the family was taken away, and the boys
were compelled to take the burden of the farm and
family upon their own shoulders.

The youngest, Thomas, was a lad of seven when his
father was murdered, and barely escaped capture at
the hands of the Indians at that time. He grew up
into a typical hunter, poor and thriftless, yet brave,
good-natured and honest. He is said to have been
an inveterate talker and to have been accustomed to
embellish his conversation with numerous stories and
anecdotes, which always gained him an appreciative
audience, whenever he entered the frontier settlements.

He partially learned the carpenter's trade, and
sometimes worked at it, but never continued long in
any occupation or place. He was noted for his physical strength, and though not anxious to exhibit it,
when aroused, he was capable of performing almost

incredible feats. At one time he is said to have
" thrashed the bully of Breckenridge County in three
minutes, and come off without a scratch."

Many of the great Lincoln's prominent traits of
character may be traced to this lazy, good-natured
Hercules of the Kentucky backwoods.

At the age of twenty-eight, he was married to
Nancy Hanks, a tall and beautiful brunette. She was
ambitious and proud, but her spirit was soon broken
by the hardships she was compelled to endure, and
her strength undermined by unceasing toil. They
settled first in Elizabethtown, in a small rudely built
house, where the young husband hoped to earn a living by working at his trade. He found this a difficult task and soon removed to a little farm in La Rue
County, which he had bought on credit, agreeing to
pay for it in instalments. The struggle that the
young couple had entered upon, was a hard one. The
land was rocky and barren, both difficult to cultivate
and unproductive, hardly yielding sufficient to supply
their immediate wants, and leaving no margin to assist in raising the debt.

Mrs. Lincoln proved to be an efficient helper to her
inefficient husband. When her housework was done,
she worked at his side with hoe or axe till sunset, or
shouldered a gun and entered the forest in search of
game to add to their scanty stock of provisions. She
was able to read and write, an unusual accomplishment among the pioneer families, but she lacked both
time and means to gratify her taste in this direction, so that they became almost forgotten accomplishments. Yet her taste made their little log-cabin,
with its rude furnishings, far more attractive than the

dwellings of their neighbors, and had she lived amid more favorable surroundings, she would, no doubt, have become a refined and cultured woman.

In the midst of such surroundings as these, and in the most abject poverty, Abraham Lincoln was born on the 12th day of February, 1809. Never was hero brought into this world under more inauspicious circumstances. There was, in the lonely life of the Lincoln family, no hint of the glory, which was to crown their name and draw the attention of the world to their humble cabin. Nor did it seem possible that, amid such surroundings and privations, a child could be born and nurtured, whose hand in after-life should wield the fate of a nation.

There were in all three children: the eldest, Sarah, and the youngest, Thomas, who lived but a short time. The family remained on the little rocky farm until Abraham was four years old, when they removed to a much better farm on Knob Creek, which might have been developed into a valuable estate. But the shiftless father, content with a diet of milk and corn-meal, and satisfied, if his physical wants were moderately well supplied, only attempted to cultivate a small patch of about six acres. He met with his usual indifferent success, although his patient wife did her best to make up for his deficiencies. He paid but little attention to the education of his children, and their overburdened mother could do but little more than clothe and feed them. Twice they attended a school in the neighborhood for a few weeks, at one time being compelled to walk four miles each way, carrying a well-worn spelling-book, their only text-book, and a scanty lunch of corn bread. The course of study included only reading, writing, spelling and a few simple arithmetical rules.

Young Abraham spent the most of his time out-of-doors hunting and fishing, or helping his father in the farm work. He was bright and active, and his free life in the open air no doubt laid the foundation of the sturdy good health which afterwards was of so much value in the terrible physical strain to which he was subjected.

Yet from childhood he was subject to the fits of melancholy which afterwards so frequently overshadowed his life. He had inherited the sensitive nature of his mother, and the gloom of his surroundings and prospects seemed to impress itself upon him, even at an age when most boys would have been oblivious to it. Whether working at his father's side, or wandering aimlessly about in the grand old forests, or fishing in the clear waters of the creek, he was still oppressed by the atmosphere of poverty and shiftlessness in which he was compelled to live.

In after-life he always looked back upon these early years with pain, and rarely alluded to them. They were characterized by no important occurrence, and their story was but " the short and simple annals of the poor." Yet the habits of simple living, of rising above hardships and of overcoming the obstacles of life, were of more value to him than schools, society and culture to many a more favored youth. The school of necessity is a hard one but it teaches its lessons well and thoroughly.

After a residence of four years in this place, Mr. Lincoln, becoming uneasy and discontented, determined to move again. He had probably been able to pay but little, if anything, on the land, and may have been compelled to seek another location. At any rate, he sold his interest in the land for ten barrels of whiskey and twenty dollars. Having built a rickety flat-boat and laden it with the whiskey, he set sail alone upon the Ohio for the purpose of seeking a new home for himself and family.

After a short voyage, his boat went to pieces, and the cargo sank to the bottom of the river. He fished it up with much labor, and leaving it at a house on the Indiana shore, he pushed into the wilderness to select a suitable spot to settle. He soon found one, and immediately moved his family and furniture from the old location to the new. The comforts of a home this poor, wandering family hardly knew. His household possessions were scanty and of little value, consisting of a little bedding, a few coarse dishes and two or three wooden stools, with his kit of carpenter's tools. His neighbors assisted him in the task of moving, ferrying the family with their goods across the river, and the remainder of the journey was made with the help of a yoke of oxen and a cart, both borrowed.

CHAPTER II.

Mr. Lincoln was no doubt influenced in his determination to leave his Kentucky home by the fact that his relations with his neighbors were becoming more and more unpleasant. His poverty and shiftlessness, together with his tendency to become implicated in disreputable affairs, all combined to make him a social outcast. Hence in leaving the State of his nativity he had but few ties to break and few friends to bewail his departure.

In Indiana, the Mecca of their pilgrimage, this forlorn family could look forward to no friendly welcome, nor even to a comfortable home. When they arrived, they were compelled to camp out until a miserable hut, commonly called a "lean-to," could be built for a temporary shelter. It was made of poles and was open on one side to the wind and weather. Here they lived for nearly a year, suffering great privations, and hardly protected at all from the storms and cold. In the mean time, Mr. Lincoln broke up a small piece of ground and planted it with corn, working in the intervals upon a rude log-hut, in which, when completed, they lived for three years, without either door or windows.

Furniture was almost wholly lacking. A few three-legged stools and a rough board for a table with a bed made of a large bag of leaves placed upon slats fas-

tened to the walls and held up by poles resting on a
crotched stick, completed the list. The children
slept on the ground, for there was no floor, except on
the coldest nights, when they crawled into the primitive bed with their father and mother.

The house was located upon an eminence about sixteen miles from the Ohio River, in what was then
known as Perry County, near the present village of
Gentryville. It was in the midst of a thickly wooded
country, where were found great oaks, maples, wal-
nuts and many other native trees, with little or no
undergrowth. The location was charming and pic-
turesque and lacked nothing but water, which had to
be brought from a considerable distance. The country abounded in deer and other inoffensive wild
animals, which furnished an abundance of meat
together with the materials of which the pioneers
were accustomed to make their clothes.

Abraham was about eight years old when the family
removed to Indiana ; yet he was possessed of considerable strength, and assisted materially in the arduous labors of the journey. He afterwards said in
regard to this period of his life : "We reached our
new home about the time that the State came into
the Union. It was a wild region with many bears
and other animals still in the woods. There I grew
up. There were some schools, so-called, but no
qualification was ever required of a teacher beyond
'readin', ritin' and cipherin' to the rule of three.' If
a straggler, supposed to understand Latin, happened
to sojourn in the neighborhood, he was looked upon
as a wizard. There was absolutely nothing to excite
ambition for an education. Of course, when I came

of age, I did not know much; still, somehow, I could read and write and cipher to the rule of three, and that was all. I have not been to school since. The little advance I have now made upon this store of education, I have picked up from time to time, under the pressure of necessity. I was raised to farm work at which I continued until twenty-two."

Life in Southern Indiana was like that in other back-woods regions, the story of which is familiar to all. Neighbors were few and distant. A sister of Mrs. Lincoln with her husband soon after settled near by, and this family furnished about the only society accessible to them for several years.

Educational advantages were few and primitive. In all, young Lincoln attended school less than a year, yet he made the most of that time and obtained a working knowledge of the rudiments, which he afterwards increased materially by home reading and study.

A man by the name of Hazel Dorsey was Lincoln's first teacher in Indiana. The school-house, which was built of logs, was distant nearly two miles from the Lincoln homestead. At school young Abraham gained the reputation of being a good scholar and soon won the affection of his teacher and playmates.

He was compelled to lose much time in school, in order to help his father split rails; yet upon his return he quickly regained his position in the class. During his short attendance upon this school he gained a knowledge of the rudiments which enabled him to continue his studies by himself and make rapid progress in them.

Farm work was never a congenial occupation, for

he seemed to feel, even then, that he was fitted for a
higher sphere and was eager to make preparation for
it. He was compelled to labor hard and incessantly,
sometimes at home, and frequently for some neighbor
who happened to be short of help. It is said that he
was inclined to slight his work, and that he had inherited something of his father's shirking propensi-
ties. It was his great delight to stop in the midst of
his labors and, mounting a stump, to make a speech
to his fellow laborers, who were always ready to hear
"Abe" speak, much to the disgust of their employer.
He would select a subject, sometimes a text from the
Bible, and embellish his harangue with stories and
jokes, which, with the contortions of his awkward figure, would keep his hearers in a roar of laughter.
When he went to the country store or to the mill, he
was generally surrounded with loafers and often forgot his errand in his attempt to amuse his rude audience.

This propensity was a source of considerable an-
noyance to his father, who strove in vain to conquer
it. One of his old neighbors[1] declared that "Abe
was awful lazy." He says, "He worked for me frequently, a few days only at a time. He once told me
that his father had taught him to work, but
never learned him to love it. He would laugh and
talk and crack jokes and tell stories all the time;
didn't love to work, but did dearly love his pay."
The following description is given of his personal
appearance at the age of fifteen.[2] "He was growing

---

[1] John Romine.
[2] Lamon.

at a tremendous rate, and two years later attained his full height of six feet and four inches. He was long, wiry and strong ; while his big feet and hands, and the length of his legs and arms, were out of all proportion to his small trunk and head. His complexion was very swarthy, and his skin was shrivelled and yellow even then. He wore low shoes, buckskin breeches, linsey-woolsey shirt and a cap made of the skin of an opossum or coon. The breeches clung close to his thighs and legs and failed by a large space to meet the tops of his shoes. Twelve inches remained uncovered, and exposed that much of shin-bone, sharp, blue and narrow."

He soon acquired an insatiable thirst for knowledge, although at first it required considerable persuasion to induce him to attend to the intellectual tasks set before him. There was no book in the house save the Bible, but this he never tired of reading, until his familiarity with it became remarkable. He used, frequently, in after-life to quote from it in his conversation and speeches, and the simplicity and clearness of his literary style was largely produced by his study of its matchless diction.

There were a few books of standard merit possessed by the different families in the neighborhood all of which he borrowed and read many times. Among them were Weem's "Life of Washington," "Esop's Fables," "Robinson Crusoe," "Arabian Nights" and the "Speeches of Henry Clay." He dearly loved to stretch himself out on the grass beneath the shadow of some great tree and pore over his book. During the long evenings he would lie at full length on the floor beside the great fireplace and read until the fire

went out. He was accustomed to write out with char-
coal on bits of board the passages, which struck him
most forcibly, and afterwards to commit them to
memory.

He became intensely interested in the speeches of
Henry Clay, many of which he committed to memory. His father was a Democrat and he had naturally inclined in that direction, but now he became an
ardent admirer of the Kentucky statesman and a determined and persistent Whig, remaining of that political belief until he became one of the leaders of the
young Republican party.

While on his way to Washington, in later years, to
assume the duties of the Presidency, he passed
through Trenton, N. J., and, in a speech before the
State Senate, made the following allusion to the deep
impression, which one of these books had made upon
him :

"May I be pardoned if, on this occasion, I mention
that, away back in my childhood, in the earliest days
of my being able to read, I got hold of a small book,
such an one as few of the younger members have
seen, Weem's 'Life of Washington.' I remember all
the accounts there given of the battle-fields and struggles for the liberties of the country ; and none fixed
themselves upon my imagination so deeply as the
struggle here at Trenton. The crossing of the river,
the struggle with the Hessians, the great hardships
endured at that time, all fixed themselves in my
memory more than any other single Revolutionary
event, and you all know, for you have all been boys,
how these early impressions last longer than any
others. I recollect thinking then, boy even though I

was, that there must have been something more than common that these men struggled for. I am exceedingly anxious that that thing which they struggled for, that something even more than national independence, that something that held out a great promise to all people of the world for all time to come, I am exceedingly anxious that this Union, the Constitution and liberties of the people, shall be perpetuated in accordance with the original idea for which that struggle was made."

This same "Life of Washington" was the first book which he ever owned. He acquired possession of it, however, in a manner not wholly satisfactory to himself. He had borrowed it from a neighbor, named Crawford, who was not noted for his generosity. One night Lincoln took it to bed with him and continued to read until his pine knot lamp burned out, when he thrust the book into a crevice between the logs in the side of the house. During the night a severe storm came up and the book was soaked. He went to Mr. Crawford in the morning, and telling him of the mishap, offered to pay for the book. Crawford set him to work pulling cornfodder, and kept him at it for three days, making the young student pay an extortionate price in labor for an old and worn-out book. Young Lincoln was much dissatisfied with such parsimony, and afterwards unconsciously following the example of an old Greek poet, wrote several bits of doggerel verse, in which he ridiculed so forcibly the personal appearance of Crawford, that his flat nose and scowling visage became a byword throughout the whole community.

When he was ten years old his mother died after a

long and distressing illness. During her sickness he
cared for her as tenderly as a girl, and often sat at her
side and read the Bible to her for hours. The dying
mother gave him much loving advice, which he stored
up in his memory as a precious legacy, and over which
he pondered deeply. Her loss must have been severely felt by the household in the long winter which
followed. The burden of the household duties fell
upon Sarah, who was hardly yet in her teens, but
was developing into a quiet, useful woman.

There was no minister in the vicinity at the time
of Mrs. Lincoln's death, and she was buried in the
grove near the house without ceremonies, beyond one
or two simple prayers from the neighbors. A few
months afterwards an itinerant preacher, Elder Elkin,
was invited by a letter composed and written with
laborious care by young Lincoln, to come and perform the simple funeral services then in vogue.

It was a clear and beautiful day when the neighbors, to the number of about two hundred, gathered
in the little grove to take part in the services. The
minister, a plain and simple man, was much
affected by the circumstances and surroundings, and
spoke with a rude eloquence that moved every heart
and made a deep impression, especially upon the
two motherless children. He spoke tenderly of the
patient Christian character of the deceased, and com-
memorated her many virtues with touching words,
commending her example for the emulation of all.

Mrs. Lincoln's life had been a dull and hard one, a
daily routine of care and trouble, yet she had made
a deep impression upon the character of her son, and
in after-life his mind often reverted to the lonely grave

by the Ohio, with love and reverence. Long afterwards, when the forest flowers had bloomed above
her grave for two score years, he said to a friend, with
tears in his eyes : " All that I am or hope to be I owe
to my angel mother—blessings on her memory."

In the autumn of the same year, Mr. Lincoln
returned to his old home in Kentucky, and married a
widow lady, who had been one of his youthful sweet-
hearts. He represented himself to be a well-to-do
farmer with considerable property, and the new Mrs.
Lincoln was much disappointed at the state of affairs
which she found at her journey's end. But like the
true woman that she was, she determined to make
the best of what she could not help. She brought
with her a large load of furniture, which the children
regarded with amazement for nothing so grand had
ever been seen in the neighborhood before, and for
the first time in his life Abe rejoiced in a warm comfortable bed. With Mrs. Lincoln came her own three
children, but she showed no partiality to them, and
the two motherless children soon learned to regard
her with warm affection. In speaking of her stepson
she once said : " Abe never gave me a cross word or
look, and never refused, in fact or appearance, to do
all I requested of him."

A new era was inaugurated in the cheerless cabin
by her arrival. Floors were laid, a door was hung,
windows were fitted into the open spaces in the walls,
and a new spirit of order and progress pervaded the
domestic economy. She not only strove to improve
the material condition of the household, but also
determined to give the children better opportunities
to secure at least the rudiments of an education.

One of his early friends says that Abe was accustomed to come in from the field after his day's labor, go to the cupboard and snatch a piece of corn-bread and sit down, literally upon his shoulder-blades, with his feet upon the mantel. In this position he would remain, absorbed in his book, until it became too dark to see, when he would crouch down by the fire and take advantage of its unsteady light. Inasmuch as writing materials were so costly as to be beyond his reach, he was accustomed to write upon strips of pine-board with charred sticks, and when the board was full would shave it down until he had a clean surface again.

It was early his ambition to become a public speaker, and he not only practiced constantly on his friends whenever he could secure an audience, but he seized every opportunity to listen to speeches. In those days, the courts were literally circuit courts, the judge and lawyers riding on horseback from one county-seat to another, where they spent a number of days or weeks trying cases. There was a great deal of oratorical display on the part of the lawyers, who made use of much bombastic eloquence in the trial of the petty cases which came up before the Court.

Young Lincoln generally managed to attend court regularly, when it was in session, and was deeply interested in its proceedings. He would arise early in the morning, "do the chores," and walk to Booneville, the county-seat, which was located seventeen miles away, returning in season to do up the evening's work. He once listened with eager interest to a speech made by John A. Breckenridge, and was so impressed with it that he ventured to congratulate the lawyer at the close of the session. After he became President, he told Mr. Breckenridge that it was listening to his speech that first inspired him with the determination to become a lawyer.

When his parents were away to church Sundays he used to take the Bible and select a text, from which he would preach a sermon to his sister and other children who happened along. His sermons may have been somewhat faulty from a doctrinal point of view, but they were entertaining. He always felt a deep compassion for any person or animal in suffering, and was exceedingly bitter in his denunciation of cruelty to animals. "One day, a boy caught a land-terrapin, brought it to the place where Abe was preaching, threw it against the tree and crushed the shell. It quivered all over and seemed to be suffering much. Abe then made a really effective speech against cruelty to animals, contending that an ant's life was as sweet to it as ours to us."

This habit of speech-making soon developed into a great nuisance, for it distracted the attention of the men who were ready to stop work at any time to hear him speak. His speeches were simple and crude, but contained many sharp points, and were illustrated with numerous stories which kept his audience in roars of laughter. Oftentimes his father was compelled to interrupt the incipient orator by the use of force, and he was dragged from his rude rostrum and hustled off to work with no gentle hand. He was not discouraged by these setbacks and difficulties, but persisted in his practice until he became recognized as a promising orator.

He commenced early to write compositions, and

soon gained a considerable rural repute by having several articles published in the country newspapers. One of his earliest efforts was an essay upon " Cruelty to Animals," which was published and was considered a marvellous production by his friends. He generally wrote with a humorous vein, and frequently directed his jokes against the failings of his friends. He was specially inclined to rhythmical composition, and possessed a rude talent in stringing together pointed couplets. Upon the page of one of his copy-books, among numerous other poetical effusions, appears the suggestive couplet :

" 'Tis Abraham Lincoln holds the pen,
He will be good, but God knows when."

He wrote several long poetical productions of a satirical character, introducing broad jokes and " take-offs " which would hardly grace a printed page. At one time there was a double wedding in the Gentry family, the leading family of the community. He was not invited, and felt the slight keenly. He was possessed of too combative a disposition to quietly put up with what he deemed to be an insult, and determined to avenge himself in poetic measures. He wrote a cutting satire, in which the members of the offending family figured as prominent characters. It was a bold, audacious thing, and created a great deal of excitement in the neighborhood, being highly applauded by his friends. The victims of the joke were highly incensed, and one of the younger members of the family challenged him to fight. He accepted the challenge, and the fight took place. Instead of fighting in person, however, he substituted his step-brother in his place, who was badly whipped. Young

Lincoln stepped into the ring, and swinging his long arms around his head, dared any one to attack him. But his strength and prowess were too well known, and he proudly left the field with his honor vindicated as the champion of the neighborhood.

His agility and strength were remarkable, and no one in the vicinity could throw him in a wrestling match.   He is said to have been able to carry a load which three men could hardly lift, and he once picked up a hen-house weighing over six hundred pounds and carried it a considerable distance.   At another time, seeing a number of men preparing sticks upon which to lift some heavy timbers, he shouldered the timbers and easily carried them to their destination. "He could strike with a maul," says Mr. Wood, "a heavier blow than any other man.   He could sink an axe deeper into the wood than any other man I ever saw."

He enjoyed being upon the water, and more than once sought to obtain employment upon the river boats.   In his leisure moments he built a small flat-boat, which he used for short excursions up and down the river.   While at work upon it one day, he was approached by a couple of gentlemen, who requested him to put their baggage upon a steamer which was passing down the river.   For this he was paid a dollar in silver, the first dollar he had ever earned. While President, he related the story to Mr. Seward and remarked : "I could scarcely believe my eyes when I received the money.   You may think it was a very little thing, and in these days it seems to me a trifle, but it was the most important incident in my life.   I could scarcely credit that I, a poor boy, had earned a dollar in less than a day—that by earnest work I had earned a dollar. The world seemed wider and fairer before me, I was a more hopeful and confident being from that time."

In March, 1828, he went to work for Mr. Gentry, who lived near by. Shortly afterwards, his employer fitted out a scow to be laden with corn, bacon and other country produce, which was to be taken down the river, and disposed of at the towns along the route. He put Abe in command of the little craft, who, in company with a young man somewhat older than himself, made the trip successfully and conducted the business to the entire satisfaction of his employer. They were accustomed to drift with the current by day, and tie up to the shore by night. One night, a number of negroes boarded the craft intent upon plunder. The young men were awakened and attacked the intruders so vigorously, that four of them were knocked into the river and the rest took to flight. But Lincoln, not content with a partial victory, leaped from the boat and pursued the marauders, with so much vigor that he overtook them and gave them a severe thrashing. It was the first and last time that Lincoln lifted his hands against any representatives of the colored race.

It was his first trip out into the world and the broad river, with its numerous steamers filled with passengers, and the villages and cities along the shores, gave him many hints of a broader life than any he was acquainted with, as well as much food for reflection. It is probable, that, on this trip, he came into actual contact with slavery for the first time and saw something of the unnatural suffering and degra-

dation caused by the iniquitous system. His heart
was tender and easily touched by suffering, even
when inflicted upon the lower animals, and the sight
of men and women bending beneath the burdens of
inhuman servitude must have been abhorrent to him.
It may not be too much to say that the Emancipation
Proclamation germinated in this trip. It is certain
that, from this time on, he pondered deeply upon the
great problems of American politics and humanity,
and sought long and patiently for their solution.

He learned much from the trip and returned home
more than ever eager to fit himself for usefulness in
a higher and wider sphere than that into which he
had been born.

The venture was a financial success, owing to his
shrewd management. Mr. Lamon says that at one
place, where they sold a quantity of provisions, they
received in payment a counterfeit bill, which they did
not discover until they were at some distance from
the town. When his companion bewailed the loss,
Lincoln remarked, by way of consolation, " Never
mind, I guess it will soon slip out of our fingers."
And it did.

CHAPTER III.

In 1830, Mr. Lincoln became once more uneasy and dissatisfied with his surroundings and determined to move again, influenced in part by the unhealthful character of the Gentryville farm and locality. Reports of the peculiar fertility of the great State to the westward had been brought to his ears and he decided to emigrate to Illinois.

This great commonwealth had been a member of the Union twelve years, and contained, at this time, a population of about a quarter of a million. The broad prairies in the central and northern portions of the State, now occupied by prosperous communities and populous cities, were then wholly without inhabitants. · The immigrants from other States passed over these great plains, uususpicious of their marvellous fertility, believing them to be only fit for pasturage, and settled in the forests and oak openings of the south or along the water-courses near the borders of the State. There were no large settlements. Cairo, Alton, Galena, Decatur and a few other villages, now developed into large and prosperous cities, were then struggling to maintain a bare existence amid the adverse influences by which they were surrounded.

Nature has been very kind to Illinois and has granted it munificent gifts. Its broad and fertile prairies, its beautiful water-courses and the great coal measures that underlie it, are treasure-houses that have developed its population from thousands to millions, and made it one of the wealthiest States in the Union. There was, however, but little to hint of its coming glory in 1830, although it attracted immigrants in increasing numbers from year to year.

The population was mostly made up of families from the border States, especially Kentucky. There were few people from the East, and the "Yankees" were not regarded with any degree of tolerance, being always the objects of suspicion and aversion.

While the people of the State had decided by a large majority not to permit slavery to be introduced, yet their sympathies were largely with the institution, sometimes even to the verge of persecuting its outspoken opponents, who lived in their midst. That there was deep feeling on the subject, is proven by the murder of Owen Lovejoy, some years later, at Alton, because he persisted in publishing an Abolition paper.

The most of the people coming from Kentucky, had become familiar with slavery in its less deplorable aspects, and, while they would not introduce it into Illinois, would suffer no one to openly stigmatize it as an unjust or iniquitous institution.

In the light of history it is easy to see how exactly the circumstances were adapted to the development of the peculiar personality of Lincoln. When he entered Illinois he was a tall, gaunt youth of twenty-one, unaccustomed to society and wholly ignorant of the ways of the world, yet with the strong, innate consciousness that he was destined to better things, and that his capabilities were greater than those of the men with whom he was accustomed to associate. Brute force and physical prowess were still in the ascendant in this pioneer State. The men of intelligence and culture were to be found almost entirely in the larger settlements and in the practice of law. Lincoln was physically stronger than his associates, and this, with his great length of limb, made him easily the champion in the rough sports in which the young men were wont to engage. His reputation spread far and wide, both for his strength and his skill in wrestling. Many a redoubted champion, who had never before met his match, came from a distance to dispute for his laurels with the new arrival and went away ignominiously defeated.

The people were generally ignorant, few of them being able to read or write. In learning, Lincoln far surpassed them all, not only being able to read and write, but having also acquired a considerable stock of general knowledge. Had he been of higher birth than his associates, this might have been an occasion for jealousy and ill feeling, but he was as poor as they and of even humbler lineage, hence they were proud of his accomplishments and boasted of his wonderful knowledge, as if credit was thereby cast upon the whole community.

His poverty and consequent struggles for a bare living contributed to strengthen his independence of character and honesty, which, in a less positive man, would have produced cringing servility and dishonesty.

One of the most marked features of his career, as it was of the career of Washington, was the profound impression he made upon everybody with whom he was brought into close personal contact.   This was, no doubt, owing to his intense and harmonious personality, and in part to the quaint charm of his conversation.

From early boyhood he had been accustomed to embellish his conversation with numberless stories and anecdotes of which he had an inexhaustible store and a skill of adaptation to the point in hand which has never been excelled. His early practice had given him a degree of proficiency in public speaking in which he made use of a rude and fervid eloquence which seldom failed to carry the audience along in sympathy with him.   In those days, when men would go thirty or forty miles to hear a lawyer's speech in court or a political discussion, this was a commanding gift and quickly earned a local reputation for its possessor.

Thomas Lincoln, with his family, settled first in Macon County; but he shortly afterwards moved to the vicinity of the present city of Mattoon, in Coles County.   Young Lincoln took hold with energy to help his father settle in his new home.   He chopped down trees and split rails and helped to fence in the whole farm.

He now told his father, that, as he was of age and the law gave him his liberty, he desired to shift for himself and left his home never to return to it again except for a brief visit.   His father, with his wandering instinct unimpaired, continued to move from one place to another, hardly able to keep the wolf from the door, until he died, at the age of seventy-three, and was buried on the old homestead near Mattoon.   Mrs. Lincoln outlived her illustrious stepson, who always treated her with tenderest consideration.

For a time he worked wherever he chanced upon an opportunity, now splitting fence rails, and again helping to plant, cultivate and harvest a crop of corn. He once made a bargain to split rails for a woman, who was to furnish cloth and make him a pair of trousers in return for his labor. He agreed to split three hundred rails for every yard of cloth used in manufacturing the garments, and faithfully carried out his part of the bargain.

Shortly afterwards a speculator, Offutt by name, came into the neighborhood looking for men to take a flatboat loaded with country produce to New Orleans and dispose of it. As young Lincoln had made one trip to New Orleans he engaged him to take charge of the expedition with two or three of his friends as helpers.

As the boat was not ready at the appointed time, they were compelled to make one, a somewhat difficult task, as the materials were scarce and hard to obtain. But the ingenuity of Lincoln overcame all obstacles, and a good serviceable boat was completed and launched in four weeks. The voyage was safely made, although on the downward trip the boat was stranded on the dam at New Salem, a small place a few miles below Springfield, and nearly lost, but was saved together with its cargo by the skill and strength of Lincoln.

New Salem was a small place, and the arrival and sad plight of the boat caused considerable excitement. The whole population gathered upon the banks of the river and watched the operation of releasing it from the dam where it had stranded and partially filled with water. After all the efforts of the crew had proven fruitless Lincoln rolled up the legs of his trousers and stepped into the water, his length of limb standing him in good stead. By sheer strength he lifted the boat upon the edge of the dam and balanced it; then borrowing an auger he bored a hole in the bottom and allowed the water to escape. Having stopped up the hole, they continued the journey. This was Lincoln's first introduction to a community of which he was destined to become a prominent and beloved member, while the people who had watched him were struck with admiration of his strength and ingenuity.

This trip made a far deeper impression upon the mind of Lincoln than the former one. At New Orleans he first came into actual contact with the most horrible features of slavery. For the first time he entered the slave-market and saw human beings put up at auction and sold like cattle. He saw families separated and the hopeless sorrow of father and mother as the children were torn from their arms to be led away into a servitude which was worse than death. He saw the whipping-post with all its attendant horrors, and heard the stinging blows of the lash and the groans of the poor victims.

He said to one of his companions as they turned away from these terrible scenes, " If I ever get a chance to hit that institution, I will hit it hard, John !" His companions remarked of him that " his heart bled, he was mad, thoughtful, abstracted, sad and depressed."

He did not at once become an Abolitionist. Indeed,

it is doubtful if he was ever an Abolitionist in the strict meaning of the term. His was not a nature to leap hastily to a conclusion. It was only after long thought and observation that his opinions attained the strength of convictions, but once formed, it was almost impossible to shake him from them. So now he observed all these things and meditated upon them, but' it was many years before he became identified with an anti-slavery movement of any kind.

There is a tradition that on this trip to New Orleans, in company with John Hanks, he visited a voodoo fortune-teller, and that during the interview "she became much excited and after various other predictions said: 'You will be President, and all the negroes will be free.'" The truth of this tradition cannot be established.

If God, in times of old, appeared to Moses and foretold the great responsibility, about to devolve upon him, of leading the Children of Israel out from the land of bondage into freedom, might not the veil of the future have been raised a little from before the eyes of this modern Moses in order that he might obtain a glimpse of the greet deeds which he was destined to perform ? However this may be, he could never again look upon slavery as a dim shadow which lay upon a section of this sunny land, but it must henceforth be a grim and horrid reality which should oppress his spirits and excite his hatred and apprehension.

Upon his return to Illinois his employer was so impressed with his ability and faithfulness that he determined to retain his services. He had recently opened a store and a flouring mill, at the little settlement of

New Salem, about twenty miles from Springfield. He
offered Lincoln the position of clerk, which was
accepted as the best opening that presented itself.

Mr. Offutt was very proud of the strength and
learning of his clerk, and frequently boasted of them.
There were at that time, living in the adjoining settlement of Clary's Grove, a number of rude, quarrel-
some boys, who had made themselves the terror of
their neighbors by their wild and lawless deeds. The
boasts of Mr. Offutt came to their ears, and they
determined to "take the impudence" out of the
young clerk. One day they went to New Salem with
this intent, and finally succeeded in provoking Lincoln to enter into a wrestling match with Jack Armstrong, their leader, who was as strong as an ox and
the champion wrestler of the neighborhood. After
struggling a few moments, Lincoln seized him with
both hands, and, holding him at arm's-length, shook
him like a child. Upon this the Clary's Grove boys
rushed forward to the assistance of their leader, when
Lincoln backed up against the side of the store and
coolly awaited their onset. Armstrong, however,
was thoroughly subdued and shouted to his followers
to stop, saying: "Boys, Abe Lincoln is the best man
that ever broke into this settlement. He shall be one
of us." After this Lincoln had no stauncher friends
than these rough men, who never lost an opportunity
to praise or to vote for him.

Although he was now recognized as the champion
of the whole region, he seldom exhibited his great
strength except in the rôle of peacemaker. At one
time, while he was waiting upon some ladies in the
store, a drunken rowdy came in and began to indulge

in abusive language. Lincoln politely requested him
not to use such lauguage in the presence of ladies,
but he became very angry and dared Lincoln to come
out and fight, declaring that he had been waiting for
a good opportunity to whip him. After the ladies
had gone, Lincoln went out with him into the street,
where he easily threw him to the ground, and picking
up a handful of smartweed, he rubbed it vigorously
into the face and eyes of the discomfited rowdy until
he fairly howled for mercy. Then Lincoln assisted
him to rise and brought him some water with which
to wash his face. He never received a challenge to
fight from the same source again.

It was here at New Salem that he acquired the
sobriquet of "Honest Abe," which clung to him
through life. The honesty of his dealings is well
illustrated by a single event. "One night, in counting the receipts of the day, he found his cash on hand
to be seven cents in excess of his sales. He concluded that he had made an error of that amount in
returning change to one of his customers, a poor
woman, who lived six or seven miles away. He immediately closed the store and walked the whole distance to restore the money to her.

He seized every opportunity to increase his store of
knowledge, and spent hours daily in study, often to
the detriment of his work. When there was too much
noise in the store he would go out into the woods and
stretch his ungainly limbs in the shadow of a tree
upon the ground, and become so absorbed in his book
as to be lost to all around.

He once heard some one speak of the science of
grammar, and immediately determined to penetrate

its mysteries.   After diligent inquiries he found and
borrowed a book on the subject from a family living
several miles away.   It took him but a short time to
master the subject.   This was considered a great
achievement by his friends of New Salem and was
made the subject of many boasts

From this time on his life increases in interest.
Hitherto he had done but little more than any active,
ambitious boy could hope to accomplish, but now his
great native ability began to develop under the
spur of his fixed determination to make something of
himself.

CHAPTER IV.

In the spring of 1832 Mr. Offutt failed in business, and Lincoln found himself without employment. Almost at the same time the Blackhawk war broke out. The State issued a call for volunteers and he was one of the first to respond.

Blackhawk was a chief of the tribe of the Sacs, who had been removed by the Government from their former home in north-western Illinois to a reservation west of the Mississippi. This Indian chief was a princely man and showed an independence and nobility of character, which belonged to few of the aborigines. Believing that his people had been unjustly deprived of their lands, he formed the determination to return and, if possible, regain possession of them. He formed an alliance between nine of the most powerful tribes of the north-west and invaded Illinois. For a time the movement seemed to threaten a serious danger to the people of the Rock River valley. But the call of the Governor was quickly responded to, and several regiments were soon in the field. After much marching and counter-marching, with many alarms and but little bloodshed, the enemy was driven from the State.

A company was formed in New Salem and vicinity of which Lincoln was elected captain. Although the troops were called out in the State service, each company was permitted to select its own officers. In the New Salem company there were two candidates for the honor, William Kirkpatrick and Lincoln. According to the custom, when the time for electing officers had arrived, the two would-be captains took their stations at some distance from each other and the men ranged themselves about the object of their choice. Lincoln's popularity was so great that he was elected by a vote of two to one.

In speaking of this event, many years afterwards, when the highest honors within the gift of the nation had been conferred upon him, he said, that he had never been more gratified in his life than by this, the first proof of public esteem he had ever received. It was the expression of the high regard in which he was held by all with whom he came into daily contact.

The war offered no opportunities to win renown or perform glorious achievements. There were no battles worthy of the name and comparatively few hardships to be endured. There were several long marches and the troops suffered somewhat from scarcity of provisions.

One day there came into the camp an old Indian, weary and hungry. Although he had a safe conduct from Gen. Cass, the men, who had become terribly incensed against all of his race, declared the letter to be a forgery and denounced him as a spy. They rushed furiously upon him, intending to put him to death, when Lincoln suddenly stepped between them and their intended victim. In an imperative tone of voice he ordered them back and told them that they should not kill the defenseless Indian. He was thoroughly aroused and his determined mien and commanding tones cowed them and compelled them suddenly to relinquish their purpose. At length, one of the men shouted from the crowd :

"Lincoln, this is cowardly of you." Lincoln looked towards him in supreme contempt and said :

"If any man thinks I am a coward let him test me."

"You are larger and braver than any of us," was the reply.

"That you can guard against," said he ; "choose your weapons."

But nothing more was said, and the men slowly dispersed. Such an occurrence could only be rendered possible by the loose discipline which necessarily prevailed among the volunteer troops. Had he attempted to arrest the insolent man, in all probability a mutiny would have resulted.

He afterwards was wont to relate, in his inimitable way, a less tragic incident which happened in this expedition. He was marching at the head of his company through a field, when he came to a gate through which it was necessary to pass.

"I could not for the life of me," said he, "remember the proper word of command to get my company through that gate endwise ; so, as we came near the place, I shouted, 'Halt! This company is dismissed for two minutes, when it will form on the other side of the gate.'" The evolution was successfully performed, and the company marched on.

Lincoln was mustered into the service by Lieut. Robert Anderson, who afterwards directed the defense of Fort Sumter.

After the evacuation of that ill-fated fortress Anderson called upon the President, and in the course of conversation Mr. Lincoln asked : "Major, do you remember ever meeting me before ?"

"No, Mr. President, I have no recollection of ever having had the honor before."

"My memory is better than yours," said Mr. Lincoln. "You mustered me into the service of the United States, in 1832, at Dixon's Ferry in the Blackhawk war."

Many of the men, with whom he was associated in early life, gained a national reputation, and some of them became his most trusted and efficient helpers in his subsequent career.

Lincoln was at this time in a painful position. He had no home and no regular occupation. His character was undeveloped, and his natural powers untrained. The difficulties that beset him, would, to another man, or in another age of the world, have been insurmountable. He had no money, and his clothes were of the poorest material : so coarse and ill-fitting that they exaggerated the natural ungainliness of his form.

On his return trip, after being discharged from military duty, he was observed to be anxious and worried about his future prospects, and, while his comrades were light-hearted and happy, he was often sad and gloomy. His determination to make something of himself, however, had been strengthened by his association with older and more cultured men, and from that time he devoted himself more earnestly than ever to his studies.

As was the custom for any one, who desired a public office, he had announced himself as a candidate for the Legislature previous to his departure from

New Salem, and had made a declaration of his principles in the county paper. Ever since he had been old enough to entertain a decided opinion upon a political question, he had been a Whig and an ardent admirer of Henry Clay. But in local elections, national politics were scarcely considered. In Sangamon County, the great local issue pertained to the navigation of the Sangamon River, and the candidate who entertained the most radical views and who could sustain them by the most telling speech, was the favorite.

The schemes, originated and championed by the aspirants for office, were visionary and impracticable and were urged more to obtain political support than with the belief that they would ever be carried into operation. The river was shallow, winding and full of obstructions, and the benefit to be derived from making it navigable was not at all commensurate with the immense expense that must have been incurred.

Lincoln was an enthusiastic advocate of this and other similar public improvements. He was, no doubt, honest in the position he had taken, but was carried away by the popular delusion, the fallacy of which his judgment was not sufficiently developed to detect.

His first political speech was made during this campaign and was as follows :

"Gentlemen and Fellow-citizens, I presume you all know who I am. I am humble Abraham Lincoln. I have been solicited by my friends to become a candidate for the Legislature. My politics are short and sweet, like the old woman's dance. I am in favor of a national bank, I am in favor of the internal-im-

provement system and a high protective tariff.
These are my sentiments and political principles. If
elected, I shall be thankful : if not, it will be all the
same."

Only ten days remained before the election, and it
was impossible to make a thorough canvas ; hence
being but little known, he was defeated.

After the election he was induced to buy a small
store in New Salem in company with one Berry, a
worthless fellow, in payment for which he gave his
personal note. They afterwards purchased the stock
of another store, thus adding to their liabilities without materially increasing the extent and profit of
their business.

It would have been hard to find two men more
totally unfitted to carry on such a business successfully. To Lincoln it was but a temporary expedient
to furnish the means of subsistence while pursuing
his studies, while his partner was drunken and disreputable. As might have been expected, from the
carelessness and inefficiency of both, the enterprise
failed and Lincoln was left with a heavy debt, which
seemed to him so large and hopeless a burden that
he often spoke of it as the national debt. His reputation for honesty did not fail him even then, and he
applied himself to the payment of the debt, which
was not fully paid for sixteen years, when he sent a
part of his Congressional salary from Washington to
Mr. Herndon to discharge the last obligation.

In 1832, he bought an old volume of Blackstone at
an auction in Springfield, and immediately commenced to master it. The determination he had
formed to enter upon the study of the law was not

hasty nor ill-considered. From the time when he was accustomed to walk fifteen miles in order to attend court and listen to the speeches, he seems to have had an earnest desire to become a lawyer. As he grew older and not only listened to speeches but began himself to gain a reputation as an orator, and as he became more acquainted with the world and recognized the many opportunities for acquiring wealth and distinction which a legal career offered, the desire was changed to a fixed determination to overcome every difficulty and fit himself for the Bar.

After mastering Blackstone, he began the systematic study of law, borrowing books from a legal friend in Springfield, whose acquaintance he had made during his brief military career. To obtain the books he was compelled to walk to Springfield, a distance of fourteen miles. He was accustomed to stride along, book in hand, unmindful of all about him. He was frequently seen at the store lying flat upon his back on the counter, absorbed in his studies. At night he went to the village carpenter's shop, and having built a fire of shavings would read by its light as long as the fuel lasted.

A friend speaks of having found him at his boarding-house, one day, stretched out at full length upon the bed, poring over a book and rocking the cradle of his landlady's baby with one foot.

He soon obtained an old book of forms and began to draw up contracts, deeds, mortgages and other legal documents for his friends and neighbors, who were filled with wonder at the great learning displayed by their favorite.

In 1833, he was appointed postmaster of New Salem

—a position which was neither arduous nor lucrative. There was but one mail a week, and this was so small that he generally carried it in his hat, and when a letter was called for he would take off his battered tile and search for it in the depths. The pay was small, but his chief compensation lay in the fact that he now had the privilege of reading all the papers that came into the neighborhood before he turned them over to their owners, and he availed himself fully of the privilege. After a time the office was discontinued, and for some reason the balance of about seventeen dollars was not called for until several years after Lincoln had moved to Springfield, during which time he had often been in want, without suitable clothes and scarcely able to obtain the necessities of life; yet when the United States Inspector called upon him, unexpectedly, for the money he went to his trunk, and taking out an old stocking poured its contents on the table. It contained the exact sum in the identical coppers and silver pieces which he had received.

It is a somewhat remarkable fact that America's two greatest heroes gained a livelihood in their youth by surveying, and that they were both masters of the art. Both surveyed many large and valuable tracts of land, the boundaries of which were in dispute, and the results attained by each were regarded as final.

Washington took advantage of the opportunities thus afforded to buy valuable tracts of land, and thus laid the foundation of a great fortune and an immense landed estate. Lincoln never speculated in land, although he had the best of opportunities, or he, too, might have become a wealthy man.

His friends secured him the appointment as deputy-surveyor from John Calhoun, the county-surveyor. This position was one of great responsibility and importance. Settlers were constantly moving in and acquiring titles in land, and speculators were buying and selling large tracts. Town sites were being marked out and subdivided, so that very much depended upon the accuracy with which the boundary lines were established.

Lincoln was entirely ignorant of the science of surveying, but with characteristic energy procured a treatise upon the subject and commenced to master it. He succeeded so well that in a short time he was put to work.

Through the kindness of his friends he secured a horse and a set of surveying instruments, and traversed the country from one end to the other, laying out claims, determining boundary-lines, and locating roads.

An incident is related which illustrates the fidelity with which he performed his tasks. Two gentlemen had a dispute in regard to the location of a corner, the stake which marked it had apparently been lost. They agreed to leave the decision to Lincoln, who carefully made a survey and located the corner. So accurate were his calculations that, upon digging down a few inches, the old corner stake was found buried in the ground.

For a time he prospered financially. His salary from the Post-office and his pay as surveyor made "good sailing," as he put it. But one of his creditors unexpectedly sued him and obtained judgment, to satisfy which his horse and surveying instruments

were levied on and sold, but were bought back and
restored to him by a friend. He had a faculty of
making loyal friends, who were always ready to
extend a helping hand.   There was something whole-
some about this awkward, ungainly young man which
attracted and attached to him those with whom he
came in contact.   His manifest unselfishness and his
readiness always to help another in every possible
way brought him many true friends.   Every effort
made in his behalf was warmly appreciated, and was
certain to bear fruit, for there was evidently no mean
future before him.

   At the next election he was again a candidate for
the Legislature and this time was triumphantly elected.   During his first candidacy he had issued a
manifesto in which he fully outlined his political views.
The closing sentences of this paper exhibit a modesty
and deference to public opinion which is not commonly expected in such compositions.   He said :

   " Upon the subjects of which I have treated, I have
spoken as I thought.   I may be wrong in regard to
any or all of them ; but, holding it a sound maxim
that it is better only sometimes to be right than at all
times wrong, so soon as I discover my opinions to be
erroneous, I shall be ready to renounce them. . . .
Every man is said to have his peculiar ambition.
Whether it be true or not I can say, for one, that I
have no other so great as that of being truly esteemed
of my fellow-men by rendering myself worthy of their
esteem.   How far I shall succeed in gratifying this
ambition is yet to be developed. . . . I was born,
and have ever remained, in the most humble walks of
life.   I have no wealthy or powerful relations or

friends to recommend me. My case is thrown exclusively upon the independent voters of the county; and, if elected, they will have conferred a favor upon me, for which I shall be unremitting in my efforts to compensate. But if the good people, in their wisdom, shall see fit to keep me in the background, I have been too familiar with disappointments to be very much chagrined."

He entered vigorously into the campaign, going all over the district, making speeches and mingling with the people. He had several advantages over his competitors—he was poor and a workingman, and he met the country people upon their own level, causing them to see that he was heartily in sympathy with them. Yet, by his evident abilities and superior attainments, he excited their respect and caused them to feel pride in him as one in whom they had a special interest.

His methods of speaking were well adapted to the people whom he addressed. His speeches were, as usual, enlivened by stories and anecdotes, which were irresistibly funny, yet always illustrated a point, and often proved more convincing than a long and labored argument. His audience was kept in good humor and expectant. It is said that he often descended to personalities, and even to the verge of vulgarity, and his stories were sometimes broad and partook too much of the corner-grocery style. Yet this was not so much his fault as that of the locality and circumstances in which he was placed.

At one time during the campaign he visited the house of Rowan Herndon, who had a number of men cradling grain in a neighboring field. He asked per-

mission to speak a few words to them, when one of
them remarked that they would vote for no man
whom they could cut out of his swath.

"Well boys," said he, "I guess you will all vote for
me then." And, seizing a cradle, he easily led them
all around the field.

After his election he found it necessary to borrow
two hundred dollars, with which to buy clothes and
to pay his expenses during the legislative term.

The capital of Illinois was then located at Vandalia in the south-central portion of the State During
the session many of the prominent men of the State
took up their residence there, either as members, or
because they were interested in the various measures
to be considered.

Lincoln eagerly availed himself of the opportunity
to meet the men of whom he had so often heard and
read. In the active work of the Legislature he took
but little part, watching closely all the details, and so
familiarizing himself with men and measures as to be
fitted in coming sessions to act as leader of his party,
which was in the minority. He is spoken of as
modest, reserved and observant, always in his seat,
and making many friends.

Upon his return to New Salem he resumed his
duties as deputy-surveyor, having been reappointed
by Thomas M. Neal, the new incumbent. He still
applied himself as closely to his studies as the duties
of the office permitted and slowly, but surely, perfected his preparation for the profession which he
had chosen.

While here in New Salem he became deeply attached to a beautiful girl, named Anne Rutledge.

She is described as being exceedingly attractive, both in appearance and character. Lincoln's love for her was deep and lasting, and she finally yielded to his suit, though never fully reciprocating his passion.

Not long after their engagement she was taken ill, and died after a short sickness. For a time, Lincoln seemed like one demented, and his friends feared, and apparently with good reason, that he would become insane and take his own life. But after his violent grief subsided he returned to his labors, though the blow had left a lasting impression upon him. His life was saddened, and the gloom induced by this bereavement never departed. Like a minor chord, it ran through all the harmony of his life, and at times became dominant.

CHAPTER V.

IN 1836 he was again a candidate for the Legislature. He had now become well known through the district, and had secured the good-will and confidence of his constituents. In the last session the Legislature, in a reapportionment bill, had increased the delegation from Sangamon County to seven Representatives and two Senators.

The days of convention rule had not then come. If a man was desirous of becoming a candidate for any local position, he issued handbills, boldly defining his views, and suing for the support of the people. In accordance with this custom Lincoln issued the following circular, which was printed in the county paper and scattered broadcast :

" NEW SALEM, June 13, 1836.

"To the Editor of the Journal :

"In your paper of last Saturday I see a communication over the signature of ' Many Voters,' in which the candidates who are announced in the *Journal* are called upon to ' show their hands.' Agreed. Here is mine. I go for all, sharing the privileges of the Government, who assist in bearing its burdens ; consequently I go for admitting all whites to the right of suffrage who pay taxes or bear arms (by no means excluding females). If elected I shall consider the whole people of the Sangamon district my constituents, as well those that oppose as those that support me. While acting as their representative I shall be governed by their will on all subjects upon which

(58)

I have the means of knowing what their will is, and upon all others I shall do what my own judgment teaches me will best advance their interests. Whether elected or not, I go for distributing the proceeds of sales of public lands to the several States, to enable our State, in common with others, to dig canals and construct railroads, without borrowing money and paying the interest on it. If alive on the first Monday in November, I shall vote for Hugh L. White for President.

" Very respectfully,

"A. LINCOLN."

The whole manifesto, so remarkable for its boldness and independence, was characteristic of the times. His radical utterances upon the question of suffrage derive added significance from the fact that, through his instrumentality, the right of suffrage was afterwards extended to four millions of people who were at this time in bondage.

The canvass upon which he now entered was more than usually exciting. There were numerous candidates, many of whom were men of well-known ability and address. Political meetings were held in different parts of the county, which were attended by great crowds of people, who assembled to hear debates or discussions by the rival candidates. Although appearing upon the platform with, and in opposition to, many old and skilled orators, Lincoln was nowhere worsted. His opponents soon learned that they could not attack him with impunity, and that in an argument he was the equal of the most adroit debater.

Among the Democrats who were stumping the county was one Dick Taylor, a pompous and self-conceited fellow, who dressed in a most gaudy manner, with ruffled shirts, embroidered vests and a large amount of flashy jewelry. Notwithstanding this he made great pretensions of being one of the yeomanry, the oppressed lower class, and ridiculed the "Rag-Barons" and "Manufacturing Lords" of the Whig party.

One day he was indulging in an unusually prolonged tirade against the Whigs, and accusing the opposing candidates of being the representatives of the aristocracy. Lincoln went up behind him, and suddenly threw his coat open, disclosing a bewildering display of ruffles and velvet and jewels. The crowd shouted with delight and Lincoln said:

"While he (Col. Taylor) was making these charges against the Whigs over the country, riding in carriages, wearing ruffled shirts, kid gloves, massive gold watch-chains and flourishing a heavy gold-headed cane, I was a poor boy hired on a flat-boat at eight dollars a month, and had only one pair of breeches to my name, and they were buckskin—and if you know the nature of buckskin, when wet and dried by the sun it will shrink—and mine kept shrinking until they left several inches of my legs bare between the tops of my socks and the lower part of my breeches ; and while I was growing taller, they were becoming shorter, and so much tighter that they left a blue streak around my legs that can be seen to this day. If you call this aristocracy, I plead guilty to the charge." [1]

As the campaign was drawing to a close he made an unusually brilliant speech at Springfield, which produced a profound impression upon the minds of

---

[1] Brown's "Life of Lincoln."

the audience. At its close a man by the name of Forquer, who was well known in the community as a man of no little ability, arose to reply to him. He had formerly been a Whig, but for some reason had seen fit to change his political faith and become a staunch Democrat. He had recently had his buildings protected from the lightning by numerous rods, which were the first ever seen in the vicinity, and were the objects of considerable curiosity and much unfavorable comment. In the beginning of his speech, he said :

"This young man must be taken down and I am sorry that the duty devolves upon me."

He then took up Lincoln's points, one by one, and answered them in a fair and logical manner, although frequently indulging in coarse personalities and an assumption of superiority that was intensely annoying to Lincoln, who stood by becoming more and more wrought up as the speaker continued. When he had closed, Lincoln stepped upon the platform to reply. His answer was dignified, forcible and convincing, and concluded as follows :

"It is for you, fellow-citizens, and not for me to say whether I am up or down. The gentleman has seen fit to allude to my being a young man, but he forgets that I am older in years than I am in the tricks and trades of politicians. I desire to live and desire place and distinction ; but I would rather die now than, like the gentleman, live to see the day that I would change my politics for an office worth $3,000 a year, and then feel compelled to erect a lightning rod to protect a guilty conscience from an offended God."

Forquer was completely answered and probably

never heard the last of this pointed allusion to his
lightning rods.

In these sentences Lincoln struck a key-note of his
life and character. Though often in a position to
profit by the tricks of politicians he never descended
to do so. In politics, as in his private life, he was
strictly honest and frank and, where a principle was
concerned, as firm and unyielding as a rock.

In this campaign he greatly increased his reputation as a speaker. He excelled especially in original
and vigorous thought, and clear, concise and pointed
expression. His appearance upon the platform was
awkward and unprepossessing, but this was soon forgotten in the interest which he never failed to excite.

The election resulted in a large Whig majority in a
county which had hitherto been a Democratic stronghold, and Lincoln's majority was larger than that of
any of the other candidates.

The members from Sangamon County were
dubbed the "long nine." They were all of great
height, averaging over six feet and more than 200
pounds in weight. They probably exerted a greater
influence in legislation than any other delegation, and
many of the extravagant and vicious laws of this
session were traceable to them.

There were many men in the Legislature with
whom Lincoln came into more or less intimate association, who afterwards gained national reputations.
There were several incipient Members of Congress
and Senators and a number who afterwards gained
distinguished military reputations. Foremost among
them all was Stephen A. Douglas, whose career was
only less brilliant than that of his great fellow-mem-

ber. Thus Lincoln was thrown into contact with
many of the brightest minds of the West, and was
much benefited by his association with them.

The principal business, considered during the session, related to a most extravagant system of internal
improvements, and many gigantic and reckless
schemes were discussed. The people were deeply
impressed with the great resources of the State, and
believed that, if they developed its natural features,
and established easy communication between the different sections, the State would immediately fill up
with inhabitants and its prosperity be assured. The
population was comparatively small, and the people
were too few and poor to bear the heavy financial
burdens thus entailed, so they determined to bond
the State for a million dollars, which would have been
but a small part of the cost of the contemplated
improvements. The Legislature represented the
extreme of public sentiment and commenced immediately to plan a system of internal improvements,
which two generations and a great commonwealth
have hardly yet completed.

Many of the small streams, as well as larger rivers,
were to be dredged, widened and made navigable.
Upon them were to be placed lines of splendid steamers, which were to connect the settlements and
develop them into large and bustling cities. There
was not a little cross-roads village or scattering hamlet that did not have its visions of metropolitan
splendors. Parks and boulevards, churches, city-halls
and great business blocks were to spring up, as if by
magic.

The State was to be crossed by a net-work of railroads connecting the North with the South, the East with the West. These sanguine legislators expected to transform in a moment a wilderness with a half a million inhabitants into an old-world country with its crowded population and improvements, a process which hitherto centuries alone had been able to perfect.

It was one of those periods of speculation and excitement through which every country must pass, and the inevitable reaction was quick to follow, retarding the general prosperity just in proportion to the extravagance of the speculation.

It is perhaps well for the State that it passed through this trying ordeal before its interests had been developed to any extent, or the crash would have been far greater and its results more lasting.

Lincoln was the recognized leader of his delegation, and hence was influential in the proceedings of the House. Into all of the extravagant measures, which were brought forward, he entered heart and soul, and exerted all his power to secure their incorporation into the statutes of the State.

The question of the permanent location of the State Capital came up at this time. Vandalia was not a desirable location for several reasons, and a number of cities were desirous of the honor and emoluments accruing from this distinction. Powerful lobbies were present from Alton, Decatur, Peoria, Jacksonville, Illiopolis and Springfield. The "long nine" were, of course, pledged to do their utmost to secure for Springfield the coveted honor, and, under the shrewd leadership of Lincoln, they gained their end, after a prolonged and bitter struggle and the beautiful city of the Sangamon was designated as the Capital of Illinois.

Near the close of the session occurred a circumstance which attracted but little attention at the time, but which, in the light of subsequent events, is worthy of more than a passing notice. As has been said, Illinois occupied a somewhat anomalous position in regard to slavery. While the institution was rigorously excluded from the State the majority of the people looked with greater abhorrence upon the Abolitionist than upon the slaveholder. But few Abolitionists ventured to settle within its borders and they were sedulously avoided by the most of the people of the community, and sometimes neglect gave place to actual ill treatment.

This sentiment was put in the form of a resolution and passed by the Legislature, near the end of the session in the following form :

" Resolved, by the General Assembly of the State of Illinois : That we highly disapprove of the formation of Abolition societies and of the doctrines promulgated by them ; that the right of property in slaves is sacred to the slaveholding States by the Federal constitution, and that they cannot be deprived of that right without their own consent; that the General Government cannot abolish slavery in the District of Columbia against the consent of the citizens of said District without a manifest breach of good faith . . ."

The Legislature thus recognized the absolute right of the slaveholding States to their peculiar institutions and sought to establish the doctrine of non-interference. The movement seemed at the time to be possessed of little significance, yet it was the cogent statement of a political doctrine which was des-

tined, in after years, to exert a baleful influence over
the whole country and to prove a great obstacle in
the path of advancing freedom.

Lincoln was not an Abolitionist. His early associations had so familiarized him with slavery as an established institution that he looked with suspicion and
alarm upon the radical doctrines of the new party
which as yet had no political status, but of which he
was in the future destined to become the leader. Yet
slavery as a fact was wholly distasteful to him; hence,
while he would not commit himself to the Abolition
movement, he would not, on the other hand, subscribe
to nor even give a silent consent to resolutions which
were essentially pro-slavery.

Accordingly, on the last day but one of the session,
he prepared a protest against the resolutions and
tried to secure the signature of his colleagues to it.
Only one, Dan Stone, could be induced to sign it, and
with but two names appended it was spread upon the
records of the House.

It reads as follows :

" Resolutions upon the subject of domestic slavery having
passed both branches of the General Assembly, at its present
session, the undersigned hereby protest against the passage of
the same. They believe that the institution of slavery is founded
upon both injustice and bad policy, but that the promulgation
of abolition doctrines tends rather to increase than to abate its
evils. They believe that the Congress of the United States
has no power under the Constitution to interfere with the institution of slavery in the different States. They believe that the
Congress of the United States has power under the Constitution to abolish slavery in the District of Columbia, but that the
power ought not to be exercised unless at the request of the
people of the District. The difference between these opinions

and those contained in the above resolutions is their reason for entering this protest.

DAN STONE,
ABRAHAM LINCOLN.

Mr. Lincoln never materially departed from the political doctrine herein enunciated and never ceased to hold that the Constitution conferred no right upon any one to interfere with slavery in the slave States.

At the close of the session he walked home from Vandalia, a distance of one hundred miles. The rest of the delegation rode upon horseback, but Lincoln was able to keep up with them and beguiled the tedium of the journey with many a story and pointed joke.

The weather was cold and his clothes were thin and worn. Complaining of the cold, one of his companions told the future President that "it was no wonder he was cold, there was so much of him on the ground." No one enjoyed the joke more than its victim.

Upon their return to Springfield they were greeted with the most extravagant manifestations of gratitude and joy. They had secured the greatly coveted honor for the city and the citizens could not do enough to show their appreciation of the service. In the midst of the feasting and rejoicing, Lincoln was observed to be sad and preoccupied. When questioned as to the cause of it he ascribed it to the unsettled condition of his life, and the uncertainty of his future. In view of his lonely situation his friends determined to secure his removal to the Capital and to assist him, as far as he would permit, to secure lucrative employment.

In April, 1837, he left New Salem and removed to Springfield, where he continued to live until he went to Washington.   His possessions were few and easily carried in his saddle-bags.   He intended to hire a small room and obtain his meals at a restaurant or boarding-house.   Upon his arrival he went into the store of Joshua F. Speed, with whom he was slightly acquainted and inquired the price of the necessary furniture, at the same time remarking that, if he succeeded in his profession, he would pay for it in full ; but if he did not succeed, he should probably never pay for it.   Struck by his appearance and apparent honesty, Mr. Speed offered to share his own room with him, an offer which Lincoln gladly accepted.

He had been licensed to practice law in the preceding month and soon entered into partnership with Major Stuart, who had superintended his legal education and was a warm and consistent friend.   He remained with him for four years when he entered into partnership with Judge Stephen T. Logan, one of the shrewdest and most successful lawyers of the State.

The Springfield bar was at this time one of the most brilliant in the country and there were several lawyers connected with it, who could have held their own against the ablest advocates of the East. Among those who afterwards achieved a national reputation were Stephen A. Douglas, the prosecuting attorney, E. D. Baker, Ninian W. Edwards, Jesse B. Thomas, Samuel H. Treat and many others.   It required a man of more than ordinary ability to make a place among such men.

Lincoln did not appear much in the society of the

place which, for a new town, was pretentious and exclusive. The population numbered less than 2,000, but there were representatives of many old Kentucky families who lived in a state of magnificence and display, which was unattainable for most of the pioneers. It is probable that Lincoln with his rude manners and uncouth appearance, together with his coarse and ill-fitting garments, could hardly find a place in the first circles. But he was intent on his work and found his amusement in more intellectual pursuits so that he did not miss the round of social gayeties.

The means of mental improvement in those days were limited. Books were costly and scarce. The few newspapers that came into the community were soon read and their contents discussed. In order to make up for this lack of material for literary culture, as far as possible, the young men were accustomed to form debating societies, where they discussed the great topics of the day and listened to addresses and papers prepared by the members. The meeting of the society was a great event in the smaller towns, and the room in which it was held was generally packed with sympathetic listeners.

Such a society was organized in Springfield under the name of the "Young Men's Lyceum," and Lincoln was an enthusiastic member of it. This was a more dignified organization than the average debating society, and contained much of the best talent of the place.

Speed's store was a popular gathering-place where, beside the great open fireplace, many an impromptu discussion took place. Here Lincoln and Douglas and Baker were often found with scores of others engaging in heated political discussions, which seldom ended with a decided advantage to either side.

In 1837, Lincoln was invited to deliver an address before the Lyceum and took for his subject, " The Perpetuation of our Free Institutions." He spent much time in its preparation and it was so favorably received as to be subsequently published in the *Weekly Journal* of Springfield. The style was florid and declamatory, yet, considering his lack of education, it was a remarkable production. It showed the profound thought and originality of a true statesman while it gave evidence of ardent patriotism and a genuine love of constitutional liberty. The style of thought and expression is in marked contrast to that exhibited in his Gettysburg address, perhaps the best example of true eloquence in the English lan-guage.

The one was at the beginning of his public career, the other, near the end. The Springfield address has the same true ring as the one made upon the great battle-field, but the development of his intellectual powers from the first product to the last contains the story of all that is most interesting in his career.

In his exordium he speaks of the peculiar blessings enjoyed by the American people in their natural surroundings and political institutions which conduce to to civil and religious liberty and then reviews the labors of our ancestors to secure to us these inestimable blessings.

" Theirs was the task, and nobly they performed it, to possess themselves and, through themselves, us, of this goodly land, and to rear upon its hills and valleys a political edifice of liberty and equal rights ;

'tis ours only to transmit these, the former unpro-
faned by the foot of an invader, the latter undecayed
by the lapse of time.   This, our duty to ourselves and
our posterity, and love for our species in general,
imperatively require us to perform. . . . . At
what point, then, is the approach of danger to be
expected?   I answer, if it ever reaches us, it must
spring up among ourselves.   It cannot come from
abroad.   If destruction be our lot, we must ourselves
be its author and finisher.   As a nation of freemen
we must live through all time or die of suicide."

He graphically describes the dangers of mob-violence and lawlessness and speaks of the different
menaces from within the people against the stability
of our institutions.

" Many great and good men, sufficiently qualified
for any task they should undertake, may be ever
found, whose ambition would aspire to nothing
beyond a seat in Congress, a gubernatorial or presidential chair.   But such belong not to the family of
the lion, or the brood of the eagle.   What?   Think
you these places would satisfy an Alexander, a Cæsar
or a Napoleon?   Never.   Towering genius disdains
a beaten path.   It seeks regions hitherto unexplored.
It sees no distinction in adding story to story upon
the monuments of fame erected to the memory of
others.   It denies that it is glory enough to serve
under any chief.   It scorns to tread in the foot-prints
of a predecessor, however illustrious.   It thirsts and
burns for distinction and, if possible, it will have it
whether at the expense of *emancipating slaves* or enslaving free men."

He closed with a tribute to the soldiers of the Rev-

olution in which he characterized them as living
histories :

" But these histories are gone. They can be read
no more forever. They were a fortress of strength ;
but what invading foemen could never do, the silent
artillery of time has—the leveling of its walls. They
are gone. They were a forest of giant oaks ; but the
all-resistless hurricane has swept over them, and left
only here and there a lonely trunk, despoiled of its
verdure, shorn of its foliage, unshading and unshaded,
to murmur in a few more gentle breezes, and to com-
bat with its mutilated limbs a few more rude storms,
then to sink and be no more. They were pillars of
the Temple of Liberty, and now, that they have
crumbled away, that temple must fall, unless we, their
descendants, supply their places with other pillars
hewn from the same solid quarry of sober reason.
Passion has helped us but can do so no more. It will,
in the future, be our enemy. Reason—cold, calculat-
ing, unimpassioned reason—must furnish all the
materials for our future support and defense. Let
these materials be moulded into general intelligence,
sound morality, and, in particular, a reverence for the
Constitution and the laws. Upon these let the proud
fabric of freedom rest as the rock of its basis and as
truly as has been said of the only greater institution,
' The gates of hell shall not prevail against it.' "

One evening, not long after, the discussion of politics in Speed's store became unusually animated
Douglas, as usual, was the Democratic champion and
not only warmly advocated his own political views,
but bitterly attacked the doctrines of the Whigs and
accused them indiscriminately of fraud, peculation

and political insincerity. In the midst of the babel
of voices he suddenly sprang to his feet, exclaiming,
"A store is no place to discuss politics," and challenged his opponents to a public debate. The challenge was accepted and a series of meetings arranged,
to be held in the Presbyterian Church to last eight
days, giving to each one an evening to present his
views. The Democrats were to be represented by
Douglas, Calhoun, Lamborn and Thomas, while the
Whigs selected Logan, Baker, Browning and Lincoln
to defend their cause. The speeches were long and
intensely partisan, and when Lincoln's turn came on
the last night, the people had become weary of the
monotony, and but a small audience assembled to listen to him. He spoke without notes and his speech
was pronounced the best of the series. He denounced
in strongest terms the short-comings and corruption
of the Administration. At times he seemed to have
almost a prophetic inspiration and the sentiments he
uttered were indicative of the most exalted patriotism. He said :

"Many countries have lost their liberties and ours
may lose hers ; but if she shall, be it my proudest
plume, not that I was the last to desert, but that I
never deserted her." Could he for a moment have
caught a glimpse of the supreme sacrifice he would
be called upon to make when he said :

"The probabilities that we may fall in the struggle
ought not to deter us from the support of a cause
which we deem just. It shall not deter me. If ever
I feel the soul within me elevate and expand to those
dimensions not wholly unworthy of its Almighty
Architect, it is when I contemplate the cause of my

country, deserted by all the world beside, and I, standing up boldly and alone, hurling defiance at her victorious oppressors. And here, without contemplating the consequences, before high Heaven and in the face of the whole world, I swear eternal fidelity to the just cause, as I deem it, of the land of my life, my liberty and my love."

When the fulfilment of this oath was called for, and the suffering country he loved so well stretched out her hands to him in her dire extremity, he hesitated not, but redeemed to the uttermost the solemn pledge he had given this night as if in anticipation of the event.

CHAPTER VI.

ALTHOUGH he was deeply interested in politics and gave up much of his time to side issues, Lincoln did not forget that it was by the practice of law that he was to make his living and, in his plodding and patient way, was slowly making a reputation. He never excelled in his knowledge of the law, unlike his partner, Judge Logan, who was ranked as the best-equipped *nisi prius* lawyer in the West. Nor did he apply himself to a single branch of the law, so as to become a recognized authority.

He had, by persistent study, gained a sufficient knowledge of common and statute law to enable him to practice successfully in the circuit courts, and his quickness to take advantage of any flaw in the evidence or to turn a point upon his adversary fully compensated for any lack of legal culture which he might have manifested.

As an example of this an interesting story is related of his defense of the son of an old friend, who was accused of murder. The incident was so striking and dramatic that it has been made the basis of a popular novel.[1] The murder was committed one Sunday evening at a camp-meeting. The victim was a young man against whom the accused had been heard to make violent threats. The principal witness was a disreputable man, who swore that he had heard the

---

[1] "The Graysons," by Edward Eggleston.

(75)

accused threaten to take the life of the victim, and that, on the night of the murder, he saw the deed performed from a thicket in which he had concealed himself. The chain of evidence seemed to be completely forged and public sentiment was strongly against the accused. To the surprise of all, Lincoln sat calmly in his seat during the trial, asked but few questions and produced no witnesses, except one or two to prove the previous good character of the young man. When it came his turn to address the jury he reviewed briefly the case and called to mind the fact that the leading witness had sworn that he had seen the foul deed performed by the light of the full moon. Producing an almanac he showed the jury that there had been no moon that night ; and then pointing his long finger at him, he accused the witness of the murder. He completed his speech with a most eloquent appeal to the jury to restore the young man to his widowed mother, and pictured so fervently the desolation of the home, deprived of the only son, that there was not a dry eye in the audience. It is needless to say that the jury returned a verdict of " not guilty," without leaving their seats.

In those days lawyers were compelled to go from place to place to attend court, making the rounds of the circuit with the Judge. The cases were generally free from legal technicalities and required but little preparation. The fees were not large and were often in kind, so that it was not a difficult matter for even a poor lawyer to secure a horse. The lawyers generally traveled in congenial groups, and enlivened the monotonous journey with stories and anecdotes, or heated political discussions.

Lincoln was always a favorite traveling-companion and made an extensive circle of friends. For a young man, ambitious for political preferment, no mode of life could have been more favorable. People from the surrounding country flocked to the court-house during the session to listen to the speeches, and they made an appreciative audience, quick to recognize ability. They knew all the lawyers by name, frequently being personally acquainted with them, and freely discussed their relative merits. Indeed, the court-session and the doings of the lawyers formed the topic of general conversation in the intervals, and the favorites were always cordially greeted.

It is needless to say that Lincoln made many firm friends during this peripatetic life. His open and frank demeanor, his good memory, which enabled him to remember the names of even casual acquaintances, his helpful disposition, and his geniality and good humor, all united to make him preferred above the most of his associates. The popularity thus acquired added to his political speeches and work soon caused him to be recognized as one of the Whig leaders in the State, and as such he gained no little prominence.

There is always a tendency on the part of posterity to idealize great heroes and to see nothing but the good and great things in their lives. This hero-worship has always been specially directed towards, Lincoln. During the last four years of his life he occupied so lofty an eminence, and performed such signal services for humanity, as to be ranked in the short list of her greatest heroes. Using this period as a starting point, men paint the halo of perfection about his whole life. As the wise men followed the star from the East to the stable at Bethlehem, so it is a common tendency to picture Lincoln passing through the minute details of his life with the star of his destiny ever in sight and pointing him out, from early boyhood, as the man upon whom the fate of the nation should depend.

This state of things was far from true. While he undoubtedly gave promise of a brilliant future, the great pre-eminence which he was to attain was but little more than hinted at. There were many more noted and learned lawyers, even in his own circuit. As an orator he had many peers, a few superiors. As a statesman he had had but little opportunity to show his mettle, but his efforts in that direction had been largely attended with failure and seemed indicative of political short-sightedness, if not of actual incapacity. Had it not been for his captivating manners and the vast fund of story and anecdote, with which he illustrated and pointed his thoughts in conversation and public addresses, he would have attracted hardly more than passing attention. That he had the elements of true greatness in youth no one can deny, but they required much training before he was fitted to occupy an exalted position in the world.

Many interesting stories are related of his sayings and doings while "riding circuit," that will be recognized as thoroughly characteristic of the man.

Two farmers, having a misunderstanding about a horse trade, went to law. By mutual consent Mr. Lincoln and his partner took the opposite sides. On the day of the trial Mr. Logan, having bought a new shirt, open in the back with a huge standing collar, dressed himself in extreme haste and put on the shirt with the bosom at the back, a linen coat concealing the blunder. He dazed the jury with his knowledge of "horse-points," and, as the day was sultry, took off his coat and summed up in his shirt-sleeves.

Lincoln, sitting behind him, took in the situation, and when his turn came remarked to the jury:

"Gentleman, Mr. Logan has been trying for over an hour to make you believe he knows more about a horse than these honest old farmers who are witnesses. He has quoted largely from his 'horse doctor,' and now, gentlemen, I submit to you (here he lifted Logan out of his chair, and turned him with his back to the jury and the crowd, at the same time turning up the enormous standing collar) what dependence can you place in his horse knowledge, when he has not sense enough to put on his shirt."

The roars of laughter that greeted this exhibition and the verdict that Lincoln got soon after gave Logan a permanent prejudice against "bosom shirts."

Mr. Lincoln never made his profession lucrative to himself. It was very difficult for him to charge any one a heavy fee, and still more difficult for him to charge his friends anything at all for professional services. To a poor client he was quite as apt to give money as to take it from him. He never encouraged the spirit of litigation. One of his old clients says that he went to Mr. Lincoln with a case to prosecute, and that Mr. Lincoln refused to have anything to do with it, because he was not strictly in the right. "You can give the other party a great deal of trouble," said the lawyer, "and perhaps beat him, but you had better let the suit alone."

About the time Mr. Lincoln came to be known as a successful lawyer, he was waited upon by a lady who held a real-estate claim which she desired to have him prosecute, putting into his hands, with the necessary papers, a check for two hundred and fifty dollars, as a retaining fee. Mr. Lincoln said he would look the case over, and asked her to call again the next day. Upon presenting herself, Mr. Lincoln told her that he had gone through the papers very carefully, and he must tell her frankly that there was not a "peg" to hang her claim upon, and he could not conscientiously advise her to bring an action. The lady was satisfied, and, thanking him, rose to go.

"Wait," said Mr. Lincoln, fumbling in his vest pocket, "here is the check you left with me."

"But, Mr. Lincoln," returned the lady, "I think you have earned that."

"No, no," he responded, handing it back to her; ' that would not be right. I can't take pay for doing my duty."

At one time he and a certain judge were bantering one another about trading horses, and it was agreed that the next morning, at nine o'clock, they should make a trade, the horses to be unseen up to that hour, and there was to be no backing out under penalty of twenty-five dollars.

At the hour appointed the judge came up, leading the sorriest-looking specimen of a horse ever seen in those parts. In a few minutes Mr. Lincoln was seen approaching with a wooden saw-horse upon his shoulders. Great were the shouts and the laughter of the crowd, and both were greatly increased, when Mr. Lincoln, on surveying the Judge's animal, set down his saw-horse, and exclaimed :

"Well, Judge, this is the first time I ever got the worst of it in a horse-trade."

It is said that Lincoln was always ready to join in a laugh at his own expense. He used to tell the following story with great glee:

"In the days when I used to be on the circuit," said he, "I was accosted on the cars by a stranger, who said:

"'Excuse me, sir, but I have an article in my possession which belongs to you.'

"'How is that?' I asked, considerably astonished.

"The stranger took a jack-knife from his pocket. 'This knife,' said he, 'was placed in my hands some years ago, with the injunction that I was to keep it until I found a man uglier than myself. I have carried it from that time to this. Allow me now to say, sir, that I think you are fairly entitled to the property.'"

Attorney-General Bates was once remonstrating with the President against the appointment to a judicial position of considerable importance of a Western man who, though upon the bench, possessed an indifferent reputation as a lawyer.

"Well now, Judge," returned Mr. Lincoln, "I think you are rather too hard upon Smith. Besides that, I must tell you, he did me a good turn long ago. When I took to the law, I was walking to court one morning with some ten or twelve miles of bad road before me, when Smith overtook me in his wagon.

"'Hullo, Lincoln!' said he; 'going to the court-house? Come in, and I will give you a seat.'

"Well, I got in, and Smith went on reading his papers. Presently, the wagon struck a stump on one side of the road, then it hopped off to the other. I looked out, and the driver was jerking from side to side in his seat; so I said, 'Judge, I think your coach-man has been taking a drop too much this morning.'

"'Well, I declare, Lincoln,' said he, 'I should not much wonder if you are right, for he has nearly upset me half a dozen times since starting.' So, putting his head out of the window, he shouted, 'Why, you infer-nal scoundrel, you are drunk.'

"Upon which, pulling up his horses, and turning around with great gravity, the coachman said: 'Be dad! but that's the first rightful decision your honor has given for the last twelve months!'"

An amusing incident occurred in connection with riding the circuit, which gives a deep glimpse into the good lawyer's heart. He was riding by a deep slough, in which, to his exceeding pain, he saw a pig struggling, and with such faint efforts that it was evident that he could not extricate himself from the mud. Mr. Lincoln looked at the pig and the mud which enveloped him, and then looked at some new clothes with which he had but a short time before arrayed himself. Deciding against the claims of the pig, he rode on, but he could not get rid of the vision of the poor brute; and, at last, after riding two miles, he turned back determined to rescue the animal, even at the expense of his new clothes. Arrived at the spot, he tied his horse, and with considerable difficulty succeeded in rescuing the pig from its predicament. Washing his hands in the nearst brook, he remounted his horse and rode on. He then fell to examining the motive that sent him back to release the pig. At first thought, it seemed pure benevolence, but at length he came to the conclusion that it was selfishness, for he certainly went to the pig's relief in order to "take a pain out of his own mind."

To a client who had carefully stated his case, to which Mr. Lincoln had listened with the closest attention, he said:

"Yes, there is no reasonable doubt that I can gain your case for you. I can set a whole neighborhood at loggerheads, I can distress a widowed mother and her six fatherless children and thereby get for you $600, which rightfully belongs, it appears to me, as much to the woman and her children as to you. You must remember that some things which are legally right are not morally right. I shall not take your case, but will give you a little advice, for which I will charge you nothing. You seem to be a sprightly, energetic man. I would advise you to try your hand at making $600 some other way."[1]

Soon after he entered upon his profession at Springfield, he was engaged in a criminal case, in which there seemed to be little chance of success. By dint of hard work he succeeded in gaining the case and received for his services five hundred dollars. A legal friend, calling upon him next morning, found him sitting before a table upon which his money was spread.

"Look here, Judge," said he, "see what a heap of money I've got from the —— case. Did you ever see

---

[1] Browne's "Life of Lincoln."

anything like it? Why, I never had so much money in my life before, put it all together." Then crossing his arms across the table, his manner sobering down, he added, " I have got five hundred dollars; if it were only seven hundred and fifty dollars, I would go directly and purchase a quarter-section of land, and settle it upon my old stepmother."

His friend said, if the deficiency was all he needed, he would loan him the amount, taking his note, to which Mr. Lincoln instantly acceded.

His friend than said : "Lincoln, I would not do just what you have indicated. Your stepmother is getting old, and will not probably live many years. I would settle that property upon her for her use during her lifetime to revert to you upon her death."

With much feeling Lincoln replied: " I shall do no such thing. It is a poor return, at the best, for all the good woman's devotion and fidelity to me, and there is not going to be any half-way business about it ;" and so saying, he gathered up his money and proceeded to carry into execution his long-cherished plan.

CHAPTER VII.

LINCOLN was again elected to the Legislature in 1838, and served his term with acceptance. In 1840 he did not seek a re-election, as his business needed his close attention. His partner, Major Stuart, had been elected to Congress, and for three or four years he had attended to all the business of the firm, rendering a scrupulous account of every transaction to his partner.

In 1841 the partnership was dissolved, and he entered the office of Judge Logan as junior partner. For the first time he was associated with a man of thorough scholarship and his influence was just that of which Lincoln stood most in need. He was thus led to closer study and to take a deeper and broader view of the duties and responsibilities of his profession.

In 1840 he had acquired sufficient political celebrity to be nominated for elector on the Whig ticket, and he spent much time speaking in its interests during the campaign in various parts of the State and in Indiana. This campaign, known as the "log-cabin and hard cider" campaign was the most unique one ever carried on in the country. General Harrison had been nominated by the Whigs, which party had been disastrously defeated in the last two Presidential campaigns. After his nomination the Democratic orators made slighting allusions to his obscure origin

(85)

and his supposed taste for hard cider. These were seized upon as the rallying cry of the campaign, and log-cabins sprang up, as if by the stroke of a magician s wand, in every part of the country. Many of these cabins were mounted on wheels, and drawn from one place to another, amid demonstrations of the wildest enthusiasm, in a sort of rude triumphal procession. The by-word and reproach of the enemy became the slogan of victory, and the tide set strongly in favor of the Whigs.

The financial measures of Van Buren's administration had been of such a character, as to weaken, for a time, the confidence of the people in the Democratic policy and leaders, and Harrison was elected by a large majority, only to die within one month of his inauguration.

Lincoln shared in the prevailing enthusiasm and contributed in no small degree to the vast increase in the Whig vote in Illinois. His peculiar ability in argument and discussion was often called into play, and several times he was pitted against Douglas, who was destined to be, in the future, his opponent in the great debates that attracted the attention of the English-speaking race. The discussions were more in the character of rough-and-tumble contests than of conflicts between trained gladiators, and Lincoln generally carried off the palm. His political work was performed at the expense of his legal practice, however, and at the end of the campaign he found himself richer in political influence, but with a financial loss which he could ill afford.

It was shortly after the close of the "Log-Cabin" campaign that he met Mary Todd, who was destined to exercise so great an influence over his after-life. She had recently come to Springfield from Kentucky, her former home, to live with her sister, the wife of Ninian W. Edwards, a prominent politician and lawyer, and who subsequently became Governor of the State.

She was descended from one of the old Kentucky families of high respectability and aristocratic connections. In appearance she was beautiful and attractive, of high culture and exceedingly bright in conversation. She joined to these agreeable attributes a high temper and a great ambition. She was once heard to say that the man she should marry would become President. Lincoln became infatuated with her wit and beauty, and began to pay his addresses to her. Douglas, his political rival, also entered the list and strove for the favor of the young stranger. Personally Lincoln could bear no comparison with Douglas, yet Miss Todd finally chose him, for what reason it would be difficult to tell, since she is said to have preferred Douglas.

Lincoln was accustomed to call upon her at the house of her sister, where he would sit for hours and listen to her brilliant conversation, as if under some magic spell. The contrast between the two could hardly have been greater, both physically and mentally. In one thing only were they in entire harmony, and that was ambition.

General Singleton, who was a young lawyer in Springfield at this time, tells the following story :

"The bevy of bright young ladies, to which Miss Todd belonged before her marriage to Mr. Lincoln, used to have a good deal of sport at this awkward young man's expense. Once evening, at a little party, Mr.

Lincoln approached Miss Todd and said, in his peculiar idiom :

" Miss Todd, I should like to dance with you the worst way."

The young lady accepted the inevitable, and hobbled around the room with him. When Miss Todd had returned to her seat, one of her mischievous companions said :

" Well, Mary, did he dance with you in the worst way ? "

" Yes," she answered, " the very worst."

His courtship was distinguished with the somewhat novel incident of a challenge to fight a duel. [1]

At this time there was living in Springfield, James Shields, a gallant, hot-headed bachelor, from Tyrone County, Ireland. Like most of his countrymen, he was an ardent Democrat, and he was also a great beau in society. Miss Todd, full of spirit, very gay and a little wild and mischievous, published in the Sangamon *Journal*, under the name of " Aunt Rebecca of the Lost Townships," some amusing satirical papers ridiculing the susceptible and sensitive Irishman. Indeed, Shields was so sensitive he could not bear ridicule, and would much rather die than be laughed at. On seeing the papers, he went at once to Francis, the editor, and furiously demanded the name of the author declaring that, unless the name of the writer was given, he would hold the editor personally responsible. Francis was a large, broad man, and Shields was very thin and slim, and the editor realized that, with his great bulk, it would be

---

[1] Arnold's " Life of Lincoln."

very unsafe for him to stand in front of Shields'
pistol. He was a warm, personal and political friend
of Lincoln, and, knowing the relations between him
and Miss Todd, in this dilemma he disclosed the facts
to Lincoln, and asked his advice and counsel. He
was not willing to expose the lady's name, and
yet was extremely reluctant himself to meet the fiery
Irishman in the field. Lincoln at once told Francis
to tell Shields to regard him as the author.

The Tazewell Circuit Court, at which he had
several cases of importance to try, being in session,
Lincoln departed for Tremont, the county-seat. As
soon as Francis had notified Shields that Lincoln was
the author of the papers, he and his second, General
Whitesides, started in hot pursuit of Lincoln. Hearing this, Dr. Merryman and Lincoln's old friend,
Butler, started also for Tremont, "to prevent," as
Merryman said, "any advantage being taken of Lincoln, either as to his honor or his life." They passed
the belligerent Shields and Whitesides in the night,
and arrived at Tremont in advance. They told Lincoln
what was coming, and he replied, that he was
altogether opposed to duelling, and would do anything to avoid it that would not degrade him in the
estimation of himself and of his friends, but if a fight
were the only alternative of such degradation, he
would fight.

In the mean while, the young lady having heard of
the demand that Shields had made, wrote another letter in which she said:

"I hear the way of these fire-eaters is to give the
challenged party the choice of weapons, which, being
the case, I'll tell you in confidence that I never fight

with anything but broomsticks, or hot water, or a shovelful of coals, the former of which, being something like a shillalah, may not be objectionable to him."

While this badinage was going on, Shields had challenged Lincoln, and the challenge had been accepted. The weapons decided on were cavalry broadswords of the largest size, and a place of meeting was selected on the west bank of the Mississippi, within three miles of Alton. The principals, and their seconds and surgeons, started for the place of meeting. As they approached the river, they were joined by Colonel Harding and others, who sought to bring about a reconciliation. Hostilities were suspended. Shields was induced to withdraw the challenge and satisfactory explanations were made. Lincoln declared that the obnoxious articles were written solely for political effect, and with no intention of injuring the personal or private character of Shields, and so the parties returned reconciled. With very heavy broadswords under the conditions of this meeting, Shields, who was a comparatively weak man, could not have injured Lincoln, and Lincoln would not have injured Shields. If the meeting had taken place, however, nothing but a tragedy could have prevented its being a farce."

The date of the wedding was set, and the invited guests were present. The bride had arrayed herself in her bridal robes, but Lincoln failed to appear. The bride and the marriage-feast—but no bridegroom. After waiting some hours, the guests slowly took their departure, the bridal-robes were laid aside, and the brilliantly lighted house was soon in darkness. As the time for the wedding had approached, Lincoln had been attacked with doubts as to his love for Miss Todd, and began to fear that he would com mit a great wrong if he married her, until he lapsed into one of his old fits of melancholy, which so closely resembled insanity. For weeks the burden of his misery seemed greater than he could bear, and his friends, fearing that he might be tempted to take his own life, stayed faithfully with him until his bosom-friend, Joshua F. Speed, invited him to spend a few months with him in his old home in Kentucky. Thither he went and spent some months of restful quiet. Speed's home was on a great estate a few miles from Louisville, and not far from Lincoln's earliest home. The peaceful surroundings and restful comforts were just what the overwrought young lawyer needed to restore his mental equilibrium.

In a few months he returned to Springfield, and took up his work again. For some time he held no communication with Miss Todd, who, after she had recovered somewhat from the mortification resulting from his desertion, had broken the engagement.

He felt great solicitude for her, and deplored deeply the injury he had done her. In some way, through the contrivance of a mutual friend, they were brought together again, the old relations were resumed, and the past was forgotten, at least forgiven.

November 4, 1842, they were married in the presence of a large concourse of friends, and with the impressive ceremonies of the Episcopal Church, a form that had never been used in Springfield before, and which attracted much attention.

Mr. and Mrs. Lincoln went to live at a hotel, where

they remained for three or four years, paying four dollars a week for their accommodations. Mr. Lincoln then bought a small, but cheery and comfortable house of the Rev. Nathaniel Dresser, where they lived until they removed to Washington to occupy the White House.

After the campaign of 1840, Mr. Lincoln had returned to his law practice, but the charm of politics had begun to exert its sway over him, and he became more and more desirous of political preferment. In 1842 he planned to secure the nomination for Congress from the Springfield district, but was compelled to withdraw in favor of his friend, Edward D. Baker, who secured the support of the delegates from Sangamon County of whom Lincoln, contrary to his wish, was one. He remarked that his case was much like the young man who had a successful rival for the affections of a young lady in whom he was interested, and was afterwards invited to act as groomsman at the wedding.

At the convention, however, Mr. Baker lost the nomination, which was given to John J. Hardin, a strong and talented man, who represented the district honorably for the next two years. In 1844 came the Presidential canvass, in which Henry Clay, the idol of the Whig party, was defeated, and James K. Polk was elected, almost as much to the surprise of the Democrats, as to the Whigs.

Lincoln, being considered the Whig leader in Illinois, was placed at the head of the electoral ticket, and again made an active canvass of Illinois and a part of Indiana. During the canvass he made a speech in Gentryville, which was near his former home.

While in the midst of his speech, an old friend, Nate Grigsby, entered the room. Lincoln recognized him on the instant, and, stopping short in his speech, cried out, "There's Nate." Without the slightest regard for the propriety of the occasion, he suspended his address totally, and, striding from the platform, began scrambling through the audience, and over the benches towards the modest Nate, who stood near the door. When he reached him, Lincoln shook his hand cordially, and, after felicitating himself sufficiently upon the happy meeting, he returned to the platform and finished his speech.

There was scarcely a character in American history for whom Lincoln entertained a more enthusiastic veneration, than for Henry Clay. This, no doubt, was due in part to the biography which he had so eagerly read in his childhood, since which time he had been a constant worshiper at the altar of the Southern sage. Hence he entered into the campaign with unusual vigor and enthusiasm, and his disappointment at the result was deep and bitter. Indeed, the defeat totally demoralized the Whig party for a time, and it hardly seemed probable that it would ever recover from the shock sufficiently to enter into the next campaign. But the events of Polk's administration unexpectedly brought about a Democratic defeat, and General Taylor, the Whig candidate, was elected in 1848, more as a result of Democratic demoralization than of Whig strength.

Lincoln and his partner, Judge Logan, were both of them prominent Whigs, and to a considerable extent rivals for political preferment. Hence their relations to each other became somewhat strained.

Logan believed that his claims should be preferred on account of his age and acknowledged ability. Lincoln based his claim upon his active services and great influence. As a result of their strained relations the partnership was dissolved, September 20, 1843, and on the same day Lincoln entered into a partnership with William H. Herndon, a young lawyer and a relative of one of the Clary's Grove boys, who had always remained his warm friends. The firm was known under the name of "Lincoln & Herndon," and continued to exist until the senior member was removed by the assassin's bullet.

In 1846 Lincoln received the long-coveted honor, and was elected to a seat in the Thirtieth Congress, being the only Whig representative from Illinois. In the nominating convention, Mr. Hardin sought a renomination, but finally withdrew in Lincoln's favor.

His competitor, on the Democratic ticket, was the Rev. Peter Cartwright, the well-known and popular preacher. There was hardly a Methodist Congregation in Illinois to which he had not preached, and his name was a family word all over the State. By his eccentricity and eminent ability, which was coupled with a bluff good-humor and warm interest in the welfare, spritual and material, of those with whom he came in contact, he had gained a great influence in the community, and was undoubtedly the strongest candidate the Democrats could have selected. It was believed that aside from his political support he would receive the votes of the church people, irrespective of party affiliations.

Lincoln was seldom seen inside of a church, and, though he had a deep reverence for true religion and

an abiding faith in God, the report was widely circulated that he was, if not an atheist, at least out of
sympathy with all things religious, and some of his
public utterances, which were susceptible of such an
interpretation, were cited against him.

What his religious belief was at this time probably
no one knows, and perhaps he had never formulated
one.   But he was a deep student of the Bible, and
was far more familiar with it than with his law-books.
Its principles wielded a lasting influence upon his life,
and the latter part of his career proves that he was
sustained by an unfaltering trust in God, and belief in
the efficacy of prayer, else he could never have carried his great burden without falling.

The agencies arrayed against him in this struggle
were powerful, but his personal popularity, and the
confidence of the people in his ability and uncompromising honesty triumphed, and he was elected by the
largest majority probably ever given a Whig candidate in that district.

In 1847 he took his seat in Congress, and from that
time on became a notable figure in national politics.
In this session of Congress he was associated with
many men who were destined to figure prominently
in national affairs in coming years.   In the House
were ex-President John Quincy Adams, whose long
and honorable career was nearly ended, Alexander
H. Stephens, the future Vice-President of the Confederacy, Robert Toombs and Cobb.   In the Senate, the
great orator and statesman, Daniel Webster still lingered with such men as Simon Cameron, John C.
Calhoun, Lewis Cass and Jefferson Davis.

In Congress Lincoln soon gained the reputation of

being an able and effective speaker, and exhibited much shrewdness and political wisdom in his Congressional relations. Whenever he addressed the House he secured and retained the attention of all, a fact indicative of more than common merit, when the usual procedure of the House is remembered. His first speech in Congress was upon an unimportant subject, and was made for the purpose of "getting the hang of the House," as he afterwards wrote to Mr. Herndon, remarking that he "found speaking here and elsewhere much the same."

During his term the Mexican war was begun, and he was naturally arrayed with the opposition against the Administration. With the rest of his party he believed the war to be without just cause, and to be carried on entirely in the interests of the pro-slavery party, in order that more slave States might be added to the Union, and the preponderating influences of the Southern States be maintained. The slave power had long been aggressive and generally triumphant. For many years no Administration had dared oppose it, and it generally held the balance of power in the Councils of the Nation.

The Southern people had long viewed with alarm the growth and development of the North-East, and the consequent increase in the number of free States. The Southern leaders saw their ascendency slowly but surely slipping from them, and to maintain it securely, they determined upon the annexation of the contiguous Mexican territory. And largely by their influence, assisted by political revolutions and entanglements in Mexico, the war was brought about.

After the declaration of war, the Whigs found themselves in a dilemma, either horn of which was an embarrassing one. If they voted in favor of war measures, they violated their oft-expressed principles ; if they voted against them, they found themselves in the position of working against the Government, and liable to the charge of unpatriotic and treasonable conduct. Some of their representatives strove to avoid the issue by absenting themselves, when the war measures were put to vote, others sturdily maintained their political principles, and consistently opposed the administration, while others, and among them was Lincoln, although condemning the principle of the war, sustained the administration in all things wherein the honor and welfare of the country were concerned.

The position which he took was one that commended itself to the better sense of the people, but was quickly taken advantage of by his political enemies to create a prejudice against him. In 1858, in one of the great debates, Judge Douglas spoke of Lincoln's having "distinguished himself in Congress by his opposition to the Mexican war, taking the side of the common enemy against his country." In reply, Mr. Lincoln said :

"The Judge charges me with having, while in Congress, opposed our soldiers who were fighting in the Mexican war. I will tell you what he can prove by referring to the record. You remember, I was an old Whig ; and whenever the Democratic party tried to get me to vote that the war had been righteously begun by the President, I would not do it. But whenever they asked for any money or land-warrants, or anything to pay the soldiers, I gave the same vote that Judge Douglas did. Such is the truth, and the Judge has the right to make all he can out of it."

On July 27, 1848, he made a strong and effective speech on "The Presidency and General Politics." He spent considerable time in ridiculing General Cass, the Democratic candidate for the Presidency. He showed vividly, and often humorously, the short-comings and unwarranted pretensions of the General, and raised many a laugh at his expense. While it was an able effort, it was intended mainly for political effect, and seems to have been sadly out of place in the great council of the nation.

During the session he introduced a bill for the gradual and compensated abolition of slavery in the District of Columbia, but the state of public affairs at that time was so disturbed that the bill was not brought before the House for consideration.

After the close of the session, and the inauguration of General Taylor, he became a candidate for the position of Commissioner of the General Land Office, and actively exerted himself to secure the honor. All the influence he could summom was brought to bear to obtain the coveted honor, and the President seemed, personally, to favor him ; but a Mr. Justin Butterfield, of Chicago, was finally appointed. While the appointment was still uncertain he went to Washington to urge his claims in person. His appearance was characteristic, but hardly prepossessing. He was six feet four inches in height, and when he stepped from the train, he was dressed in a suit of light summer clothing with an old linen duster on, neither well-fitting nor clean. His pants came only to his ankles, showing the woolen socks above his coarse brogans. With his great length of limb and ill-fitting garments he was a noticeable object in the street, but there was something in his general mien, as well as in the expression of his face, notwithstanding the sadness and gloom apparent there, that made him a marked man, and led those who saw him, to feel that he was of no ordinary mould.

He was deeply disappointed and chagrined at his failure, and afterwards adverted to it, when, during his Presidential term, he was asked to give an appointment to the son of his successful rival. When the application was presented, the President paused and, after a moment's silence said :

" Mr. Justin Butterfield once obtained an appointment I very much wanted, and in which my friends believed I could have been useful, and to which they thought I was fairly entitled ; and I hardly ever felt so bad at any failure in my life. But I am glad of an opportunity of doing a service to his son." And he gave an order for his commission.

CHAPTER VIII

LINCOLN would unquestionably have been glad to return to Congress for another term, for the life and duties at Washington were far more attractive to him than his law business. For certain reasons he felt disinclined to seek the nomination, and, as his course in Washington had not been generally popular among his constituents, he failed to secure a renomination.

Upon his return to Springfield, he applied himself closely to his law-practice, and from 1849 to 1859 was actively engaged in it. Though taking part in the political movements of the day, with more or less interest, he held no important public office during that time. It was largely a period of preparation, during which he was finding out the ground upon which he stood, and his principles were becoming more fully developed and established. It was an important and interesting period, and one in which his intellectual and moral growth were plain. He was analyzing the political situation, and defining more clearly to himself its vital points. Many of his most eloquent speeches and finest sayings were uttered during this time, and much that is immortal in literature issued from his pen.

During his Congressional term the affairs of the firm had been conducted by the junior member, so that, when he returned, he found a flourishing business ready to be taken up. He entered into his labor

(100)

with great earnestness, as if his profession afforded a pleasing change from the responsibilites and frictions of a political life. It was during this time that he largely earned his legal reputation, which gradually extended beyond the borders of the State.

Had he died in 1849, he would have been unknown to posterity. Had this event occurred in 1859, he would have occupied a position in the history of the State, second only to Douglas, perhaps surpassing even him.

His character as a lawyer was in many respects unique. He would never undertake a case unless reasonably certain that the cause was a just one. And he was several times known to surrender a case in the midst of a trial when unexpectedly convinced that his client was in the wrong.[1]

"At a term of court in Logan county, a man named Hoblet had brought suit against a man named Farmer. The suit had been appealed from a justice of the peace, and Lincoln knew nothing of it until he was retained by Hoblet to try the case in the Circuit Court. Judge Treat, afterwards on the United States bench, was the presiding judge at the trial. Lincoln's client went upon the witness-stand and testified to the account he had against the defendant, gave the amount due, after allowing all credits and set-offs, and swore positively that it had not been paid. The attorney for the defendant simply produced a receipt in full, signed by Hoblet prior to the beginning of the case. Hoblet had to admit the signing of the receipt, but told Lincoln he supposed the defendant had lost

---

[1] Browne.

it. Lincoln at once arose and left the court-room. The judge told the parties to proceed with the case; and Lincoln not appearing, he directed a bailiff to go to the hotel and call him. The bailiff ran across the street to the hotel, and found Lincoln sitting in the office with his feet on the stove, apparently in a deep study, when he interrupted him with : 'Mr. Lincoln, the Judge wants you.' 'Oh, does he?' replied Mr. Lincoln. 'Well, you go back and tell the Judge I cannot come. Tell him I have to *wash my hands*.' The bailiff returned with the message, and Lincoln's client suffered a non-suit. It was Lincoln's way of saying that he wanted nothing more to do with such a case."

He was entirely innocent of all the tricks, which so many lawyers use to influence judge or jury. In his conduct of a case he was always straightforward and honest, often conceding points which the opposition had difficulty in establishing, apparently against his own interest, but the vital points he always grasped with unerring precision and presented them so clearly and pointedly that he seldom failed to win his case.

There were many of his associates who excelled him in knowledge of the details of the law, but few who could seize and apply a general principle so forcibly and appropriately.

He practiced not only in the common courts, but also in the Supreme, District and Circuit courts, and had equal success in them all. When he had an important case, or one in which some great principle was involved, he was absolutely invincible, asking comparatively few questions but such as would elicit facts directly bearing upon the case in hand. When he addressed the jury, his view of the testimony was so pointed and straightforward as to carry conviction.

He sometimes became so eloquent in his address to the jury that he moved the whole audience, judge, jury and spectators, to tears. At such times he was exceedingly impressive. His tall figure, now drawn up to its full height, and then bent over until his hands nearly touched the floor, acquired an unusual dignity. His gestures were simple, but exceedingly striking, while he would give utterance to vivid descriptions, or paint the sufferings and adversities of his client in living colors.

Though holding himself from active participation in political affairs, he never faltered in his interest, and ardently longed to reënter the arena, yet he patiently bided his time, and when the supreme opportunity came, he was ready and fitted to the uttermost to take advantage of it.

During the campaign of 1852, he made a few speeches for General Scott, the Whig candidate, but they were not marked by much display of ability. Douglas, in opening the campaign for the Democrats, at Baltimore, had made an exceedingly partisan speech, and one which contained many utterances upon slavery which were obnoxious to the people of Illinois. Lincoln was asked to reply to the statements and arguments of Douglas, but for some reason made one of the poorest and least effective speeches of his life, failing to make an impression upon his audience.

Slavery had always been the great disturbing element in American politics. More than any other issue, it had tended to divide the people on sectional lines, and was always developing and fomenting hostility between them.

In colonial times it had secured a foothold, not because the colonists specially desired or needed it, but because it suited the interests of European slave-traders to encourage its growth in the New World. It was the survival of an Old World custom, which, in former times, had obtained in every civilized country. It was like a serpent charming its conscious victim only to destroy him. In every country property declined in exact ratio to the advance of slavery. The more extensively the system was developed, the weaker the country became, and more than one great power fell in utter ruin because the slave-power became predominant.

As civilization advanced in Europe, slavery became more and more distasteful to the people, until the nefarious trade, which had been a mine of wealth, almost ceased. In order that a better market might be opened up, the institution was forced upon the American colonies and, England, who could not tolerate the blight on her own fair soil, even abetted its introduction into her colonies. For a time it languished and several petitions were handed into the Crown looking towards a prohibition of the traffic, but George III. received them in contemptuous silence, and did nothing to prevent or even to check it in any way.

The peculiar conditions of climate and soil in the Southern States rendered slave labor both agreeable to the people and profitable. The climate was so hot as to discourage active effort on the part of the white man, but was adapted to call out the best energies of the warm-blooded African. The products, too, could be raised to advantage in large plantations, which would require the labor of hundreds of men to cultivate. As land was plenty, the population sparse, and the products in good demand, especially after the invention of the cotton-gin, made that material available for the manufacture of a cheap fabric, the landed proprietors gradually acquired great estates, requiring hundreds of laborers to till them.

Thus the system became firmly rooted, and seemed to be an absolute necessity to the indolent and aristocratic Southerners. They had no difficulty in persuading themselves that slavery was morally and legally right, and were ready to defend it with their best efforts, and even with their lives, if necessary. What the fathers looked askance upon, the sons came to regard as a right, and succeeding generations as a fixed institution which it was treason to attack. It was but natural that each assault upon it should intrench them more firmly in their position, and widen the breach between them and their Northern neighbors.

They early learned that, when they were compelled to assume the defensive, they were at a disadvantage, hence they became aggressive and combative, in society as well as in the State and national councils, making their pet institution the dominant question, and were ready to do battle for it even when no one attacked.

The political situation, at the time of the adoption of the Constitution, had been so confused, and the grounds for dissension so numerous, that the insertion of a clause forbidding slavery would have insured its rejection. Yet the majority of its framers were undoubtedly opposed to the institution and believed that the best welfare of the nation would be subserved by its abolition, to such an extent that they made it possible for the Government to prevent the importation of slaves, after twenty years had elapsed, by a special provision.

Through the efforts of Henry Clay, during the administration of Monroe, Missouri was admitted to the Union as a slave State in 1821, but the extension of slavery in all territory west of the Mississippi river and north of the southern boundary of Missouri, latitude 36°, 30′, was forever forbidden. This seemed to assure the development into free States of the vast territory of the North-west, and to seal the final doom of slavery. For, as the North-west should gradually be populated and organized into free States, the balance of power would pass from the slave to the free States, and the latter would have it in their power to crush the institution out of existence.

But the South would not give up without a struggle. A vast territory was acquired from Mexico, and the question of its organization came up in Congress in 1850 for settlement. The "irrepressible conflict" broke out afresh, and again the representatives of freedom and slavery were pitted against each other. The conflict resulted in a compromise, again established through the efforts of Clay. California was to be admitted as a free State. Territorial governments were to be organized in New Mexico and Utah, and slavery was to be tacitly admitted. Texas' claim to nearly ninety square miles, north of the parallel of 36°, 30′ was to be recognized, and slavery was to be extended into it. Ten millions of dollars were to be paid to Texas as compensation for the territory of New Mexico. The slave-trade was to be abolished in Washington, but a new fugitive-slave law, more stringent and inhuman than any before enacted, was placed upon the national statute books. Evidently the South would not rest content with this success, and both sides began to prepare for the more deadly conflict which was to ensue.

The Thirty-third Congress assembled December 5, 1853. One of the Senators from Illinois was Stephen Arnold Douglas, whose name was destined to become a noted one in American history. He was a native of Vermont, but had emigrated to Illinois in 1833, at the age of twenty, feeble, friendless and almost penniless, seeking bread and a career in the great West.

The history of his subsequent life reveals a marvelous career. Success greeted his every effort, and glory and renown came at his bidding. At the age of twenty-one he was admitted to the bar, where he made such rapid progress that only one year later he stood at the head of his profession in his district. At the age of twenty-three he was a member of the State Legislature ; at twenty-seven he was appointed Secretary of State in Illinois ; at twenty-eight, Judge of the Supreme Court. At thirty he was a Member of Congress, and at thirty-two United States Senator, and recognized as the leader of the great Democratic party. At forty-three he was a candidate for the nomination to the Presidency, and was nominated at forty-six, but was defeated by an irreconcilable division in his party. In his forty-eighth year he died in the prime of life, yet with a well-rounded career behind him.

His life is inseparably connected with that of Lincoln. They were both admitted to the bar in the same year, and often practiced in the same courts. They served in the Legislature together, and were afterwards rivals for the hand of the same lady. Senatorial honors were contested for between them in one of the most brilliant State campaigns ever carried on. And finally they became rival candidates for the Presidency, and both died prematurely at apparently the very culminating point of their careers, and for each the country mourned irrespective of party. In all things they were consistently opposed to each other, yet each entertained a profound respect and admiration for the other, if not a feeling of genuine friendship.

The contrast between the two was in every way most striking, with all the advantage, to a superficial observer, on the side of Douglas. Lincoln expressed one phase of this contrast very forcibly in a speech at Springfield, July, 17, 1858, during the Senatorial canvass:

"There is still another disadvantage," said he, "under which we (the Republicans) labor. It arises out of the relative positions of the two persons who stand before the State as candidates for the Senate. Senator Douglas is of world-wide renown. All the anxious politicians of his party, or who have been of his party for years past, have been looking upon him as certainly, at no distant day, to be President of the United States. They have seen in his round, jolly, fruitful face, post-offices, land-offices, marshalships and cabinet appointments bursting and sprouting out in a wonderful exuberance, ready to be laid hold of by their greedy hands.

"On the contrary, nobody has ever expected me to be President. In my poor, lean, lank face nobody has ever seen that any cabbages were sprouting out."

In this session of Congress Douglas introduced a bill for the organization of the Territories of Kansas and Nebraska, which became the absorbing topic of thought and conversation all over the land, the one issue which overshadowed all others.

The Kansas-Nebraska bill, as it was called, contemplated the organization of these Territories into States, without insisting upon the prohibition of slavery, which the Missouri compromise had established. Indeed, it was a virtual nullification of that compromise. The measure took the country by surprise. It had not been demanded by the South, nor expected by the North, but each entered heart and soul into the controversy.

Douglas was untiring in his efforts to procure the passage of the bill, and was seconded by others, who, if inferior to him in ability, were equal in enthusiasm, and the bill finally passed the Senate by a small majority, despite the efforts of those grand apostles of freedom, Sumner, Chase and Seward, who were arrayed against it. The struggle in the House was prolonged, but the bill was finally successful, and became a law. Thus at a single blow the whole statutory opposition to the spread of slavery was swept away, and there was nothing to hinder the introduction of the institution into any territory over which the American flag floated. Especially since, in the Dred Scott case, the Supreme Court had decided slavery to be constitutional. For the moment the slave-power seemed to be absolutely triumphant, but its very success was a potent element in its overthrow.

As a result of the Kansas-Nebraska bill, "squatter-sovereignty" was proclaimed in the disputed territory. This term, which was widely used, contained the essence of the new policy promulgated by Douglas as the central principle of his party. It was in effect that each State was sovereign, within its own limits, and had the power to adopt or exclude slavery as it desired. Hence each State was to decide upon its status, in regard to the institution, by ballot. The new doctrine was tersely summed up by Lincoln in a speech at Springfield as follows: "That if any one man choose to enslave another, no third man shall be allowed to object." The argument used by Douglas was incorporated in the bill in the following language:

"It being the true intent and meaning of this act not to legislate slavery into any Territory or State, nor to exclude it therefrom; but to leave the people thereof perfectly free to form and regulate their domestic institutions in their own way, subject only to the Constitution of the United States."

The subsequent agitation in Kansas, resulting in bloodshed and mob-violence, and the final admission of the Territories as free States, are familiar to every school-boy, and need not to be repeated here.

Lincoln viewed the proceedings with deep interest and no little apprehension. Although he deprecated the necessity of agitation, he saw clearly that the whole question had come to a square issue, and that it must be firmly met, and he felt that the time for action had come. Many enthusiastic Abolitionists were starting for Kansas, and he was invited to make one of an armed band to go there and fight for freedom, but he refused to go, and earnestly counselled them to abstain from all violence, and to obey the laws of the country, showing that it was better to bear oppression from rulers than to enter into a rebellion against the government.

The passage of the bill proved the death-knell of the Whig party, indeed it introduced the utmost confusion into political councils on every side, and for a time it was impossible to analyze the situation. Many Democrats were dissatisfied with the policy of the party, and joined with the Whigs, Abolitionists, Free-soilers and miscellaneous elements to form a new party, which was in the future to be known as the Republican party.

Lincoln, without hesitation, joined his fortunes with the new movement, and became its recognized leader in Illinois. This party, which was soon to become the dominant power in American politics, numbered many strong and influential men in its ranks, and, although of conflicting political opinions previously, they now united upon the single issue of hostility to the extension of slavery and its prohibition in all Territories.

A convention of all those who were in sympathy with these principles was called to meet in Bloomington, May 29, 1856, and the Republican party was formally organized in the State. A national convention was called to meet in Philadelphia in June, which nominated a national ticket, at the head of which was placed the illustrious name of John C. Fremont. Lincoln's prominence in political circles was so great that he received one hundred and ten votes for the position of Vice-President. The party became wholly committed to the opposition to the spread of slavery, and, for the first time in the history of the country, the slave-holders found themselves squarely opposed by a great and compactly organized political party. The fact that the working forces of the new party must be drawn necessarily from the free States, and that the opposition must come mainly from the slave States, not only increased sectional antagonism, but led to a disruption of the Democratic party, each section following radical or conservative leaders. Although this division did not take place in the campaign of '56, it so weakened the Democratic party in the next presidential campaign that the election of a Republican President followed.

The campaign of '56 was one of the most animated and closely contested political campaigns since the formation of the government up to that time. However, the time was not ripe. Indiana and Pennsylvania, two doubtful States, were carried by the Democrats by narrow majorities, and Buchanan was elected. Lincoln, up to this time, had not been outspoken in regard to slavery. He had always looked upon it with horror and detestation. The horrors of the slave-mart, the barbarous cruelty of plantation life in many of its phases, and the utter disregard of human rights, shown on every side, had been inexpressibly shocking to him, yet he had never taken a prominent stand against it, and had looked with suspicion upon the Abolitionists and their bold efforts to

overthrow it. He stated clearly and tersely his attitude upon the subject in a speech in reply to one of
Judge Douglas in Chicago, July 10, 1858, as follows :

" I have always hated slavery, I think, as much as
any Abolitionist—I have been an old-line Whig—I
have always hated it, but I have always been quiet
about it until this new era of the introduction of the
Nebraska bill began. I have always believed that
everybody was against it, and that it was in the
course of ultimate extinction. The great mass of the
nation have rested in the ultimate belief that slavery
was in the course of extinction."

If he had held his peace hitherto, on the great
topic, he was to do so no more. From this time
on no heart was more earnest nor tongue more
eloquent in behalf of the down-trodden millions
than his. With him it was an ever-present evil, becoming more and more appalling as time went on,
and more and more did he become impressed with
the magnitude and imminence of the struggle, and
the stupendous catastrophe threatened by it.

He was always ready to assist fugitive slaves, and
more than once put himself to great inconvenience
and some personal danger by reason of his sympathy
for the suffering slave fleeing from bondage.

One afternoon an old negro woman came into his
office, and told the story of her trouble. It appears
that she and her offspring were born slaves in Kentucky, and that her owner had brought the whole
family into Illinois, and given them their freedom.
Her son had gone down the Mississippi as a waiter
or deck-hand on a steamboat. Arriving at New Orleans, he had imprudently gone ashore, and had been

snatched up by the police, in accordance with the law then in force concerning free negroes from other States, and thrown into confinement. Subsequently he was brought out and tried. Of course, he was fined, and, the boat having left, he was sold, or was in immediate danger of being sold, to pay his fine and expenses. Mr. Lincoln was very much moved, and requested Mr. Herndon to go over to the State House and inquire of Governor Bissell, if there was not something he could do to obtain possession of the negro. Mr. Herndon made the inquiry, and returned with the report that the Governor regretted to say that he had no legal or constitutional right to do anything in the premises. Mr. Lincoln rose to his feet in great excitement, and exclaimed : " By the Almighty, I'll have that negro back soon, or I'll have a twenty years' agitation in Illinois, until the Governor does have a legal and constitutional right to do something in the premises." He was saved from the latter alternative—at least in the direct form which he proposed. The lawyers sent money to a New Orleans correspondent—money of their own—who procured the negro, and returned him to his mother.

In 1854 Lincoln was nominated for the State Legislature, but refused to accept the proffered honor. His name, however, was presented to the people, and he was elected. But, feeling that he had earned a higher honor than this, he refused to take his seat. One of the duties of this session was to elect a United States Senator to succeed General Shields, the colleague of Douglas. Lincoln ardently desired the position, and once, in speaking of it, said that he had rather have one full term in the Senate than the

Presidency. His prospects seemed good to secure the coveted honor, but, through certain unexpected complications, his election became doubtful, and he magnanimously withdrew his name in favor of Judge Trumbull, who was immediately elected. When consulted in the dilemma, he said: "You ought to drop me and go for Judge Trumbull, that is the only way you can defeat Mathison (the Democratic candidate)." Judge Logan came up and insisted on making one more effort to secure Lincoln's election ; but the latter said: " If you do, you will lose both Trumbull and myself, and I think the cause in this case is to be preferred to men." This was certainly a rare instance of political self-sacrifice.

CHAPTER IX

At the Bloomington Convention Mr. Lincoln was called upon to make a speech. It proved to be the inauguration speech of the new party in Illinois, and in it he advanced to higher political ground than he had ever done before. He seemed like one inspired as he gave utterance to the grandest political truths, and made close application of them to the condition of the country.

One of the delegates says : " Never was an audience more completely electrified by human eloquence. Again and again, during this speech, the audience sprang to their feet, and by long continued cheers expressed how deeply the speaker had affected them." Herndon characterizes this speech as the grand effort of his life.

The movement, thus enthusiastically inaugurated, gathered strength rapidly, and the young, but vigorous party soon became a recognized power in the State. Lincoln had been one of the ruling spirits of the old Whig party, and he now became the recognized leader of the Republican party, its great defender in the furious onslaughts made upon it, and its champion in the aggressive fight it was about to make upon the old parties.

In the following national campaign, the first in which the Republican party had figured, his services

(116)

were in great demand. Earnest requests to speak upon the principles of the party came to him from every district in Illinois, from Indiana, Ohio, Iowa and Wisconsin, and so far as possible he accepted the invitations.

At one of the meetings, which he was addressing, an old Democrat arose from his seat and strode away, driving his cane viciously into the ground at every step, exclaiming: "He's a dangerous man, a dangerous man! He makes you believe what he says in spite of yourself."

The Republicans generally believed that Fremont would be elected, but Lincoln did not share in this confidence. He was too clear-sighted, and realized too fully the strength of the opposition, to be thus deceived by a false hope. During the campaign he said to Mr. Noah Brooks, a Chicago Journalist: "Don't be discouraged if we don't carry the day this year. We can't do it, that's certain, but we shall sooner or later elect our President. I feel confident of that."

The event proved the truth of his forecast. Although the new party made a gallant fight, its ticket was defeated, and Buchanan was elected President. The closeness of the contest so alarmed the slave-holders that they began, even then, to perfect their plans for a revolution in the event of a Republican victory at the next national election. In this they were materially aided by the weakness of the President who, though no doubt desirous of maintaining the Union intact and upholding the Constitution, yet found himself powerless in the hands of the slave element.

Lincoln, since the passage of the Kansas-Nebraska bill, had become recognized as the champion of the anti-slavery element in Illinois. Even before the formation of the new party, he had ably and persistently opposed the measure as ill-advised and revolutionary. His opinions were always freely expressed on the subject both publicly and privately, and were well sustained by logical argument.

When Douglas returned from Washington, after the passage of the bill, he found himself, more than once, compelled to defend his policy to his constituents, who were generally indignant at his course. Nor was he lacking in the ability to do this. Fresh from the Halls of Congress, where he had carried the bill by his fiery eloquence and power of logical reasoning, in the face of an opposition led by such masters of debate as Sumner, Chase and Seward, flushed with victory, and more than ever confident of his ability to overcome opposition, he appeared before great audiences in Illinois eager to hear his vindication from his own lips.

Soon after his return to Chicago, the State Fair opened in Springfield, and he was invited to address the assembled crowds upon the repeal of the Missouri Compromise. His task was a difficult one, for the majority of the audience were hostile to the measure. Incited by the adverse sentiment, he made a masterly address. He gave an historical review of the whole situation, and presented, in their most plausible form, the arguments by which he had won his victory in the Senate.

Lincoln was present and listened intently, and, at the close of the address, it was announced that he would speak in opposition to the measure on the following day.

A large audience assembled in the State House to hear him. He spoke three hours, and most effectively answered the arguments brought forward on the previous day. The great audience was deeply affected, and gave close attention. Never before had he displayed so much feeling in public. At times his voice quivered and the tears filled his eyes, while loud and continued applause attested that his arguments struck home.

Douglas went from Springfield to Peoria, where he again made a lengthy address, explaining and defending his course in Congress. He was followed and again answered by the indefatigable Lincoln, who sought to prove the fallacy of Mr. Douglas's position from an historical, political and moral standpoint. One by one he took the arguments of his opponent, and demonstrated their weakness. The following extract will convey some idea of his convincing eloquence.

"Slavery is founded in the selfishness of man's nature; opposition to it, in his love of justice. These principles are in eternal antagonism, and when brought into collision so fiercely as slavery extension brings them, shocks, throes and convulsions must ceaselessly follow. Repeal the Missouri Compromise; repeal all compromises; repeal the Declaration of Independence; repeal all past history—you still cannot repeal human nature. It still will be the abundance of man's heart, that slavery extension is wrong; and, out of the abundance of his heart, his mouth will continue to speak. . . . Thus we see the plain, unmistakable spirit of that early age towards slavery, was hostility to the princi-

ple, and toleration only by necessity. But now it is
to be transformed into a 'sacred right.' Nebraska
brings it forth, places it on the high road to extension
and perpetuity, and with a pat on its back says to it,
'Go and God speed you.' Henceforth, it is to be the
chief jewel of the nation, the very figure-head of the
ship of State. Little by little, but steadily as man's
march to the grave, we have been giving the old for
the new faith. Nearly eighty years ago we began by
declaring that all men are created equal ; but now
from that beginning we have run down to that other
declaration, 'that for *some* men to enslave others is
a sacred right of self-government.' . . . In our
greedy chase to make profit of the negro, let us
beware lest we cancel and tear to pieces even the
white man's charter of freedom. . . . Our Republican robe is soiled, trailed in the dust. Let us repu-
rify it. Let us turn and wash it white, in the spirit,
if not the blood, of the revolution. Let us turn
slavery from its claims of 'moral right,' back upon its
existing legal rights and its arguments of 'necessity.'
Let us return it to the position our fathers gave it,
and then let it rest in peace. Let us re-adopt the
Declaration of Independence, and with it the practices and policy which harmonize with it. Let North
and South—let all Americans—let all lovers of liberty
everywhere—join in the great and good work. If
we do this, we shall not only have saved the Union,
but we shall have so saved it as to make and to keep
it forever worthy of the saving. We shall have so
saved it that the succeeding millions of free and
happy people, the world over, shall rise up and call
us blessed to the latest generations."

In the course of his speeeh at Peoria, Mr. Douglas had remarked that the Whigs were all dead. When Mr. Lincoln arose to speak, he said: " Fellow-citizens : —My friend, Mr. Douglas, made the startling announcement to-day that the Whigs are all dead. If this be so, fellow-citizens, you will now experience the novelty of hearing a speech from a dead man, and I suppose you might properly say, in the language of the old hymn :

"'Hark! From the tombs a doleful sound.'"

Douglas felt that, perhaps for the first time in his life, he had been worsted in the field of debate, and upon his proposal it was agreed between them that neither should make any more speeches, or rather that, if Lincoln would let him alone, he would quit.

April 21, 1858, the Democratic State Convention met at Springfield, and heartily indorsing the course of Senator Douglas, announced him as the candidate of the party for another Senatorial term.

June 16 following, the Republican State Convention met at the same place and unanimously declared that : " Abraham Lincoln is our first and only choice for United States Senator, to fill the vacancy about to be created by the expiration of Judge Douglas's term of office."

This action had been foreseen, and Mr. Lincoln had prepared a speech accepting the honor. In this speech, he uttered more exalted sentiments and proclaimed higher political doctrines than any great party-leader had ever ventured to do before ; so high, indeed, that it alarmed his partisans and delighted his opponents, who believed that he had sounded the death-knell of his own political career as well as that of his party.

Although he suffered defeat at this time, the sequel showed that he was possessed of more foresight than the party, and demonstrated the wisdom which had made him a party-leader as well as his fitness for that position.

The opening paragraph of the speech which occasioned much comment and criticism, was as follows : " Mr. President and Gentlemen of the Convention : If we could first know where we are and whither we are tending, we could better judge what to do and how to do it. We are now far into the fifth year since a policy was initiated with the avowed object and confident promise of putting an end to slavery agitation. Under the operation of that policy, that agitation has not only not ceased but has constantly augmented. In my opinion it will not cease until a crisis shall have been reached and passed. ' A house divided against itself cannot stand.' I believe this Government cannot endure, permanently, half slave and half free. I do not expect the Union to be dissolved—I do not expect the house to fall—but I do expect it will cease to be divided. It will become all one thing or all the other. Either the opponents of slavery will arrest the further spread of it and place it where the public mind will rest in the belief that it is in the course of ultimate extinction, or its advocates will push it forward, until it shall become alike lawful in all the States, old as well as new, North as well as South."

This statement was afterwards greeted with a perfect storm of disapproval, and formed the subject of many a speech and political debate throughout the country. It was a startling proposition, and, from a superficial point of view, it seemed to be entirely unwarranted by the facts. For almost three-quarters of a century the Government had endured, over a country half slave and half free ; nor had the country, during that time, ever been at a standstill. In material progress and the development of its vast domain, it was the marvel of the world. From a little confederacy of puny states grouped on the Atlantic seaboard, it had developed into an imperial nation numbering thirty millions of souls. Its progress had been steady and almost uninterrupted, and its prosperity seemed to rest upon a secure foundation. How absurd then, said his opponents, to assert that this country is on the verge of disruption, nay, of destruction, because of differing opinions in regard to a single institution. Yet history proved his perfect vindicator, and more certainly than arguments or specious philosophy did coming events demonstrate the wisdom of his position.

His friends, to whom he read the speech before delivering it, urged him to omit the first paragraph, all except his partner, Mr. Herndon, who said : "Lincoln, deliver that speech as read, and it will make you President." A prophecy destined to be wonderfully fulfilled, but seeming at the time to pass credence.

One of his friends, after the speech, remonstrated with him against such "foolishness," to whom Lincoln replied that, if he were compelled to destroy every utterance of his life save one, he would select that one for preservation. He remarked to Mr. Herndon, who asked him if he deemed it wise or ex-

pedient to commit himself in such a way at that time :
" I had rather be defeated with this expression in the
speech, and have it held up and discussed before the
people, than to be victorious without it." [1]

The speech was mainly directed against the en-
croachments of the slave-power upon the free domain,
as exemplified by the Kansas-Nebraska bill, and the
subsequent " Dred Scott " decision. He showed, in
support of his main position, that every effort of the
Southern party, open and insidious alike, was directed
towards an opening up to slavery of the whole national domain, and he clearly demonstrated the active
instrumentality of Senator Douglas in bringing about
this result. To him the danger seemed more imminent and startling than ever before. " We shall lie
down, pleasantly dreaming," said he, " that the people of Missouri are on the verge of making their
State free ; and we shall awake to the reality, instead,
that the Supreme Court has made Illinois a slave
State. To meet and overthrow the power of that
dynasty is the work now before all those who would
prevent that consummation—that is what we have to
do. . . . Our cause, then, must be intrusted to and
conducted by its undoubted friends—those whose
hands are free, whose hearts are in the work—who
do care for the result. Two years ago the Republicans of the nation mustered over one million three
hundred thousand strong. We did this under a
single impulse of resistance to a common danger,
with every external circumstance against us. Of
strange, discordant and even hostile elements, we

---

[1] Herndon's " Lincoln."

gathered from the four winds, and formed and fought this battle through, under the constant, hot fire of a disciplined and pampered enemy. Did we brave all to falter now?—now, when that same enemy is wavering, dissevered and belligerent. The result is not doubtful. We shall not fail—if we stand firm, *we shall not fail*. Wise counsels may accelerate or mistakes delay it, but sooner or later the victory is sure to come."

A little incident occurred during the campaign that illustrated Mr. Lincoln's readiness in turning a political point. He was making a speech at Charleston, Coles County, when a voice called out, " Mr. Lincoln, is it true that you entered this State barefoot, driving a yoke of oxen?" Mr. Lincoln paused for a full half a minute, as if considering whether he should notice such cruel impertinence, and then said that he thought he could prove the fact by at least a dozen men in the crowd, any one of whom was more respectable than his questioner. But the question seemed to inspire him, and he went on to show what free institutions had done for himself, and to exhibit the evils of slavery to the white man wherever it existed, and asked if it was not natural that he should hate slavery, and agitate against it. " Yes," said he, " we will speak for freedom, and against slavery, as long as the Constitution of our country guarantees free speech, until everywhere on this wide land the sun shall shine and the rain shall fall and the wind shall blow upon no man who goes forth to unrequited toil." [1]

---

[1] Holland's " Life of Lincoln."

It was at about this time that Lincoln made his
first visit to Cincinnati, where he met the Hon. E. M.
Stanton, with whom he was afterwards to be so intimately associated.   Among his law cases was one
connected with the patent of the McCormick reaper,
and it became necessary for him to visit Cincinnati,
to argue the case before Judge McLean of the United
States Circuit Court.   It was a case of great importance, involving the foundation patent of the machine
which was destined to revolutionize the harvesting of
grain.   Reverdy Johnson was on one side of the case,
and E. M. Stanton and George Harding on the other.
It became necessary, in addition, to have a lawyer
who was a resident of Illinois ; and inquiry was made
of Hon. E. B. Washburne, then in Congress, as to
whether he knew a suitable man.   The latter replied,
"that there was a man named Lincoln, at Springfield,
who had considerable reputation in the State."   Lincoln was secured, and came on to Cincinnati with a
brief.   Stanton and Harding saw "a tall, dark, uncouth man," who did not strike them as of any account, and, indeed, they gave him hardly a chance.
Mr. Lincoln was a little surprised and annoyed, after
reaching Cincinnati, to learn that his client had also
associated with him Mr. Stanton of Pittsburgh, and
a local lawyer of some repute ; the reason assigned
being that the importance of the case required a man
of the experience and power of Mr. Stanton to meet
Mr. Johnson.   The trial of the case came on ; the
counsel for the defense met each morning for consultation.   On one of these occasions, one of the
counsel moved that only two of them should speak
on the case.   This motion was acquiesced in.   It had

always been understood that Mr. Harding was to speak, to explain the mechanism of the reapers. So this motion excluded either Mr. Lincoln or Mr. Stanton. By the custom of the bar, as between counsel of equal standing, and in the absence of any action by the client, the original counsel speaks. By this rule Mr. Lincoln had the precedence. Mr. Stanton suggested that Mr. Lincoln make the speech. Mr. Lincoln answered, "No, you speak." Mr. Stanton replied, "I will;" and taking up his hat, said he would go and make preparation. Mr. Lincoln acquiesced in this, but was deeply grieved and mortified ; he took but little more interest in the case, though remaining until the conclusion of the trial. He seemed to be greatly depressed, and gave evidence of that tendency to melancholy which so marked his character in after years. His parting words on leaving the city cannot be forgotten. Cordially shaking the hand of his hostess, he said : "You have made my stay here most agreeable, and I am a thousand times obliged to you ; but, in reply to your request for me to come again, I must say to you I never expect to be in Cincinnati again. I have nothing against the city, but things have so happened here as to make it undesirable for me ever to return."

If Mr. Lincoln was "surprised and annoyed" at the treatment he received from Mr. Stanton, the latter was no less surprised, and a good deal more disgusted, on seeing Mr. Lincoln and learning of his connection with the case. He made no secret of his contempt for the "long, lank creature from Illinois," as he afterwards described him, "wearing a dirty linen duster for a coat, on the back of which the perspiration had splotched wide stains that resembled a dirty map of the· continent." He blurted out his wrath and indignation to his associate counsel, declaring that if " that giraffe " was permitted to appear in the case, he would throw up his brief and leave it. Mr. Lincoln keenly felt the affront, but his great nature forgave it so completely that, recognizing the singular abilities of Mr. Stanton beneath his brusque exterior, he afterwards, for the public good, appointed him to a seat in his Cabinet.

CHAPTER X.

THE memorable campaign opened vigorously on both sides. Each of the leading candidates entered the field, seeking to so influence the State election that the new legislature might be in his favor. Speeches had been made by both, in Springfield, Chicago and Bloomington, where Mr. Lincoln addressed the following note to his opponent :

"*Hon. S. A. Douglas.*

"MY DEAR SIR—Will it be agreeable to you to make an arrangement for you and myself to divide time, and address the same audiences during the present canvass ? Mr. Judd, who will hand you this, is authorized to receive your answer, and, if agreeable to you, to enter into the terms of such arrangement.

"Your obedient servant,

"CHICAGO, ILL. July 24, 1858. A. LINCOLN."

In the correspondence which followed, Douglas acceded to the request, though demurring somewhat at first; and it was finally agreed that they should meet in joint discussion at seven different places, viz., Ottawa, Freeport, Jonesboro, Charleston, Galesburg, Quincy and Alton. In closing his last letter Mr. Douglas said :

"I agree to your suggestion that we shall alternately open and close the discussion. I will speak at Ottawa one hour. You can reply, occupying one

hour and a half, and I will then follow you for a half
an hour. We will alternate in like manner at each
successive place." It was arranged that the first debate should be held August 21, and the last one
October 15.

These seven discussions now rank among the ablest
forensic debates that have ever taken place in
America, perhaps in the world. They were widely
reported in the newspapers, but, as they were delivered without manuscript, the reports failed to do
justice to them, and conveyed but an inadequate idea
of their effectiveness. The whole country followed
the course of the debates with great interest, and from
that time Lincoln's reputation transcended sectional
bounds and spread throughout the nation. The man
who could meet and overcome in debate, Judge
Douglas, the redoubted champion of the Senate,
could no longer remain unknown.

The personality of the principals was reflected in
their speeches. Douglas was fiery and impetuous,
making his points with the brilliancy and dash of one
who was assured of victory, because he had never
known defeat, and with the adroitness which characterized the successful politician.

Lincoln was calm and straightforward. He was
quick to see and able to take advantage of any weak
point in his adversary's argument, relying less upon
his eloquence and magnetism than upon frank statements and clear reasoning to convince his audience.

Douglas excited the more feeling at the time ; Lincoln made the deeper and more lasting impression.
Douglas was greeted with applause and congratulation for the brilliancy of his efforts ; Lincoln made

friends for his cause and influenced votes. The more self-sacrificing of the two, he sought to magnify the cause while he held his own personal interests in the background. A declaration in his Chicago speech well illustrates this. He said : "I do not claim, gentlemen, to be unselfish. I do not pretend that I would not like to go to the United States Senate, I make no such hypocritical pretense; but I do say to you that, in this mighty issue, it is nothing to the mass of the people of the nation, whether or not Judge Douglas or myself shall be heard of after this night ; it may be a trifle to either of us, but in connection with this mighty question, upon which hang the destinies of the nation, perhaps, it is absolutely nothing."

The contrast between the two men, in every way, could hardly have been greater, yet each felt that to win the victory would require his very best efforts, and went into the conflict with every power on the alert and every faculty in operation.

When Douglas was congratulated in advance upon the ease with which he would vanquish his opponent, he replied that " he would rather meet any other man in the country in this joint debate than Abraham Lincoln." At another time, he said : "I have known Lincoln for nearly twenty-five years. There were many points of sympathy between us when we first got acquainted. We were both comparatively boys, and both struggling with poverty in a strange land. I was a school-teacher in the town of Winchester, and he a flourishing grocery-keeper in the town of Salem. He was more successful in his occupation than I was in mine, and hence more fortunate in this world's goods. Lincoln is one of those peculiar men who

perform with admirable skill whatever they undertake. I made as good a school-teacher as I could, . . .
but I believe that Lincoln was always more successful in his business than I in mine, for his business
enabled him to get into the Legislature. I met him
there, however, and had sympathy with him, because
of the up-hill struggle we both had had in life. He
was then just as good at telling an anecdote as now.
He could beat any of the boys in wrestling or running
a foot-race, in pitching quoits or in pitching a copper,
and the dignity and impartiality with which he presided at a horse-race or a fist-fight, excited the admiration, and won the praise of everybody that was
present. I sympathized with him because he was
struggling with difficulties and so was I. Mr. Lincoln served with me in the Legislature of 1836, when
we both retired, and he subsided, or became sub-
merged and was lost sight of as a public man for some
years. In 1846, when Wilmot introduced his celebrated proviso, and the Abolition tornado swept over
the land, Lincoln again turned up as a Member of
Congress from the Sangamon District. I was then
in the Senate of the United States and was glad to
welcome my old friend." [1]

The following estimate of Douglas by Lincoln is
of interest in connection with the above : "Twenty-
two years ago Judge Douglas and I first became
acquainted. We were both young then, he a trifle
younger than I. Even then we were both ambitious,
I, perhaps, quite as much as he. With me, the race
of ambition has been a failure—a flat failure ; with

[1] Browne.

him it has been one of splendid success. His name
fills the nation, and is not unknown even in foreign
lands. I affect no contempt for the high eminence
he has attained; so reached, that the oppressed of my
species might have shared with me in the elevation, I
would rather stand upon that eminence than wear the
richest crown that ever pressed a monarch's brow."

Around the institution of slavery centred all the
arguments of the joint debate. The positions taken
upon this subject constituted the main issues between
the Democratic and Republican parties. It was the
absorbing topic of the nation. Lincoln's stand upon
the question was firm, elevated and positive, and he
sustained it with logical argument and close reasoning. Douglas sought to avoid the issue, attempting
rather to overthrow the arguments of his opponent
than to enunciate any decided policy other than that
contained in his public measures.

The debates everywhere attracted great crowds.
At first both of the disputants refrained from offensive personalities. But afterwards each accused the
other of unfair conduct, of misrepresentation and
even falsehood. The points brought forward and
the arguments used to sustain them, were substantially the same in all the speeches, the methods of presenting them being adapted to the circumstances and
audience. In his first speech Douglas attacked the
position taken by Lincoln in his previous speeches,
especially on the three points that Lincoln had laid
stress upon, viz., that the Union could not remain
half free and half slave, but must become either one
or the other ; his opposition to the Kansas-Nebraska
bill, and to the Dred Scott decision. He maintained

that the first proposition was not only an absurdity
upon the face of it, but that it was treasonable in its
tendency, as, if insisted upon, it must result in civil
war between the two sections, and either the slave-
holders must carry slavery into all the free States at the
point of the bayonet, or the Abolitionists must drive
it into the sea before the muzzles of their cannon. He
sustained his position on the other two points by the
same arguments which he had so often advanced
before, modified, only, to meet the present exigency.

Upon Lincoln's opposition to the Dred Scott decision he made the following startling and dramatic
comment, the truth of which Lincoln afterwards
emphatically denied :

" His conscientious scruples led him to believe that
the negro is entitled by divine right to the civil
and political privileges of citizenship on an equality
with the white man. For that reason he wishes the
Dred Scott decision reversed. He wishes to confer
those privileges of citizenship on the negro. Let us
see how he will do it. He will first be called upon to
strike out of the constitution of Illinios that clause
which prohibits free negroes and slaves from Kentucky
or any other State coming into Illinois. When he blots
out that clause, when he lets down the door, or opens
the gate for all the negro population to flow in and
cover our prairies, until at midday they will look
dark and black as night : when he shall have done
this, his mission will yet be unfulfilled. Then it will
be that he will apply his principles of negro equality,
that is, if he can get the Dred Scott decision reversed
meantime. He will then change the Constitution
again, and allow negroes to vote and hold office,

and will make them eligible to the Legislature, so that, thereafter, they can have the right men for United States Senators. He will allow them to vote to elect the Legislature and the Governor, and will make them eligible to the office of Judge or Governor or to the Legislature. He will put them on an equality with the white man. What then? Of course after making them eligible to the Judiciary, when he gets Cuffee elevated to the Bench, he certainly will not refuse his Judge the privilege of marrying any woman he may select. I submit to you whether these are not the legitimate consequences of his doctrine."

Lincoln's reply was direct and forcible. He accused Douglas of misrepresenting him, and denied the truth of many of his assumptions. His reply to the allegation that he favored the admission of the negro to social and civil equality could leave no doubt as to his sentiments. He said: "I have no purpose, directly or indirectly, to interfere with the institution of slavery in the States where it exists. I believe I have no lawful right to do so, and I have no inclination to do so. I have no purpose to introduce political and social equality between the white and black races. There is a physical difference between the two which, in my judgment, will probably forever forbid their living together on a footing of perfect equality, and inasmuch as it becomes a necessity that there must be a difference, I, as well as Judge Douglas, am in favor of the race to which I belong having the superior place. I have never said anything to the contrary, but I hold that, notwithstanding all this, there is no reason in the world why the negro is not entitled to all the natural rights enumerated in the Declaration of Independence, the right to life, liberty and the pursuit of happiness. I hold that he is as much entitled to these as the white man. I agree with Judge Douglas that he is not my equal in many respects—certainly not in color, perhaps not in moral or intellectual endowment. *But in the right to eat the bread, without the leave of anybody else, which his own hand earns, he is my equal, and the equal of Judge Douglas, and the equal of any living man.*"

At Ottawa Judge Douglas propounded seven questions to Mr. Lincoln, to which he wished explicit answers. These answers Lincoln gave clearly and pointedly, and then propounded other questions to Douglas, some of which he had difficulty in honestly answering.

In the course of Lincoln's reply, at Alton, occurred the following interesting and significant passage : "I have stated, upon former occasions, and I may as well state again, what I consider to be the real point of controversy between Judge Douglas and myself. On the point of my wanting to make war between the free and slave States, there has been no issue between us. So, too, when he assumes that I am in favor of introducing a perfect social and political equality between the white and black races. These are false issues, upon which Judge Douglas has tried to force the controversy. There is no foundation in truth for the charge that I maintain either of these propositions. The real issue in this controversy— the one pressing upon every mind—is the sentiment on the part of one class, that looks upon the institution of slavery as wrong, and of another class that does not look upon it as wrong. The sentiment that contemplates the institution of slavery in this country as a wrong is the sentiment of the Republican party. It is the sentiment around which all their actions—all their arguments—circle; from which all their propositions radiate. They look upon it as being a moral, social and political wrong ; and while they contemplate it as such, they nevertheless have due regard for its actual existence among us, and the difficulties of getting rid of it in any satisfactory way, and to all the constitutional obligations thrown around it. Yet having a due regard for these, they desire a policy in regard to it that looks to its not creating any more danger. They insist that it should, as far as may be, be treated as a wrong ; and one of the methods of treating it as a wrong is to make provision that it shall grow no larger. They also desire a policy that looks to a peaceful end of slavery at some time. These are the views they entertain in regard to it, as I understand them ; and all their sentiments—all their arguments and propositions come within this range. I have said, and I repeat it here, that if there be a man among us, who does not think that the institution of slavery is wrong in any one of the aspects of which I have spoken, he is misplaced, and ought not to be with us. And if there be a man among us who is so impatient of it as a wrong as to disregard its actual presence among us, and the difficulty of getting rid of it suddenly in a satisfactory way, and to disregard the constitutional obligations thrown about it, that man is misplaced if he is on our platform. We disclaim sympathy with him in practical action. . . . That is the real issue—

that is the issue that will continue in this country,
when these poor tongues of Judge Douglas and myself shall be silent. It is the eternal struggle between
these two principles, right and wrong, throughout
the world. They are the two principles that have
stood face to face since the beginning of time, and
will ever continue to struggle. The one is the common right of humanity; the other is the divine right
of kings. It is the same principle in whatever shape
it develops itself. It is the same spirit that says,
'You work and toil and earn bread, and I will eat it.'
No matter in what shape it comes—whether from
the mouth of a king, who seeks to bestride the people of his own nation, and live upon the fruit of their
labor, or from one race of men as an apology for
enslaving another race, it is the same tyrannical principle."

"The contest between Douglas and Lincoln," says
Dr. Newton Bateman, "was one between sharpness
and greatness. Mr. Lincoln seemed a man strongly
possessed by a belief to which he was earnestly striving to win the people over; while the aim of Mr.
Douglas seemed rather to be simply to defeat Mr.
Lincoln."

So serious did Lincoln consider his task that he
departed from his custom and indulged in few pleas-
antries; yet, occasionally, his sense of the humorous
led him to make some sharp hits against his opponent. In his speech at Galesburgh, Douglas remarked,
with a sneer, that "honest Abe" had once been a
liquor-seller. Lincoln replied that, when a young
man, he had been compelled by poverty to work in a
store where one of his duties was to retail liquor;

"but," said he, "the difference between Judge Douglas and myself is just this, that while I was behind the bar, he was in front of it."

At another time Douglas said that his father, who was an excellent cooper, had apprenticed him to learn the cabinet business. Lincoln seized the opportunity to remark that he had long known that Douglas was in the cabinet business, but he had never known that his father was a cooper; " But," said he, "I have no doubt that he was a good one, for he made one of the best whiskey casks I have ever seen," at the same time bowing to his opponent, who was sitting near him. The allusion was instantly understood by the audience, and was greeted with roars of laughter.

During the campaign Mr. Lincoln spoke about fifty times, yet when he made his last speech his voice was as clear and vigorous as ever, and he "seemed like a trained athlete, ready to enter, rather than one who had closed a conflict." There is no question but that the advantage in the contest lay with Mr. Lincoln rather than with Mr. Douglas, yet he failed to secure his election to the Senate ; for, although the Republican State officers were elected, the Legislature remained Democratic on account of the hold-over Representatives, and Judge Douglas was re-elected to his third Senatorial term.

It is unnecessary to say that Lincoln was deeply disappointed. Yet the splendid results of his great debates were exceedingly gratifying to him. They really formed the opening to the last great period in his career—the period for which all the preceding years of his life had been but the preparation, though unconsciously to himself. To the student of his life and times it is plainly to be seen that every element and influence of his life tended to give him the most complete preparation for his last five years. His Presidential term was but the blossom of which his previous life had furnished the stalk and leaf ; but, alas, the blossom was destined never to develop into the ripe fruit.

CHAPTER XI.

HENCEFORTH Lincoln was looked upon, throughout the country, as a new factor in politics, unexpected and unique, but original and forcible. And the eyes of the Republican party turned towards him as a possible candidate for the Presidency. As the Democracy was dividing itself into two factions, the moderate and radical, of which the former was represented by Judge Douglas, so the Republicans found a similar division in their ranks. Mr. Seward, the recognized leader of the party, represented the extreme Abolition element, and Lincoln, the more moderate wing. Whereas the former had said and done much to alienate from him many of the rank and file of the party, Lincoln, by his splendid, yet moderate, championship of the party principles, had gained the friendship of all, the enmity of none. From this time on he continued to grow in the estimation of the party, and his every act served to confirm his popularity. He was a politician as well as a statesman, and to assume that he remained unconcernedly at home, and did nothing to accelerate the current which was carrying him towards the Presidential chair, is to ignore historical facts. He was ambitious, and his still more ambitious wife did much to arouse and urge him on. By letters, addresses and consultations he labored to strengthen his hold upon his

(141)

party and his title to preferment. Never indulging
in underhanded methods nor seeking to undermine
his rivals, he yet did all an honorable and shrewd man
could do to bring about the desired result.

He has been frequently represented as sitting
quietly down and laying hold of the honors, which
Providence showered upon him, without an effort on
his part to secure them. But this is a mistake;
political preferment comes to few men without effort
and solicitation, in this age of the world, and Lincoln
formed no exception to the rule.

After the great debates the idea of presenting him
as a presidential candidate came to many of his
friends, some of whom approached him on the subject. At first he opposed the suggestion ; " What is
the use of talking of me," he said, " when we have
such men as Seward and Charles Sumner, and every
body knows them, while scarcely anybody outside of
Illinois knows me ? Besides, as a matter of justice, is
it not due them ? " His friends admitted the claims
of these eminent men upon the party but showed
that, on account of their radical opinions and utterances, they could never be available candidates ;
while he had kept himself clear from all political
entanglements and was not known to be openly an
Abolitionist, and his political creed of " opposition
to the further extension of slavery " was so simple
and moderate that it commended itself to both wings
of the party. As time passed on, he became more
and more deeply absorbed in the political life of the
country and began to neglect seriously his law business.

In the autumn of 1859, Senator Douglas was invited

to address the Democracy at Columbus and Cincinnati during the campaign preceding the State election. There was a magic in the very name of Douglas. It was only necessary to announce that he would speak to fill the largest halls to be secured in any part of the country. So, here in Ohio, he was greeted with the usual display of enthusiasm and his speeches were able and effective. But the name of Lincoln had been too closely associated with that of Douglas to be forgotten now, and the Republicans made arrangements for him to speak in both the cities, where Douglas had been. His audiences were large and attentive, and contained many representatives of the opposing political party. Many went out of mere curiosity to see and hear the man who had proved himself to be more than the peer of Douglas, but all acknowledged his ability as an orator and his political sagacity. His work in the State contributed, in no small degree, to the Republican victory which followed.

At Cincinnati there were many pro-slavery men from Kentucky in the audience and to them he addressed part of his speech. In the directness and force of his arguments, and his earnest and logical exposition of party principles, his speech had not been excelled by any previous effort.

In concluding that part of his speech, which was addressed to the Kentuckians, he asked the following pointed questions. " I often hear it intimated that you intend to divide the Union whenever a Republican, or anything like it, is elected President of the United States. . . . I want to know what you are going to do with your half of it? Are you going to

split the Ohio down through and push your half off
a piece? Or are you going to keep it right alongside
of us outrageous fellows? Or are you going to build
up a wall some way between your country and ours,
by which that movable property of yours can't come
over here any more, to the danger of your losing it?
Do you think you can better yourselves on that subject, by leaving us here under no obligation, whatever, to return those specimens of your movable
property which came hither? You have divided the
Union because we would not do right with you, as
you think, upon that subject; when we cease to be
under obligations to do anything for you, how much
better off do you you think will be? Will you make
war upon us and kill us all? Why, gentlemen, I think
you are as gallant and brave men as live, that you
can fight as bravely in a good cause, as any other
people living; that you have shown yourselves
capable of this upon various occasions; but, man for
man, you are not better than we are, and there are
not so many of you as there are of us. You will
never make much of a hand at whipping us. If we
were fewer in numbers than you I think that you
could whip us; if we were equal it would likely be a
drawn battle; but being inferior in numbers you will
make nothing by attempting to master us."

From time to time reports of the eccentric sayings
and doings of the Illinois statesman had found their
way East. These had served to amuse the people and
excite their curiosity, rather than to impress them
with his ability as a party-leader or as a statesman,
but when he met and overcame, on the forensic arena,
the man who bore the reputation of being the most

finished and forcible debater in the United States
Senate, and who had never, up to that time, met his
equal, they were surprised, and became possessed
with the desire to see and hear the "rude, Western
orator." Accordingly he was invited to deliver a
lecture in a course to be given in the Plymouth
Church, in Brooklyn. He consented, with the under-
standing that he be permitted to speak upon some
political subject. When he arrived in New York, on
February 25, 1860, he found, to his surprise, that the
arrangements had been changed, and that he was
advertised to speak in Cooper Institute.

Never had he bestowed so much study upon a
speech before. For months all his thought and
research had been directed to its preparation, yet,
when he found that he was to speak in New York, and
in this famous hall, he expressed the fear that he was
not equal to the occasion and that the effort would
result in failure.

A large part of the audience had assembled, either
from curiosity or to be amused by "the buffoonery of
the low-born speaker." But never was an audience
more surprised, for instead of jokes and stories, the
address was scholarly and refined, and with nothing
offensive to the most fastidious taste. The scene was
an impressive one, and the audience of a character
such as Lincoln had never before addressed. Upon
the platform sat many of the leaders of the new
party, and the meeting was presided over by William
Cullen Bryant, whose voice had early been attuned to
the song of freedom.

Mr. Lincoln afterwards remarked that it was worth
a journey East "only to see such a man." Mr.

Bryant introduced the speaker with a flattering reference to his record as an orator. "Mr. Lincoln began his address in a low, monotonous tone, but as he advanced, his quaint but clear voice rang out boldly and distinctly enough for all to hear. His manner was, to a New York audience, a very strange one, but it was captivating. He held the vast meeting spellbound, and as one by one his oddly-expressed, but trenchant and convincing arguments confirmed the soundness of his political theories, the house broke out in wild and prolonged enthusiasm."

A large part of the address was historical, tracing the origin and growth of slavery, the various causes and influences by which it had been affected and then defining its present status, with words of sage advice to the young Republican party. He took as his subject, or rather point of departure, a short passage from one of Senator Douglas's speeches, as follows: "Our fathers, when they framed the government, under which we live, understood this question just as well, and even better than we do now."

The question referred to by Douglas, he stated concisely as: "Does the proper division of local from federal authority, or anything in the Constitution forbid our federal Government to control, as to slavery, in federal territories? Upon this Senator Douglas holds the affirmation and the Republicans the negative. This affirmative and denial form an issue, and this issue—this question—is precisely what the text declares, 'our fathers understood better than we.'"

The great Cooper Institute speech made a strong and abiding impression and convinced the people of the East that Lincoln was not only master of the political situation, but was possessed of the elements of true greatness. The speech was widely reported and was afterwards published in pamphlet form and used for campaign purposes. In the preface of one of the editions the editors[1] made the following statement, which well expresses the estimate in which the speech was held :

" No one who has not actually attempted to verify its details can understand the patient research and historical labor it embodies. The history of our earlier politics is scattered through numerous journals, statutes, pamphlets and letters ; and these are defective in completeness and accuracy of statement, and in indexes and tables of contents. Neither can any · one, who has not traveled over this precise ground, appreciate the accuracy of every trivial detail, or the self-denying impartiality with which Mr. Lincoln has turned from the testimony of the 'fathers' on the general question of slavery, to present the single question which he discusses. From the first line to the last, from his premises to his conclusion, he travels with a swift, unerring directness, which no logician ever excelled—an argument complete and full, without the affectation of learning, and without the stiffness, which usually accompanies dates and details. A single, easy, simple sentence, of plain Anglo-Saxon words contains a chapter of history, that, in some instances, has taken days of labor to verify, and must have cost the author months of investigation to acquire ; and though the public should justly estimate the labor bestowed on facts which are stated, they can-

---

[1] Nott and Brainard.

not estimate the greater labor involved in those which are omitted. How many pages have been read—how many works examined—what numerous statutes, resolutions, speeches, letters and biographies have been looked through? Commencing with this address, as a political pamphlet, the reader will leave it as an historical work—brief, complete, profound, impartial, truthful—which will survive the time and the occasion that called it forth and be esteemed hereafter no less for its intrinsic worth than for its unpretending modesty."

The address revolutionized the Republican sentiments of the East. As the aristocratic Jews of old regarded Galilee, so did the East regard the West. "Can anything good come out of the West?" was the thought, if not the expression of the East, and the feeling was natural. The Atlantic border had been so long settled that the wildness of nature had passed away. From the earliest colonization of the country the centre of civilization had been here, and the measure of refinement and culture had diminished exactly as the distance from the sea-board increased. That the interior had been the scene of the most remarkable development of all time, the people of the older States could not deny, but that it had, as well, acquired an intellectual prestige equal to their own, and a culture and refinement which would enable its sons to meet their own statesmen and orators on equal terms, was a yielding of proud superiority of which they were not capable.

That Lincoln was pre-eminent among the Western pioneers they were willing to admit, but they could not for a moment imagine him standing upon the same platform with, and the peer of such men as Seward, Chase, Sumner and others, before whose genius the whole American people did homage. For a moment, Lincoln's ungainliness and diffidence seemed to justify their preconceived opinion, but, as he entered more and more deeply into the spirit of his theme, and his awkwardness gave place to a simple majesty of demeanor, the whole audience felt his power, and from that time no one questioned his ability or his right to be called a statesman.

This address was the turning-point in his career. He stepped upon the platform a comparatively unknown politician, before he left it his right to the name of statesman was conceded. When he began, he had but little pretension to political preferment; when he ended, he was recognized as a formidable candidate for the Presidency. Before, he was reported to be a western boor, who strove to entertain his audiences by clownish buffoonery; after, he was ranked in ability and culture with the few choice spirits of the East. The address did for him what the debates could not, for it was recognized as the calm and deliberate utterance of a thoughtful man, uninfluenced by the intense partisanship of a heated political campaign.

The address was, in the highest sense, political, and in it, more fully than before, he committed himself to the single issue of opposition to the further extension of slavery. As an institution, he did not oppose it, because "wrong as we think slavery is, we can yet afford to let it alone where it is, because that much is due to the necessity arising from its actual presence in the nation, but can we, while our votes will prevent

it, allow it to spread into the National Territories
and to overrun us here in these free States." The
platform, thus enunciated, was so simple that not
only could all Republicans accept it, but it exactly
represented the political belief of many Northern
Democrats. Thus, both the personality of the
man and his political doctrines commended him
to the party at large as its most available candidate.

While in New York, at this time, Mr. Lincoln visited
the famous Five Points Sunday-school. The following touching account of the visit is from his
own lips :

"'When Sunday came, I didn't know exactly what
to do. Washburne asked me where I was going. I
told him I had nowhere to go ; and he proposed to
take me down to the Five Points Sunday-school, to
show me something worth seeing. I was very much
interested by what I saw. Presently, Mr. Pease, the
Superintendent, came up and spoke to Mr. Washburne, who introduced me. Mr. Pease wanted us to
speak. Washburne spoke, and then I was urged to
speak. I told them I did not know anything about
talking to Sunday-schools, but Mr. Pease said many
of the children were friendless and homeless, and that
a few words would do them good. Washburne said
I must talk. And so I rose to speak ; but I tell you
I didn't know what to say. I remembered that Mr.
Pease said that they were homeless and friendless,
and I thought of the time when I had been pinched
by terrible poverty. And so I told them that I had
been poor ; that I remembered when my toes stuck
out through my broken shoes in winter ; when my

arms were out at the elbows ; when I shivered with
the cold. And I told them there was only one rule: That
was, always do the very best you can.   I told them
that I had always tried to do the very best I could ;
and that, if they would follow that rule, they would
get along somehow.   That was about what I said.
And when I got through, Mr. Pease said it was just
the thing they needed.   And when the school was
dismissed, all the teachers came up and shook hands
with me, and thanked me for it ; although I did not
know that I was saying anything of any account.
But the next morning I saw my remarks noticed in
the papers.'   Just here Mr. Lincoln put his hand in
his pocket, and remarked that he had never heard
anything that touched him as had the songs which
those children sang.   With that he drew forth a
little book, remarking that they had given him one of
the books from which they sang.   He began to read
a piece to the friends to whom these remarks were
addressed, with all the   earnestness of his great
earnest soul.   In the middle of the second verse his
auditors became deeply affected and soon the tears
were falling from their eyes. · At the same time they
noticed the great blinding tears in the eyes of Lincoln, who was reading straight on, so that he could
not see the page.   He was repeating that little song
from memory.   How often he had read it, or how its
sweet and simple accents continued to reverberate
through his soul, no one can know." [1]
   Mr. Pease, the Superintendent of the school, gives
the following interesting account of this event :

---

[1] Edward Eggleston in Browne's " Life of Lincoln."

"One Sunday morning, I saw a tall, remarkable-look-
ing man enter the room and take a seat among us.
He listened with fixed attention to our exercises, and
his countenance expressed such genuine interest that
I approached him and suggested that he might be
willing to say something to the children. He accepted
the invitation with evident pleasure ; and, coming
forward, began a simple address which at once fasci-
nated every little hearer and hushed the room into
silence. His language was strikingly beautiful, and
his tones musical with intense feeling. The little
faces would droop into sad conviction as he
uttered sentences of warning, and would brighten
into sunshine as he spoke cheerful words of promise.
Once or twice he attempted to close his remarks, but
the imperative shout, 'Go on ! O, do go on !' would
compel him to resume. As I looked upon the gaunt,
sinewy frame of the stranger, and marked his powerful head and determined features, now touched into
softness by the impressions of the moment, I felt an
irrepressible curiosity to learn something more about
him, and while he was quietly leaving the room I
begged to know his name. He courteously replied :
'It is Abraham Lincoln, from Illinois.'"

After spending a day or two in New York, Mr. Lincoln made a short tour through New England, and
spoke at a number of places. On the morning after
his speech at Norwich Conn., Rev. Mr. Gulliver met
him upon the train, and entered into conversation
with him. In referring to his speech, Mr. Gulliver
said that he thought it the most remarkable one he
had ever heard. "Are you sincere in what you say ?"
inquired Mr. Lincoln.

" I mean every word of it," replied the minister.
" Indeed, sir," he continued, " I learned more of the
art of public speaking last evening, than I could from
a whole course of lectures on rhetoric."

Then Mr. Lincoln informed him of a most "extraordinary circumstance" that occurred at New Haven a
few days previously. A professor of rhetoric in Yale
College, he had been told, came to hear him, took
notes of his speech, and gave a lecture on it to his
class on the following day, and, not satisfied with
that, followed him to Meriden the next evening, and
heard him again for the same purpose. All of this
seemed to Lincoln to be " very extraordinary." He
had been sufficiently astonished by his success in the
West, but he had no expectation of any marked success in the East, particularly among refined and literary men.

" Now," said Mr. Lincoln, " I should very much
like to know what it was in my speech which you
thought so remarkable, and which interested my
friend, the professor, so much ? "

Mr. Gulliver's answer was : " The clearness of your
statements, the unanswerable style of your reasoning and especially your illustrations, which were
romance and pathos and fun and logic welded
together." After Mr. Gulliver had fully satisfied his
curiosity by a further exposition of the politician's
power, Mr. Lincoln said :

" I am much obliged to you for this. I have been
wishing for a long time to find some one who would
make this analysis for me. It throws light upon a
subject which has been dark to me. I can understand
very readily how such a power as you have ascribed

to me, will account for the effect which seems to be produced by my speeches.   I hope you have not been too flattering in your estimate.   Certainly, I have had a most wonderful success for a man of my limited education " [1]

---

[1] Mr. Gulliver in the New York *Independent.*

CHAPTER XII.

Mr. Lincoln's candidacy for the Presidency was quietly but efficiently promoted by judicious friends, as well as by his own efforts, during the months which intervened before the National Convention.

Meantime affairs were so shaping themselves as to contribute more and more to the certainty of Republican success. Judge Douglas was actively engaged in a canvass to insure his own nomination by the Democratic Convention, which was to meet in Charleston, April 23, 1860. He sought to propitiate the hostile element of the South and, at the same time, not to alienate the friendly element of the North. Instead of standing firm upon his own convictions he tried to trim his course midway between the extreme elements of the Democracy and retain the support of both. In this he failed. While the majority of the delegates to the Charleston Convention favored him, he failed to secure the necessary two-thirds. The South had lost their confidence in him since his political integrity had caused him to refuse to support the Lecompton Constitution and by no effort could he regain it. The Southern wing withdrew from the Convention to meet later, in Richmond, while the Douglas party adjourned to Baltimore, where the great Illinois statesman was put in nomination for the Presidency.

The Richmond Convention nominated John C.

Breckenridge of Kentucky. Thus Democratic discord resulted in a party division, which rendered the
success of the Republican party almost certain.

The Republican National Convention was called to
meet in Chicago, May 16, 1860. Six days previous to
this, the State Convention met in Decatur, where the
movement to secure the nomination for Mr. Lincoln
was publicly inaugurated in such a manner as to
attract the attention of the nation and furnish a rallying cry for the campaign. The Convention was
made up of representative men of the party, who felt
that this meeting, held just before the greater Convention, should be one of special note. Lincoln was
present, apparently out of mere curiosity and with no
idea that he would receive more than passing notice
from the delegates. "A few minutes after the Convention organized, Governor Oglesby arose and said
amid increasing silence : 'I am informed that a distinguished citizen of Illinois, and one whom Illinois
will ever delight to honor, is present ; and I wish to
move that this body invite him to a seat upon the
stand.' Here the Governor paused, as if to tease and
dally, and work curiosity up to the highest pitch ;
but at length he shouted the magic name, 'Abraham
Lincoln.' Not a shout but a roar of applause, long
and deep, shook every board and joist of the building."[1] Some of those standing nearest seized him and
hoisting him on their shoulders passed him struggle-
ing and kicking over the heads of the audience to the
platform, where with clothing disarranged and face
flushed, he tried to regain his composure.

---

[1] Lamon's " Life of Lincoln."

Later on Governor Oglesby again arose and said that there was an old Democrat outside, who wished to present something to the Convention. A motion was made and carried that he be admitted. The doors swung open and a sturdy, open-featured old man entered bearing upon his shoulders two weather-beaten fence rails, with a banner floating above them bearing the inscription, " Two rails from a lot made by Abraham Lincoln and John Hanks in the Sangamon bottom in the year 1830." He was met with the wildest enthusiasm and a babel of shouts and applause. As soon as the tumult subsided, Lincoln was called upon for a speech and afterwards a resolution was passed to the effect that " Abraham Lincoln is the first choice of the Republican party of Illinois for President,' and instructing the delegates to Chicago to use all honorable means to secure his nomination and to cast the vote of the State as a unit for him.

The Chicago Convention was one of the most notable of all the great political meetings which have become historic during the present century. The majority of the delegates were young men with enough gray-haired men to temper their actions and measures with moderation. Many of the delegates were afterwards prominent in public life. Not less than sixty were destined to be sent to Congress, many became Governors of States or occupied other prominent positions of public trust.

The Convention was sectional, being made up of delegates from the free States, and the five border States with a few representatives from Texas. David Wilmot, the author of the famous Proviso, was made temporary chairman, and George Ashmun, of Massachusetts, representing the Conservative element, was made permanent chairman.

Mr. Seward had been for a long time the leading candidate and by many was regarded as certain of the nomination. The other candidates, besides Lincoln, were Edward Bates of Missouri, Salmon P. Chase of Ohio, Simon Cameron of Pennsylvania, and Jacob Collamer of Vermont. There were none, however, with the exception of the two leading candidates, who received any material support outside of their respective States.

The platform, which was adopted early in the session, affirmed the right of all men to "life, liberty and the pursuit of happiness" and declared the Convention to be in favor of the immediate admission of Kansas, of a general system of river and harbor improvements and a railroad to the Pacific Coast. It was largely made up of negatives denouncing disunion, extension of slavery, the re-opening of the slave-trade and popular or "squatter" sovereignty.

The utmost enthusiasm pervaded the Convention at each meeting, and the great wigwam, a wooden structure erected for the occasion on the lake-front, constantly rung with cheers and acclamations. The delegates felt that the candidate for the Convention would be the next President, yet they knew that he must be a sectional President. That the country was approaching a great crisis and that upon the Republican party and its President must devolve the task of defending and preserving the Union and set tling the vexed question forever, must have been

dimly realized by all. But the young and vigorous party was eager for the fray and ready to
assume the responsibility ; how great, none could
foresee.

From the first the tide turned strongly towards Lincoln. On the first ballot Seward received 173½ votes
and Lincoln 102. The remainder were cast for the
various local candidates. On the second ballot many
of the complimentary votes came to Lincoln, while
but few were given to Seward, who received 184½ to
181 for Lincoln. The result of the next ballot was
not doubtful, and long before it was completed the
news flashed all over the land that Lincoln "the
pioneer statesman" "honest old Abe" "the rail-
splitter," "the flatboatman," was the Republican
nominee.

In a moment the multitude in the streets joined
their shouts to the deafening roar within the wigwam.
Cannon were fired on the lake-front and bonfires
were lighted. In the most extravagant manner was
the approbation of the people manifested.

The Convention closed its labors by nominating for
the Vice-Presidency, Hon. Hannibal Hamlin of Maine,
than which a wiser selection could not have been made.
During the Convention Mr. Lincoln remained in
Springfield anxiously awaiting the result. When the
first ballot was announced, he considered it very favorable as he believed that Seward would show nearly
his full strength at the outset. The second ballot
convinced him of the certainty of his nomination.
And he repaired to the *Journal* office to await the
result. When news of his nomination came, he was
surrounded by excited friends who alternately

cheered and congratulated him. He soon remarked : "Well, gentlemen, there is a little short woman at our house who is probably more interested in this dispatch than I am ; and if you will excuse me I will take it up and let her see it."

During the day a hundred guns were fired at Springfield and the nomination was ratified in the evening by a monster mass meeting, at which Lincoln was present and spoke briefly.

The morning after adjournment, the committee appointed by the Convention, headed by Hon. George Ashmun, went to Springfield to officially notify Mr. Lincoln of his nomination. They arrived at his home at about eight o'clock in the evening. The notification was given in a few well-chosen words and Mr. Lincoln's reply, which was short and dignified, made a very favorable impression upon the committee. A few days afterwards his letter of acceptance was sent to the National Committee. It consisted of a declaration of his acceptance of the Convention platform, and of the nomination, and closed with these words : "Imploring the assistance of Divine Providence, and with due regard to the views and feelings of all who were represented in the Convention ; to the rights of all the States and Territories and all the people of the Nation ; to the inviolability of the Constitution and the perpetual union, harmony and prosperity of all, I am most happy to co-operate for the practical success of the principles declared by the Convention."

Crowds of people came to visit the Republican nominee, either out of curiosity or to ingratiate themselves into his favor, as his election seemed to be assured. His little house was found to be too small to receive the large delegations which frequently came to interview him, and, hence, the Governor's room in the State House was placed at his disposal. There he spent the summer and autumn of the campaign, in company with his private secretary, John G. Nicolay, receiving visitors from all parts of the country and of all ranks and conditions. For every one who came he had a warm hand-shake and a kindly word, and he listened as respectfully to the rough words of the laborer as to the polished sentences of the millionaire.

In his character and antecedents Mr. Lincoln appealed strongly to the popular regard. He was a man of the people, simple, plain and modest. His words and his actions convinced the masses that he was one of their own number, who, by his great ability, and incorruptible honesty had been raised to an exalted station. They thoroughly believed in him, and were confident that he was in every way qualified to manage the affairs of state in the dark times which were then seen casting their shadows over the land. Hence from the very first the tide of popular feeling in the North set strongly in his favor. Yet many, who should have been found naturally among his supporters, became his active opponents. Especially was this true of church people, who believed him to be irreligious if not actually an atheist, and they hesitated to elevate to the Presidency a man of such principles as they believed him to hold. The misapprehension was a lamentable one, and caused Mr. Lincoln much sorrow.

As an illustration of this Mr. Holland quotes a conversation[1] which Mr. Lincoln held with Dr. Newton Bateman, Superintendent of Public Instruction, whose office in the State House adjoined the Governor's room, which was used by the President-elect as a reception room.

A canvass had been made of the voters of Springfield to ascertain their political standing and the results had been tabulated and given to Mr. Lincoln. In company with Mr. Bateman he carefully examined the list and then, with a face full of sadness, said :

"Here are twenty-three ministers of different denominations and all of them are against me except three : and here are a great many prominent members of the churches, a very large majority of whom are against me. Mr. Bateman, I am not a Christian— God knows I would be one—but I have carefully read the Bible and I do not so understand this book," and he drew from his bosom a pocket New Testament. "These men well know that I am for freedom in the Territories, freedom everywhere, as the laws and Constitution permit, and that my opponents are for slavery. They know this and yet, with this book in their hands, in the light of which human bondage could not live a moment, they are going to vote against me. I do not understand it at all." Here Mr. Lincoln paused, and then he arose and walked up and down the room in the effort to retain or regain his self-possession. Stopping at last he said with a trembling voice and his cheeks wet with tears : "I

---

[1] The authenticity of this conversation has been discredited by many of Mr. Lincoln's biographers, but Mr. Arnold has taken pains to verify the statements and is convinced that they are substantially correct.

know that there is a God and that He hates injustice and slavery. I see the storm coming and know His hand is in it. If He has a place and work for me—and I think He has—I believe I am ready. I am nothing, but truth is everything. I know I am right because I know that liberty is right, for Christ teaches it and Christ is God. I have told them that a house divided against itself cannot stand ; and they will find it so. Douglas doesn't care whether slavery is voted up or voted down, but God cares and humanity cares and I care ; and with God's help I shall not fail. I may not see the end, but it will come, and I shall be vindicated : and these men will find that they have not read their Bibles aright."

After a pause, he resumed : "Doesn't it appear strange that men can ignore the moral aspects of this contest ? A revelation could not make it plainer to me that slavery or the Government must be destroyed. The future would be something awful, as I look at it, but for this rock upon which I stand," alluding to the New Testament which he held in his hand, "especially with the knowledge of how the ministers are going to vote. It seems as if God had borne with this thing, (slavery) until the very teachers of religion have come to defend it from the Bible and to claim for it a divine character and sanction : and now the cup of iniquity is full and the vials of wrath will be poured out."

He had never so fully shown out his inner nature to any one. Few people believed that he was possessed of religious convictions, yet his whole life showed that he was dominated by high religious principle, that if he did not talk and preach Christianity, he lived it.

As his life now appears on the pages of history it
seems almost incredible that he should have been so
misjudged by his contemporaries, and yet it was no
doubt largely his own fault as he was intensely secre-
tive and seldom spoke upon the subject of religion.
Mr. Herndon says of him : "Mr. Lincoln had the
very genius of silence and high cunning and is not
understood at all by the world." Nor was his true
position on the slavery question generally understood. Though so often misapprehended his principles were very simple and he had so often expressed
them, both publicly and privately, that it seemed
strange that he should be so persistently misrepresented. He reverenced the Constitution and would
have its mandates obeyed in every function of government and citizenship. He hated slavery with an
intensity that gathered strength as he saw more of its
cruelty and injustice and as the arrogance and pretensions of the slaveholders increased. Yet slavery
had been recognized as an institution in one section
of the country longer than the Constitution had
existed, and he did not believe there was any Constitutional warrant for interference with it while confined to the States in which it originated. He would,
however, prevent, by all available means, its further
extension into free territory. Let it remain, if remain
it must, but it must not pass beyond its Constitutional
limits.

Douglas's pet theory of "Squatter Sovereignty" he
vigorously opposed as calculated to break down every
restriction and throw open the whole country, event-
ually, to the entrance of the hateful institution.

His moderation subjected him to violent criticism

and animadversion from both sides. The pro-slavery men classed him with the Abolitionists and coupled with his name every vulgar and derisive epithet they could devise. Their opposition was based upon passion, not upon reason, and was abusive in the extreme. On the other hand many of the Abolitionists ranked him, unjustly, with the pro-slavery sympathizers because he never advised nor favored the use of what he deemed unconstitutional measures to rid the country of the evil. His attitude in regard to the fugitive-slave law gave some color to their accusations, and one of the more prominent Abolitionists of the East went so far as to speak of him as the "Illinois slave-driver."

His position in regard to this inhuman law was generally misunderstood. It is well illustrated by an incident which occurred at this time, related by A. J. Grover. "Mr. Lincoln detested the law, but argued that until it was declared unconstitutional, it must be obeyed. This was a short time after the rescue of a fugitive slave at Ottawa, Ill., by a number of Abolitionists after Judge Caton, acting as United States Commissioner, had given his decision remanding him into the custody of his alleged owner; and the rescuers were either in prison or out on bail." Says Mr. Grover: "When Mr. Lincoln had finished his argument, I said, 'Constitutional or not, I shall never obey the fugitive-slave law, I will never catch and return slaves in obedience to any law or constitution. I do not believe a man's liberty can be taken from him, constitutionally, without a trial by jury. I believe the law to be not only unconstitutional but most inhuman ' 'Oh,' said Mr. Lincoln, 'it is ungodly!

it is ungodly! no doubt it is ungodly! but it is the law of the land and we must obey it as we find it.'"

So great was his veneration for the majesty of law that he would bow to it even though his whole nature protested against it.

Mr. Lincoln took no active part in the Presidential canvass nor was he consulted to any extent in regard to its conduct. Yet his personality was potent in winning votes wherever he was known. No one realized his greatness or believed that he could in any way lay claim to genius. His warmest friends could only recommend him as a plain man, one of the people, a commanding orator and a good fellow generally; but that he would prove the most consummate statesman and the profoundest observer of the great political movements of the day no one for a moment suspected. He had filled well his previous station, but had nowhere given evidence that he was especially qualified for the great position for which he was a candidate, either by nature or by culture. Nor did he himself, feel any degree of confidence in his fitness for the position. His ambition had naturally led him to seek the honor, but with it almost in his grasp he felt more and more the weight of the responsibilities which came with it and began to shrink from assuming them in doubt of his ability to faithfully discharge them. Hence he became more and more habitually melancholy and his face, when at rest, was full of sadness and despondency. For him, henceforth, the glamour, which his ambition had thrown over the Presidential office, was gone and he saw but the burdens and embarrassments, the jealousies and tumults, with which he must contend.

Many pleasing incidents occurred in the interval between his nomination and election to relieve the tedium of the campaign.[1] "One day there entered his room a tall Southerner, a Colonel from Mississippi, whose eyes' hard glitter spoke supercilious distrust and whose stiff bearing betokened suppressed hostility. 'It was beautiful,' says Dr. Bateman, 'to see the cold flash of the Southerner's dark eye yield to a warmer glow and the haughty constraint melt into frank good-nature under the influence of Mr. Lincoln's words of simple earnestness and unaffected cordiality. They got so far in half an hour that Mr. Lincoln could say, in his hearty way, 'Colonel, how tall are you?' 'Well, taller than you, Mr. Lincoln,' replied the Mississippian. 'You are mistaken, there,' retorted Mr. Lincoln. 'Dr. Bateman will you measure us?' So a big book was adjusted above the head of each, and pencil-marks made upon the white wall. Mr. Lincoln's height, as thus indicated, was a quarter-inch greater than the Colonel's. 'I knew it,' said Mr. Lincoln. 'They raise tall men down in Mississippi, but you go home and tell your folks that 'Old Abe tops you a little.' The Colonel went away much mollified and impressed. 'My God,' said he to Dr. Bateman, as he went out, 'there is going to be a war; but could my people know what I have learned in the last half-hour, there would be no need of war.'"

A New York gentleman thus describes a meeting with Mr. Lincoln at Springfield, soon after the nomination: "I was in Chicago when Mr. Lincoln was nominated, and, being curious to see the man

---

[1] Browne's "Life of Lincoln."

every one was going wild over, I went to Springfield
I called at his office, but he was not in.   Then I went
to his residence and learned that he had a room in
the Capitol Building and that I would find him there.
Arrived at the room, I rapped at the door.   It was
opened by a tall, spare man, plain of face.   I told him
I had come to see Mr. Lincoln.   Inquiring my name,
he took me by the arm and introduced me to some
half dozen persons who were in the room, and then
remarked, 'My name is Lincoln.'   In ten minutes I
felt as if I had known him all my life.   He had the
most wonderful faculty I have ever seen in a man to
make one feel at ease.   I left him, feeling that he
was an extraordinary man and that I should vote for
him and influence all I could to do the same."

At one time when Hon. George S. Boutwell, of
Massachusetts, was present, together with a number
of other men of distinction, an old lady from the
country entered, dressed in awkward, old-fashioned
garments, with a tanned and wrinkled face looking
out from the depths of a large sunbonnet.   She had
come to present " Mr. Linkin " with a pair of home-
made stockings at least a yard long.   He received
them with kindly thanks and, holding one in each
hand for inspection, he gravely assured her that he
would take them to Washington with him, and that
he was sure he should be unable to find any like
them there.   After she had gone, Mr. Boutwell
remarked that the lady had evidently made a very
correct estimate of Mr. Lincoln's latitude and longi-
tude.

CHAPTER XIII.

THE campaign of 1860, with all its evil passions and boisterous enthusiasm, finally ended with the election of Mr. Lincoln by a large majority of electoral votes, but with a minority of nearly a million in the popular vote. It was with an ominous presage that the result was announced. Not an electoral vote south of Mason and Dixon's line was given to him. He was to become the first sectional President. The South understood neither Lincoln's character, nor his policy. Then, as to a great extent since, he was totally misapprehended, his character maligned and his motives impugned. Yet, the bitter hostility to the man was but a cloak for the enduring enmity felt towards the principles he was supposed to represent.

The campaign had been pre-eminently a conflict between opposing principles rather than persons. Douglas, in one of his speeches, remarked substantially, that the great principle involved in the contest was that of "interference" or "non-interference." The Republicans who opposed, and the Buchanan Democrats who favored the extension of slavery, were, to all intents, committed to the same policy, while the American party, headed by Mr. Bell and the Douglas wing of the Democracy, could easily coalesce, being pledged to the principle of non-interference, a policy which would leave to each

(169)

State the decision of the question, whether it should be free or slave.

Many times before had slavery and anti-slavery met at the polls in violent, though nominally, peaceful strife. But the crisis had now come, when the decision of the ballot was no longer deemed authoritative. For the sake of slavery the South was ready to cast away all the memories of the past, fraught with the glory achieved by the heroes of an united country ; to renounce the presage of future greatness and prosperity, which harmony alone could bring ; to haul down the "Stars and Stripes" which had waved over many a battle-field where their fathers had stood, shoulder to shoulder, with the now hated heroes of the North in defense of a common country against a common tyranny. For slavery they would destroy the Government, disrupt the country and enter into a war which should devastate the land, destroy their homes and stain the soil with the blood of their beloved sons.

The question of secession was not a new one, nor was the issue hastily raised. It had its root in the opposition to the adoption of the Constitution. That instrument, efficient and able as it has since proven itself to be, was then viewed with disfavor and distrust by a majority of the people in New York, Massachusetts, New Hampshire, Rhode Island and South Carolina. Yet the emergency of the hour and the ability of its advocates overrode the objections and secured its adoption. There was a constantly increasing party which believed that the Union was but a federation, a compact into which the States had voluntarily entered and from which they possessed the

power to withdraw at their discretion. The Union
party believed that by the adoption of the Constitution, the States had merged their existence into that
of the Nation, permanently surrendering their rights
to the central government, except such as the Constitution should delegate to them. According to this
view the events of 1789 constituted a revolution as
radical as that of 1776, though of a different character. The one established the independence of the
individual States, the other took away the independence of the States and made them component parts
of a nation, laying emphasis upon their nationality.

The doctrine of State sovereignty was first distinctly stated in 1798, after the passage of the " Alien
and Sedition " laws by Congress. The Legislatures
of Kentucky and Virginia passed resolutions, prepared by Jefferson and Madison, respectively, which
asserted that the Constitution was of the nature of a
compact to which the separate States were parties,
and that each State had the exclusive right to decide
for itself when the compact had been broken and the
mode and measure of redress. At different times one
or more of the States had asserted the right of secession, but had either been restrained by wiser counsels
or by force. Calhoun's doctrine of nullification,
which was tried in South Carolina in 1832 and failed,
was a legitimate offspring of this political theory.
Another outbreak was imminent in 1850, but was
subdued by compromise and popular vote. The sentiment was not destroyed, but reposed in the faith
of its ultimate triumph, and awaited an opportunity
for an outbreak. The election of Lincoln brought
the opportunity and a nominal provocation.

During the memorable winter preceding Lincoln's inauguration, secession was the all-absorbing topic. The South energetically maintained its right to secede, and proceeded to exercise it; while the North was loth to believe that the secession movement was not conceived in a spirit of mere bravado, and that the Union would be broken.

The subject was discussed in the press and pulpit, and in the national Legislature. Thaddeus Stevens of Pennsylvania, in a speech in the House of Representatives, said:

"The secession and rebellion of the South have been inculcated as a doctrine for twenty years past among slaveholding communities. At one time the tariff was deemed a sufficient cause; then the exclusion of slavery from the Territories; then some violation of the Fugitive Slave Law. Now the culminating cause is the election of a President who does not believe in the benefits of slavery or approve of that great missionary enterprise, the slave-trade. The truth is, all these things are mere pretenses. The restless spirits of the South desire to have a slave empire, and they use all these things as excuses. Some of them desire a more brilliant and stronger government than a republic. Their domestic institutions and the social inequality of their free people naturally prepare them for a monarchy, surrounded by a lordly nobility, for a throne founded upon the neck of labor."

The extreme Southern view was partially presented in a short speech in the Senate, December 4, by Thomas Clingman of North Carolina, which he began as follows:

"My purpose was not so much to make a speech, as to state what I think is the great difficulty ; and that is, that a man has been elected because he has been and is hostile to the South. It is this that alarms our people ; and I am free to say, as I have said upon the stump this summer repeatedly, that if an election were not resisted, either now or at a day not far distant, the Abolitionists would succeed in abolishing slavery all over the South. . . . Therefore, I maintain that our true policy is to meet this issue *in limine*, and I hope it will be done. If we can maintain our personal safety let us hold on to the present Government, if not, we must take care of ourselves at all hazards. . . . The current of resistance is running rapidly over the South. It is idle for men to shut their eyes to consequences such as these."

The views of the ultra-secessionists were presented much more elaborately in the same place, January 7, by Robert Toombs of Georgia. He formulated the grievances of the South into five demands : "First, that the people of the United States shall have an equal right to emigrate and settle in the present or future acquired Territories, with whatever property they may possess (including slaves), and be securely protected in its peaceable enjoyment until such a Territory be admitted as a State into the Union, with or without slavery as she may determine, on an equality with existing States. . . . The second proposition is, that property in slaves shall be entitled to the same protection from the Government of the United States, in all its departments, everywhere, which the Constitution confers upon it the power to extend to any other property, provided that nothing herein contained shall be construed to limit or restrain the right now belonging to every State to prohibit, abolish or establish and protect slavery within its limits. We demand of the common Government to use its granted powers to protect our property as well as yours. . . . We demand, in the next place, that persons committing crimes against slave property in one State and fleeing to another, shall be delivered up in the same manner as persons committing crimes against other property and that the laws of the State from which persons flee shall be the test of criminality. . . . The next stipulation is, that fugitive slaves shall be surrendered under the provisions of the Fugitive Slave Act of 1850, without being entitled either to a writ of *habeas corpus* or a trial by jury or other similar obstructions of legislation in the State to which he may flee. . . . The next demand, made in behalf of the South is, that Congress shall pass effective laws for the punishment of all persons in any of the States who shall, in any manner, aid and abet invasion or insurrection in any other State, or commit any other act against the laws of nations tending to disturb the tranquility of the people or government of any other State. . . . In a compact where there is no common arbiter, where the parties finally decide for themselves, the sword, at last becomes the real, if not the constitutional arbiter. Your party says that you will not take the decision of the Supreme Court. What are you going to do? You say we shall submit to your construction. We shall do it—if you can make us ; but not otherwise, or in any other manner. That is settled. You may call that secession or you may call it revolution ; but there is a big fact stand-

ing before you ready to oppose you, and that fact is
—freemen with arms in their hands. The cry of the
Union will not disperse them ; we have passed that
point ; they demand equal rights, you had better
heed their demands."

With such specious words as these did the party-
leaders seek to justify their course. If it be granted
that slavery was morally and legally right, their
arguments were conclusive. Few of them claimed
that they had any constitutional right to secede ;
for such a claim there were no plausible grounds.
They, therefore, justified secession as a revolutionary
measure and used, practically, the same arguments as
the patriots of 1775 in severing their connection from
England—the oppressive character of the Government and the impossibility of maintaining their
rights under the Constitution.

The speeches in Congress were but the echoes of
aggressive deeds throughout the South. One of the
orators boldly said :[1] " And while this Congress is debating the constitutionality and expediency of seceding from the Union, and while the perfidious authors of
this mischief are showering down denunciations upon
a large portion of the patriotic men of this country,
those brave men are coolly and calmly voting what
you call revolution.—Ay, sir, better than that, arming
to defend it. They appealed to the Constitution
they appealed to justice, they appealed to fraternity,
until the Constitution, justice, fraternity, were no
longer listened to in the legislative halls of their
country, and then, sir, they prepared for the arbitra-

---

[1] Robert Toombs.

ment of the sword ; and now you see the glittering bayonet, and you hear the tramp of armed men from your Capital to the Rio Grande."

The great conspiracy was almost perfected in the South before the North did more than suspect its existence. No sooner was Lincoln's election assured than active preparations for secession were begun. When the result of the election was announced, a Convention was called in South Carolina, a State which had always been the leader in revolutionary movements, to consider the question of secession. After a heated discussion, an ordinance of secession was adopted, November 17. Mississippi, Georgia, Alabama, Florida and Louisiana followed her example in January, and Texas in February. Not only were the people of the North powerless to prevent the catastrophe but the National Government was practically in the hands of the Confederacy. The President weakly deplored the state of affairs, but announced his inability to cope with it. In a message to Congress he announced it as his belief, that no State had the constitutional right to secede, but once seceded that the Government had no right nor power to bring them back by force. Congress was powerless to effect anything and the suffering country could only wait and pray for the advent of a stronger administration. And as comparatively few had any faith in the ability of Lincoln to successfully cope with such a momentous state of affairs, the outlook was gloomy indeed, perhaps more so than at any time during the succeeding war.

President Buchanan's Cabinet was a very hot-bed of treason. Traitors, high in the Councils of State, neglected no opportunity to serve the South and to cripple the Government. Men who had taken a solemn oath to uphold the Constitution, deliberately broke its most binding provisions. Howell Cobb, Secretary of the Treasury, emptied its vaults and impaired the public credit and then resigned because "his duty to Georgia demanded it." Isaac Toucey, Secretary of the Navy, placed as many of the ships of war as possible in the hands of traitors and sent the rest on cruises to remote ports in other parts of the world. John B. Floyd, Secretary of War, transferred nearly all the effective munitions of war, from Northern to Southern arsenals, where they could be easily seized by the rebels, and scattered the regular army along the frontier, whence it could with difficulty be recalled. And all of this was done openly with scarce a pretense of concealment. Nor were these men at all loth to proclaim their disunion sentiments, even while occupying positions of trust under, and drawing their salaries from the Government they were seeking to destroy. Anxious patriots, powerless to prevent, watched the bespoiling of the country and the gathering of armed forces, the clouds of rebellion darkening upon the Southern horizon, with feelings akin to despair.

The seceding States appointed delegates to meet at Montgomery, Ala., on February 4, to form a provisional Government. They organized a Federal Government, with a Constitution similar to the old one, excepting that it recognized slavery and the paramount rights of the States. Jefferson Davis was appointed President and Alexander H. Stephens, Vice-President.

February 15, Congress, in joint session, counted the electoral votes and declared Messrs. Lincoln and Hamlin, President and Vice-President-elect. The event had been looked forward to by the loyal North with fear and foreboding. The turbulent element was apparently in the supremacy in the National Capital, and there seemed to be reason to fear that the counting of the electoral votes would be interfered with, if not violently prevented. But nothing occurred in any way to obstruct the ceremony, whether because the plans of the Southern leaders were so far advanced that they did not care to interfere or because they did not believe that Lincoln would attempt to force them back into the Union.

During this time, Mr. Lincoln was remaining quietly at home, watching closely the course of events and trying to avert the catastrophe in every way possible. He was in close communication with the leaders of the party and many prominent men both North and South, striving to assure them of his pacific intentions. He insisted emphatically that he did not intend to interfere with slavery in the slave States, but he would not abate one iota of his opposition to its further extension, nor would he permit his friends to take any measures looking toward a compromise. December 13 he wrote the following letter to Hon. E. B. Washburne, Chairman of the House Congressional Committee : " Your long letter received. Prevent, as far as possible, any of our friends from demoralizing themselves and our cause by entertaining propositions for compromise of any sort upon slavery extension. There is no possible compromise upon it, but which puts us under and all our work to do over again.

Whether it be a Missouri line or Eli Thayer's popular sovereignty, it is all the same. Let either be done, and immediately fillibustering and slavery extension recommences. On that point hold firm as a chain of steel."

In an interview published in the New York *Tribune*, January 30, 1861, he reiterates the same sentiments with increased emphasis :

"I will suffer death before I will consent, or advise my friends to consent, to any concession or compromise which looks like buying the privilege of taking possession of the Government, to which we have a constitutional right ; because, whatever I might think of the merit of the various propositions before Congress, I should regard any concession in the face of menace as the destruction of the Government itself, and a consent on all hands that our system shall be brought down to a level with the existing disorganized state of affairs in Mexico. But this thing will hereafter be, as it is now, in the hands of the people, and if they desire to call a convention to remove any grievances complained of, or to give new guarantees for the permanence of vested rights, it is not mine to oppose."

Mr. Lincoln's firmness, at this time, prevented all attempts at compromise which could only have been consummated by such a surrender of constitutional rights as would have been disastrous to the unity and prosperity of the country. Secession and war were evils to be avoided if possible, but not by compromise or concession which could at best but defer the appeal to arms for a short time. The points in dispute were too vital to be settled by anything short of war, and the sooner the issue was faced the better it was for the country.

Mr. Lincoln appreciated the situation much better than many of the party-leaders, and his dignified firmness in refusing all compromise that contemplated a sacrifice of principle, has been proven by subsequent events to have been the wisest policy.

February 11 he left Springfield with his family and a few friends to go to Washington and enter upon the arduous duties of his office. It was a solemn moment and one fraught with the deepest anxiety and apprehension. Elected to the highest and most honorable office within the gift of the people of the great Republic, he should have started upon his journey joyfully, with bright anticipations of a brilliant and glorious career. Not as a tried General, confident of success, did he go to his task, but rather as one called upon to go out and do fierce battle with mighty foes, without preparation, and feeling his own incompetency. Hence it was not with the pride of assured success, that he bade adieu to the friends who gathered at the railway-station for one last shake of the hand and a parting look at a face which they should see no more until, with a martyr's crown, it should return to find a resting-place forever in the spot he so dearly loved. A feeling of sadness pervaded the group and none felt more sorrow than the one to whom the attention of all was directed. As he stepped upon the platform of the car he turned around and uttered the following beautiful and touching words:

"My Friends: No one, not in my position, can realize the sadness I feel at this parting. To this people I owe all that I am. Here I have lived more than a quarter of a century. Here my children were born and here one of them lies buried. I know not how soon I shall see you again. I go to assume a task more difficult than any which has devolved upon any other man since the days of Washington. He never would have succeeded except for the aid of Divine Providence, upon which he at all times relied. I feel that I cannot succeed without the same Divine blessing which sustained him ; and on the same Almighty Being I place my reliance for support. And I hope you, my friends, will all pray that I may receive that divine assistance, without which I cannot succeed, but with which success is certain. Again, I bid you an affectionate farewell."

With many a hearty "God bless you and keep you," the train pulled out of the depot. The plan of the journey contemplated a trip through the States of Indiana, Ohio, Pennsylvania, New York, New Jersey and Maryland. When the distinguished party reached Indianapolis, the Legislature was in session. Mr. Lincoln visited the State House, and was warmly greeted. Here, as elsewhere, when the opportunity offered, Mr. Lincoln made a short speech, the burden of which was intended to allay the excitement and distrust in the South, and to gain the confidence of the people. He could not yet believe that the people of the South were determined in their attempts to break up the Union, and he desired that they might become convinced of his good-will and his intention not to interfere with their peculiar institutions any further than his construction of the Constitution demanded. Everywhere his speeches were pacific and moderate, and appealed to the highest

patriotism of the people. Yet his temperate words
at no time led the people to suspect that he lacked
in firmness. "I shall do all that may be in my power,"
said he, "to promote a peaceful settlement of our
difficulties. The man does not live who is more devoted to peace than I am—none who would do more
to preserve it. But it may be necessary to put the
foot down firmly."

He visited the cities of Cincinnati, Columbus and
Cleveland and was everywhere received with the
greatest enthusiasm. At Cincinnati he approached
the borders of a slave State, and his speech here was,
as on a previous occasion, directed largely to the
Kentuckians, who might almost hear the echoes of
his voice from the opposite shore. The burden of
his utterances was everywhere the same. At Buffalo,
Albany, New York, Trenton, Philadelphia and Harrisburg he attempted to allay fear and encourage confidence. Never had he before been brought into
contact with so many people in so short a time. His
journey was a veritable triumphal march. At every
station and crossroad crowds waited patiently to see
the Presidential train pass by, and the larger cities,
where stops were to be made, were thronged with
eager crowds, some of whom had come to criticise and
others to counsel, some out of mere curiosity and
others out of a warm, hearty good-will towards him
who was to assume a greater responsibility and bear
a heavier burden than any President since Washington. The general impression made upon the people
was pleasing, and many who came to ridicule his
ungainliness, went away to praise his manliness.
The Ohio *State Journal* spoke in highest terms of

the impression made by Mr. Lincoln upon the people.

"His great height was conspicuous even in that crowd of goodly men. At first the kindness and amiability of his face strikes you; but, as he speaks, the greatness and determination of his nature are apparent. Something in his manner, even more than in his words, told how deeply he was affected by the enthusiasm of the people, and when he appealed to them for encouragement and support, every heart responded with a mute assurance of both. There was the simplicity of greatness in his unassuming and confiding manner that won its way to instant admiration."

When he reached Albany, the Legislature of the Empire State was in session, and he was invited to address it. The scene was an impressive one. Not only was the audience a notable one, but the memories associated with the place were impressive. That so distinguished an audience, in so noted a place, had assembled to greet him, touched him deeply. In commencing his speech, he said:

"It is with feelings of great diffidence and, I may say, feelings of awe, perhaps greater than I have recently experienced, that I meet you here in this place. The history of this great State, the renown of its great men who have stood in this chamber, and have spoken their thoughts, all crowd around my fancy and incline me to shrink from an attempt to address you. Yet I have some confidence given me by the generous manner in which you invited me, and the still more generous manner in which you have received me. You have invited me and received me

without distinction of party. I could not for a moment suppose that this has been done in any considerable degree with any reference to my personal self.
It is very much more grateful to me that this reception and the invitation preceding it were given to me,
as the representative of a free people, than it could
possibly have been were it but the evidence of devotion to me or to any one man. It is true that, while
I hold myself, without mock modesty, the humblest
of all the individuals who have ever been elected
President of the United States, I yet have a more difficult task to perform than any of them has ever
encountered."

At Trenton, the historic capital of New Jersey, he
was also tendered a reception by the Legislature.
The memories of the dangerous passage of the Dela-
ware and the great victory which followed were intimately associated in his mind with his childhood's
days, when he eagerly read and re-read Weem's attractive but unreliable " Life of Washington," by the
light of a pine knot, long after the rest of the family
had retired for the night. He alluded modestly, but
impressively, to the toils and privations of those early
days, proving once more that he was not ashamed of
his lowly origin, but that he rather gloried in the fact
that he was one of the masses and thus in deepest
sympathy with them.

At Philadelphia he unfurled a splendid flag in the
presence of a great concourse, and made an elaborate
address, in which he spoke of his political life and
feelings more freely than at any other time on the
journey, and when, for a moment, he admitted his
apprehensions of the future in almost prophetic

words. The whole speech, which was delivered in Independence Hall, is too long to be quoted, but a single passage will well illustrate its character.

"You have kindly suggested to me that in my hands is the task of restoring peace to the present distracted condition of our country. I can say in return, sir, that all the political sentiments I entertain have been drawn, so far as I have been able to draw them, from the sentiments which originated in, and were given to the world from this hall. I have never had a feeling, politically, that did not spring from the sentiments embodied in the Declaration of Independence. I have often pondered over the dangers which were incurred by the men who assembled here and framed and adopted that Declaration of Independence. I have pondered over the toils that were endured by the officers and soldiers of the army that achieved that Independence. I have often inquired of myself what great principle or idea it was that kept this Confederacy so long together. It was not the mere matter of the separation of the Colonies from the mother country, but that sentiment in the Declaration of Independence which gave liberty, not alone to the people of this country but, I hope, to the world for all future time. It was that which gave promise that, in due time, the weight would be lifted from the shoulders of all men. This is a sentiment embodied in the Declaration of Independence. Now, my friends, can this country be saved on this basis? If it can, I shall consider myself one of the happiest men in the world if I can help save it. If it cannot be saved on that principle, it would be truly awful. But if this country cannot be saved without giving up that principle, I was about to say, *I would rather be assassinated on this spot than surrender it.*"

This was not the first time that he had declared his' veneration for and allegiance to the principles of the immortal Declaration. Again and again had he reiterated it in the Douglas debates and other political speeches. In it he found his political creed and upon the permanence of its principles he based all his hope for the future welfare of the country.

On the next day he visited Harrisburg and addressed the Pennsylvania Legislature there assembled, and here his public journey ended. There had been many vague rumors afloat in regard to conspiracies formed by Southern sympathizers to prevent his inauguration. Baltimore was intensely disloyal and numerous threats had been made that the President-elect should never pass through the city alive. Much alarm was felt by his friends and everything possible had been done to unearth the conspiracy, if one existed. Detectives had been engaged and evidence of the existence of such a plot was apparently secured. Mr. Lamon, who accompanied Mr. Lincoln, criticises the evidence and casts grave doubts upon its reliability. But that there was good reason to apprehend danger, even if none existed, was excuse enough for more than ordinary caution. His friends had advised Mr. Lincoln to cancel his engagements in Philadelphia and Harrisburg and hastily and secretly make the journey to Washington. This he refused to do, but, after his address at Harrisburg, he secretly boarded a special car, and without the knowledge of any one, save two or three of his most intimate friends, he went to Philadelphia, where he boarded the night train, passed through Baltimore in safety and reached the Capital in the morning, before it was generally known that he had left Harrisburg.

This hurried journey to Washington was sharply criticised and mercilessly ridiculed and caricatured in the papers of the day. Some went so far as to impute its motive to cowardice. It must be admitted that there are at least grave doubts that any such conspiracy existed or that there was any danger to be apprehended from the passage through Baltimore. The suspicions, however, were strong enough and the condition of the country sufficiently critical to justify the most extraordinary precautions to protect the person of the President-elect from all possible danger.

CHAPTER XIV

LINCOLN had practically constructed his Cabinet before he left Springfield. It was a task of unusual difficulty, yet he executed it with judgment and moderation. The Republican party had been formed in large part, by recruits from the Whig and Democratic parties, the latter being in the majority. Something of the old-time antagonism existed between the quondam political foes and the great difficulty presented itself, in the formation of the Cabinet, of recognizing both wings in such a manner that satisfaction would be given to both and cause for jealousy to neither.

Here, at the very outset, Lincoln gave intimations of the fixed principle that was to guide him in his political appointments during his administration. He would recognize true patriotism as a standard for political preferment and not party affiliations. Other things being equal he made but little distinction between Democrats and Republicans, provided that the loyalty of the candidate was unquestioned. Never since Washington had a President placed so high a premium upon patriotism, and paid so little attention to politics. It made him many political enemies but brought him multitudes of friends from the masses of the people who recognized his earnest desire to administer the affairs of the Government for the general good. And later on, when the gathering storm of war burst upon the land and the adherents of the South strove to show that it was a war inspired and brought on by the " black Republicans," instead of choosing his officers exclusively from the party which had elected him, he gave full proof of the fact that he considered the question of suppessing the Rebellion to be a purely national one, and he made it his policy to gather to the national standard all loyal men of whatever party. The peril of the nation annihilates party, and he did not fail to appreciate the fact. Beyond a question he will be recognized in history as the most purely national and loyal Chief Magistrate of the century.

From the day of his election he had been beset by hordes of hungry office-seekers, who demanded that he should dismiss all the appointees of previous administrations and divide the spoils among those who had helped to elect him. A strong pressure was early brought to bear upon him to this end, but, although he listened courteously to all suggestions and advice, he remained firm in his determination to make removals from office only upon patriotic and not upon partisan grounds, and in many cases he even went further than this and showed his willingness to appoint his political enemies and rivals to the most important offices on grounds of qualification alone.

This principle was exemplified in the selection of Cabinet officers. Many men were recommended to him by influential politicians, who believed they had a claim upon him; yet he was for the most part uninfluenced by their representations, and made his selections solely with a view to the public good. He de-

sired to enroll some moderate, but influential Southern men in the Cabinet, hoping that such action
might materially assist in averting the war which
was threatened.   To this end he made overtures to
Hon. John A. Gilmore, then a member of Congress
from North Carolina.   In a letter personally delivered
by Thurlow Weed, he explained briefly his views
upon the situation, and outlined the policy he intended to pursue.   He then offered Mr. Gilmore a
Cabinet portfolio which, however, he reluctantly
refused in view of the probable secession of his
State.

Before his election Mr. Lincoln had determined to
offer the two leading positions, the State and Treasury Departments, to his two prominent rivals for the
nomination, Messrs. Seward and Chase.   And afterwards the Cabinet was completed by the selection of
Hon. Simon Cameron as Secretary of War, Hon.
Gideon Welles as Secretary of the Navy, Hon. E. H.
Bates as Attorney General, Hon. Caleb Smith as Secretary of the Interior and Judge Montgomery Blair
as Postmaster General.

The Cabinet, thus constituted, was a strong one,
and every member of it was eminently qualified to
fulfill the arduous duties of his position; yet there was
not a single appointment which failed to excite bitter
criticism and, in some cases, from within the party
itself.

Mr. Seward was the most prominent and widely
known of these gentlemen.   He had been one of the
founders of the party, and was noted for the earnestness with which he had entered into the struggle with
the slave power.   By his eloquent and forcible speeches

he had done much to bring together the diverse elements of the party, and to unite them for a victorious campaign. In a speech at Rochester he had been the first to predict the "irrepressible conflict," and, even sooner than Lincoln, he had announced his belief that the Government could not long exist half free and half slave. He was a cultured gentleman and a thorough scholar. He believed in a pacific policy and, as far as the dignity of the Government would permit, he believed concessions should be made to the South.

Salmon P. Chase had also been a prominent candidate for the Presidential nomination. His ability was unquestioned, and his mind clear and logical. In character he was above reproach, and yet, while he always commanded the highest respect, he lacked the elements which conduce to popularity, and never wielded much influence over the masses. His position was, undoubtedly, the most difficult and perplexing in the Cabinet. The expenses of a great war must be met from an empty Treasury and by a nation which was in the throes of civil war. Never had financial problems of greater magnitude been forced upon a government, and never had a man better fitted to deal with them been at the head of the Treasury. He had been a radical Abolitionist from the first and had never faltered in his principles, though in the midst of the most determined opposition.

Hon. Simon Cameron was given the position of Secretary of War, rather because of arrangements made before the Convention and his assistance during the campaign, than on account of his popularity. When it was understood that Mr. Lincoln contem-

plated giving him a Cabinet position, numerous pro-
tests were received from all over the North, alleging
that he was an unscrupulous and dishonest politician
and that his presence in the Cabinet would bring
discredit upon the Administration. He was descended from the Scotch clan of the Camerons and
had inherited many of the characteristics of his High-
land ancestors. He was said never to forget a friend
or an enemy. Much opposition was also manifested
to the appointment of Judge Blair. He came from a
distinguished family which had been possessed of
considerable political influence. He was a gentleman of the old school, hasty, selfwilled, but able.
The affairs of the Postal Service have never been better administered than during his incumbency.

Mr. Lincoln spent the few days intervening between his arrival in Washington and his inauguration in consultation with his political advisers, in receiving delegations which came to pay their respects
to the Chief Magistrate-elect and in listening to the
claims of candidates for office. As the date of the inauguration approached, the popular interest and apprehension became more intense. Threats had been
freely made that Lincoln should never be inaugurated. Washington lay within the bounds of a slave
State, and contained a large element which was in
sympathy with the South, and, moreover, the city had
become a rendezvous for many desperate radicals who
would hesitate at nothing to carry out their incendi-
ary designs. General Scott, the veteran hero of the
Mexican War, who was the Commander of the United
States' Armies, was aware of the danger and announced his intention of protecting the person of

the President from assault with the whole army if necessary.

When the day came the whole North waited with bated breath as if almost expecting to hear the echoes of insurrection and carnage at the national Capital, proclaiming the disruption of the Union. The great crowds which usually attend these quadrennial ceremonies were, in large part, absent. For few dared to face the evident danger to gratify curiosity. On the eastern front of the Capitol was erected a platform upon which were grouped the Members of Congress, the Supreme Court Judges, the high officers of the Army and Navy, many of the Diplomatic Corps, resplendent in their decorations of tinsel and gold. The crowd that had assembled to view the proceedings was such a one as had never before been seen in the Capital City. There were patriots who beheld their beloved country on the verge of ruin and who could see no hope for the future save such as was held out by the grave, gaunt man before them. Despondent and hopeless, they could see no guiding light through the black clouds that lowered so thickly around them. And there were traitors there, who waited but the opportunity to tear down and trample underfoot the Stars and Stripes that floated above their heads, men, whose hearts were full of malice towards him, whose election to the Presidency they had chosen to assign as the cause for the fulmination of their evil designs against the Government.

Upon the platform stood, with bowed head, President Buchanan, whose administration was to be known to posterity as the feeblest and most fraught with evil in the history of the country. There too,

prominent in the eyes of the people, was Douglas,
Lincoln's great rival, now, for the first time suffering
the bitter pangs of defeat, yet in every way considerate of his old friend.   From this time no man was
more loyal or more earnest in the defense of the
Union than Douglas, he, who had been ranked as the
champion of the slaveholders.   Henceforth he would
forget party allegiance and political animosity, and
join heart and hand with all good patriots who strove
to preserve the Union.   And to-day, his piercing eye
restlessly scanned the crowds before him as if to
observe the first signs of outbreak or violence.

Everywhere was disquiet and uncertainty.   The
spirit of violence was abroad and none knew where
he would first manifest his flaming presence.   One
man, alone, was calm and self-reliant.   Without a
tremor or a fear for his personal safety Lincoln stood
before the people, unconscious of self and eager to
impress upon the world, for he knew the world would
listen to his utterances, his peaceful sentiments and
the assurance of his belief that the unity of the Government would not be destroyed by violence.   He
was not insensible to the danger, but he believed that
the better sense of the South would ultimately triumph over the hasty passions of the men so eager to
work a revolution.   Above all he believed in the permanence of the Government and the vitality of republican institutions, and especially in the power of the
Constitution to perpetuate itself.   He forgot his own
personality in the presence of the tremendous issues
thronging upon him and stood before the people,
calm and fearless, the embodiment of the might of the
Constitution and the offended Genius of Liberty.

He stood, bareheaded, and read his address in a voice so clear and penetrating that each word was heard distinctly by every one of the thousands present. Beholding the dark clouds of war hanging low over the country, he yet planted his feet firmly upon the rock of peace. His enemies had cast the gauntlet of defiance at his feet and he, in return, extended to them the right hand of amity.

His address was conciliatory but firm, dignified but confidential. As no other man had ever done he blended the loftiest utterances with perfect candor and honesty towards the people. Nevertheless, the address, which, in the unprejudiced judgment of history, will rank among the great masterpieces of oratory and not the least among them, was greeted with carping and criticism. The South characterized it as the rabid utterance of the most radical republicanism, and many who should have sustained him in the North, spoke of him as a traitor to his party principles and accused him of seeking to compromise with the secessionists. Time, the great vindicator, proves the mistake of both and places the correct estimate upon the great inaugural speech. Its length forbids its entire insertion here, but some of the most striking passages are quoted below :

" Fellow-citizens of the United States. In compliance with a custom as old as the Government itself, I appear before you to address you briefly and to take in your presence the oath prescribed by the Constitution to be taken by the President before he enters upon the execution of his office. . . . Apprehension seems to exist among the people of the Southern States that by the accession of a Republi-

can administration their property and their peace and
personal security are to be endangered. There has
never been any reasonable cause for such apprehension. Indeed, the most ample evidence to the contrary
has all the time existed and been open to their inspection. It is found in nearly all the published speeches
of him who now addresses you. I do but quote from
one of those speeches when I declare that ' I have no
purpose, directly or indirectly, to interfere with the
institution of slavery in the States where it exists. I
believe I have no lawful right to do so, and I have
no inclination to do so.' Those who nominated and
elected me, did so with the full knowledge that I had
made this and many similar declarations and had
never recanted them. And, more than this, they
placed in the platform for my acceptance, and as a
law to themselves and me, the clear and emphatic
resolution which I now read : ' Resolved, that the
maintenance inviolate of the rights of the States, and
especially the right of each State to order and control its own domestic institutions according to its own
judgment exclusively, is essential to that balance of
power on which the perfection and endurance of our
political fabric depends, and we denounce the lawless
invasion by armed force of any State or Territory, no
matter under what pretext, as the gravest of crimes.'
I now reiterate these sentiments ; and, in doing so,
I only press upon the public attention the most conclusive evidence of which the case is susceptible, that
the property, peace and security of no section are to
be in anywise endangered by the now incoming
administration. I add, too, that all the protection
which, consistently with the Constitution and the laws,

can be given will be cheerfully given, to all the States, when lawfully demanded, for whatever cause —as cheerfully to one section, as to another. . . . I take the official oath to-day with no mental reservations and with no purpose to construe the Constitution or laws by any hypercritical rules. And while I do not choose now to specify particular acts of Congress as proper to be enforced, I do suggest that it will be much safer for all, both in official and private stations, to conform to and abide by all those acts which stand unrepealed, than to violate any of them trusting to find impunity in having them held to be unconstitutional.

"It is seventy-two years since the first inauguration of a President under the national Constitution. During that period fifteen different and greatly distinguished citizens have, in succession, administered the executive branch of the Government. They have conducted it through many perils and, generally, with great success. Yet with all this scope of precedent, I now enter upon this same task, for the brief constitutional term of four years, under great and peculiar difficulty. A disruption of the Federal Union, hitherto only menaced, is now formidably attempted. I hold that, in contemplation of universal law and of the Constitution, the union of the States is perpetual. Perpetuity is implied if not expressed in the fundamental law of all national Governments. It is safe to assert that no Government proper ever had a provision in its organic law for its own termination. Continue to execute all the express provisions of our national Constitution and the Union will endure forever—it being impossible to destroy it except by some action not provided for in the instrument itself.

"Again if the United States be not a Government proper, but an association of States in the nature of a compact merely, can it, as a contract, be peaceably unmade by less than all the parties who made it. One party to a contract may violate it—break it, so to speak, but does it not require all to lawfully rescind it? . . . It follows from these views, that no State, upon its own mere motion, can lawfully get out of the Union ; that resolves and ordinances to that effect are legally void ; and that acts of violence within any State or States, against the authority of the United States, are insurrectionary or revolutionary, according to the circumstances. I therefore consider that, in view of the Constitution and laws, the Union is unbroken ; and to the extent of my ability, I shall take care, as the Constitution itself expressly enjoins upon me, that the laws of the Union be faithfully executed in all the States. Doing this, I deem to be only a simple duty on my part ; and I shall perform it, so far as practicable, unless my rightful masters, the American people, shall withhold the requisite means, or in some authoritative manner direct the contrary. I trust this will not be regarded as a menace, but only as a declared purpose of the Union that it will constitutionally defend and maintain itself. In doing this, there need be no bloodshed or violence ; and there shall be none unless it is forced upon the national authority. The power confided to me will be used to hold, occupy and possess the property and places belonging to the Government and to collect the duties and imposts ; but beyond what may be necessary for these objects, there will be no invasion, no using of force against or among the people anywhere. . . . That there are persons in one section or another who seek to destroy the Union at all events, and are glad of any pretext to do it, I will neither affirm nor deny; but if there be such, I need address no word to them. To those, however, who really love the Union, may I not speak? Before entering upon so grave a matter as the destruction of our national fabric, with all its benefits, its memories and its hopes, would it not be wise to ascertain precisely why we do it? Will you hazard so desperate a step while there is any possibility that any portion of the ills you fly from have no real existence? Will you, while the certain ills you fly to are greater than all the real ones you fly from—will you risk the commission of so fearful a mistake? All profess to be content in the Union, if all constitutional rights can be maintained. Is it true, then, that any right, plainly written in the Constitution has been denied? I think not. . . . Plainly the central idea of secession is the essence of anarchy. A majority held in check by constitutional checks and limitations, and always changing easily with deliberate changes of popular opinion and sentiments, is the only true sovereign of a free people. Whoever rejects it, does, of necessity, fly to anarchy or to despotism. Unanimity is impossible; the rule of a minority, as a permanent arrangement, is wholly inadmissible; so that rejecting the minority principle, anarchy or despotism in some form, is all that is left. . . . One section of our country believes slavery is right, and ought to be extended, while the other believes it is wrong and ought not to be extended. This is the only substantial dispute. . . . Physically speaking we cannot separate. We cannot remove our respective sections from each other, nor build an impassable wall between them. A husband and wife may be divorced and go out of the presence, and beyond the reach of each other, but the different parts of our country cannot do this. They cannot but remain face to face and intercourse, either amicable or hostile, must continue between them. Is it possible to make that intercourse more advantageous or more satisfactory after separation than before? Can aliens make treaties easier than friends can make laws? Can treaties be more faithfully enforced among aliens than treaties among friends? Suppose you go to war, you cannot fight always ; and when, after much loss on both sides, and no gain on either, you cease fighting, the identical old questions as to terms of intercourse are again upon you. . . . My Countrymen, one and all, think calmly and well upon this whole subject. Nothing valuable can be lost by taking time. If there be an object to hurry any of you in hot haste to a step which you would never take deliberately, that object will be frustrated by taking time ; but no good object will be frustrated by it. Such of you, as are now dissatisfied, still have the old Constitution unimpaired and, on the sensitive point, the laws of your own framing under it ; while the new administration will have no immediate power, if it would, to change either. If it were admitted that you, who are dissatisfied, hold the right side in the dispute, there is still no single good reason for precipitate action. Intelligence, Patriotism, Christianity and a firm reliance on Him, who has never yet forsaken this favored land, are still competent to adjust, in the best way, all our present difficulty. In your hands, and not in mine, is the momentous issue of civil war. The Government will not assail you. You can have no conflict, without being yourselves the aggressors. You have no oath registered in Heaven to destroy the Government, while I shall have the most solemn one 'to preserve, protect and defend it.' I am loth to close. We are not enemies, but friends. We must not be enemies. Though passion may have strained it must not break our bonds of affection. The mystic chords of memory, stretching from every battlefield and patriot grave to every loving heart and hearthstone, all over this broad land, will yet swell the chorus of the Union when again touched, as they surely will be, by the better angels of our nature."

At the close of the address Chief Justice Taney, white-haired and venerable with age, stepped forward and administered the simple oath of office. It was a striking scene, the Judge, whose decision in the Dred Scott case had opened all the avenues of contention and civil war, confirming the authority of the man who had been most potent in opposition to the principle he had enunciated, and who was destined to overthrow the institution in whose favor it had been made. It was the old dispensation handing its sword to the new; the might of law triumphing over the confusion of anarchy and secession. From that moment the ill-omened institution was doomed, yet it had so entered into and permeated the life of the South that it required all the horrors of a civil war to

tear it out. It had been rooted in tyranny, and prop-
agated and nourished in the midst of sectional
strife and jealousy, until the mighty force of the
Government was all but inadequate to overthrow
it.

When Mr. Lincoln came upon the platform he
appeared awkward and ill at ease. He was clad in a
new suit of clothes and carried in his hand a new silk
hat, a style which he had never before worn. As he
stepped to the front he looked helplessly around for
some place to put his hat but could find none. For a
moment he stood holding it in his hands, evidently
unwilling to trust it upon the floor, when Mr. Douglas, who had seen his embarrassment and its cause,
stepped forward and took the hat and held it during
the address, while he listened with eager interest to
every word that fell from the lips of the speaker and
from time to time showed plainly his approval of the
sentiments expressed.

When the ceremonies were ended, the hearers slowly
dispersed and went to their homes and the new
administration entered upon its difficult duties amid
embarrassments far greater than could have been
expected and which were destined to increase rapidly
both in numbers and extent.

Of all the congratulations extended to Mr. Lincoln
none were more sincere and heartfelt than those of
Mr. Douglas who, realizing the magnitude of the task
undertaken by his erstwhile rival, gave him the assurance that he would aid him to the utmost in upholding the Constitution and enforcing the laws of the
country. And he nobly kept his pledge.

Mr. Arnold, in his " Life of Lincoln," relates the following remarkable story of a prophecy made by Mr. Douglas at this time :

"Senator Douglas and his wife, one of the most beautiful and fascinating women of America, occupied one of the houses which formed the Minnesota block. On New Year's Day, 1861, General Stewart, of New York, was making a New Year's call on Senator Douglas and, after some conversation, asked him : 'What will be the result, Senator, of the efforts of Jefferson Davis and his associates, to divide the Union ?'

"'We were,' says Stewart, 'sitting on the sofa together, when I asked the question. Douglas rose, walked rapidly up and down the room for a moment, and then, pausing, he exclaimed, with deep feeling and excitement :

"'The cotton States are making an effort to draw in the border States to their schemes of secession, and I am but too fearful they will succeed. If they do, there will be the most fearful civil war the world has ever seen, lasting for years.'

"Pausing a moment, he looked like one inspired, while he proceeded : 'Virginia, over yonder, across the Potomac,' pointing to Arlington, 'will become a charnel-house ; but, in the end the Union will triumph. They will try to get possession of this Capital, to give them *prestige* abroad, but in that effort they will never succeed ; the North will arise *en masse* to defend it. But Washington will become a city of hospitals, the churches will be used for the sick and wounded. This house,' he continued, 'the *Minnesota block*, will be devoted to that purpose before the end of the war.'

" Every word of this prediction was literally fulfilled; nearly all the churches were used for the wounded and the Minnesota block and the very room, in which this declaration was made, became the 'Douglas Hospital.'

"'What justification is there for all this?' asked Stewart.

"'There is no justification,' replied Douglas. 'I will go as far as the Constitution will permit to maintain their just rights. But,' said he, rising to his feet and raising his arm, 'if the Southern States attempt to secede, I am in favor of their having just so many slaves, and just so much slave territory, as they can hold at the point of the bayonet, and no more.'"

Five months after this remarkable conversation Stephen A. Douglas was no more.

CHAPTER XV.

WHEN Mr. Lincoln entered the White House on the night of March 4, 1861, he was nominally the President of the United States, but in fact his recognized authority extended only over the Northern and border States. the Southern tier was in a state of open revolt. The Union was disintegrated, the Constitution nullified and the opposing political theories of States' rights and centralization, brought into hostile relations by the unholy institution of slavery, were now preparing to decide the great dispute by force of arms.

Seven States had already passed ordinances of secession and had set up a provisional government, with Montgomery as the capital. North Carolina was the only Southern State that still hesitated. At first, the majority of its people were opposed to secession. This grand old State had special reason to cling to and reverence the Union. Within its borders had been fought some of the most sanguinary conflicts of the Revolution and, in the past, no State had been more loyal to the Constitution or more ready to sacrifice blood and treasure in its defense. Her patriotic feelings, however, were strongly opposed by the common sentiment of her sister States, to whom she was bound by ties of strongest sympathy and common interest. The disunion influences were thus too

(205)

strong to be resisted and the secession ordinance was passed, May 21, and the Southern Confederacy was complete.

The fight in the border States of Maryland, Kentucky and Missouri was long and bitter. The people were about equally divided, but the Union party finally triumphed, assisted, as it was, by the active sympathy and support of the North and the earnest co-operation of the administration. Mr. Lincoln clearly perceived the importance of retaining these States in the Union, not only for their moral influence but also because they formed a belt of neutral territory between the loyal and disloyal States. Had these States seceded, the war would, no doubt, have been greatly prolonged, the National Capital could not have been held against the enemy, and the issue would have been more doubtful than it was.

The difficulties that surrounded the administration were almost insuperable. There was incipient war, and no means of crushing it; rebellion, but the hands of the Government were tied. The majority of the army officers, who had been educated at West Point, and had gained skill from actual experience, violated their oaths and entered the armies of the South. The army and navy were demoralized and almost disorganized. The munitions of war had been largely transported to the South, and were now in the hands of the recalcitrants. The Treasury was empty, and the public credit exhausted. The administration was in the hands of men who were untried and inexperienced in the details of the governmental machinery. Moreover, the constant defections of men, who were believed to be thoroughly loyal, and the outbreak of treasonable sentiments in quarters least expected, filled the hearts of loyal citizens with distrust and deepened their apprehensions. For a time, no active or aggressive policy was announced by the Government, and the people, forgetting that the new officers must have time to become accustomed to their duties before any decided change could be inaugurated, bewailed the apathy of the Government and began to hint that it was secretly in sympathy with the South. In addition to all this the European world either looked coldly on or extended sympathy and the implied promise of support in the future to the seceding States.

Mr. Lincoln had announced in his inaugural that he should never make war upon the South. If war must come, the disaffected people would themselves be the aggressors. Therefore, he awaited patiently the issue, all the time making active preparations for an emergency, but avoiding all appearance of hostility or any overt action which could be regarded as a provocation or excuse for war on the part of the South. Meantime, events in the seceding States were moving rapidly on towards the catastrophe. The leaders had determined upon separation at all hazards, and while the Northern States had been uncertain as to the course of events and disturbed by conflicting counsels and the embarrassments incident upon a change of administration, the fullest opportunities had been offered to the violent spirits of the South to conceive and carry out their treasonable plans. In South Carolina, the discontent was greatest and the disunion sentiment most violent. Here, naturally, the first outbreak occurred. The Confed-

erate Government saw that a loyal garrison in Fort
Sumter, in Charleston harbor, would materially interfere with their plans, and they determined to secure
possession of the stronghold. When Major Anderson, the officer in command, refused to surrender,
they opened fire upon the old flag, Friday morning,
April 12.

Never before had the roar of hostile cannon so
convulsed a mighty nation. The majority of the
Northern people, while deeply troubled by the manifest hostility of their Southern brethren, could not
yet believe that they would deliberately commence a
great civil war. For more than a generation there
had been no war of any magnitude upon American
soil. Great industries and an immense traffic between the different sections, nurtured by peaceful
influences, had banished the memories of the horror
and carnage of war, and men now stood aghast at
the thought that a war, whose consequences none
could foresee, had suddenly come upon them, and
that the great cities, the product and abode of the
peaceful arts, might soon be given over to rapine and
flames. There was no hamlet so remote but it might
fear the coming of the ruthless invader, no home-
circle which might not be broken. Yet the shock
was not one of paralysis, but rather the blow which
awakens from the lethargy of inaction and brings
every faculty into instant and vigorous exercise.
Much could be forgiven, but the insult to the old
flag, around which clustered so many hallowed memories, and which represented all that was noble and
enduring in republican institutions, could not be
condoned.

A wave of awakening patriotism swept over the North to its remotest limits. Orators in the public squares, and ministers in the pulpits, preached in fervent words the duty of patriotism and loyalty to the Government. For the time all political antagonisms were forgotten. Party strifes and sectional jealousies were laid aside and Democrats vied with Republicans, Nationals with Abolitionists in their eagerness to defend the majesty of the Government and to sustain its imperiled interests. Nor were the feelings of the people expressed alone in words. Men hastened to lay upon their country's altar, their influence, their property, themselves. Never had there been such a patriotic uprising. Companies were formed and drilled in every village and hamlet. The militia assembled. Muskets and flint locks, which had done service in the Revolution and the Mexican War, were taken down from the hooks, where they had long reposed untouched, and were cleaned and burnished and made ready for use. Meantime, every eye was turned towards Washington and him, upon whose shoulders devolved the responsibility of directing the efforts made to uphold the honor and integrity of the Government. At last had come the crucial test, the hour that would prove the metal of the man and expose to the world the flaw if one existed. Would the pioneer President rise to the demands of the hour and prove himself a master in the untried sphere into which he had been called; or would the reins of power fall from his nerveless hand ? Upon the answer to this question depended the fate of the Nation, and to a large extent the weal or woe of modern civilization.

The world was not long left in doubt. During the trying weeks previous to the assault upon Sumter, Mr. Lincoln had not swerved from his expressed policy and more than once had he reiterated and emphasized it. Even at the time, when the siege of Sumter was in progress and when it would appear that all hope for securing a peaceful solution should have been abandoned, Mr. Lincoln in his reply to a committee, appointed by the Virginia convention, which afterwards passed the secession ordinance, for the purpose of ascertaining definitely his policy, referred in emphatic terms to the statements made in his inaugural address, saying:

"By the words 'property and places belonging to the Government' I chiefly allude to the military posts and property which were in the possession of the Government when it came into my hands. But if, as now appears to be true, in pursuit of a purpose to drive the United States authority from these places, an unprovoked assault has been made upon Fort Sumter, I shall hold myself at liberty to repossess like places which had been seized before the Government was devolved upon me; and in any event I shall, to the best of my ability, repel force with force."

The attitude of Mr. Douglas at this time was a source of great strength to the administration and to the cause at large. His last days were his most glorious, and go far towards wiping away the stains which his course had left upon his reputation. In a newspaper interview, which was published all over the land, he proclaimed himself as "unalterably opposed to the administration in all its political issues, but prepared to fully sustain the President in the exercise of all his constitutional functions, to preserve the Union, maintain the Government, and defend the Federal Capital." He furthermore said:

"The Capital is in danger and must be defended at all hazards, and at any expense of men and money. A firm policy and prompt action is necessary." The whole weight of his influence was used to inculcate these principles, especially among his political associates, until, but a few weeks later, he was cut off in the midst of his career and the country stopped for a moment to drop a tear on his grave.

On the 15th day of April, soon after the fall of Sumter was announced, the President issued a proclamation calling for seventy-five thousand volunteers and summoning Congress to meet in extra session, July 4. In the proclamation he said: "I deem it proper to say that the first service assigned to the forces hereby called out will probably be to repossess the forts, places and property which have been seized from the Union; and in every event the utmost care will be observed, consistently with the objects aforesaid, to avoid any devastation and destruction of or interference with property, or any disturbance of peaceful citizens of any part of the country."

The call was instantly answered and the full number asked for was ready to start for the scene of war before the end of the week. Indeed, more than one detachment of troops were on the way to the National Capital almost before the telegraphic instrument had ticked out its startling message.

Although the number of troops called for was soon at hand, they were far from being ready for service. Recruited from the farm, counting-room and store,

they were totally inexperienced in war and ignorant
of its art.   It was almost as difficult a task to organ-
ize and drill them as it was afterwards to lead them
on to victory.   It takes time to convert raw recruits
into disciplined armies and time was wanting.   So
the President and his co-laborers exerted every energy and strained every nerve in the efforts to meet the
emergency.

In its every feature the situation was a trying one.
The present was thick with perplexities and the future dark with portents.   The one bright feature
which gladdened the heart of the President and made
it possible for him to carry out the great lines of policy which he had inaugurated was the attitude of the
loyal people of the North, who heartily supported
the administration regardless of party, at least for a
time.   More clearly than the people could did he appreciate the magnitude of the struggle and the great
principles involved.   With him it was not a question
whether ten States should be permitted to withdraw
from the Union and set up a separate government,
but whether Republican Institutions possessed inher-
ent vigor sufficient to perpetuate themselves against
violent assaults from within.   The blow was directed
not alone against the American Republic, but against
the great principle of popular sovereignty.   Never had
there been so advantageous a field for the development of this form of government, as in America, and
if it should fail here it would receive its death blow.
In his first message to Congress he states this principle clearly and concisely:

"This is essentially a people's contest.   On the
side of the Union it is a struggle for maintaining in the

world that form and substance of government, whose leading object is to elevate the condition of man ; to lift artificial weights from all shoulders ; to clear the paths of laudable pursuits for all ; to afford all an unfettered start and a fair chance in the race of life. Yielding to partial and temporary departures, from necessity, this is the leading object of the Government for whose existence we contend. I am most happy to believe that the plain people understand and appreciate this."

The Congress, which met July 4, was a noteworthy assembly. Many seats were vacant and the deliberations were marked by a solemnity never before manifested in the Capitol. The discordant element was, for the time being, withdrawn. The halls which had so often in the past echoed with fierce contentions, were now the scenes of earnest, united action. The reality of the war was mutely attested by the empty chairs. Turn which way they would, the members were met with the evidences of rebellion. The responsibility laid upon them developed wise statesmen out of men hitherto unknown, as it developed, in the field, skillful generals out of the raw soldiery. In Congress were men who had grown gray in the honored service of their country and others just entering the political arena, whose names were to become household words and whose influence would be potent in directing the affairs of the Government. In the Senate, presided over by Vice-President Hamlin, were such men as Sumner, Collamer, Foote, Anthony, Hall, Trumbull, Wilmot and Lane. In the House were Conkling, Thad Stevens, Colfax, Logan and Cox.

The prevailing sentiment of the House was favorable to the President and his policy. The majority were ardent and wise patriots, quick to appreciate the demands of a situation and to wisely satisfy them so far as possible. Their first act was to indorse, unreservedly, the action and policy of the President, and to pledge themselves to vote for any amount of money and number of men which might be necessary to quell the insurrection. The military situation soon began to present serious difficulties. A splendid army of volunteer soldiers had assembled at Washington, eager for service, but utterly unskilled in the art of warfare. The North was impatiently demanding that an attack be made without delay, and many believed that an immediate and crushing blow would end the war. A general movement was therefore planned. General McClellan, who had succeeded General Scott, with a large army attempted to drive the Confederates out of West Virginia, while General McDowell attacked their main army at Manassas. On the 21st of July occurred the battle of Bull Run, and the disastrous flight of the Federal army. The blow was a severe one, and yet it served to awaken the North more fully to the serious character of the war, and to prove that it could not be ended by a single campaign. The defeat was a surprise to Mr. Lincoln and caused him deep sorrow, yet, even when overwhelmed by anxiety, he did not lose his sense of humor or his readiness to illustrate a point by a humorous story. Indeed, this propensity seemed to afford him relief from the pressure of his work, acting much like the safety-valve of a steam-engine.

Two or three days after the battle some gentlemen, who had been on the field, visited him and related the details as they had observed them, putting as good a face upon them as possible. After listening to them, he said, " So it is your notion that we whipped the rebels and then ran away from them ! " Soon after the battle he visited the army at Georgetown, and, while inspecting the arrangements in company with Colonel Sherman, a subordinate officer approached him, evidently very angry, and complained of the unjust treatment which, he alleged, had been accorded him by Colonel Sherman, who had threatened to shoot him. " Well," said Mr. Lincoln in a loud whisper, which was easily heard by all in the vicinity, " if I were you and he threatened to shoot me, I wouldn't trust him, for I believe he would do it."

Military operations on a large scale were now entered upon. A great army was concentrated around Washington, which was believed to be in immediate danger of attack. Fresh troops were constantly arriving from all parts of the North and going into camp in the vicinity of the city. The labor of converting the great masses of raw troops into an effective force of disciplined soldiery, was long and arduous, and for some months but little progress seemed to be made by the National arms. Again, so many of the best and most efficient officers had deserted the " Stars and Stripes " and enrolled themselves in the Confederate army, that the National forces had been left without tried leaders. The generals must be educated as well as the soldiers, and nothing but service in the field could test their skill and ability. Hence the National cause was greatly retarded and the war prolonged. General Scott, the hero of the Mexican War, was too old and infirm to carry the burden of the war and had resigned his position of Commanding General early in October. General McClellan, a young and dashing officer, was appointed his successor. He was a thorough patriot, having what he believed to be the best interests of the country at heart, but slow and unprogressive, impatient of criticism and obstinate in his self-esteem. He lacked the most important qualifications of a military leader, and allowed many opportunities to distinguish himself and win success for the cause to slip through his hands. The President was disposed to place the utmost confidence in him and to give over into his hands the general control of the army, and to listen to his suggestions and comply with his advice so far as possible.

On the 21st of October occurred the battle of Ball's Bluff, a mere skirmish, which was distinguished only by the death of the gallant Colonel Baker, who had left his seat in the Senate to lead his regiment into battle. Baker was an old and trusted friend of Lincoln, who keenly felt his loss and, in common with the whole country, lamented it. The loss of Baker, though of less vital importance, had much the same effect upon the people as the loss of Hampden in the great English rebellion. In many respects the two men were counterparts.

On the 8th of November occurred an event which threatened a violent rupture of the already strained relations existing between the National Government and England. The sympathies of England were largely with the South, and her Government had hastened to recognize the Confederate States as a belligerent power. It was no secret that private individuals were actively engaged in England in fitting out ships of war and blockade runners for the use of the rebellious States, besides rendering much material aid in other ways, if not with the connivance of, at least ignored by the Government. Hence when news came that Captain Wilkes, of the *San Jacinto*, had taken the Confederate commissioners from the British mail steamer *Trent*, the act was greeted with the most enthusiastic commendation from every side. Indignation and hostility against England had never, since the War of 1812, been so violent and demonstrative.

The Confederate representatives were brought to Boston and confined in Fort Warren. Not only were the people at large loud in the praises of Captain Wilkes, but he even received official thanks from his superior officers. Congress hastily passed a resolution of thanks ; the Secretary of the Navy wrote a letter of congratulation on the " great public service " rendered by the capture of the rebel emissaries, and Secretary Stanton applauded the deed. The whole people were ready to rush into a hasty war with England while the South rejoiced at every manifestation of such sentiment, knowing that a declaration of war would be followed by a close alliance between their own Government and that of Great Britain.

The incident placed Mr. Lincoln in a difficult position, one where a less clear-sighted and resolute man would have utterly failed. He was quick to see that the act was of the very same nature as those on the part of England which brought on the War of 1812 and was a violation of all maritime law. It is true that no British subject was interfered with in the exploit of Captain Wilkes. But the principle, which had been established by the force of arms, was as applicable in 1860 as in 1812, against the Americans now as against the English then.

The temper of the people and the injudicious words of more than one member of his Cabinet, made the task devolving upon him all the more difficult. England immediately, and in terms by no means conciliatory, made a demand for the surrender of the prisoners to the English Minister at Washington, and for an ample apology from the Government. If the demand should be refused, war would be inevitable and that at a time when the country was involved in the most extensive and costly civil war ever known. The result could hardly have been doubtful. On the other hand, if the demand was complied with, the scarce concealed hostility of the English must still be expected as well as the indignation and, perhaps, disaffection of a large party of the Northern people. Popular sentiment was forcibly expressed in a speech made afterwards in Congress by Owen Lovejoy, who was one of Lincoln's warmest supporters. He said : " Every time this *Trent* affair comes up, . . . I am made to renew the horrible grief which I suffered when the news of the surrender of Mason and Slidell came. I acknowledge it, I literally wept tears of vexation. I hate it ; and I hate the British Government. I have never shared in the traditional hostility of many of my countrymen against England. But I now here publicly avow and record my inex-

tinguishable hatred of that Government. I mean to
cherish it while I live, and bequeath it as a legacy to
my children when I die."

Against such a sentiment as this did Lincoln declare
when he ordered the return of the prisoners. He
could not do otherwise than share in the prevailing
indignation against England, but his cool judgment
caused him to rise above the prejudice of passion and
to grasp the broad principles involved and to carry
them out at whatever risk of popularity to himself.
The same high principle guided him in his private as
in his public life. He was always above mean jealousies and animosities, and never was he known to
cherish resentment against any public or private
enemy. He showed the highest degree of magnanimity towards any one who had injured him and
never sought to wreak vengeance upon him. And
this was not because he was insensible to insult. His
nature was sensitive and unjust attack and ridicule
caused him much suffering, but his dignity of character and complete self-control enabled him to triumph
over them.

It required nerve and moral courage to take such
a stand in regard to the *Trent* affair in the face of
the opposition of the whole North, but while he was
roundly denounced in the heat and excitement of the
hour, the calmer judgment of the people thoroughly
approved his course. Nowhere had Lincoln been so
mercilessly ridiculed, so unjustly and persistently
misrepresented, so maligned and scoffed at, as in
England. The papers were filled with squibs, and
society laughed and jeered over burlesque descriptions of his awkward appearance. This feeling was

aptly referred to in a stanza of a poem published after
his death, in Punch, as follows :

> "You, who with mocking pencil wont to trace
> Broad for the self-complacent British sneer
> His length of shambling limb, his furrowed face,
> His gaunt, gnarled hands, his unkempt, bristling hair,
> His garb uncouth, his bearing ill at ease,
> His lack of all we prize as debonnaire,
> Of power or will to shine, of art to please."

Yet all this could not cause him to swerve from the
course of right and justice to satisfy national hostilities or avenge a private wrong.   He was satisfied to
do his duty as it became plain to him and leave to
time his vindication, and nobly did it come at last.

The diplomatic correspondence carried on by Mr
Seward, in regard to the affair, is characterized by
remarkable ability and clear-sightedness.   The President assisted, in no small degree, in its preparation,
both by advice and direction.   He afterwards said
that the affair occurring at a critical time in the conduct of the war occasioned him much anxiety and
apprehension.   When asked if he was not reluctant
to surrender the two Commissioners to England, he
said : "Yes, that was a bitter pill to swallow, but I
contented myself with believing that England's triumph in the matter would be short-lived, and that,
after ending our war successfully, we should be so
powerful that we could call her to account for all the
embarrassment she had inflicted upon us.   I felt a
good deal like a sick man in Illinois, who was told
that he had but a few days more to live and that he
ought to make peace with his enemies.   He said that
the man he hated worst of all was a fellow in the

next village named Brown, and he guessed he had better commence on him first. So Brown was sent for and when he came, the sick man began to say, in a voice as meek as Moses, that he wanted to die at peace with all his fellow-creatures, and hoped he and Brown could now shake hands and bury all their enmity. The scene was becoming altogether too pathetic for Brown, who had to get out his handkerchief and wipe the gathering tears from his eyes. It wasn't long before he melted and gave his hand to his neighbor and they had a regular love-feast. After a parting that would have softened the heart of a grindstone, Brown had about reached the door, when the sick man rose upon his elbow and said, ' But, see here, Brown, if I *should* happen to get well, mind, that old grudge stands ! ' So I thought if this nation should get well we might want that old grudge against England to stand."

One of the greatest difficulties that embarrassed the administration was the lack of skillful and energetic commanders. Soldiers were recruited more rapidly than they could be used, but it was necessary to experiment long, and, as it proved, disastrously, with untried officers, before the men were found who were qualified to lead the Union army on to victory. The President was often and severely criticised for his appointments and removals, and elements of discord were thus introduced which threatened to bring on a national calamity.

That thousands of precious lives were lost on account of unskillful and careless leadership is unquestionably a fact. That the administration made the best possible use of the inefficient material

at hand the impartial testimony of history proves.
The story of General McClellan's career is well-
known and has been the subject of much acrimonious
discussion. He had presented to him magnificent
opportunities which he failed to take advantage of.
While he succeeded Scott as General in command,
he was yet inferior in rank to the President, who
was clothed by the Constitution with the power of
Commander-in-Chief of the Army and Navy. Yet he
refused to heed the advice of his superior officer and
delayed to obey his commands until the occasion
which had called them forth had lost its significance.
Again and again he permitted the enemy to make
raids into Maryland, and carry on offensive campaigns
in Virginia without making an effort to repulse them
though he had a splendid army under his command
much larger and more efficient than that of the
enemy. His constant appeals for re-inforcements ;
his ill-concealed contempt for the orders of the President and Secretary of War ; his inactivity and constant failure to make use of the armies intrusted to
his charge and his jealousy of his inferior officers are
all so directly at variance with his vehement asservera-
tions of loyalty and love of his country's cause as to
be almost inexplicable, except upon the grounds of
insincerity. His personality was attractive and his
ability was generally admitted. Yet his ability was
not of the kind which fitted him to control the movements of great armies or to direct the conduct of complicated campaigns. Had General McClellan never
been elevated to the chief command, his career would,
no doubt, have been distinguished and his rank in
history second to that of none of the minor generals.

Many of the peculiar qualities of Mr. Lincoln's character were shown in his dealings with General McClellan. In the first place, McClellan was a Democrat and strongly opposed to the political policy of the administration. Yet this did not deter the President from appointing him, for he believed him to be not only the most available man but the best equipped in every way for the position. The appointment was not a popular one among the friends of the administration but as long as it was evidently for the good of the nation the President was little moved by the complaints of his friends, and long after General McClellan had proved himself, to the satisfaction of the majority, totally unfit for the position, Mr. Lincoln continued to have faith in him and did his utmost to urge him on, nor did he withhold his hearty support as long as there seemed to be a single chance of his achieving success. Only the most long-suffering patience would have ignored his sneers and reproaches or his persistent disregard of orders.

These embarrassments and the subsequent failure of a number of generals to successfully fill the requirements induced Mr. Lincoln to make a close study of the science of war. He became deeply dissatisfied with the lack of skill and energy on the part of the commanders and of progress on the part of the armies and endeavored to infuse something of his own vigor and enthusiasm into the hearts of his subordinates. The metamorphosis from the plain country lawyer unversed in the technical details of either war or government into the most accomplished ru.er and commander of the day, was one to which history hardly presents a parallel. Slowly he gathered up the details of the war and directed the multitudinous movements in the various departments with a sagacity, wise judgment and determination which finally brought victory out of impending defeat and saved the Union. General Keep says: "The elements of selfishness and ferocity, which are not unusual with first-class military chiefs, were wholly foreign to Mr. Lincoln's nature. Nevertheless, there was not one of his most trusted warlike counsellors in the beginning of the war, who equalled him in military sagacity."

CHAPTER XVI.

It is an old saying that " Circumstances make the man," and it is also true that man impresses much of his character upon his surroundings. As the foot imprints its form upon the sand, man impresses his character upon his environment and moulds it to the peculiarities of his taste and temperament. The very rooms in which a man of affairs does his work will bear the stamp of his activity and be suggestive of his presence.

This was true of Mr. Lincoln to an unusual degree. He always dressed plainly and made no attempt at personal adornment. The conventional garb of society sat awkwardly upon his long gaunt body. He was most at ease when most simply clad and was always glad to exchange his dress suit for his working clothes. His mind seemed to be far above the petty details of dress and chafed when compelled to give attention to them.

In the furnishing of his house his tastes were equally simple. The old kitchen, where the whole family were wont to gather around the fireplace and read or work by the bright blaze, was to him the most comfortable room in the house.

He never felt at home in the broad and ornate rooms of the White House and spent the most of the time in his office, which he often spoke of as his "workshop."

(225)

Mr. Arnold thus describes this historic room:

" It was about 25x40 feet in size. In the centre on
the west was a large, white marble fireplace, with big,
old-fashioned brass andirons and a large, high brass
fender. A wood fire was burning in cool weather.
The large windows opened upon the beautiful lawn
to the south with a view of the unfinished Washington Monument, the Smithsonian Institute, the Potomac, Alexandria and down the river towards Mount
Vernon. Across the river were Arlington Heights
and Arlington House, late residence of Robert E. Lee.
On the hills around, during nearly all his administration, were the white tents of soldiers and field fortifications and camps, and in every direction could be
seen the brilliant colors of the national flag. The
furniture of this room consisted of a large oak table,
covered with cloth, extending north and south, and it
was around this table that the Cabinet sat when it
held its meetings. Near the end of the table and between the windows was another table, on the west
side of which the President sat in a large arm-chair,
and at this table he wrote. A tall desk with pigeon-
holes for papers stood against the south wall. The
only books usually found in this room were the Bible,
the Constitution of the United States and a copy of
Shakespeare. There were a few chairs and two plain
hair-covered sofas. There were two or three map
frames from which hung military maps on which the
position and movements of the armies were traced.
There was an old and discolored engraving of General Jackson on the mantel and a later photograph of
John Bright. Doors opened into this room from the
room of the Secretary, and from the outside hall run-

ning east and west across the house. A bell-cord within reach of his hand extended to the Secretary's office. A messenger stood at the door opening from the hall, who took in the cards and names of the visitors. Here in this plain room Mr. Lincoln spent most of his time while President. Here he received every one, from the Chief Justice and Lieutenant General to the private soldier and humblest citizen. Custom had fixed certain rules of precedence and the order in which official visits should be received. Members of the Cabinet and the high officers of the Army and Navy were generally admitted promptly. Senators and Representatives were received in the order of their arrival. Sometimes there would be a crowd of Members of Congress awaiting their turn. While thus waiting, the loud ringing laugh of Mr. Lincoln —in which he would be joined by those inside, but which was rather provoking to those outside—would be heard by the waiting and impatient crowd. Here, day after day, from early morning till late at night, Lincoln sat, listened, talked and decided. He was patient, just, considerate and hopeful. The people came to him as to a father. He saw every one, and many wasted his precious time. All classes approached him with familiarity. This incessant labor, the study of the great problems he had to decide, the worry of constant importunity, the quarrels of the officers of the army, the care, anxiety and responsibility of his position, wore upon his vigorous frame."

Mr. Deming in commenting upon his personal appearance, says: " As the world has rung with ridicule of the ungainliness of his manners, I may be permitted to say, that without any pretensions to superfine polish, they were frank, cordial and dignified, without rudeness, without offense and without any violation of the proprieties and etiquettes of his high position. To borrow one of his own conversational phrases, ' he did not brag on deportment.' He stood and moved and bowed without affectation, and without obtrusive awkwardness, pretty much as nature prompted, and as if he regarded carriage about as bad a criterion as color, of the genuine nobility of the soul."

The White House was constantly thronged with office-seekers, men and women with complaints or advice to proffer, and people with private or public business to transact, until the weary President was hardly given time to attend to the more important demands upon him. He was gentle and sympathetic with those in trouble and quick to help, if possible. He listened patiently to honest complaints, but was quick to detect dishonesty and selfishness, and bitter and scathing in his denunciation of it.

Among the callers at the White House, one day, was an officer who had been cashiered from the service. He had prepared an elaborate defense of himself, which he consumed much time in reading to the President. When he had finished, Mr. Lincoln replied that, even upon his own statement of the case, the facts would not warrant Executive interference. Disappointed and considerably crestfallen, the man withdrew.

A few days afterwards, he made a second attempt to alter the President's convictions, going over substantially the same ground, and occupying about the same space of time, but without accomplishing his end.

The third time he succeeded in forcing himself into Mr. Lincoln's presence, who, with great forbearance, listened to another repetition of the case to its conclusion, but made no reply. Waiting for a moment, the man gathered from the expression of his countenance that his mind was unconvinced. Turning very abruptly, he said: "Well, Mr. President, I see you are fully determined not to do me justice!"

This was too aggravating, even for Mr. Lincoln. Manifesting, however, no more feeling than that indicated by a slight compression of the lips, he very quietly arose, laid down a package of papers he held in his hand, and then suddenly seizing the defunct officer by the coat-collar, he marched him forcibly to the door, saying, as he ejected him into the passage :

"Sir, I give you fair warning never to show yourself in this room again. I can bear censure, but not insult!"

In a whining tone, the man begged for his papers, which he had dropped.

"Begone, sir," said the President. "Your papers will be sent to you. I never want to see your face again!"[1]

In February, 1862, Mr. Lincoln was visited by a severe affliction, in the death of his beloved son, Willie, and the extreme illness of his son, Thomas, familiarly known as "Tad." This was a new burden, and the visitation which, in his firm faith in Providence, he regarded as Providential, was also inexplicable. A Christian lady from Massachusetts, who was

---

[1] Lincoln's Stories, by T. B. McClure.

officiating as nurse in one of the hospitals, at the time, came to attend the sick children. She reports that Mr. Lincoln watched with her about the bedside of the sick ones, and that he often walked the room, saying, sadly:

"This is the hardest trial of my life; why is it? why is it?"

In the course of conversation with her, he questioned her concerning her situation. She told him that she was a widow, and that her husband and two children were in heaven; and added that she saw the hand of God in it all, and that she had never loved Him so much before as she had since her affliction.

"How is that brought about?" inquired Mr. Lincoln.

"Simply by trusting in God, and feeling that he does all things well," she replied.

"Did you submit fully under the first loss?" he asked.

"No," she answered, "not wholly; but, as blow came upon blow, and all were taken, I could and did submit, and was very happy."

He responded: "I am glad to hear you say that. Your experience will help me to bear my affliction." On being assured that many Christians were praying for him, on the morning of the funeral, he wiped away the tears that sprang in his eyes, and said: "I am glad to hear that. I want them to pray for me. I need their prayers." As he was going out to the burial, the good lady expressed her sympathy with him. He thanked her gently, and said, "I will try to go to God with my sorrows." A few days afterwards, she asked him if he could trust God. He replied:

"I think I can, and I will try. I wish I had that childlike faith you speak of, and I trust He will give it to me." And then he spoke of his mother, whom so many years before he had committed to the dust among the wilds of Indiana. In this hour of his great trial, the memory of her who had held him upon her bosom, and soothed his childish griefs, came back to him with tenderest recollections. "I remember her prayers," said he, "and they have always followed me. They have clung to me all my life."

He received a great many visits from men who came to criticise his actions and offer him gratuitous advice in regard to matters wherein they believed themselves to be better qualified to judge than he. One day, a number of gentlemen called who were greatly excited ove what they believed to be the shortcomings of the administration. He listened patiently to them, and, in reply, said :

"Gentlemen, suppose all the property you were worth was in gold, and you had put it in the hands of Blondin to carry across the Niagara River on a rope ; would you shake the cable, or keep shouting out to him : 'Blondin, stand up a little straighter ! Blondin, stoop a little more—go a little faster—lean a little more to the north—lean a little more to the south.' No, you would hold your breath as well as your tongue, and keep your hands off until he was safe over. The Government is carrying an immense weight. Untold treasures are in their hands. They are doing the very best they can. Don't badger them. Keep silence and we will get you safely across."

Many people came to him asking for information which it was often not proper or possible for him to give. He had a very effective way of dealing with such people. A visitor once asked him how many men the Confederates had in the field. The President answered, very seriously, " Twelve hundred thousand, according to the best authority." The questioner was thunderstruck, for everything about the President's manner indicated that he was in earnest. " Yes, sir," said Mr. Lincoln, "twelve hundred thousand—no doubt of it. You see, all of our generals, when they get whipped, say the enemy outnumbered them, from three or five to one, and I must believe them. We have four hundred thousand men in the field, and three times four makes twelve. Don't you see?"

After the appearance of the rebel ram *Merrimac* in 1862, the President was waited upon by fifty gentlemen from New York who informed him that they represented in their own right $100,000,000 and who were greatly alarmed at the comparatively defenseless condition of New York. After magnifying as much as possible, the cause of their apprehension, they requested that a gunboat be detailed for the defense of the city. Mr. Lincoln listened very attentively to their statements and seemed much impressed by them. When they had finished, he replied, very deliberately :

" Gentlemen, I am by the Constitution Commander-in-Chief of the Army and Navy of the United States ; and, as a matter of law, can order anything done that is practicable to be done. But, as a matter of fact, I am not in command of the gunboats or ships of war ; as a matter of fact, I do not know exactly where they are, but presume they are actively engaged. It is impossible for me, in the present condition of things, to furnish you a gunboat. The credit of the Government is at a very low ebb; greenbacks are not worth more than forty or fifty cents on the dollar; and in this condition of things, if I was worth half as much as you gentlemen are represented to be, and as badly frightened as you seem to be, I would build a gunboat and give it to the Government."

One day in the spring of 1862, a gentlemen made a very earnest request for a pass to Richmond. "A pass to Richmond," exclaimed the President, "why, my dear sir, if I should give you one it would do you no good. You may think it very strange, but there's a lot of fellows between here and Richmond, who either can't read or are prejudiced against every man who totes a pass from me. I have given McClellan and more than two hundred thousand others passes to Richmond, and not a single one of them has gotten there yet."

Although of a sensitive disposition, Mr. Lincoln never permitted himself to be disturbed by violent criticism or denunciation. To show how much attention he paid to the attacks made upon him, he once told the following story:

"Some years ago," said he, "a couple of immigrants fresh from the 'Emerald Isle,' seeking labor, were making their way towards the West. Coming suddenly one evening upon a pond of water, they were greeted with a grand chorus of bull-frogs—a kind of music they had never before heard. Overcome with terror, they clutched their 'shillalahs,' and crept cautiously forward, straining their eyes in every direction to catch a glimpse of the enemy; but he was not to be found. At last a happy idea seized the foremost one—he sprang to his companion and exclaimed, ' An' sure, Jamie, it's my opinion it's nothing but a noise.' "

On one occasion, while a great battle was being fought and he was waiting anxiously for news, he entered the room where a Christian lady was engaged in nursing a member of the family, looking worn and haggard and saying he was so anxious that he could eat nothing. The possibility of defeat depressed him greatly; but the lady told him that he must have faith, and that he could at least pray. "Yes," said he, and taking up a Bible he started to his room. Shortly afterwards a telegram was received announcing a victory. He immediately re-entered the room, his face beaming with joy and said : "Good news ! Good news ! The victory is ours, and God is good."

"Nothing like prayer," suggested the pious lady, who believed the news to be the direct result of the prayer.

"Yes there is," he replied—"praise—prayer and praise."

The lady afterwards said : "I do believe he was a true Christian, though he had very little confidence in himself."

CHAPTER XVII.

When the Southern States decided upon secession, they staked the institution of slavery upon the result of the war. If they were to be victorious it was their purpose to found a slave republic. If they were defeated the penalty could be nothing less than its abolition, how much more—they hardly realized. Many eager Sprits of the North felt that the issue should be squarely met and decided at once and they called upon the President to issue an emancipation edict without delay. As time passed on and the course of the war seemed to be unfavorable to the national cause, the demand became stronger that the President should make the issue a distinctive one between slavery and freedom. Not only was he constantly beset with advice and entreaty and sometimes with a vehemence which almost changed the prayers to threats, but a number of strong, influential Republican papers began to reproach him for his hesitancy which some went so far as to denominate moral cowardice.

No Republican paper took a more decided stand or found more fault with Mr. Lincoln on this score than the New York *Tribune*. Mr. Greeley was, beyond question, a true patriot, and had the best interests of the country, as he conceived them, at heart. Both his disposition and environment were peculiar. He had always been in favor of Abolition and he seems now to have become convinced that the affairs of the country were faring ill and that its only salvation consisted in creating a moral issue, which would rally to its support all right-minded patriots. He manifested both impatience and petulance at the course of the President and strove in every way to compel him to adopt his own views. But Mr. Lincoln's perceptions were much clearer than those of Mr. Greeley, and his judgment calmer. He listened patiently and attentively but he could not be persuaded to change his policy against his own judgment and more clearly than any-one else could, did he apprehend the part which he was to play in the great drama. His duty was not to be guided by the dictates of sentiment, however elevated, nor to preserve one institution and overthrow another. He realized that he was the representative of the soverign people and that his powers and privileges were strictly defined by a most solemn obligation, which he had voluntarily taken upon himself and he summoned all the strength of his resolution to his aid to keep inviolate his oath of office. He had solemnly sworn to preserve the Constitution and this meant the perpetuation of the Government and the uninvaded rights of the people.

In a letter to Mr. Greeley in reply to one ungenerously chiding him, he stated clearly his views upon this subject, as follows :

" . . . As to the policy 'I seem to be pursuing' as you say, 'I have not meant to leave any one in doubt.' I would save the Union. I would save it in the shortest way under the Constitution. The sooner the national authority can be restored the sooner the

Union will be—the Union as it was. If there be
those who would not save the Union unless they
could at the same time save slavery, I do not agree
with them. If there be those who would not save
the Union unless they could, at the same time, destroy
slavery, I do not agree with them. My paramount
object is to save the Union and not either to save or
destroy slavery. If I could save the Union without
freeing a slave I would do it. And if I could do it
by freeing all the slaves, I would do it. And if I
could do it by freeing some and leaving others alone,
I would also do that. What I do about slavery and
the colored race, I do because I believe it helps to
save the Union and what I forbear, I forbear because
I do not believe it would help to save the Union. I
shall do less, whenever I believe what I am doing
hurts the cause, and shall do more whenever I believe
doing more will help the cause."

Mr. Lincoln's position on this question can only be
fully understood in the light of the circumstances by
which he was surrounded. It had been his policy,
persistently maintained, to retain in the Union, so far
as possible, the border States, at a time when the
Union and secession elements nearly balanced each
other. In the most of these States, slavery was a
recognized institution and any intimation from the
President that he proposed to interfere with it, would
have precipitated them into immediate secession. In
the Northern States there was far from an united
sentiment in favor of immediate emancipation. A
large party were opposed to it, partly upon principle
and partly because they believed the proper time had
not arrived. Hence any precipitate movement in this

direction would have alarmed and perhaps alienated
many active supporters at a time when the Government was most in need of support from every one of
its loyal citizens. But perhaps the most potent influence acting in the mind of Mr. Lincoln was that of
the high principle upon which the war was being
fought. If slavery were made the issue, in either
event of the struggle, the great constitutional question would remain unsettled and at some future time
another sectional dispute might once more array
different portions of the nation against each other in
armed conflict. By making the preservation of the
Union the one great issue and subordinating all other
questions, however vital to it, the conflict once fought
would be forever finished and no difference of interest
or opinion could ever renew it again. It was fortunate for the country that the man in the Presidential
chair had a mind sufficiently broad to grasp fully the
situation, and a purpose sufficiently fixed to stick
closely to the one great principle unmoved by all the
influences that could be brought to bear upon him.

The experiment of military emancipation had been
tried early in the war. When, in the midst of the
struggle to retain Missouri in the Union, General
Fremont had been placed in command of that military department, almost his first important step was
to issue an order declaring all slaves held in that district to be free. The proclamation would probably
have lost Missouri to the Union had not the President promptly annulled it and forbidden the issuance
of a similar order in the future without his own
express consent. It is unnecessary to enter into the
details of the controversy with General Fremont,

which excited so much ill-feeling at the time and led many to believe that the distinguished General had not met with generous treatment at the hands of the President. Succeeding events proved that the policy of the President was not a selfish or vindictive one.

In March, 1862, Mr. Lincoln transmitted a special message to Congress in which he recommended the adoption of a system of general emancipation. He proposed that the Government should take measures to co-operate with any State, which should adopt gradual abolition of slavery and to reimburse it in part for any public or private loss accruing from such a measure. He earnestly recommended that Congress take the matter into immediate consideration. April 16 a bill passed both Houses of Congress abolishing slavery in the District of Columbia. This measure had been first proposed in Congress by Mr. Lincoln himself in 1849. It was then passed over as unworthy of consideration, but now, as President, he had the satisfaction of enrolling it among the laws of the land.

That a great revolution was taking place in public opinion was shown by the constantly increasing boldness of Congress and its progress towards the final step. June 19 slavery was prohibited forever in all present and future Territories of the United States. Thus the question, which had so often divided Congress and formed political issues, which had been ably debated upon every platform in the land and which had figured as the animus of the Lincoln-Douglas debates, was finally and forever settled. Had Douglas used his great ability and commanding eloquence to prevent rather than to favor the repeal

of the Missouri Compromise, the appeal to arms
might never have occurred and the vexed question
might have been settled by natural rather than by
violent agencies.

July 17 a bill was passed authorizing the employment of negroes as soldiers and conferring freedom
upon all who should regularly enlist in the army.
Since the beginning of the war the camps of the
Union forces had been beset by hordes of fugitive
slaves, who believed that their only hope of freedom
and safety consisted in getting under the shadow of
the "Stars and Stripes" as soon as possible. They
frequently came in such numbers as to seriously
embarrass the movements of the army, and the question of their disposition became a grave problem.
The bare suggestion that they would be enrolled in
the Federal Armies, threw the Southern States into
the most violent rage. Scathing were the denunciations hurled against the Government that should dare
to take such a step. Rumors of slave insurrections
and the horrible scenes attendant upon them spread
far and wide. The rebel leaders proclaimed that no
white officer connected with colored troops would be
treated as a prisoner of war, if captured, but would
be shot upon the spot. These threats and denunciations did not deter the Government from inaugura-
ting the measure nor skillful officers from taking command of colored regiments. The negroes afterwards
proved themselves good and faithful soldiers and the
equal of their white brethren in bravery and daring.
And so greatly did the Southern sentiment change
that long before the close of the war many negroes
were regularly enlisted into the Confederate armies.

Meantime, in the North, public sentiment was becoming more firmly fixed in favor of emancipation. And the pressure brought to bear upon the President became increasingly strong. Many delegations visited him and frequently with ill-timed arguments sought to induce him to proclaim freedom to all slaves. Among them was a Quaker delegation, the spokesman of which seemed to Mr. Lincoln to unfairly criticise him, and he replied somewhat sharply and was just on the point of dismissing the visitors, when one of the women requested permission to detain him with a few words. Her remarks contained a plea for the emancipation of the slave, urging that he was the appointed minister of the Lord to do this work, and she enforced her argument with many Scriptural quotations. At the close he asked :

"Has the Friend finished?" And, receiving an affirmative answer, he said : "I have neither time nor disposition to enter into discussion with the Friend and end this occasion by suggesting for her consideration the question whether, if the Lord has appointed me to do this work, it is not probable he would have communicated knowledge of the fact to me as well as to her."

It is certain that he had long been earnestly and prayerfully considering the question. To him it was the most momentous step of his life and the one fraught with the greatest personal consequences. After the proclamation was issued, he said to a friend : "As affairs have turned, it is the central act of my administration and the great event of the nineteenth century."

Moses had led out from bondage two millions of

Hebrews, guided by the hand of God. Lincoln's task was no less God-given, and he waited anxiously for the pillar of cloud to lead the way. And as Moses never entered into the promised land, so he seems to have had a presentiment that he should not live to see the results of emancipation. He still clung to the idea of gradual and compensated emancipation. In speaking to a number of Congressmen from the border States in July, he said : " I intend no reproach or complaint when I assure you that, in my opinion, if you had all voted for the resolution in my gradual emancipation message of last March, the war would now be substantially ended. . . . I do not speak of an emancipation at once but of a decision to emancipate gradually."

To Mr. Channing, who visited him in this trying time and spoke warmly in favor of the measure, he said : " When the hour comes for dealing with slavery, I trust I shall be willing to do my duty, though it costs my life. And, gentlemen, lives will be lost."

It is evident that Mr. Lincoln, early in the summer of 1862, had made up his mind to take the decisive step, and that he was only waiting for the right time to come. Not long before he had said to a Southern Unionist, who had warned him against meddling with slavery : " You must not expect me to give up this Government without playing the last card." And there can be no doubt that his last card was emancipation. In September a number of Chicago clergymen visited him to urge upon him the immediate issuance of an emancipation proclamation. In the course of his reply to their address, he said : " I do not wish to issue a document that the whole world will see must necessarily be inoperative, like the Pope's bull against the comet. . . . Do not misunderstand me, because I have mentioned these objections. They indicate the difficulties which have thus far prevented my action in some such way as you desire. I have not decided against a proclamation of liberty to the slaves, but hold the matter under advisement. And I can assure you that the subject is on my mind, by day and night, more than any other. Whatever shall appear to be God's will I will do."

The following interesting account of the circumstances attending the preparation and issue of the proclamation was given by Mr. Lincoln himself to Mr. Carpenter, who was engaged upon a painting of Lincoln and his Cabinet discussing the proclamation, as representing the new epoch in the national history. Said Mr. Lincoln:

"It had got to be mid-summer, 1862. Things had gone on from bad to worse, until I felt that we had reached the end of our rope on the plan of operations we had been pursuing; that we had about played our last card, and must change our tactics or lose the game. I now determined upon the adoption of the emancipation policy, and without consultation with or the knowledge of the Cabinet, I prepared the original draft of the proclamation and, after much anxious thought, called a Cabinet meeting on the subject. This was the last of July or the first part of the month of August, 1862. I said to the Cabinet that I had resolved upon this step, and had not called them together to ask their advice, but to lay the subject matter of the proclamation before them; suggestions as to which would be in order after they had heard it read. Mr. Lovejoy," said he, "was in error when he informed you that it excited no comment, excepting on the part of Secretary Seward. Various suggestions were offered. Secretary Chase wished the language stronger in reference to the arming of the blacks. Mr. Blair, after he came in, deprecated the policy, on the ground that it would cost the administration the Fall elections. Nothing, however, was offered that I had not already fully anticipated and settled in my own mind, until Secretary Seward spoke. He said in substance, 'Mr. President, I approve of the proclamation, but I question the expediency of its issue at this juncture. The depression of the public mind, consequent upon our repeated reverses, is so great that I fear the effect of so important a step. It may be viewed as the last measure of an exhausted Government, a cry for help; the Government stretching forth its hands to Ethiopia, instead of Ethiopia stretching forth her hands to the Government.' His idea," said the President, "was that it would be considered our last shriek, on the retreat." (This was his precise expression.)

"'Now,' continued Mr. Seward, 'while I approve of the measure, I suggest, sir, that you postpone its issue, until you can give it to the country supported by military success instead of issuing it, as would be the case now, upon the greatest disasters of the war!'" Mr. Lincoln continued: "The wisdom of the view of the Secretary of State struck me with very great force. It was an aspect of the case that, in all my thought upon the subject, I had entirely overlooked. The result was that I put the draft of the proclamation aside, waiting for a victory. From time to time I added or changed a line, touching it up here and there, anxiously watching the progress of events. Well, the next news we had was of Pope's disaster at Bull Run. Things looked darker than ever. Finally, came the week of the battle of Antietam. I determined to wait no longer. The news came, I think, on Wednesday, that the advantage was on our side. I was then staying at the Soldiers' Home (three miles out of Washington). Here I finished writing the second draft of the preliminary proclamation ; came up on Saturday ; called the Cabinet together to hear it, and it was published the following Monday."

At the final meeting of September 20, another interesting incident occurred in connection with Secretary Seward. The President had written the important part of the proclamation in these words: "That, on the first day of January, in the year of our Lord, one thousand eight hundred and sixty-three, all persons held as slaves, within any State or designated part of a State, the people whereof shall then be in rebellion against the United States, shall be then, thenceforward and forever free ; and the Executive Government of the United States, including the military and naval authority thereof, will recognize the freedom of such persons, and will do no act or acts to repress such persons, or any of them, in any efforts they may make for their actual freedom." "When I finished reading this paragraph," resumed Mr. Lincoln, "Mr. Seward stopped me, and said, 'I think, Mr. President, that you should insert after the word "recognized," in that sentence, the words "and maintain.'" I replied that I had already fully considered the import of that expression, in this connection, but I had not introduced it, because it was not my way to promise what I was not entirely sure that I could perform, and I was not prepared to say that I thought we were exactly able to ' maintain ' this."

" But," said he, " Seward insisted that we ought to take this ground; and the words finally went in !" "It is a somewhat remarkable fact," he subsequently remarked, " that there were just one hundred days between the dates of the two proclamations, issued on the twenty-second of September and the first of January. I had not made the calculation at the time."

In the preliminary proclamation he reiterated his intention to prosecute the war for the purpose of restoring the constitutional union between the United States and each of the States and people thereof, in which States that relation is or may be suspended. He affirmed his purpose to again recommend to Congress, at its next meeting, the adoption of a practical measure "tendering pecuniary aid to the free acceptance or rejection of all slave States, so-called, the people whereof, may not then be in rebellion against the United States, and which States may then have voluntarily adopted, or thereafter may voluntarily adopt, immediate or gradual abolishment of slavery within their respective limits; and that the effort to colonize persons of African descent, with their consent, upon this continent or elsewhere, with the previously obtained consent of the governments existing there, will be continued."

In his second annual message transmitted to Congress in December, 1862, Mr. Lincoln thus feelingly referred to the subject of the emancipation about to be consummated by Presidential decree: "The dogmas of the quiet past are inadequate to the stormy present. The occasion is piled high with difficulty and we must rise to the occasion. As our case is new, so we must think anew and act anew. Fellow-citizens, we cannot escape history. We of this Congress and of this administration will be remembered in spite of ourselves. No personal significance or insignificance can spare one or another of us. The fiery trial through which we pass will light us down, in honor or dishonor, to the latest generation. We say we are for the Union. The world will not forget that we say this. We know how to save the Union. The world knows we do know how to save it. We—even we here—hold the power and bear the responsibility. In giving freedom to the slave, we assure freedom to the free—honorable, alike, in what we give and what we preserve. We shall nobly save, or meanly lose, the last, best hope of earth. Other means may succeed, this could not fail. The way is plain, peaceful, generous, just—a way, which, if followed, the world will forever applaud and God will forever bless."

The final proclamation was issued January 1, 1863, and was a document which will ever live in history and occupy the most honorable place in the nation's annals. After quoting some sections from the preliminary proclamation and designating, in detail, the revolted districts to which the proclamation should apply, Mr. Lincoln proceeds as follows: "And by virtue of the power and for the purpose aforesaid, I do order and declare that all persons held as slaves, within designated States and parts of States, are and henceforward shall be free; and that the Executive

Government of the United States, including the military and naval authorities thereof, will recognize and maintain the freedom of said persons. And I hereby enjoin upon the people, so declared to be free, to abstain from all violence, unless in necessary self-defence ; and I recommend to them that, in all cases when allowed, they labor faithfully for reasonable wages. And I further declare and make known that such persons, of suitable condition, will be received into the armed service of the United States to garrison forts, positions, stations and other places and to man vessels of all sorts in said service. And upon this act, sincerely believed to be an act of justice, warranted by the Constitution, upon military necessity, I invoke the considerate judgment of mankind and the gracious favor of Almighty God."

Soon after this in conversation with George Thompson, the great anti-slave orator, he said : [1]

" When the rebellion broke out my duty did not admit of a question. That was, first, by all strictly lawful means to endeavor to maintain the integrity of the Government, I did not consider that I had a right to touch the ' State ' institution of ' slavery ' until all other measures for restoring the Union had failed. The paramount idea of the Constitution is the preservation of the Union. It may not be specified in so many words, but that this was the idea of its founders is evident ; for without the Union the Constitution would be useless. It seems clear then, that, in the last extremity, if any local institution threatened the existence of the Union, the Executive

---

[1] Carpenter.

could not hesitate as to his duty. In our case, the moment came when I felt that slavery must die that the nation might live. I have sometimes used the illustration in this connection, of a man with a diseased limb, and his surgeon. So long as there is a chance of the patient's restoration, the surgeon is solemnly bound to try to save both life and limb ; but when the crisis comes, and the limb must be sacrificed as the only chance of saving the life, no honest man will hesitate. Many of my strongest supporters urged emancipation before I thought it indispensable, and I may say, before I thought the country was ready for it. It is my conviction that had the proclamation been issued even six months earlier than it was, public sentiment would not have sustained it. . . . We have seen this great revolution in public sentiment slowly but surely progressing so that, when final action came, the opposition was not strong enough to defeat the purpose, I can now solemnly assert that I have a clear conscience in regard to my action on this momentous subject. I have done what no man could have helped doing, standing in my place."

The influence of the proclamation upon the national cause cannot be overestimated, yet it failed to meet with universal approval. As there had been previously many who had strenuously blamed the President for his hesitation, so now there were many who accused him of precipitate action and foreboded evil as the result of the proclamation. But the effect of it was immediately manifest in the conduct of the war. Little progress had been made up to this time by the Federal army. Dissensions had dissipated the strength of the leaders and opposing counsels

had condemned great armies to comparative inaction
or to ill-judged movements which had resulted disastrously and produced universal distrust and apathy.
The victorious arms of the South, the growing disaffection manifest in the army, the increasing lack of
confidence in the leaders and their policy, throughout
the North, all tended towards a crisis, when either
some new and decisive policy must be inaugurated or
the collapse of the National cause was inevitable.
Just the right moment was selected by the unerring
judgment of the President, the proclamation was
issued, and from that time on it needed no inspired
prophet to tell what the ultimate result would be.
True it was that many cruel battles must yet be
fought, that much blood must be shed and great
treasures expended, for the strength of the South
was, as yet, unbroken, but, from that time on, the
power of the Confederacy began to wane, its main-
stay was taken away, and from January 1, 1863,
Appomattox was in view.

The proclamation was a moral fortification, the inauguration of a decisive policy which declared that
the preservation of the Union was of more importance
than the perpetuation of slavery or any other institution ; that the President had the determination to
exert his full power in all lawful channels to put down
the insurrection. It showed the rebels in arms that
the Government was just as determined as they, and
would as relentlessly use every weapon for the preservation of the Constitution as they for its destruction. The institution was a vital one to the South,
and every blow struck against it was keenly felt, just
at the point where it would do the most harm. It was

the source of the war and soon became its strength.
Though the white man would scorn to fight beside
the negro, or to strike a blow in his behalf, personally, yet to maintain his property rights in him he
chose to enter upon the most disastrous war of
modern times. Yet all the time, behind the battling
hosts, was the negro patiently toiling to give greater
strength to the Confederacy than the shot and shell
which mangled and murdered the opposing ranks of
loyal citizens who strove to uphold the majesty of
law and the might of a constitutional government.
Slavery was the vital principle of the rebellion, which
destroyed must drain the life of secession.

The Government did not hesitate to confiscate
property, capture arms and fortresses by force, nor
to kill as many of the enemy as possible ; all this was
lawful, nor had it any less the right to attack an institution, especially when that institution was hostile
not only to the best interests of the nation, but to
its very existence. The act was plainly a legitimate
military measure, dictated by common-sense. In its
scope it was nothing less than a national purification,
while its temporary intention was the maintenance
of the Union and of national government, its ultimate result was permanent peace and prosperity,
founded upon the only principle that could secure
either.

It is given to but few men to formulate a great
principle in a political doctrine, and to afterwards
demonstrate the correctness of its application by
actually working it into the fabric of the nation's
life. To Mr. Lincoln belongs this distinction. When
he first announced his abiding belief in the principle

that the nation could not long endure half slave and
half free, Cassandra-like, he prophesied to a scoffing
crowd ; but many who ridiculed lived to acknowledge
their error, and the justness of his conclusions. His
friends believed that he had ended his public career
by the annunciation of this unpopular principle, and
it is undoubtedly true that to it he owed his defeat
in his second Senatorial campaign and his temporary
retirement from the political field. But never was
the triumph of principle more signal or vindication
more complete than his. Like the old statue, the
nation had one foot of iron, strong and enduring, and
one of clay, which could not long withstand the force
of the elements, but must inevitably crumble away
and bring ruin and destruction upon the whole social
edifice. Strong in liberty, weak in slavery ! The
proclamation not only marked the crisis of the war,
but it also proved a most important landmark in the
life of the President. Hitherto he had pursued his
steady course undisturbed, at least uninfluenced by
the wild uproar of the war. Few men would have
been sufficiently independent to pursue the course
marked out by their convictions when so hard beset
on every side. Before his inauguration he had been
openly slandered by his enemies ; after it his influence had been secretly undermined by his friends.
Because he and his Secretary of State, who had
always been known to be friendly to the peaceful
annihilation of the power of the slaveholding interests in the Government, did not immediately advocate
emancipation, they were pursued by bitter suspicions
of cowardice and incapacity, or still worse with the
stern rebuke of treachery to their political friends.

Slowly the policy of the President unfolded itself, developing, as circumstances demanded, rather than along a rigid line defined by arbitrary rules. Again and again was the trend of his thoughts indicated or hinted at by some incisive utterance, just as the fluttering leaves in the tree-tops indicate the direction of the atmospheric currents. More than a hint of his policy is given in a single sentence or two of his December message, when he says:

"The Union must be preserved, and hence all indispensable means must be employed." Again: "We should not be in haste to determine that radical and extreme measures, which may reach the loyal as well as the disloyal, are indispensable."

Mr. Lincoln's career is, as yet, too recent to place a complete and proper estimate upon it or to say what has been the crowning achievement in his career. The din and turmoil of a hundred battle-fields have not ceased echoing through the country, nor has the smoke of burning cities been yet entirely dissipated from the atmosphere. The glorious achievements of his administration, the evolutions of mighty armies, the daring deeds of prowess and the hard-won conquest of a valiant foe, all cast a glamour over the great struggle, which blinds the eyes of beholders and renders them incapable of judging as to the single achievement which shall stand pre-eminent over all others as the most far-reaching and beneficent in its results. Shall it be the preservation of republican institutions, the perpetuation of constitutional governmen or the elevation of four millions of slaves to the status of manhood and womanhood? Whatever may be the ver-

dict, it is certain that the name of Abraham Lincoln
will always be associated with the sacred cause of
freedom, that his example will be an inspiration in
the great struggle between the powers of right and
wrong, and one of the greatest glories of the final
victory which his life has done so much to assure.
His career is inseparably connected with the history
of the American slaves, and to them his name will
ever be a sacred one.

His achievements were in no sense accidental, nor
did he act as an unreasoning instrument in the hands
of Providence, to bring about a foreordained result.
It is true that the whole history of the country leads
up, in concentering lines, to the grand *denouement*;
that all the forces of political and social life were unconsciously exerted to hasten the crisis ; and all the
tendencies of modern civilization, together with the
example of foreign countries, were towards the ele-
vating of the lowly and the freeing of those who
were in bondage. These agencies would either have
brought about the desired result in the course of
time, or would have relegated all slaveholding
countries to the lowest position in the scale of
nations and to a condition of comparative barbarism.

The powerful forces of advancing civilization demanded a Lincoln to concentrate, and apply them,
and, though the operation nearly rent the continent
in twain and caused the rivers to pour crimson tides
into the sea, it proved effectual, and the terrible curse
of American slavery was forever blotted out.   To
bring about this result it is safe to say that Lincoln
contributed more than any other man.   The cause of
Abolition had been made unpopular, in the North as

well as in the South, by the radicalism of its champions. Lincoln was the first to rescue it from the slough of sentimentalism and plant it upon the firm ground of political principle. Before his entrance into the field, it had been recognized only as the visionary scheme of a few enthusiasts. In only a few limited localities had it attained a respectable degree of influence. The Douglas debates and the Cooper Institute speech raised it to the dignity of a great political issue.

No consideration of the question should detract from the value of the immortal deeds of such men as Phillips, Garrison, Sumner, Seward and Whittier, yet it is certain that that their lives were in a large sense only preparatory to the giant achievements of Lincoln. Their extreme utterances appealed to but a small portion of the people ; his earnest moderation and reasonable policy aroused far less antagonism and made multitudes of friends among those who would otherwise have been lukewarm or even hostile. A more self-assertive policy would no doubt have wrecked the Government and broken up the country; less resolution and earnestness of purpose would have allowed the opportunity of a century to pass or long years of contention or divided sovereignty would have been the result. In view, then, of the mighty interests preserved, and the weighty problems solved, it is probably not too much to say that Abraham Lincoln will be recognized as the central figure of the nineteenth century in American history.

CHAPTER XVIII.

DURING the first year of the war the prestige had been with the Southern armies. The Confederate leaders had made elaborate preparations and had not only taken the Government unawares but had deprived it, to a large extent, of the means of waging offensive warfare, and compelled it to act mainly upon the defensive until its resources could be recuperated. The first year, therefore, was largely a period of self-fortification on the part of the national Government and of preparation of a vantage-ground from which the war might be successfully fought. As next in importance to recruiting and disciplining large armies, the administration directed its energies towards retaining the border States in the Union, for the possession of which the Confederacy was exerting every effort.

It was only through the skillfully planned movements of the Government that a number of these States did not find their way into the Confederacy. Thus were saved to the Union the States of Maryland, West Virginia, Kentucky and Missouri, which afterwards rendered gallant service in its defense.

One of the greatest achievements of the year was the blockade of the South. The rebellious commonwealths were virtually placed in a state of siege; the fleets upon the ocean and the armies on the north and

(256)

west almost entirely shutting off communication with the outside world. Never before had an attempt been made to actually enforce so extensive a blockade. Napoleon's famous Berlin decree and the resulting Orders in Council on the part of Great Britain covered an extensive seaboard but both Governments were powerless to enforce them by actual blockade. When the policy was first announced military men abroad sneered at the idea and arrogantly proclaimed its utter impracticability. And the obstacles did seem insurmountable. The numerous harbors of the South, its navigable rivers and complex system of estuaries and sounds seemed to offer so many opportunities for blockade-runners that nothing short of an actual patrol of the entire coast would apparently effect the desired result. Yet in less than a year the South was practically cut off from outside markets and was neither able to sell her own products abroad nor buy the many luxuries which, from common use, had almost come to be necessities. The moral effect of this move was great, both at home and abroad. More than was possible in any other way the whole disaffected district was made to feel the rigor of war, and the serious character of the situation was brought close home to every door, while the loss of Southern products, especially of cotton, brought much suffering upon foreign communities and led the different powers to feel a deeper personal interest in the struggle.

But two great battles had been fought, and in each the National armies had been signally defeated, and though victorious in a number of minor engagements, the laurels of the contest thus far rested on Southern

brows. For the second year the administration had
conceived a policy looking towards the achievement
of three different things, viz.—the continued blockade of Southern ports, the opening of the Mississippi
and the capture of Richmond. Early in the year the
country was electrified by news of the capture of
Forts Henry and Donelson by General Grant, assisted
by Commodore Foote. The cool and resolute bearing of General Grant attracted the attention of the
people, but especially that of the President, who was
eagerly watching for the appearance of some military
genius who should be able to lead the grand armies
of the Republic on to victory. Between Lincoln and
Grant there were many things in common and each
conceived a warm admiration for, and complete confidence in the other. In each was to be noted the same
unaffected simplicity and earnest resolution. Each
was self-reliant in critical times and quick to discern
merit in another and each was capable of grasping
the broad principles of a situation, unembarrassed by
minor details, which enabled them to frame compre-
hensive policies or plan great and successful campaigns. To Grant, Lincoln was the greatest man of
the times, and to Lincoln, Grant was the ablest general of the age. Yet neither arrived at this conclusion until each had been thoroughly tested and proven
worthy. And it was only after his ability had been
demonstrated in many a hard fought field and complicated siege that Grant was advanced from one position to another until he was put in command of the
united armies of the nation.

Then came the movements looking towards the
forced evacuation of Kentucky and Tennessee, involv-

ing the fiercely fought battle of Shiloh and the gradual rolling southward of the rebel tide which had
threatened to inundate the States of the Northwest.

The administration early saw the importance of
gaining possession of the Mississippi River. As in
early times this magnificent highway of inland waters
had been the subject of many a controversy and in-
ternational complication, so once more its peaceful
waters were to be the witness of a tremendous struggle between the free Northwest and the slave Southwest for its possession, which foreboded final defeat
to the loser. In April a fleet under the command of
Commodore Farragut captured the city of New Orleans after passing through the defenses at the mouth
of the river and running by the forts which guarded
the city. While on the north the Federal forces were
advancing slowly and surely southward to form a
junction with the blue-coated armies at the mouth of
the river.

Early in the year the people of the North were
dismayed by the news that the *Merrimac*, whose construction and formidable character had been widely
heralded, had attacked the fleet off Hampton Roads,
and had sunk or disabled a number of the stanchest
ships, which were powerless to harm their adversary.
Anxiously did they throng the telegraph offices the
next day, awaiting news which the most sanguine
could not hope to be favorable. But a new factor
had appeared upon the scene, one of those products
of man's ingenuity which special emergencies sometimes call forth. The story of the *Merrimac* and
Monitor has passed into history, and is familiar to
every school-child.

It is not generally known that Mr. Lincoln was, in a large measure, responsible for the building of the *Monitor*. The plans had been presented to the Navy Department, but had excited but little interest. Finally, the projectors of the enterprise solicited an interview with the President, at which Captain Ericsson's plans were displayed and fully described. After making a thorough examination of them, Mr. Lincoln said : " Well, I don't know much about ships, though I once contrived a canal-boat, the model of which is down in the Patent Office, the great merit of which was that it could run where there was no water, but I think there is something in this plan of Ericsson's." And, shortly afterwards, the Government entered into a contract for the construction of the boat as a result of this interview. The result amply vindicated the claims of the great inventor and his friends.

At the time of the capture of Norfolk and the destruction of the *Merrimac*, the President was at Fortress Monroe with several of his Cabinet. He had witnessed with deep interest one of the struggles between the little *Monitor* and the rebel iron-clad, and awaited anxiously the result of the expedition against Norfolk. His account of the reception of the news of its downfall is as follows :

" Chase and Stanton," said he, " had accompanied me to Fortress Monroe. While we were there, an expedition was fitted out for an attack on Norfolk. Chase and General Wool disappeared about the time we began to look for tidings of the result, and after vainly waiting their return until late in the evening, Stanton and I concluded to retire. My room was on the second floor of the commandant's house, and

Stanton's was below. The night was very warm, the moon was shining brightly, and, too restless to sleep, I sat for some time by the table reading. Suddenly hearing footsteps, I looked out of the window and saw two persons approaching, whom I knew by the relative size to be the missing men. They came into the passage, and I heard them rap at Stanton's door, and tell him to get up and come upstairs. A moment after, they entered my room. 'No time for ceremony, Mr. President,' said General Wool—'Norfolk is ours!' Stanton here burst in, just out of bed, clad in a long night-gown, which nearly swept the floor, his ear catching, as he crossed the threshold, Wool's last words. Perfectly overjoyed, he rushed at the General, whom he hugged most affectionately, fairly lifting him from the floor in his delight. The scene altogether must have been a comical one, though at the time we were all too greatly excited to take much note of mere appearances." [1]

The North had become impatient at the meager results of the war hitherto, and from east to west, from Canada to the border-land, the imperious cry resounded, "On to Richmond!" A vast and well-disciplined host lay upon its arms within sight of the great dome of the Capitol at Washington, and impatiently demanded that it be led against the enemy. The time was ripe, the opportunities favorable, and the men were ready; but the great leader, unerring in judgment, quick to strike and cool in temper, was wanting. McClellan started out with the most brilliant prospects, a good soldier, an honest patriot, but

---

[1] Browne.

unfitted to conduct a great campaign. The onward movement was undertaken with undue deliberation and utter neglect of caution. Opportunities were overlooked which might have contributed much towards the success of the expedition, and yet the great army arrived almost within sight of the defenses of Richmond, carrying consternation to the inhabitants, but was then compelled to turn back by the adroit manœuvres of the opposing generals. Then followed the skillfully-conducted but disastrous retreat, the seven days' fighting and the bloody struggle in the Wilderness, and, at last, the broken fragments of the once splendid Army of the Potomac returned, with banners torn and laurels gone, leaving behind a pathway strewn with the mangled remains of the husbands and sons of the North. How the eyes of the people were turned towards that spot on Virginia's sacred soil, and how the hearts of mothers and wives and children were breaking, as they pictured their loved ones bleeding and dying in that lonely swamp! Such scenes of woe the pen can never describe nor the brush picture. The broken heart alone knows the depth of its suffering.

The retreat of McClellan was followed by an advance of the rebel armies into Maryland. Flushed with victory, General Lee permitted his forces to become widely separated, when he was suddenly confronted by the Federal army, which was much superior in numbers, at Antietam. But McClellan, with characteristic inactivity and indecision, delayed until the scattered forces of the Confederates could be collected, and then engaged the enemy. What might have been a glorious victory, resulted practi-

cally in a drawn battle, and Lee was permitted to
retire unmolested across the Potomac.   The battle of
Antiétam ended General McClellan's military career,
and he was succeeded by General Burnside, who was
shortly afterwards disastrously defeated at Fredericksburg, and was in turn succeeded by General
Hooker.

It is related that, on the morning after the battle
at Fredericksburg, Hon. I. N. Arnold called on the
President, and, to his amazement, found him engaged
in reading "Artemas Ward."   Making no reference
to that which occupied the universal thought, he
asked Mr. Arnold to sit down while he read to him
Artemas' description of his visit to the Shakers.
Shocked at this proposition, Mr. Arnold said : " Mr.
President, is it possible that, with the whole land
bowed in sorrow and covered with a pall in the presence of yesterday's fearful reverse, you can indulge
in such levity ? "   Throwing down the book, with the
tears streaming down his cheeks, and his huge frame
quivering with emotion, Mr. Lincoln answered, " Mr.
Arnold, if I could not get momentary respite from
the crushing burden I am constantly carrying, my
heart would break ! " [1]

At the beginning of the year 1863, the situation was
not materially changed from the preceding year. The
emancipation proclamation had been issued, and the
result of the step was anxiously awaited.   The disasters in the East had inspired a feeling of gloom and
discouragement, which the victories in the West had
hardly been able to counteract. General Grant was per-

Browne.

sistently continuing his efforts to open the Mississippi, and had gained possession of the territory on both sides of the river as far south as Vicksburg, which was now the only important Confederate stronghold on the river. The city was in an exceptionally strong position, and was seemingly impregnable. Moreover, as it was the last position held by the Confederates, it was believed that their Government would exert every effort to maintain it. Hence there were few who believed that it could be captured. General Grant, however, in spite of all obstacles, determined to invest the city. He tried one plan after another and failed, yet, with a tenacity of purpose which has rarely been equalled, he persisted in the effort and, finally, July 4, 1863, had the satisfaction of planting the "Stars and Stripes" upon the ramparts, and taking possession of Vicksburg in the name of the Federal Government. Like an electric shock, the news passed through the North, and gave birth to exultation and a renewed feeling of confidence in ultimate success. No one was more delighted by this achievement than Mr. Lincoln, and he took an early opportunity to write the following congratulatory letter to him:

"EXECUTIVE MANSION,
"WASHINGTON, D. C., July 13, 1863.

"*Major-General Grant.*

"MY DEAR GENERAL—I do not remember that you and I ever met personally. I write this now as a grateful acknowledgment for the almost inestimable service you have done the country. I write to say a word further. When you first reached the vicinity of Vicksburg, I thought you should do what you finally did—march the troops across the neck, run the

batteries with the transports, and thus go below ; and I never
had any faith, except a general hope that you knew better than
I, that the Yazoo Pass expedition, and the like, could succeed.
When you got below, and took Port Gibson, Grand Gulf and
vicinity, I thought you should go down the river, and join General Banks ; and when you turned northward, east of the Big
Black, I feared it was a mistake. I now wish to make the personal acknowledgment that you were right, and I was wrong.

" Yours truly,
" A. LINCOLN."

Vicksburg's capture was undoubtedly the greatest
achievement of the war up to this time, yet General
Grant's work was but begun. The Department of
the Tennessee was under the command of General
Rosecrans but, after the disastrous battle of Chicka-
mauga, he was superseded by Grant who arrived
just in time to fight the battle of Chattanooga and to
witness the gallant and desperate ascent of Missionary Ridge. A more glorious spectacle is not
described in the annals of war. The rugged mountain lifting its precipitous heights into the clouds,
where might be seen the Confederate lines intrenched
behind formidable defenses of rocks and crags. At
its base a long slender line of blue-coated soldiers,
whose eyes swept the heights and whose faces were
eagerly set towards the foe so far above them. Once,
twice, six times the signal cannon bellowed forth its
thunderous sound and like a sword from its scab-
bard the impatient line sprang forth, impetuous,
undaunted by the rugged heights and frowning
redoubts. From crag to crag, amid the tempest of
iron, which raged round about them, splintering the
rocks and hurling many a brave soldier to the ground

in his death agony, they dash onward and upward, with the starry flags leading far in the advance. The foe was met and despite his advantage of position was hurled back by the avalanche of steel, thus turned back from its natural course. So the battle of the clouds was fought and the proud banner of freedom floated over another State rescued from the polluting clutch of treason.

In the East affairs began to take a more favorable turn. Encouraged by his almost unbroken career of victory General Lee determined to carry the war into the enemy's country. The broad and fertile fields of Pennsylvania and the wealthy and populous cities of New York and Philadelphia offered tempting prizes to the invader, whose soil had been the scene of so many sanguinary conflicts and whose resources had been exhausted by destructive war. Swiftly the legions of the South moved down the Shenandoah and crossed the Potomac, hotly pursued by the Federal army under the command of General Meade, which now, for the first time, found a hostile army between itself and the North.

Upon Northern soil, in a State founded upon the principles of peace and good-will towards all, in a place where the echoes of the guns could almost be heard in the " City of Brotherly Love," was the decisive battle of the war destined to be fought. Neither general had planned to fight here but by accident, or rather by the hand of Providence, a collision occurred between a squadron of Federal .cavalry and a division of Lee's army and the great engagement was brought on. For three days the battle continued ; each side recognizing that then and there the issue must be fought out. Deeds of bravery and daring were performed which will ever redound to the glory of American heroism. Charges and counter-charges, artillery duels and broadsides of musketry, together with the minor refrain of groans and dying prayers, mingling with the shrill shrieks of death and hoarse cries of command, all go to make up the battle of Gettysburg. But at last the tide of invasion was turned and the rebel army, in full retreat, sought the regions which it had left so hopefully, but a few days before, defeated but not dishonored. No braver men ever breathed or more gallant hearts ever beat than those in the gray coats, save alone those in the blue, whose greatest mead of praise was that they had beaten their brethren of the South.

The tide of the war had turned. With the beginning of 1864, the last act in the great tragedy opened. General Grant was made Commander-in-Chief of the National forces and now for the first time all the tremendous power of the army was swayed by one mind, intelligently to the accomplishment of one purpose—the putting down of the rebellion as quickly and effectively as possible. Obedient to command, General Sherman, who was soon to be ranked in ability as a commander only second to the great chief himself, set out, in pursuit of Johnston, on his great march to Atlanta and thence to the sea. Straight across the very centre of the Confederacy he marched, overcoming all opposition and capturing Atlanta, then breaking loose from all communications, in the heart of the enemy's country, he started with sixty thousand men for the Atlantic coast. In five weeks he had marched three hundred miles and

captured Savannah. The effect of this daring expedition cannot be over estimated. The enemy's country had once more been cut in two and the interior,
for the first time, was made to feel the rigors of destructive and uncompromising war.

The advantage of having all the Federal armies
under the direction of one cool, vigilant and unweary-
ing mind soon became apparant. The operations of
the national forces covered a vast field, but they were
no longer conducted at cross purposes; each army,
division and brigade became like the pieces in the
hands of a chess-player, and were skilfully and harmoniously manipulated. Sherman in the South,
Thomas in Tennessee, Sheridan in the Shenandoah
Valley, Butler in eastern Virginia, Dupont along the
Atlantic seaboard, and Porter and Farragut in the
Gulf of Mexico with the great General himself at the
head of the vast armies advancing towards Richmond
worked with a vigor and unity of purpose which,
exhibited in the earlier stages of the war, would have
brought it to a close long before. Once more was
Richmond the objective point and slowly but relentlessly the Union armies were closing around the Confederate Capital. All the genius of Lee and his
accomplished generals was exerted to turn back the
tide of invasion, quick marches, flank movements and
bloody battles were all unavailing, and in the spring
of 1865 the Wilderness had been once more passed in
the face of the Confederate hosts. The army left a
broad swath behind strewn with its dead but still it
pressed on past the numerous defenses until the
strongholds of the rebellion were one by one secured
and the victorious but sore-stricken lines were at

last within sight of the city. Its defense was bravely
conducted but ineffectual and, at last, on the morning
of April 3, the "Stars and Stripes" were borne in triumph through the streets and flung once more to the
breezes fresh from the South, where for four years
the proud but ill-fated "St. Andrew's Cross" had
flaunted.

Close upon the capitulation of Richmond followed
Appomattox and the shattered remnants of the gallant foe laid down their arms and their cause was lost
forever. The fearful penalty of the nation's sin, conceived in her infancy and cherished and strengthened
in her vigorous youth, was now paid and a united
country was ready to take its place among the nations
on a firmer basis and with grander prospects than
ever before.

The conflict was inevitable. It had been begun at
the time of the adoption of the Constitution. It had
gained strength amid strife and mutual distrust.
More than once it had broken out in open rebellion,
and finally it burst like a tempest upon the land. It
can hardly be believed that the election of Lincoln
hastened secession, much less that it was the cause of
it. The time had come and a pretext only was sought.
In the dark days that succeeded his inauguration he
was confronted with a situation whose difficulty had
never been surpassed in the history of the country.
Though few had believed him to be possessed of the
elements of greatness he exhibited an adaptability to
circumstances, a keenness of foresight and a readiness
to adapt means to the accomplishment of a desired
end that will undoubtedly rank him among the great
rulers of the world. In his energy and versatility he

was the peer of Cæsar ; in the magnitude of the operations which he conducted, he vied with Alexander ;
while his patience, persistence and devotion to the
right were never excelled by Washington.

To what extent the success of the war was due to
him cannot be estimated. The North was far stronger
than the South, both in material resources and
the men from whom armies are recruited. Her im·
mense extent of seacoast, east and west, would have
prevented a successful blockade; or, if successful, her
vast domain of fertile territory would have rendered
it nugatory. Her people were patriotic and devoted
and equal, at least, man for man to their Southern
brethren. On the other hand, they were taken unawares and were for the time helpless in the presence
of armed rebellion. It was Lincoln who combined
and utilized the giant forces, which were otherwise
helpless, because without a rallying point. It was
Lincoln who planned and organized, who encouraged
the people in their gloom, and pointed out the way to
victory, not only pointed it out but led the advance,
often but a forlorn hope, until the desired end was attained. What Washington was to the Revolution Lincoln was to the Rebellion and more. More, because
a domestic foe is more formidable than a foreign enemy; because the interests he controlled and conserved
were immeasurably greater than those in the hands of
Washington.

CHAPTER XIX.

NOWHERE in the management of the war did the Government show greater weakness than in the selection of commanders. It is hardly just to blame the President or his advisers exclusively for this. The difficulty was largely the result of circumstances, entirely beyond the control of the administration. In 1860 there were comparatively but few men, North or South, who were trained in the art of war. The Mexican War had been too short and on too limited a scale to educate many men in military tactics, and the officers of the regular army, in large part, deserted their colors to enlist in the Southern armies. Nor were the President and his Cabinet prepared for the emergency suddenly thrust upon them. Mr. Lincoln was obliged to feel his way slowly and carefully along an unknown track without precedent to guide him. It was evident that the proper man to guide and control the affairs of the great armies could be found only by experiment and in large measure must be educated up to his position. Mr. Lincoln realized most keenly the difficulties of the situation and exercised the utmost patience as long as he saw his appointees progressive and earnest He still continued to have faith in McClellan after the country had begun to clamor for his removal, and still upheld and offered him full

support if he would only make an effort to redeem
his reputation.

His policy was vigorous and he earnestly advised
and finally directed a general advance towards the
centre of the Confederacy, and yet, in spite of all, he
constantly saw his advice rejected and his plans dis-
concerted. No one will ever realize the keenness of
his disappointment when he became convinced that
he was mistaken in his man and that only disaster
could be expected so long as McClellan remained at
the head of the army. Nor was his disappointment
entirely upon public grounds. He felt a sense of personal bereavement in the wholesale slaughter to
which the army had been subjected and his grief was
all the more poignant because he recognized the fact
that much of it was unnecessary and useless. The suffering and misery occasioned by the war met him on
every side. In Washington more than any other city
of the North was the terrible physical suffering, the
mutilation and sickness of the soldiers seen. The
city was full of hospitals and the streets were thronged
with ambulances bearing the sore-stricken soldiers
from battlefield to hospital.

He once said to a friend, while gazing at a long line
of ambulances, with an expression of deepest dejec-
tion on his face, "Look at those poor fellows, I cannot bear it ! This suffering, this loss of life is dreadful ! "

From his windows he could see the rebel flag floating at Arlington while the magnificent Union army
lay idly upon its arms. Yet he seldom criticised the
inactivity of McClellan, except in a humorous way.
He once said to a friend: " If McClellan does not

want to use the army for some days, I should like to borrow it and see if it cannot be made to do something." At another time he said: "General McClellan is a pleasant and scholarly gentleman. He is an admirable engineer, but he seems to have a special talent for a *stationary* engine."

After the battle of Antietam he visited the army with Hon. O. M. Hatch, a former Secretary of State of Illinois. He arose early in the morning and with Mr. Hatch walked out upon a hill and looked down upon the great expense of white tents extending as far as the eye could reach. As they looked upon the wonderful scene the deepest emotions were stirred within them as they thought of the multitudes, who were already sleeping their last long sleep on Southern soil, and the unknown but terrible possibilities of the future. The President suddenly leaned forward and said in a whisper:

"Hatch, Hatch, what is all this?"

"Why, Mr. Lincoln," said he, "that is the Army of the Potomac."

The President hesitated a moment, and then said: "No, Hatch, no. This is General McClellan's body-guard."

Mr. Lincoln was often reproached for his levity and was often misjudged. People thought that he had but little feeling or appreciation of the gravity of the situation. As in many other things the people failed to understand the character of their President. The stories and humorous illustrations, which he constantly used in his conversation, were a relief to him and for the moment diverted his mind from the distressing responsibilities resting upon him, and, without such distraction, the burden would have been too great for him to bear. Without it he once said he should die.

He realized as fully as any one the necessity of some positive movement which would enable the army to retrieve its former defeats, and, despairing of any independent action on the part of McClellan, towards the end of January, 1862, he issued a proclamation known as "the President's General Order, No. 1," directing a general onward movement of the whole army, to take place Feb. 22. While no great result followed, it indicated the temper of the administration and tended to awaken the army out of its apathy.

General Burnside's lack of qualification was shown in the battle of Fredricksburg, and Chancellorsville revealed the same in regard to Hooker. Mr. Lincoln had never fully approved of Hooker and when he appointed him cautioned him pointedly against the repetition of several mistakes which he believed him to have previously made. The news of Chancellorsville was a terrible blow to Mr. Lincoln. Still his main thought was for its effect upon the country. "Oh, what will the country say, what will the country say?" was his first ejaculation. The country's welfare, not his own, was always in his heart, and for that was his greatest anxiety. He often spoke of himself as the attorney for the people, and, as he quaintly expressed it, "was the lead horse in the team and must not kick over the traces."

He found himself compelled to defend his policy to his friends, and to that end made speeches, held interviews and wrote letters, explaining and justifying his course. He felt that the people had a right to know everything in regard to his measures which could be divulged without injury to the cause. No President has been more indefatigable in his efforts to make himself understood by the people. He was, in a measure, compelled to resort to this course by the open opposition of his political enemies and the continual carping of those who should have been his friends.

He was frequently called upon to make speeches to the troops who were passing through the city, as well as to delegations of citizens who were continually appealing to him upon some subject. Although quick to detect insincerity or selfishness, and unsparing in his rebuke of it and frequently manifesting weariness or impatience, he never made a mistake in his speeches. His utterances were always dignified and pointed. In them he frequently alluded to the trenchant points of his policy, especially if they had been criticised, and in plain terms made clear the points misunderstood or criticised so that the reasons for his actions might be seen. Although he seemed to speak extemporaneously, he generally prepared the principal points of his speech with great care in order that he might allow no unguarded expression to escape his lips.

Not one of the least elements of his greatness was this power of saying just the right thing at the right time, and the fact that although the opportunities were many and the temptation great, he never indulged in intemperate language or said anything which would in the end prejudice his cause. His care and painstaking are especially shown in his public papers.

No President has left behind a collection of more able and dignified State-papers. His reasoning was always cogent and convincing. He had a way of getting at the important features of a matter and presenting them clearly in a few words, overriding opposition and carrying conviction.

During the whole continuance of the war no influence was more potent in forming and directing public sentiment than that of the President. The country anxiously scanned his utterances and awaited the expression of his opinions and guided their actions by them. It is probably not too much to say that no President had ever before exercised so powerful an influence in the halls of Congress as he. His messages were deemed almost oracular and his advice was eagerly sought by both Senators and Representatives. The impress of his thought may be distinctly seen upon the legislative acts of his administration and is preserved in the archives of the nation.

In his message of December, 1862, he felt called upon to demonstrate the utter impracticability of the formation of two Governments upon the American continent, and never was the foolishness of the attempt to sever the Union more conclusively shown. It may be that at this trying time he was disheartened and feared that the North might, after all, be defeated and thus sought to strengthen the hearts and hands not only of Congress, but also of the people. He said :

" . . . That portion of the earth's surface which is owned and inhabited by the people of the United States, is well adapted to be the home of one national family ; and is not well adapted for two or

more. Its vast extent and its variety of climate and productions are of advantage in this age for one people,
whatever they may have been in former ages. Steam,
telegraph and intelligence have brought these to an
advantageous combination for one united people.
. . . . There is no line, straight or crooked, suitable for a national boundary, upon which to divide.
Trace through from east to west upon the line
between free and slave territory and we shall find a little more than one third of its length are rivers, easy
to be crossed, and populated, or soon to be populated,
thickly on both sides ; while nearly all its remaining
length are merely surveyors' lines over which the
people walk back and forth without any consciousness of their presence. No part of this line can be
made any more difficult to pass by writing it down
upon paper or parchment as a national boundary. . . . But there is another difficulty. The
great interior region bounded east by the Alleghanies, north by the British Dominions, west by the
Rocky Mountains and south by the line along which
the culture of corn and cotton meets, already has
above ten millions of people and will have fifty millions within fifty years, if not prevented by any political folly or mistake. It contains more than one-
third of the country owned by the United States,
certainly more than one million square miles. A
glance at the map shows, that, territorially speaking,
it is the great body of the Republic. The other parts
are but marginal borders to it. The magnificent
region, sloping west from the Rocky Mountains to
the Pacific, being the deepest and also the richest in
undeveloped resources. In the production of provi-

sions, grains, grasses, and all which proceed from
them, this great interior region is naturally one of the
most important in the world. . . . And yet this
region has no seacoast, touches no ocean anywhere.
As a part of one nation its people may find, and may
forever find their way to Europe by New York, to
South America and Africa by New Orleans and to
Asia by San Francisco. But separate our common
country into two nations, as designed by the present
rebellion, and every man of this great interior region
is thereby cut off from some one or more of these
outlets, not perhaps by a physical barrier but by
embarrassing and onerous trade regulations."

His appreciation of the services rendered by General Grant was keen. Up to the capture of Vicksburg it had not been satisfactorily shown whether
Grant was a great general or whether his successes
had been partly the result of circumstances. But the
conquest of the stronghold of the Mississippi, in the
presence of almost insuperable difficulties proved his
metal. The knight had won his spurs. The eyes of
the nation were turned upon him, and the President
became convinced that at last he had found the man
who could lead the armies of the North to victory.
There were strong bonds of sympathy between the
sorely tried President and the plain but successful
general. They were both men of the people who
had risen to commanding positions from the lower
walks of life by the force of sterling character and
native ability. Each retained his sympathy with the
masses and utter carelessness for all the pomp and
display of high official position. Each one formed
opinions and plans deliberately but adhered to a

principle or line of action, once adopted, with a tenacity that at times amounted almost to obstinacy.
Each was unexcelled in the sphere to which the
exigency of the war had called him. Grant leading
the great armies in the field and executing long and
complicated campaigns, was the exact complement
of Lincoln directing the vast affairs, military, political and civil, of a disrupted country, and framing and
carrying out policies requiring the most consummate
wisdom and tact. Lincoln had followed Grant's
career with profound interest and had more than
once congratulated him upon his achievements.
After the relief of Knoxville, in December, 1863, he
said in a letter : "   .   .   .   I wish to tender you and
all under your command my more than thanks, my
profoundest gratitude for the skill, courage and per-
severance with which you and they, over so great
difficulties, have accomplished that object.   May God
bless you all."

Lincoln never hesitated to speak in highest terms
of him. Soon after the capture of Vicksburg, he
said : "I guess I was right in standing by Grant,
although there was a great pressure made after Pitts-
burg Landing to have him removed. I thought I saw
enough in Grant to convince me that he was one
upon whom the country could depend. That 'uncon-
ditional surrender ' message to Buckner, at Donelson,
suited me.   It indicated the spirit of the man."

It was not until Grant had been appointed Lieut-
enant-General that Lincoln first saw him. He was
much pleased with his appearance, and afterwards
commented upon his unobtrusive and quiet character,
saying, "The only evidence you have that he is in

any place, is that he makes things *git*. Wherever he is things move."

Being afterwards asked for his estimate of Grant, he said that he was the first general he had had. His other generals had been accustomed to form plans for campaigns and ask him to shoulder the responsibility for their outcome ; "but," said he, " Grant does nothing of the kind. He hasn't told me what his plans are. I don't know, and don't want to know. I am glad to find a man who can go ahead without me. . . . He doesn't ask impossibilities of me and he is the first general I have had that didn't. The great thing about him is his cool persistency of purpose. He is not easily excited, and he has the grip of a bulldog. When he once gets his teeth in, nothing can shake him off."

After the fall of Vicksburg there was some dissatisfaction manifested by captious people, because Grant had permitted Pemberton's men to leave on parole, to re-enforce the ranks of the enemy, as they said. A delegation of these men visited Lincoln and voiced their complaint. He answered with a characteristic story. "Have you ever heard," said he, " the story of Sykes' dog? Well, I must tell you about him.

"Sykes had a yellow dog he set a great store by; but there were a lot of small boys about the village and that's always a bad thing for dogs, you know. These boys didn't share Sykes' views and they were not disposed to let the dog have a fair show. Even Sykes had to admit that the dog was getting unpopular ; in fact, it was soon seen that there was a prejudice growing up against that dog that threatened to wreck all his future prospects in life. The boys, after meditating how they could get the best of him, finally fixed upon a cartridge with a long fuse, put the cartridge in a piece of meat in the road in front of Sykes' door, and then perched themselves on the fence, a good distance off, with the fuse in their hands. Then they whistled for the dog. When he came out he scented the bait and bolted the meat, cartridge and all. The boys touched off the fuse and in about a second a report came from that dog that sounded like a clap of thunder. Sykes came bouncing out of the house and yelled, ' What's up ? Anything busted ? ' And looking up, he saw the air filled with pieces of yellow dog. He picked up the biggest piece he could find—a portion of the back with the tail still hanging to it—and, after turning it around and looking it all over, he said : ' Well, I guess he'll never be of much account again—as a dog.' And I guess Pemberton's forces will never be of much account again—as an army." [1]

Grant's opinion of Lincoln was most favorable. Shortly before his (Lincoln's) death, he said of him : " I regard Lincoln as one of the greatest of men. The more I see him and exchange views with him the more he impresses me. I admire his courage and respect the firmness he always displays. Many think from the gentleness of his character that he has a yielding nature ; but while he has the courage to change his mind, when convinced that he is wrong, he has all the tenacity of purpose which could be desired in a great statesman. His quickness of perception often astonishes me. Long before the state-

[1] Browne.

ment of a complicated question is finished, his mind will grasp the main points, and he will seem to comprehend the whole subject better than the person who is telling it. He will rank in history alongside of Washington."

The battle of Gettysburg marked the turning of the tide. It was the decisive struggle which was to determine the future of the land. The anxiety of the North during those eventful first three days of July was intense and feverish. Would the invasion be turned back or would the peaceful regions of the North be devastated by the cruel hand of war. Would Lee be checked in his victorious career, or would he bear the St. Andrew's Cross in triumph over the blood-stained soil of Gettysburg and plant it in the heart of the North to wave over burning cities and desolated firesides.

It was a struggle for life or death, and the gloomiest forebodings were indulged in on every side. The revulsion of feeling which occurred, when the telegraph announced that Lee was in full retreat, and the Union army, though shattered, was victorious, is past description. The President was overwhelmed with congratulations and, being serenaded on the night of the 4th, said: "I do most sincerely thank Almighty God for the occasion of this call. . . . Eighty odd years since, on the Fourth of July, for the first time in the history of the world, a nation, by its representatives, assembled and declared as a self-evident truth, that all men are created equal. That was the birthday of the United States of America. And now, at this last Fourth of July just past, we have a gigantic rebellion, at the bottom of which is an effort to overthrow the principle that all men are created equal. We have the surrender of a most important position, and an army, on that very day."

On July 15, he issued a proclamation to the people in which he referred to the great victory that had been won and the brightening prospects of the national cause, not failing to speak in touching words of the sorrow and suffering, the broken homes and stricken hearts. He then called upon the people to assemble, August 4, for thanksgiving, praise and prayer, and to render homage to the "Divine Majesty" for the wonderful things He had done in the nation's behalf. He asked the loyal people to pray that the hearts of the insurgents might be turned to better counsels, and the officers of the Government might have their hands upheld and their judgments directed by divine wisdom; and that the Great Father might console and comfort the stricken ones, and lead the nation through all the trials and vicissitudes of war to unity and fraternal peace.

There were many things that combined to make Gettysburg the most notable battle of the war. It was the only great battle that was fought on Northern soil, and was the most stubbornly contested. Deeds of individual valor and daring, such as grace the annals of chivalry, were here performed in countless numbers. There was hardly a community in the North which did not feel a sense of personal bereavement, when Gettysburg was mentioned. The tear-dimmed eyes of a great people were turned towards its fields and hills rendered sacred by the precious blood in which it was baptized. Hence it was peculiarly fit that the spot should be chosen as the site of a great national cemetery, where the Nation's dead, the soldiers, who had offered up their lives on her altars, might sleep their last sleep. And where the serried columns of armed men once stood in martial array, now stretches long avenues of funeral mounds, with their white headboards, recording the simple annals of the dead or marking the resting-places of those whose names earth has long since forgotten, but whose deeds shall be remembered as long as the "Stars and Stripes" wave over an united country. Where once the roar of battle convulsed the earth and echoed through the air, is now heard the song of birds and the soft moaning of winds. Once, a pall of sulphurous smoke, lit up by the cannon's glare, now the clear blue sky or the summer clouds gently weeping o'er the slain!

It is fitting, too, that the great commonwealths of the North should erect obelisks and monuments to commemorate the resting-place of their heroes, until the great mausoleum shall become the most hallowed spot on American soil, save only that place where the Pilgrims first landed to found a nation, for whose maintenance these Boys in Blue so bravely died.

On the 19th of November, the cemetery was dedicated, with solemn and imposing ceremonies. The President and his Cabinet were present, together with Members of Congress, Governors and the representatives of foreign Powers. The principal address was delivered by Edward Everett, one of the most accomplished scholars and eloquent speakers of the day. His oration was long and masterly and the audience did homage to the polished orator, whose faultless style and flowing sentences excited a feeling of admiration for the living speaker as well as for the voiceless dead. After the oration was ended Mr. Lincoln was called upon to speak. He had bestowed but little time and thought upon his speech. On the cars, while on his way to the battlefield, he had called for a pencil and piece of paper and had hastily written out the few sentences which were destined to produce so profound an impression. He arose slowly, adjusted his spectacles and, with his whole frame quivering with emotion and his voice shrill and penetrating, read the following address :

"Four score and seven years ago, our fathers brought forth upon this continent a new nation, conceived in liberty and dedicated to the proposition that all men are created equal. Now we are engaged in a great civil war, testing whether that nation, or any nation so conceived and so dedicated, can long endure. We are met on a great battlefield of that war. We are met to dedicate a portion of it as the final resting-place of those who here gave their lives that that nation might live. It is altogether fitting and proper that we should do this.

" But, in a larger sense, we cannot dedicate—we cannot consecrate—we cannot hallow this ground. The brave men, living and dead, who struggled here, have consecrated it far above our power to add or detract. The world will little note nor long remember what we say here, but it can never forget what they did here. It is for us, the living, rather to be dedicated here to the unfinished work that they have thus far so nobly carried on. It is rather for us to be here dedicated to the great task remaining before us, that from these honored dead we take increased devotion to the cause for which they here gave the last full measure of devotion, that we here highly resolve that the dead shall not have died in vain ; that the nation shall, under God, have a new birth of freedom ; and that government of the people, by the people and for the people, shall not perish from the earth."

But a few minutes were necessary for the address, yet, never before had words so wrought upon the feelings of an audience. The devotion and self-forgetfulness of the simple man before them, himself the central figure of the scene, as he was the inspiration of the whole people, affected them as the words of the polished orator had not.

As Mr. Lincoln finished amid the tears and sobs and cheers of the audience, he turned to Mr. Everett and, grasping him by the hand, warmly congratulated him upon his oration, seemingly unconscious that he had himself said anything worthy of note. " Ah, Mr. President," said Mr. Everett, " how gladly would I exchange all my hundred pages to have been the author of your twenty lines !" Though short, the address ranks as one of the greatest American classics, and as such it is recognized both at home and abroad. The Westminster *Review* said of it :

" It has but one equal, in that pronounced upon those who fell in the first year of the Peloponnesian war, and in one respect it is superior to that great speech. It is not only more natural, fuller of feeling, more touching and pathetic, but we know with absolute certainty that it was really delivered. Nature here takes precedence of art—even though it be the art of Thucydides."

A great meeting of all Union men in Illinois was

called to assemble at the State Capitol, September 3, 1863, for the purpose of strengthening the Union sentiment and upholding the hands of the administration. The movement was timely and grateful to the President. It seems almost incomprehensible that many of his worst enemies should have been found in the ranks of his professed friends, yet such was the case. Open opposition and honest criticism every public official must expect, but he has a right to the earnest, unreserved support of those who have raised him to the position of responsibility which he may occupy, just so long as he shall honorably fulfill the duties of that office to the best of his ability. Even though he shall prove himself unfitted naturally for the position, a lack of support will only aggravate the difficulty of the situation. What then shall be said of numerous influential men, who assisted to raise Mr. Lincoln to the Presidency and then afterwards, because of differences of opinion, deliberately sought to break down his influence and prejudice the people against him.

The opposition of such men as Horace Greeley, whose patriotism and honesty of purpose were undoubted, though captious and annoying, could be forgiven. But there were multitudes of men, more or less influential, who never lost an opportunity to assail him and his policy, by open attack or secret innuendo; they were scattered throughout the country and were found even in the halls of Congress, where opposition might be made especially embarrassing to the President. As the Hon. A. G. Riddle, of Ohio, once aptly said in a speech :

" The outspoken comments here and elsewhere have

at least the merit of boldness ; but what shall be said of that muttering, unmanly, yet swelling undercurrent of complaining criticism, that reflects upon the President, his motives and capacity, so freely indulged in by men having the public confidence? Whisperings and complainings and doubtings and misgivings and exclamations, predictions by men who are never so happy as when they can gloat over the sum of our disasters, which they charge over to the personal account of the President."

In the midst of such opposition it was more than pleasant for the President to receive assurances of confidence and hearty support from the people of his own State by whom he was best known. Two years and a half had passed since he had left Illinois. During that time his neighbors had eagerly watched his career and observed with surprise the ability he displayed in coping with the adverse circumstances that were constantly closing around him. It was with constant astonishment that they watched the development of the greatness of his character. Nowhere had he more ardent supporters tnan among these, his old time friends. On the other hand he delighted in the revival of old memories and always greeted with hearty cordialty any of his Illinois friends. He earnestly desired their approval and rejoiced when he received evidences of it.

He was deeply disappointed that his duties in Washington would not permit him to be present at the September meeting and sent a long letter in which he gave his neighbors and friends a simple, frank and complete exposition of his principles, showing that he both desired and merited their confi-

dence. In the course of the letter he said : "There
are those who are dissatisfied with me. To such I
would say : You desire peace, and you blame me that
we do not have it. But how can we attain it ? There
are but three conceivable ways : First—to suppress
the rebellion by force of arms. This I am trying to
do. Are you for it ? If you are, so far we are agreed.
If you are not for it, a second way is to give up the
Union. I am against this. Are you for it ? If you
are, you should say so plainly. If you are not for
force nor yet for dissolution, there only remains some
imaginable compromise. I do not believe that any
compromise, embracing the maintenance of the
Union, is now possible. All that I learn leads to a
directly opposite belief. The strength of the rebellion, is its military, its army. That army dominates
all the country and all the people within its range.
Any offer of terms made by any man or men within
that range, in opposition to that army, is simply
nothing for the present, because such man or men
have no power whatever to enforce their side of the
compromise, if one were made with them. . . .
You dislike the emancipation proclamation, and perhaps would have it retracted. You say it is unconstitutional. I think differently. I think the Constitution invests its Commander-in-Chief with the law
of war in time of war. The most that can be said, if
so much, is, that slaves are property. Is there, has
there ever been, any question that by the law of war,
property, both of enemies and friends, may be taken
when needed ? And is it not needed whenever it
helps us and hurts the enemy ? Armies, the world
over, destroy enemies' property when they cannot

use it ; and even destroy their own to keep it from the enemy. Civilized belligerents do all in their power to help themselves or to hurt the enemy, except a few things regarded as barbarous or cruel. Among the exceptions are the massacre of vanquished foes and non-combatants, male and female. . . . The signs look better. The 'Father of Waters' again goes unvexed to the sea. Thanks to the great Northwest for it ; nor yet wholly to them. Three hundred miles up they met New England, Empire, Keystone and Jersey, hemming their way right and left. The sunny South, too, in more colors than one, also lent a helping hand. On the spot their part of the history was jotted down in black and white. The job was a great national one and let none be slighted who bore an honorable part in it. . . . Peace does not appear so distant as it did. I hope it will come soon and come to stay ; and so come as to be worth the keeping in all future time. It will then have been proved that among freemen there can be no successful appeal from the ballot to the bullet, and that they who take such appeal are sure to lose their cause and pay the cost. And there will be some black men, who can remember that with silent tongue, and clinched teeth and steady eye and well-poised bayonet, they have helped mankind on to this great consummation, while I fear there will be some white ones unable to forget that, with malignant heart and deceitful speech they have striven to hinder it. Still let us not be over-sanguine of a speedy, final triumph. Let us be quite sober. Let us diligently apply the means, never doubting that a just God, in His own good time, will give us a rightful result."

The letter was enthusiastically received and heartily indorsed. Its hopeful spirit was infectious; its calm logic was convincing, and the Illinois Convention sent back its congratulations and its prayers for the success of the cause. Not alone on the broad prairies of Illinois was this letter read, but from east to west it went, with its cheering message, and everywhere was confidence in the final outcome renewed, and a more cheerful view taken of existing circumstances. Still more was this feeling fostered and strengthened by the Thanksgiving proclamation of October 3.

As time passes on the words of Lincoln are assuming more and more significance and are perused with an increasing interest. Many writers conceal their personality and give no single glimpse of it in their works. This is necessarily not the case with Lincoln. For while he has left behind a great many works of literary merit, he did not distinctly enter the field of literature. The occasions that called forth his productions and the productions themselves were of such a character as to call out more or less of his opinions and personality. While his autobiography was never written, his published works afford a better ground for character-study than the story of his life otherwise. In view of this fact no biography is complete which does not contain copious selections from his own words. His October proclamation contains many noteworthy sentiments, a few of which are quoted below :

" The year that is drawing towards its close has been filled with the blessings of fruitful fields and healthful skies. To these bounties, which are so constantly enjoyed that we are prone to forget the source from which they come, others have been added which are of so extraordinary a nature that they cannot fail to penetrate and soften even the heart which is habitually insensible to the ever-watchful providence of Almighty God. In the midst of a civil war of unequalled magnitude and severity, which has sometimes seemed to invite and provoke the aggression of foreign States, peace has been preserved with all nations, order has been maintained, the laws have been respected and obeyed, and harmony has everywhere prevailed, except in the theatre of military conflict, while that theatre has been constantly contracted by the advancing armies and navies of the United States. . . . Population has steadily increased notwithstanding the waste that has been made in the camp, the siege and the battlefield ; and the country, rejoicing in the consciousness of augmented strength and vigor, is permitted to expect a continuance of years with a large increase of freedom. No human counsel hath devised, nor hath any mortal hand worked out these great things. They are the gracious gifts of the most high God, who, while dealing with us in anger for our sins, hath nevertheless remembered mercy. It has seemed to me fit and proper that they should be solemnly, reverently and gratefully acknowledged, as with one heart and voice, by the whole American people."

The President had awaited anxiously the Fall elections of 1863, for their result would proclaim the popular verdict upon his policy. The general drift of public opinion could be readily discerned in the larger places, but the pulse of the great agricultural districts could not be so readily felt, hence the party leaders awaited the result with much anxiety. The news was more than reassuring and showed that the nation reposed abiding confidence in its rulers and their ability. Every State gave large majorities for the Republican tickets, except New Jersey. In Ohio the notorious Vallandigham was the Democratic candidate for Governor and was defeated by over one hundred thousand majority. When the news was announced to Lincoln he telegraphed back the words: "Glory to God in the highest! Ohio has saved the Nation."

The name of Lincoln is inseparably connected with the abolition of American slavery. While, owing to the stress of circumstances, he had issued the proclamation of emancipation, it was contrary to his often-expressed belief as to the best method of dealing with the evil. As a war measure the proclamation was a success, but could not be permanent and complete in its results. Until it should become a part of the fundamental law of the land the doom of American slavery would not be sealed. The only way to accomplish this was by securing a constitutional amendment. On February 10, 1864, Senator Trumbull, the old-time political friend of Mr. Lincoln, introduced into the Senate what was destined to be known as the Thirteenth Amendment, as follows:

"ARTICLE XIII, Section 1.—Neither slavery nor involuntary servitude, except as a punishment for crime, whereof the parties shall have been duly convicted, shall exist within the United States or any place subject to their jurisdiction.

"Section 2.—Congress shall have power to enforce this article by appropriate legislation."

The question was long and ably discussed and finally passed the Senate, April 8, 1864, by a vote of 38 to 6. In the House the hostility to the bill was pronounced and uncompromising. For nearly three months the battle was waged and finally lost as the vote did not show a necessary two-thirds majority. Lincoln was disappointed at the result and feared that the cause of freedom had received a serious setback. In his annual message, December 5, 1864, he declared himself to be uncompromisingly in favor of the bill, and urged that Congress take immediate and favorable action upon it. He closed by saying that whatever should be the action of Congress, he would not retract or nullify the emancipation proclamation, nor would he retire from his position on the subject. If the people desired to return the former slaves to servitude he would not be the instrument to do it. He did not content himself with simply urging this matter in his message, but he personally sought to induce the opponents of the measure to change their votes. He was entirely committed to the measure and determined to use his whole influence to secure its adoption, and this time he was not disappointed. January 13, the bill passed by more than the requisite majority, and the amendment was now ready to be presented to the States for their ratification or rejection. The feelings of Lincoln can hardly be appreciated. At last the crowning achievement of his life was to be perpetuated in the organic laws of the Nation, which was destined once more, as the fruit of his labors, to be united and harmonious. Well might he say:

"The great job is ended. The occasion is one of congratulation, and I cannot but congratulate all present, myself, the country and the whole world upon this great moral victory."

The work thus begun he never saw completed. On December 18, 1865, Secretary Seward made proclamation that the Thirteenth Amendment had been ratified by the requisite number of States, and hence had become a part of the organic law. Thus was the great revolution, begun with bullet and blood, irrevocably settled and established by the ballot. But its illustrious leader, the "defender of the Constitution," never lived to see the result. Already the shadow was approaching and wrapping the doomed President in its folds. His work was nearly done ; a few more victories and defeats; a few more anxieties and wearying cares, and then the triumph. His work had been well done, and the results were substantial and permanent.

From the time when he had been brought first into contact with the horrors of the system, in New Orleans, to the time when the last blow had been struck and its doom sounded, he had been more or less active in opposition to it. Not with the opposition of the fanatic, who would achieve his ends at any sacrifice of justice and happiness, but rather with the feelings of a patriot who recognized the enormity of the evil, but would suppress it by just and lawful measures. He had not plunged into the struggle suddenly, without preparation, but was rather led gradually up to it by the irresistible logic of events which, all unseen and unrecognized, was gradually fitting him for, and advancing him to the great career which was destined to place his name among the few great liberators of earth.

It is said that the President of the United States can have no domestic life; that he is so constantly and prominently in public, that the opportunities for privacy and retirement with his family, which the ordinary citizen enjoys, are entirely lacking for him. Nor is this to any large extent untrue of Lincoln. Even before he became President he was so constantly engaged in business that occupied him away from home, that his homelife was limited and unsatisfying. No doubt this was increased by a certain lack of congenialty and harmony of tastes. In his family he was always kind and forbearing, patient with his children, almost to the verge of indulgence. He knew nothing about severe discipline and could never bear to see his children punished. He loved them with all the strength of his great heart, and when one of them, William Wallace, died in the White House, he could hardly be comforted. During the latter years of the war, Robert was away at college, leaving only Thomas, or " Tad," as he was universally called, at home. He was a general favorite everywhere, and free to go and come as he pleased. His father was never too busy to welcome him, nor too tired and weary to enjoy his companionship. They frequently took long walks together, and more than once Tad accompanied his father while reviewing troops, and the boy was generally received with as much enthusiasm as his father. He even had free entrance into the Cabinet meetings which he more than once interrupted with some tale of childish woe.

Mr. Lincoln was possessed of a wonderfully reten-

tive memory. If he liked anything, after once reading or hearing it, "it just seemed to stick." He
delighted especially in poetry, and could repeat
poems, that struck his fancy, after once hearing them.
Shakespeare was his especial favorite. Early in the
war, in company with a number of Cabinet officers
he visited Fortress Monroe, and, on his way down the
river, he sat for hours repeating from memory the
finest passages of Shakespeare's works, page after
page of Browning and whole cantos of Byron, to the
intense surprise of his auditors. He was not a Latin
scholar and was not ashamed to acknowledge his
ignorance and he once stated that he had never read
an entire novel in his life.

As the duties of his position began to weigh more
heavily upon him and his trials and perplexities continued to increase, he came more and more to look to
Divine Providence for aid and strength. Feeling the
insufficiency of his own powers, and noting the
perils which assailed the nation on every side, he
early recognized the fact that there was no help in
man, that God alone could rescue the nation by his
providence. He not only possessed the true spirit of
religion, but so far as possible he observed its requirements and ordinances. The following proclamation
in regard to the observance of the Sabbath by the
army well illustrates this point.

" The President, Commander-in-Chief of the Army
and Navy, desires and enjoins the orderly observance
of the Sabbath by the officers and men in the military
and naval service. The importance to man and beast
of the prescribed weekly rest, the sacred rights
of Christian soldiers and sailors, a becoming defer-

ence to the best sentiment of Christian people, and a due regard for the Divine Will, demand that Sunday labor in the army and navy be reduced to the measure of strict necessity. The discipline and character of the national forces should not suffer, nor the cause they defend be imperiled by the profanation of the day or name of the Most High. 'At the time of public distress,' adopting the words of Washington in 1776, 'men may find enough to do in the service of their God and their country, without abandoning themselves to vice and immorality.' The first general order ever issued by the 'Father of his Country,' after the Declaration of Independence, indicates the spirit in which our institutions were founded and should ever be defended : 'the General hopes and trusts that every officer and man will endeavor to live and act as becomes a Christian soldier defending the dearest rights and liberties of his country.'"

CHAPTER XX.

THE approach of the national elections in the autumn of 1864 was viewed with grave apprehensions by patriotic men generally. The heated campaigns incident upon a general election always have a depressing effect upon trade and in many localities, especially where the opposing parties are of nearly equal strength, a spirit of rivalry and jealousy is engendered that sometimes leads to serious results. It is a trying ordeal for a country to pass through even when everything is in a normal condition. How much more trying, then, when in the midst of civil war, when business is interfered with, resources taxed to the uttermost and evil passions and distrust excited, in a struggle with a captious minority which was bitterly hostile to an administration whose every energy was engaged in the prosecution of the greatest war of the century. Every one realized that the coming election would be the severest test to which republican institutions had ever been subjected. Could they stand the test? Patriotic citizens hoped for the best but feared the worst, hence, as the season approached, a feeling of gloomy apprehension overspread the North and infected many of the leaders with a fear approaching a panic.

Meantime he, who was personally most interested

in the outcome of the election, seemed to be the least concerned in regard to its dangers. This was not because he was insensible to them but because he had an abiding faith in Providence and the American people and he believed that their better sense and the strength of the Constitution would triumph over all dangers. While he was anxious for a re-election and would have been deeply wounded if he had failed to receive it, he yet was ready to surrender his claims whenever the welfare of the country seemed to demand it. He desired a re-election both as showing the approval of his past actions by the people and to give him the opportunity of completing the arduous labors which had occupied his attention during his first term. He said to a friend, in speaking on the subject, before the Baltimore Convention, that [1] "he was not quite sure whether he desired a renomination. Such had been the responsibilities of the office—so oppressive had he found its cares, so terrible its perplexities—that he felt as though the moment, when he could relinquish the burden and retire to private life, would be the sweetest he could possibly experience. But, he said, he would not deny that a re-election would also have its gratification to his feelings. He did not seek it, nor would he do so ; he did not desire it for any ambitious or selfish purpose, but after the crisis the country was passing through under his Presidency, and the efforts he had made conscientiously to discharge the duties imposed upon him, it would be a very sweet satisfaction to him to know that he had secured the approval of his fellow-citi-

---

[1] Browne.

zens, and earned the highest testimonial of confidence they could bestow."

There was a strong opposition to his candidacy manifesting itself within the party. This opposition, which amounted almost to hostility, centred in Horace Greeley and his paper, the New York *Tribune*. This paper circulated widely through the rural districts and probably was more influential than any other paper published in America. Mr. Greeley believed that the war was being unnecessarily prolonged and that blood and treasure were being needlessly expended. He appealed again and again to the President, beseeching him to make peace by compromise or concession, anything to put an end to the war, which was exhausting the " poor, suffering, distracted country." Had his counsel been heeded the war would have been stopped on the verge of its triumphant issue ; the country would have been divided and all the fruits of the terrible struggle would have been lost. But the *Tribune* went on its daily and weekly mission sowing the seeds of distrust and apprehension and doing much to enhance the difficulty of the situation. Mr. Greeley, however, was not the only prominent party-leader to withdraw his confidence and support from the President. The seeds of disaffection were sown in his very Cabinet. Mr. Chase, the Secretary of the Treasury, had long been ambitious to be Mr. Lincoln's successor. He had administered the affairs of the Treasury with signal ability. As a financier he had shown himself incomparable. Not Necker nor Calonne found greater problems to deal with than did Chase, and the European bankers met with failure where the American minister triumphed over the entangled and almost hopeless state of affairs with which he was compelled to cope. Not only had he rendered distinguished services in the Treasury Department, but he was recognized as the most stalwart champion of the Abolition party. Severe and uncompromising, he hated with righteous hatred both slavery and the slaveholder, both sin and the sinner. Moreover, his character was far more self-centred than that of the President, leading him to do full credit to his own transcendent abilities and in some instances to disparage those of his rivals. He had early conceived the idea of becoming a candidate, in opposition to Mr. Lincoln, for the Republican nomination, and he used all the tremendous influence of his great office to further his ambition. His self-aggrandizing efforts early came to the notice of Mr. Lincoln, but he magnanimously refused to take notice of them, preferring to leave the whole matter to the decision of the people and even went so far as to assure Mr. Chase that he need fear no opposition from him, if he (Chase) should prove to be the choice of the party. But his candidacy was as short-lived as it was inauspicious. He soon perceived that the tide of popular opinion was setting strong towards Mr. Lincoln and he acquiesced as gracefully as possible in the situation. He exhibited such a spirit, however, towards the President that his resignation was asked for and accepted. Senator Fessenden was appointed to take his place. Shortly afterwards Mr. Lincoln happened to meet Mr. Chase, and upon an inquiry by the future Chief Justice as to how matters looked generally, Mr. Lincoln quietly remarked :

"Oh, pretty well! pretty well! The only thing is that I've had a litte trouble about the Cabinet, but it's all happily settled now, I'm glad to say."

"Why, how is that, Mr. President?" queried Chase, in earnest and sympathetic tones; "I'm sure it could not have been anything very serious."

"No, not at all, not at all!" cried the President, in his cheery way. "You see," he continued, dropping his voice a little, and with a merry twinkle in his eye, "although I am by no means an extremist myself, still I have always been devoured by an overmastering anxiety regarding the religious tenets and profession of faith held by the various members of my official family. Now, Fessenden is quite a recent addition to the Cabinet and I have been a little undecided where to place him, in a religious point of view."

"Well, Mr. President," timidly ventured Chase, "I'm glad you satisfied yourself upon such an important point."

"Oh, yes!" responded Lincoln. "I haven't the slightest doubt upon the subject now. You see Fessenden is a pretty evenly-balanced man, but once in a while he gets real, hoppin' mad, and then he swears so all-fired hard, just like Seward, that I know, sure as faith, that he's an Episcopalian."

In 1864 Chief-Justice Taney died, the man whose decision in the "Dred Scott" case had done so much to precipitate the rebellion and who had lived to see his decision nullified by force of arms and the institution which he had done so much to foster abrogated and destroyed. After a short delay Mr. Lincoln appointed Mr. Chase to the position overlooking all the criticism and animadversion to which Mr.

Chase had subjected him with a rare forbearance and magnanimity.

The National Republican Convention had been called to meet at Baltimore, June 8, 1864. May 31, a convention met at Cleveland, made up of disappointed politicians and a few visionary spirits who had from the first arrayed themselves with General Fremont against the administration. Many of the prominent men, who had been expected, failed to attend and the proceedings were characterized by neither dignity nor fairness. The movement very soon "petered out," to use Mr. Lincoln's phrase, and the only vestige of the convention that survived the early summer was the candidacy of General Fremont. He had been nominated as Lincoln's successor and had accepted in a letter in which he severely attacked Mr. Lincoln's course, alleging incompetency and a needless disregard of the rights and privileges of American citizens. The nomination was received with so much apathy that General Fremont finally withdrew his name but seized the opportunity to renew his denunciations of Mr. Lincoln. He said :

"I consider that his administration has been politically, militarily and financially a failure and that its necessary continuance is a cause of regret to the country." The attitude of General Fremont was one to be deplored, not because of any material influence it might exert upon the country, but because he was one of the founders of the Republican party, its first nominee for President, and because his name was held in highest esteem and veneration by those who had grown old in the struggle against slavery.

The Republican Convention met at Baltimore,

June, 1864. It was a foregone conclusion that Mr.
Lincoln would be the nominee of the Convention.
Nothing could influence popular opinion against him.
The masses of the people were more than satisfied
with his conduct of the war, indeed they regarded
him much as the Israelites did Moses, and believed
that the interests of the country were safer in his
hands than in those of any one else. The intrigues of
politicians and the open and covert attacks that were
made upon him had no appreciable effect. The
Convention did little beyond reiterating the fundamental principles of the party. They cordially indorsed the administration and then quickly made the
nominations. The platform in brief pledged the
party to aid the Government unreservedly in quelling
the rebellion ; approved the acts of the administration in regard to slavery and its refusal to enter
into any compromise ; returned thanks to the soldiers
and sailors who were so nobly fighting to preserve
the Union; and especially deprecated any interference
by European powers in American affairs. The nomination of Mr. Lincoln was made unanimously, except
that Missouri, at first, cast her twenty votes for Grant.
Andrew Johnson, of Tennessee, a pronounced Union
man, who had rendered valuable service to the national
cause in a State where a severe contest had been
carried on between rebels and patriots, and whose
retention in the Union was largely due to his efforts,
was nominated for Vice-President. Though the
nomination afterwards proved an unfortunate one, at
the time it seemed a graceful recognition of faithful
service on the part of a true patriot and an able man.
Washington was so near Baltimore that a com-

mittee waited upon the President the same day the nominations were made and presented him with a copy of the platform and officially notified him of the action of the Convention. He spoke to them as follows:

"Having served four years in the depths of a great and yet unended national peril, I can view this call to a second term in nowise more flattering to myself than as an expression of the public judgment that I may better finish a difficult work, in which I have labored from the first, than could any one less severely schooled to the task. In this view and with assured reliance on that Almighty Ruler who has so graciously sustained us thus far, and with increased gratitude to the generous people for their continued confidence, I accept the renewed trust, with its yet onerous and perplexing duties and responsibilities."

His letter of acceptance, written June 27, was brief, expressing his concurrence in the resolutions passed by the Convention and its platform, and gratefully accepting the nomination. He said:

"I am especially gratified that the soldier and the sailor were not forgotten by the Convention, as they forever must and will be remembered by the grateful country, for whose salvation they devote their lives."

The Democratic Convention had been called for August 29, in the hope that in the interval the events of the war might be of such a character as to prepare the people to accept a peace policy and thus they would be able to create a distinct issue. Nor was the situation without elements of encouragement to the opposition. The political situation, in the intervening months, had taken on grave aspects. Congress,

just before its adjournment, had prepared and passed
an elaborate plan for reconstruction, but the President
had failed to sign it, giving the reasons for his disapproval in a proclamation soon after issued, in
which he presented the plan to the public and offered
executive support to any rebel State which should
decide to adopt it, but declining to commit himself
and the Government to any one method of reconstruction, especially if that plan should require the undo-
ing of the work which had been done in the already
partially reconstructed States. His course was
severely criticised and two of the most prominent
Republican members of Congress, Messrs. Wade and
Davis, issued a manifesto, which was printed in the
New York *Tribune* and which contained a most bitter
and uncalled for attack upon the President's motives
and course. Another thing which militated against
Mr. Lincoln was the outcome of a proposed peace
conference to be held between representatives of the
Confederate Government and of the President. It
was undertaken at the earnest solicitation of Mr.
Greeley. The circumstances turned out to be not as
represented and the Conference was broken off.
Mr. Lincoln's course in regard to it was consistent
and dignified, but being misunderstood gave another
weapon to his enemies to be wielded against him.
It is very evident now that the South was not ready
to accept peace upon the only terms upon which it
could be offered and that the President could not
have entered into negotiations without stultifying
himself.

The approaching Democratic Convention was
anticipated with apprehension by the Republicans.

It is true that the Democrats were numerically in the minority, but there was not only a discontented element in the Republican party, but also many who had become tired of the war and who would be glad to purchase peace at almost any price. How large this element was no one could tell, but its very existence was cause for alarm. When the Convention assembled Mr. Vallandigham, of Ohio, appeared as one of its leading spirits and, was himself, the author of the platform. The Convention was especially emphatic in its condemnation of the President and his policy, and demanded the cessation of the war. Mr. August Belmont, in opening the Convention said :

"Four years of misrule by a sectional, fanatical and corrupt party have brought our country to the very verge of ruin. The past and present are sufficient warnings of the disastrous consequences which would befall us if Mr. Lincoln's re-election should be made possible by our lack of patriotism and unity. The inevitable results of such a calamity must be the utter disintegration of our whole political and social system amid bloodshed and anarchy, with the great problems of liberal progress and self-government jeopardized for generations to come."

These words formed the keynote of the Convention and of the platform and upon the issue thus made the campaign was to be fought. After a long discussion General McClellan, a war Democrat, was nominated for President and George H. Pendleton, a consistent member of the peace-party, was nominated for the Vice-Presidency. The promulgation of the peace platform was followed by a storm of popular indignation, which in many cases branded those who had taken part in the Convention as cowards and traitors. A large part of the Democracy disapproved of the policy and General McClellan hastened to repudiate it in his letter of acceptance.

While the Convention was in session the clouds had already begun to lift from the political and military horizon, and every occurrence tended to strengthen Mr. Lincoln's position. The persistent campaign which General Grant had been pursuing around Richmond began to break the spirit of the rebels and lessen the power of their resistance. Already the end could be seen in the near future. Appomattox was foreshadowed and that at no distant day. Four days after the Democratic party had declared that the war was a dismal failure and had demanded peace at any price, President Lincoln issued a proclamation of Thanksgiving for the Union victories. Irresistibly the tide of victory swept on, each success proving a potent campaign speech, each advance increasing the majority for the administration. Mr. Lincoln said in regard to the prospects: "With reverses in the field the case is doubtful at the polls. With victory in the field the election will take care of itself."

The majority was strong and decisive. Indeed, Mr. Lincoln lacked but little of being unanimously elected, his competitor securing but three out of the twenty-two States voting. The victory in the nation was the most complete ever achieved in an election so hotly contested. It could no longer be said that Mr. Lincoln was a sectional President, for four Southern States had given him their electoral votes. He

would have been less than human if he had not
been gratified with this result.   Yet his rejoicing was
utterly free from the taint of a selfish ambition or of
personal triumph.   He said to a number of gentlemen
who had called to congratulate him upon the result :

"I am thankful to God for this approval of the
people.   But while deeply grateful for this mark of
their confidence in me, if I know my heart, my gratitude is free from any taint of personal triumph.   I
do not impugn the motives of any one opposed to
me.   It is no pleasure to me to triumph over any
one ; but I give thanks to the Almighty for this evidence of the people's resolution to stand by free government and the rights of humanity."

He subsequently said : "It has demonstrated that
a people's government can sustain a national election
in the midst of a great civil war.   Until now it has
not been known to the world that this was a possibility.   It shows also how strong and sound we still
are. . . . Being only mortal, after all, I should have
been a little mortified if I had been beaten in this
canvass before the people ; but that sting would have
been more than compensated by the thought that
the people had notified me that all my official responsibilities were soon to be lifted off my back."

Mr. Lincoln's re-election took away the last hope
of the Confederacy.   There was to be no change in
policy or in leaders.   The war was to be pushed just
as persistently and uncompromisingly as before.   No
ill-judged mercy would be extended to rebels in arms,
and peace could only be hoped for when all armed
opposition to the Government should cease.   The
prospects still continued to brighten and when Con-

gress assembled the President greeted it with a hopeful and encouraging message. He reviewed the situation and showed the substantial results attendant upon the year's campaigns, speaking of General Sherman's march to the sea, which was then in progress, as the most remarkable feature of the military operations for the year. The message was, however, mainly concerned with arguments in favor of the passage of the Thirteenth Amendment.

The winter's work was eminently satisfactory, both in the field and in Congress. Although the fall of the Confederacy was imminent, no precaution was neglected, no preparation omitted, which looked towards the completion of the war. When the day of Mr. Lincoln's second inauguration dawned, General Sherman had captured Savannah and was marching northward ; General Grant was slowly but surely approaching Richmond and directing the operations of his magnificent army, with the almost certain assurance of success. The military power of the Confederacy had been destroyed in the West and Southwest and the field of operations was rapidly narrowing down to the territory of Virginia.

The day was indeed an auspicious one and it was joyously saluted by the people of the nation which was now on the verge of a peaceful union. The contrast between this day and the one four years before, when Mr. Lincoln had stood before the people of the country, untried and distrusted, was most remarkable. Then the gulf of civil war yawned before him, the partially fulfilled threat of a divided sovereignty. He stood anxiously, almost timidly, in the presence of a future dark and uncertain. He had sought to

console and reassure the people and to heal the
breach if possible. Earnestly, almost plaintively, he
had pleaded with the discontented spirits to pause
and reflect before taking action and urged upon them
his own friendliness and the absence of any intention
to inflict upon them the evils which they foreboded.
Now—the tempest of civil war had nearly spent its
power, the clouds were dispersing and the sun of
peace was breaking through the gloom to shed his
joyful rays upon a country shattered and bleeding,
but saved. The triumph was not far off and surely
the President would find cause for gratulation and
glorying. But not so. His address was pitched in a
minor key. He indulged in no boastings of victories
won or predictions of coming triumph. His memory
was too active with the terrible scenes of the past four
years. He saw the laurel crown but dimly through
the tears flowing for the dead. His eyes were turned,
not to the future, but to the battlefields of the past.
He saw the wounded and the dying, the "Stars and
Stripes" tattered and bullet-riven, stained with the
life-blood of its gallant defenders. And may it not
have been that his prophetic eye discerned dimly the
shadow into which he had already entered, the crowning catastrophe, the last sacrifice, and the greatest,
upon the country's altar?

Heroic figure! Standing there in all the majesty of
thy greatness! Great, because self has been lost in
others good! Sublime, indeed, was the picture, with
the glorious achievements of the past in the background, and the central person of them all standing,
unconscious, face to face with death! Where can history show the counterpart?

The morning of March 4 was stormy, but towards noon the rain ceased, the clouds rolled away and the sun shone brightly. Vast crowds had gathered to witness the inaugural ceremonies. Congress, as usual, adjourned at noon, but the Senate was called to meet in special session, at which Hon. Andrew Johnson appeared, took the oath of office and became its presiding officer. The Senate-chamber was filled with a brilliant and distinguished assembly, in the midst of which were seen many an uniform whose wearer had become distinguished during the last four years.

Mr. Lincoln was accompanied by the Judges of the Supreme Court, in their judicial robes, many representatives of the Diplomatic Corps, in their national costumes, and a large number of military and naval officers, resplendent in their glittering uniforms. As he stepped upon the platform the air was filled with cheers and acclamations, which did not cease until he waved his hand in the air to indicate that he was ready to speak. The crowd, which had gathered in front of the Capitol, was vast, extending far beyond the reach of Mr. Lincoln's voice, but enthusiastic and contented if their eyes could but rest upon his form. The most touching and suggestive feature of the crowd was the large number of maimed and crippled soldiers, whose eager attention and hearty applause were but faintly indicative of their devotion to their illustrious chief. The simple oath of office was administered by Chief Justice Chase, after which, in a clear but melancholy voice, Mr. Lincoln read his second inaugural as follows:

"Fellow-Countrymen:—At this second appearing to take the oath of the Presidential office, there is less

occasion for an extended address than there was at
the first. Then, a statement somewhat in detail of a
course to be pursued, seemed very fitting and proper.
Now, at the expiration of four years, during which
public declarations have been constantly called forth
on every point and phase of the great contest, which
still absorbs the attention and engrosses the energies
of the Nation, little that is new could be presented.
The progress of our arms, upon which all else chiefly
depends, is as well known to the public as to myself,
and it is, I trust, reasonably satisfactory and encouraging to all. With high hope for the future, no
prediction in regard to it is ventured.

"On the occasion corresponding with this, four
years ago, all thoughts were anxiously directed to an
impending civil war. All dreaded it, all sought to
avoid it. While the inaugural address was being delivered from this place, devoted altogether to saving
the Union without war, insurgent agents were in the
city, seeking to destroy it with war—seeking to dis-
solve the Union, and divide the effects by negotia-
tion. Both parties deprecated war, but one of them
would make war rather than let the Nation survive,
and the other would accept war rather than let it
perish; and the war came. One-eighth of the whole
population were colored slaves, not distributed generally over the Union, but localized in the southern
part of it. These slaves constituted a peculiar and
powerful interest. All knew that this interest was
somehow the cause of the war. To strengthen, perpetuate and extend this interest, was the object for
which the insurgents would rend the Union by
war. While the Government claimed no right to

do more than to restrict the territorial enlargement of it.

"Neither party expected for the war the magnitude or the duration which it has already attained. Neither anticipated that the cause of the conflict might cease with, or even before the conflict itself should cease. Each looked for an easier triumph, and a result less fundamental and astounding.

"Both read the same Bible, and pray to the same God, and each invokes His aid against the other. It may seem strange that any men should dare to ask a just God's assistance in wringing the bread from the sweat of other men's faces. But let us judge not, that we be not judged. The prayer of both could not be answered. That of neither has been answered fully. The Almighty has His own purposes. 'Woe unto the world because of offenses, for it must needs be that offenses come, but woe to that man by whom the offense cometh.' If we shall suppose that American slavery is one of these offenses, which, in the Providence of God, must needs come, but which, having continued through His appointed time, He now wills to remove, and that He gives to both North and South this terrible war as the woe due to those by whom the offense came, shall we discern there any departure from those divine attributes which the believers in a living God always ascribe to Him? Fondly do we hope, fervently do we pray, that this mighty scourge of war may speedily pass away. Yet, if God wills that it continue until all the wealth piled by the bondsman's two hundred and fifty years of unrequited toil shall be sunk, and until every drop of blood drawn with the lash shall be paid by another drawn by the sword, as was said three thousand years ago, so still it must be said, that 'the judgments of the Lord are true and righteous altogether.'

"With malice towards none, with charity for all, with firmness in the right, as God gives us to see the right, let us finish the work we are in, to bind up the Nation's wounds, to care for him who shall have borne the battle, and for his widow and his orphans, to do all which may achieve and cherish a just and a lasting peace among ourselves and with all nations."

Never had more impressive words been uttered by a nation's ruler. Did his character need aught to prove his greatness, this address would fully establish the claim.

As the procession moved from the Capitol to the White House a star was observed to be shining with a brilliancy which made it visible, even in the midst of the sunlight, and it was joyously hailed as a harbinger of brighter times; like that other star whose appearance was the heralding of "peace on earth, good-will to men."

CHAPTER XXI.

In the latter part of March, it became apparent that Richmond could not hold out much longer, and, as Mr. Lincoln had always been desirous of visiting the army while engaged in the work of actual warfare, he made arrangements to spend several days with General Grant at City Point.

He was much interested in the details of the siege, and would sit and watch the soldiers for hours. He did not wish to interfere with the military movements in any way, and hence took pains not to inquire into the plans of the campaign. It was here that the famous conference occurred between Generals Grant and Sherman and Admiral Porter, at which the President was present, and which was subsequently made the subject of a notable painting by Healy, now in the possession of the Calumet Club of Chicago. The object of the conference was to perfect the details of the closing campaign, in order that the army and navy might work harmoniously together. Mr. Lincoln was much interested in the discussion and, when the conversation turned upon the probability of another great battle being fought before the war could be ended, he asked more than once: "Must more blood be shed? Cannot this last bloody battle be avoided?"

April 3, Lee evacuated Richmond, and the city was taken possession of by the Union troops. Mr. Lincoln expressed a desire to visit the city, and in company with Admiral Porter and a file of marines succeeded in reaching it by water. The remarkable scenes that followed are thus graphically described by the admiral: [1]

"There was a small house on the landing, and behind it were some twelve negroes digging with spades. The leader of them was an old man, some sixty years of age. He raised himself to an upright position as we landed, and put his hands to his eyes. Then he dropped his spade, and sprang forward : 'Bress de Lord,' he said, 'dere is de great Messiah ! I knowed him as soon as I seed him. He's bin in my heart fo' long yeahs, an' he's come at las' to free his chillun from deir bondage ! Glory, Hallelujah !' And he fell upon his knees before the President, and kissed his feet. The others followed his example, and in a minute Mr. Lincoln was surrounded by these people who had treasured up the recollection of him caught from a photograph, and had looked up to him for four years as the one who was to lead them out of captivity. It was a touching sight—that aged negro, kneeling at the feet of the tall, gaunt-looking man, who seemed in himself to be bearing all the grief of the nation, and whose sad face seemed to say, 'I suffer for you all, but will do all I can to help you.' Mr. Lincoln looked down on the poor creatures at his feet; he was much embarrassed at his position. 'Don't kneel to me,' he said, 'that is not right. You

---

[1] Porter's Leading Incidents in the Civil War.

must kneel to God only, and thank Him for the liberty you will hereafter enjoy. I am but God's humble instrument; but you may rest assured that, as long as I live, no one shall put a shackle on your limbs, and you shall have all the rights which God has given to every other free citizen of this Republic.'

"It was a minute or two before I could get the negroes to rise and leave the President. The scene was so touching, I hated to disturb it, yet we could not stay there all day; we had to move on; so I requested the patriarch to withdraw from about the President, with his companions, and let us pass on. 'Yes, mars,' said the old man, 'but after bein' so many yeahs in de desert widout water, it's mighty pleasant to be lookin' at las' on our spring of life. 'Scuse us, sir; we means no disrespec' to Mars' Lincoln; we means all love an' gratitude.' And then, joining hands together in a ring, the regroes sang a hymn, with melodious and touching voices, only possessed by the negroes of the South. The President and all of us listened respectfully while the hymn was being sung. Four minutes, at most, had passed away since we first landed at a point where, as far as the eye could reach, the streets were entirely deserted; but now what a different scene appeared as that hymn went forth from the negroes' lips! The streets seemed to be suddenly alive with the colored race. They seemed to spring from the earth. They came tumbling and shouting from over the hills and from the waterside, where no one was seen as we had passed. The crowd immediately became very oppressive. We needed our marines to keep them off. I ordered twelve of the

boats' crew to fix bayonets to their rifles and sur-
round the President—all of which was quickly done;
but the crowd poured in so fearfully that I thought
we all stood a chance of being crushed to death.

"At length the President spoke. He could not move
for the mass of people—he had to do something.
'My poor friends,' he said, 'you are free—free as air.
You can cast off the name of slave and trample upon
it ; it will come to you no more. Liberty is your
birthright. God gave it to you as he gave it to others, and it is a sin that you have been deprived of it
for so many years. But you must try to deserve this
priceless boon. Let the world see that you merit it,
and are able to maintain it by your good works.
Don't let your joy carry you into excesses. Learn
the laws and obey them ; obey God's Commandments
and thank Him for giving you liberty, for to Him
you owe all things. There, now, let me pass on ; I
have but little time to spare. I want to see the Capitol, and must return at once to Washington to secure
to you that liberty which you seem to prize so
highly.'

"The crowd shouted and screeched as if they would
split the firmament, though while the President was
speaking you might have heard a pin drop."

As he proceeded through the streets, the windows
on either side were full of people who were curious
to see the "dreaded Lincoln." There was no
unfriendly manifestation and many of the citizens
gave him a cordial welcome. He passed through the
city, visiting several places of interest and especially
the deserted mansion of Mr. Davis, the President of
the now defunct Confederacy.

Admiral Porter, relates an incident occurring in this trip, which well illustrates Mr. Lincoln's feelings, towards the South and his intentions in regard to reconstruction. He says:

"In the strife between the North and South there was no bitterness in Mr. Lincoln's composition; he seemed to think only that he had an unpleasant duty to perform and endeavored to perform it as smoothly as possible. He would, without doubt, have yielded a good deal to the South, only that he kept his duty constantly before his eyes, and that was the compass by which he steered at all times. The results of a battle pained him as much as if he were receiving the wounds himself for I have often heard him express himself in pained accents over some of the scenes of the war. . . . I know that he was determined the Confederacy should have the most liberal terms. 'Get them to plowing once,' he said, 'and gathering in their own little crops, eating pop-corn at their own firesides, and you can't get them to shoulder a musket again for half a century. . . .

"One morning, at ten o'clock, Mr. John A. Campbell, late Justice of the Supreme Court of the United States, sent a request to be allowed to come aboard with General Weitzel. He wanted to call upon the President. He came on board, and spent an hour. The President and himself seemed to be enjoying themselves very much, to judge from their laughter.

"I did not go down into the cabin. In about an hour, General Weitzel and Mr. Campbell came on deck, asked for a boat, and were landed.

"I went down below for a moment, and the President said: 'Admiral, I am sorry you were not here

when Mr. Campbell was on board. He has gone on
shore happy. I have given him a written permission
to allow the State Legislature to convene at the
Capitol, in the absence of all other government!

"I was rather astonished at this piece of information. I felt that this course would bring about complications, and wondered how it had all come to
pass. . . .

"When the President told me all that had been
done, and that General Weitzel had gone on shore
with an order in his pocket to let the Legislature
meet, I merely said: 'Mr. President, I suppose you
remember that this city is under military jurisdiction,
and that no Courts, Legislature or Civil Authority
can exercise any power without the sanction of the
General commanding the Army. This order of yours
should go through General Grant, who would inform
you that Richmond was under martial law; and i am
sure he would protest against this arrangement with
Mr. Campbell.'

" The President's common sense took in the situation at once. 'Why,' he said, 'Weitzel made no
objection, and he commands here.'

"'That is because he is Mr. Campbell's particular
friend, and wished to gratify him.'

"'Run and stop them,' exclaimed the President,
'and get my order back! Well, I came near knock-
ing all the fat into the fire, didn't I?'

"To make things sure, I had an order written to
General Weitzel, and signed by the President, as fol-
lows: 'Return my permission to the Legislature of
Virginia to meet, and don't allow it to meet at all.'
There was an ambulance wagon at the landing and,

giving the order to an officer, I said to him: 'Jump into that wagon, and kill the horse if necessary, but catch the carriage which carried General Weitzel and Mr. Campbell, and deliver this order to the General.'

" The carriage was caught after it reached the city. The General and Mr. Campbell were surprised. The President's order was sent back, and they never returned to try and reverse the decision."

The same writer relates the following incident, which occurred a little later:

" He was one day discussing the generals of the war—what difficulties he had in making appointments, etc. He illustrated each case with a story. In speaking of one general, he said it reminded him of a friend of his, a blacksmith, he knew out in the West when he was a boatman.

" This old friend was celebrated for making good work, especially axes, which were in great demand at that day. No boatman had a complete outfit unless he had a good ax.

" 'One day,' he said to me, 'Lincoln, I have the finest piece of steel you ever saw; I got it on purpose to make an ax for you, and if you will sit down and tell me a good story, you shall have the ax when it is finished.'

" 'Go ahead,' I said, and I sat down to tell the story, while he made the ax.

" My friend, the blacksmith, first put on a huge piece of fresh coal, and blew it until it was at a proper heat—the coals glowing; he picked up the piece of steel, and locked at it affectionately, patted it all over, then, 'Lincoln,' he said, 'did you ever see a piece of steel equal to that ? It will make you

a companion you will never want to part with; and
when you are using it, you will think of me.' Then
he put it into the fire, and began to work his bellows,
while I began to tell my story.

"He blew and blew until the steel was at a deep
red heat, when, taking it out of the fire and laying
it on the anvil, he gave it a clip with a four-pound
hammer. Lord bless you, how the sparks flew, and
the big red scales also ! 'Lincoln,' he said, 'here's
a go, and a bad one too. This lump of steel ain't
worth the powder that would blow it up. I never
was so deceived in anything in all my life. It won't
make an ax. But I'll tell you what it will make. It
will make a clevis,' and he put it in the fire again,
and went through the same performance as before.
Then, when it was heated, he laid it upon the anvil,
and commenced to hammer it. The sparks flew, and
so did the scales, and in a minute half of it was
gone.

"The blacksmith stopped and scratched his head,
as men often do under difficulties. 'Well,' he said,
'this certainly is an onery piece of steel, but it may
get better nearer the heart of it. I can't make a
clevis out of it, but it will make a clevis-bolt. It may
have some good in it yet. After all, a good clevis-
bolt is not a bad thing.'

"He put it into the fire again, and this time got it
to a white heat. 'I think I have it now, Lincoln,'
and he pounded away at it until I was nearly blinded
by the scales.

"'This won't do,' he said, 'I certainly don't know
my trade to let a thing like that fool me so. Well,
well, it won't make a clevis-bolt, but I have one resort

yet; it will make a tenpenny nail. You will have to wait for your ax,' and he put the metal into the fire again.

"This time he didn't blow it ; he let it get red-hot naturally, and when it was as he wanted it, he put it on the anvil again.

"'This,' he said, 'is a sure thing. I am down to the heart of the piece. There must be a tenpenny nail in this.' But he was mistaken; there was only a small piece of wire left. He was actually dazed.

"'Durn the thing !' he said, 'I don't know what to make of it. I tried it as an ax, and it failed me. Then it failed me as a clevis. It failed me as a clevis-bolt, and the thing won't even make a tenpenny nail ! But I'll tell you, old fellow, what it will make,' and he put it in the fire again until it and the tongs were at a white heat. Then, turning around, he rammed it into a bucket of water. 'There, you will make a big fizzle, and that is all you will make.' And it sputtered and fizzled until it went out, and there was nothing left.

"Now that is the case with the person I am speaking of,' continued the President. 'I tried him as an ax. I tried him as a clevis. He was so full of shakes, he wouldn't work into one. I tried him as a clevis-bolt. He was a dead failure, and he wouldn't make even a tenpenny nail. But he did make the biggest fizzle that has been made in this war, and fizzled himself out of the army."

On Sunday, April 9, he returned to Washington and there received the tidings of Lee's surrender and that of his entire army. His joy at the news can be imagined. For the time he seemed to have had a new life infused into his worn and weary frame, and he showed his happiness like a great, overgrown school-boy. His enthusiasm was shared by the whole country. Business was suspended as the tidings were borne through the length and breadth of the land ; flags were flung out to the breeze ; cannon boomed, and there was one constant scene of wild jubilation. For the moment the horrors of the war were forgot-ten, and every man helped to swell the grand chorus of thanksgiving, whose echoes were borne on every wind to the remotest shores of the world. In Wash-ington, which had suffered more than any other city from the gloom and shadow of the war, the celebra-tion of the news was most unrestrained. The White House was thronged by those who were anxious to extend their congratulations to the President and to share in his joy. He appeared at the window over the main entrance in view of the multitude and in declining to make a speech, said :

"I am very greatly rejoiced that an occasion has occurred so pleasurable that the people can't restrain themselves. I suppose that arrangements are being made for some sort of formal demonstration, perhaps this evening or to-morrow night. If there should be such a demonstration, I of course shall have to respond to it, and I shall have nothing to say if I dribble it out before. I see you have a band. I propose now closing up by requesting you to play a certain air or tune. I have always thought 'Dixie' one of the best tunes I ever heard. I have heard that our adver-saries over the way have attempted to appropriate it as a national air. I insisted yesterday that we had fairly captured it. I presented the question to the

Attorney General and he gave his opinion that it is our lawful prize. I ask the band to give us a good turn upon it."

On the evening of April 11, the city was illuminated and a vast crowd gathered around the east window to listen to the last speech Mr. Lincoln ever made. He began with the following modest words: "We meet to-night not in sorrow but in gladness of heart. No part of the honor or praise is mine. To General Grant, his skillful officers, and brave men, all belongs."

The greatest problem that presented itself in the closing up of the war was that of reconstruction. The difficulty of dealing with the rebellious States and of establishing the terms upon which they might regain their proper status in the Union was a colossal one. The policy which Mr. Lincoln had outlined was liberal. He did not wish to witness the humiliation of the commonwealths nor the execution of American citizens as traitors even though they had raised their hands in rebellion against the Constitution. When asked what he intended to do with the leaders of the revolt, he answered with a characteristic story:

"A Springfield boy once caught a coon which he took home in triumph to his parents. For a time the animal was the pet of the household and attracted much attention. But after a time the novelty wore off and the awkward beast became a nuisance, yet no one could suggest a way to get rid of it. One day, the boy was observed sitting on the doorstep, holding a cord to which the coon was attached, while his attention was turned earnestly in another direction. A passer-by noticing the boy's disconsolate appearance stopped, and asked what was the matter. 'Oh,' was the reply, 'this coon is such a bother to me.'

"'Why don't you get rid of him, then?' said the gentleman.

"'Hush,' said the boy, 'don't you see he is gnawing his rope off? I am going to let him do it, and then I will go home and tell the folks he got away from me.'"

Mr. Lincoln continued: "This talk about Mr. Davis tires me. I hope he will mount a fleet horse, reach the shores of the Gulf of Mexico, and drive so far into the waters that we shall never see him again."

Mr. Lincoln's wise and merciful policy of granting amnesty to all rebels except a few of the most culpable leaders and not to make a special effort to secure their persons was undoubtedly the best that could have been put in force, yet it could not have been wholly popular. When the people of the North reflected upon the war which had been brought on by the South, and the terrible cost of it, both in resources and human life, they felt that leniency was not a virtue, but rather a condoning of crime. The men who had desolated their homes and all but ruined their country should be made an example of so that in the future all such efforts would be discouraged. Had Lincoln lived he would have encountered much opposition and adverse criticism. He might have found a large wing of his own party opposed to his policy. Yet his persistence and carelessness of opposition, when he had once decided upon a policy, would undoubtedly have enabled him to overcome all opposition, and, in the end, carry into operation the policy which had, to some extent, been outlined in the States already partially reconstructed. So far as it is possible to forecast the future from the past, it is certain that if he had lived, many of the unfortunate complications would have been avoided which were destined to leave a lasting impress upon the South in sectional bitterness perpetuated in crippled prosperity, and a general feeling of distrust between the sections which two and a half decades have scarcely been able to heal.

But it is useless to speculate as to what might have been. It is certain that there was no moment in his whole career so fitted to bring about his apotheosis. Had he lived longer his career might have been clouded by adverse circumstances over which he could have had no control ; for it is well known that, when a country is at war, in a condition of great peril, all the diverse elements are concentrated to the support of a government, which, in times of peace, many of them would violently oppose. Hence much might have occurred to tarnish his brilliant reputation and lower him from the high place to which his successful conduct of the war had raised him. The bullet struck him at the zenith of his glory. The war was ended. The country was once more united. The fresh woven wreath of victory was on his temples. The country rejoiced in its preservation and revered him as its preserver. Riding on the crest of the tidal wave of success naught but the martyr's crown could add to his laurels. It came, and Lincoln's memory was forever enshrined in the hearts of his countrymen. It is heartrending to think of the great chief, bearing all the terrible burden of the conflict and passing hence just when the fruits of the victory were to be enjoyed ; the pilot, bringing the ship safely into port through raging tempests and opposing tides but not permitted to step upon the solid land of peace and union.

Yet it was not his loss. The earthly crown he laid aside for a brighter and eternal one. He left the field of battle for the realms of everlasting peace. The tired head and weary heart were forever at rest.

CHAPTER XXII.

THE season of rejoicing had come. For the moment the gloom and darkness which had overspread the land had been dispelled. The cruel war was over. No longer would the papers be scanned eagerly, yet with sickening dread to find the news of some battle and tidings of dear ones overwhelmed, perchance, by the crimson tide of war. Gayly the old flag floated from every masthead. Joy and gladness abounded. Friends joyfully greeted each other, the smile of gladness breaking over faces even yet suffused with tears. But amid the blare of trumpets and the sounds of martial music, amid the clanging chimes and ringing cheers, might be heard the monotone of tolling bells and the sobs of a country about to be bereft of its ruler.

As sometimes on a summer's day a dark cloud passes quickly over the face of the sun, and its black shadow falls upon the earth, rejoicing in the brilliancy of day, like a pall upon the landscape, gliding over the distant hillsides, approaching noiselessly, perhaps unseen, until suddenly it covers the whole champaign with its sable mantle, leaving in its wake darkness and gloom, where but a moment before had been all light and joy and peace. So now amid the festivities and rejoicing, when all fears had been laid aside and naught of harm was dreaded, the shadow

(331)

of death was fast approaching. Already it was gliding down the distant hillsides and none saw it. Its
sable folds were growing thicker and blacker as it
approached, and yet the sun was shining never more
brightly. So sudden was the transition from hope
to despair, from joy to mourning.

His last day was a memorable one and largely free
from the care and anxieties which had weighed him
down with their burdens in the days and months that
had passed. He had often been oppressed by pre-
monitions and forebodings, but to-day he caught no
glimpse of the shadow so close upon him. He was in
exceptionally good spirits and was already beginning
to enter with keen zest upon the new duties and
questions suggested by the closing war. In the
morning the family lingered long at the breakfast-
table listening to a description of Lee's surrender
given by Robert Lincoln, who had just returned from
the front on a short furlough. He had been present
at the historic scene and gave many details which the
President had not before heard, and in which he was
deeply interested.

After breakfast, he proceeded to his office, where
he despatched some routine business and received a
number of calls from Senators and Representatives,
and from one or two of his old Illinois friends, all
anxious to congratulate him upon the glorious close
of the war. He greeted them all with cordiality, and
afterwards went out for a short drive with General
Grant, who was spending a few hours in Washington
on business connected with the army. The sight of
the illustrious General and his still more illustrious
chief, was greeted with enthusiastic cheers, which

they smilingly acknowledged. After his return, Mr. Lincoln attended a Cabinet meeting, his last on earth. After congratulations, inquiries were made into the condition of the army, and the terms of surrender. General Grant, who was present, was asked regarding the whereabouts of General Sherman, but could not give much information on the subject, as he had not recently heard from him. Mr. Lincoln seemed especially anxious about him, and pressed the inquiry. Finding that nothing further could be ascertained, he said:

"Gentlemen, I feel sure we shall hear news of Sherman, either good or bad, before night." Upon being asked why he thought so, he replied that he had had a dream the night before, which he had regularly had the night before some great event, and, as there was no other place in which to apprehend a catastrophe, he feared it for Sherman. He said that he had had it before the great battles of Bull Run, Antietam, Stone River and others. Some one asked him what the dream was, and he replied that he seemed to be on a great ship, under full sail on the ocean, approaching an unknown shore. The dream had never failed, and he believed that something would happen. Yet he did not seem to attach any personal meaning to it, nor apprehend that the disaster might be to himself.

After lunch, he went out for a drive with Mrs. Lincoln, for the day was a beautiful one, such a day as only the spring can bring, and that in the latitude of the Capital City. During the ride, he recalled many old memories and familiar scenes of his Springfield life, and a vein of sadness came over him, such

as memories of by-gone days, forever past, produce.
He spoke of the trials and worries of the last four
years, recalling rather the sad scenes they had passed
through than the glorious triumphs he had achieved,
and speaking in tenderest terms of the son, William
Wallace, who had died at the White House and whose
memory he cherished with the warmest affection. He
then spoke hopefully of the future, remarking that
they would be able to save but little from the Presidential salary, and that, at the close of his term, they
would return to Chicago or Springfield, buy a house
and he would resume his law practice, and they
would pass the remainder of their lives in peace and
quiet. He longed for the time to come when he
might throw aside the cares that were so oppressive,
and enjoy the much-needed rest. Sweet and com-
forting was this planning for the future. But abiding
rest was much nearer the weary frame than he knew.
Already the darkness of the shadow was upon him.

Upon his return he found on his desk an application for the discharge of a rebel prisoner, upon taking
the oath of allegiance. He took his pen, which had
always been so ready to do an act of mercy and so
reluctant to confirm a sentence which law and justice
had passed, and wrote across the back of it the words,
" Let it be done." His last official order !

He had that morning accepted an invitation to
attend Ford's Theatre that evening and witness the
presentation of the popular play, " Our American
Cousin." He seldom allowed himself time for rest
and recreation, but he felt that he could better do so
now. He did not stop to consider the danger that
he incurred by thus appearing in a public resort,

without an escort or any means of protection. But during the whole war he had been accustomed to expose himself, at times almost recklessly, upon the streets unattended at all hours of day and night, and at times when the streets were thronged with desperate characters in sympathy with the South, and who would hesitate at nothing to bring about their nefarious ends. It is marvellous that he had never before suffered from violence. Opportunities had been numerous, and more than once attempts had been made on his life but had failed. During the latter part of the war, he was out riding one evening, when the officer in charge at the White House heard a pistol-shot down the avenue, and a moment later the hoof-beats of a horse galloping furiously. A moment later the President rode up hurriedly without his hat. Upon being asked what the matter was, he replied, that some one had fired off a pistol unexpectedly, down the street and had frightened his horse, causing him to run, and he had thus lost his hat. A search was made and his hat was found with a bullet-hole through it. Even when he saw this evidence he ridiculed the idea of any one trying to shoot him, claiming that it must have been an accidental shot, but at the same time requesting that nothing be said about it lest it frighten the people and excite their apprehensions.

How many plots were formed during the administration, which were in one way and another frustrated, no one will ever know.

On the evening of the fourteenth, the President conversed for some time with Hon. George Ashmun, who had acted as President of the Convention which had nominated him, and with Hon. Schuyler Colfax, whom he invited to go to the theatre with him, but who pleaded a previous engagement.

Mr. and Mrs. Lincoln entered the theatre at about nine o'clock. As they approached the door of the box, which had been reserved for them, the whole audience arose and cheered them, waving their hand-kerchiefs and applauding. Mr. Lincoln stopped and bowed, then entered the box, which was profusely decorated with flags in honor of the event. And the cloud which had been so swiftly approaching closed in about the doomed President and enveloped him in its sable folds. In the midst of a scene of extraordinary brilliancy, with blazing gas-jets, glitter-ing jewels, fair women and brave men on every side. Surely if there were any scene which could dispel the shadow and drive away grim death, it was this! Did the victim feel any dim prescience of the swift approaching fate? Did that sensitive brain perceive aught of the enveloping darkness? Truly the "grand ship was approaching an unknown country." The tempest was filling the sails; the roar of the breakers was heard louder and louder; the harbor lights shone full upon the view; and soon, ah, so soon, the anchor would drop in the fair haven of rest.

At half-past ten a pistol-shot was heard in the direction of the President's box, a wreath of smoke lingered for a moment in the air, then a man, a demon in human form, leaped from the President's box upon the stage. His spurred heel caught in the draperies of the flags, as if the banner whose defender he had slain would detain him in his flight until the hand of justice had seized him. He fell, arose again, ran across the stage, flourishing a bloody dagger in

his hand, shouting, "*Sic semper tyrannis*," and disappeared through one of the stage-doors, whence a
second later came the sound of horse's hoofs in furious
flight over the pavement. Meantime, a woman's form
leaned far out over the railing and pointed towards
the fleeing figure, while a woman's voice, in all the
agony of despair shrieked out, "He has killed the
President." Who can picture the scene of wild confusion which followed! For a moment the audience
sat, struck dumb, as when the rumble of some earth-
quake, mysterious, awful, paralyzes the limbs which
fain would flee, the tongue as it struggles to utter the
cry of despair, and then, there were shouts and
screams and curses; women fainted or rushed aimlessly about, a hundred rushed towards the box
where lay the prostrate form of the President. The
stage was thronged in an instant with frantic men,
eager to be of service but knowing not what to do.
And through it all that prostrate form was lying
quiet, unheeding, with the precious life-blood oozing
slowly out upon the velvet carpet and dyeing to a
deeper crimson the draperies around. The panic
spread. From lip to lip passed the words, "The
President is killed." On into the street it echoed.
A platoon of soldiers rushed in with bayonets fixed
and charged upon the helpless throng, burning with
passion, ready to die for their beloved leader or to
stain the ground with the blood of his murderers.

The conspiracy to murder him had originated in
the brain of John Wilkes Booth, an actor of hitherto
illustrious name, but henceforth to be hurled to a
deeper gulf of infamy, and to bear a reputation more
cursed and black than any master of crime painted

by Shakespeare's matchless hand, whom he was wont
to personate upon the stage in mimic life. The
details of the plot have never, perhaps, been fully
revealed, but it contemplated not only the murder of
the President, but also of his leading advisers.
Whether there were those back of the plot whose
names have never been revealed, will probably never
be ascertained. Booth, learning that the President
was to visit the theatre on the evening of the fourteenth, chose that day for the culmination of the plot.
He entered the theatre and made his plans for the
accursed deed.

When the fatal shot was fired the attention of the
President was directed towards the stage, and no one
saw the assassin enter. The box was occupied by
Miss Harris, the daughter of Senator Harris of New
York, who sat at the right, next the stage ; close to
her sat Mrs. Lincoln, while in the rear sat Major
Rathbone and the President. Booth placed his pistol, a small Derringer, close to the head of Mr. Lincoln and fired. The bullet entered the brain and he
fell to the floor. Major Rathbone, hearing the shot,
sprang up and grappled with the murderer who
struck at him with a knife which he held in his hand,
wounding him in the shoulder. Booth then leaped
over the rail to the stage below, a distance of ten or
fifteen feet, and running across the stage he passed
out into the alley in the rear where he had a
swift horse awaiting, which he mounted and rode
away.

The inanimate form of the President was tenderly
lifted and carried to a house opposite, where a cur-
sory examination showed that the wound was fatal.

There quickly gathered around the bedside of the man, whose life was evidenced only by the faint breathing and feebly beating heart, a crowd of sorrowing friends: Secretaries Welles and Stanton, the Surgeon-General, Vice-President Johnson and many others, who sadly awaited the end. Robert Lincoln spent the sad hours of the night with his almost frantic mother in an adjoining room, striving to comfort her who could not be comforted. In the gray dawn of the morning, just as the sun was rising, the last feeble breath was drawn, the last fluttering beat came and the great heart was still. Slowly and sadly they bore his mortal remains to the White House, his "shop," as he used to call it, while the dark cloud which had enveloped him, borne on by the swift currents that carried the news, settled down dark and forbidding, sorrow-breeding and tear-laden upon the length and breadth of the land ; nay, and wherever throughout the world there was a heart that loved liberty, there was sorrow for its brave champion whose career had been so rudely cut off. The news fell like a blight upon the land. Men started to their labors, blithe and gay, and they returned to their homes stricken and mourning. The newsboys stood on the street corners and silently handed their black-bordered papers to their customers, while they wiped with tattered sleeves the tears of genuine sorrow from their eyes. Men looked at each other in dismay. The shock was too sudden, too terrible, to bring at first its most acute suffering, dazed and shocked they could but stand in mute horror. Men returned from their offices and children from their schools, and the wives and mothers meeting them at the door

with anxious inquiry received the simple answer,
"Our President is shot."

The flags which had floated so proudly at the mast-
heads were lowered to half-mast. Crape fluttered at
every door and hung in funeral folds from the
windows. Stores were closed and business was suspended. In the cities the very car-horses seemed to
feel the prevailing gloom and proceeded to their
tasks with hanging heads and dejected mien. "Our
President is dead," was echoed from the tolling bells
as their solemn cadences lingered in the tremulous
air. "Our President is dead," the very birds hushed
their songs and flitted disconsolately from tree to
tree. "Our President is dead," were the words that
fell sadly from every tongue and brought to each
heart a grief such as all the exigencies of a cruel war
had not yet inflicted. Nor was the grief confined to
the western continent Dispatches of sympathy and
condolence, genuine and hearty, poured in from all
over the civilized world. He had once been the sport
of Europe ; his awkward and homely figure had been
the object of jest and ridicule, at the court and in the
cabin ; but prince and peasant had, long ere this,
learned to respect the plain, simple man, whose
character and deeds had given to their scoffs the lie
and taken from their ridicule its sting. No grander
man or one better fitted to rule ever sat upon European throne, or held the sceptre of power. They
recognized it now and did honor with sorrowing
hearts to the dead peasant prince.

The President had been shot on Friday, an ill-
omened day, dark with sorrow and anguish. The
body was removed to the White House, Saturday

morning where, after being embalmed, it was placed in a coffin resting upon a great catafalque, embowered in flowers. Memorial services were held Sunday throughout the land, and from thousands of pulpits were spoken words of heartfelt sorrow and eloquent eulogies upon the life now ended. The week which was thus ushered in was one of the most remarkable in the annals of the country. Never before had a whole people mourned a hero so spontaneously and with such a unanimity of grief. Never before had there been such elaborate manifestations of popular sorrow, funeral orations, imposing processions, martial bands with muffled drums and solemn dirges, while in palace and cottage alike the swift-flowing tears, the choking sob and breaking voice attested to the sincerity of the almost universal grief.

Monday morning there was a meeting of the Congressional Committee appointed to make the arrangements for the funeral. In the afternoon their report was made, outlining the exercises and appointing the pall-bearers and the committee to attend the remains on their long journey to their resting place on the far-distant prairies of Illinois. At ten o'clock, Tuesday morning, the doors of the White House were thrown open and the public were permitted to file in, and take their last look at the face of the dead lying enshrined in beds of roses and lilies not whiter or more unstained than the character of him whose inanimate form they pillowed.

All day in ceaseless procession the people passed across the grounds, up the marble steps and through the corridors to the coffin, paused to drop a tear and departed, rich and poor, white and black, in satins and in rags, made one by the community of their grief. The simple funeral occurred Wednesday morning. All the public offices were closed and business was suspended, while the Government buildings were all heavily draped with crape. Vast crowds gathered around the White House and thronged its spacious rooms. In the East room stood the catafalque and around it were grouped the family and friends of the deceased, save only Mrs. Lincoln, who was too much prostrated to attend, the high State officials and the representatives of foreign governments.

The ceremonies were solemn and impressive, being participated in by Rev. Dr. Hale of the Episcopal Church, Bishop Simpson, who was a special friend of Mr. Lincoln, and Rev. Dr. Gurley of the Presbyterian Church which Mr. Lincoln and his family had been wont to attend. Dr. Gurley paid a noble and worthy tribute to the memory of the dead, in the course of which he said :

"Probably no man since the days of Washington was so firmly and deeply imbedded and enshrined in the hearts of the people as Abraham Lincoln. Nor was it a mistaken confidence and love. He deserved it ; deserved it well ; deserved it all. He merited it by his character, by his acts and by the tenor and tone and spirit of his whole life. . . . His integrity was thorough, all-pervading, all-controlling and incorruptible."

In speaking of the power of Mr. Lincoln to rise to an emergency, he truly said : "He rose to the dignity and momentousness of the occasion ; saw his duty as the Chief Magistrate of a great and imperilled people ;

and he determined to do his duty and his whole duty, seeking the guidance and leaning upon the arm of Him of whom it is written, ' He giveth power to the faint, and to them who have no might he increaseth strength.' Yes, he leaned upon His arm. He recognized and received the truth that the kingdom is the Lord's."

After the services were over, the casket was taken from its resting place, and borne to the rotunda of the Capitol, where it lay in state until April 21. The funeral procession was long and the route over which it passed was thronged with people, with sad eyes, waiting to pay their simple tribute of sorrow. The trees were just bursting out into leaf; the air was sweet and fragrant; and all nature seemed to be pointing to the resurrection and the new life into which he, who was not dead, had now entered. As the hearse entered the Capitol grounds, drawn by six white horses, there was a burst of martial music as the great bands played requiem and dirge, while all the guns of the fortifications added their roar to swell the solemn chorus.

It was a scene never to be forgotten, and probably never to be repeated in the future history of the country. Nor were such scenes witnessed alone in Washington. In New York, Philadelphia, Chicago and all the great cities, in smaller towns and villages, and in the sparsely-settled country, men and women left their daily avocations and assembled in the churches to participate in memorial services, and join in great and imposing processions where all the solemn pageantry of sorrow was displayed.

Thus did a nation mourn its dead ; thus did the all-

absorbing grief penetrate each heart, as the thought
came of the great and good man who had died in
their behalf ; not as Cæsar had died, the victim of
his own ambition ; not as Alexander II. had died, the
oppressor, suffering at the hands of the oppressed ;
nor yet as died the soldier upon the battlefield, fighting for his country in the hour of her sorest need
against an open enemy. But his life had been offered
up after the tide of battle had flowed and ebbed, and
the victory had been declared ; when thoughts of
peace and harmony filled the hearts of all ; at the
time when the nation had laid aside the weeds of
mourning for the laurels of triumph, then had been
raised the hand of the assassin, more accursed than
Ravaillac of old, of memory more execrable than any
whose hands have been stained with innocent blood,
save only he whose arch-treason had delivered up his
Master, the Saviour of a lost humanity ; and then had
fallen the blow that pierced the heart of the nation
and wounded all mankind. And yet the horror of
the blow had for the moment led the people to forget
the author of it. Their sorrow was too deep to
admit of the feelings of hatred and revenge which
would, in less heartfelt sorrow, have been in the
ascendency.

It was decided that the funèral cortège should
return, as nearly as possible, over the same route as
Mr. Lincoln had followed in coming to Washington
in the beginning of the eventful four years. It
seemed almost cruel to subject the worn body to so
long a journey, but the people, whose he was,
demanded the right once more to look upon his features and to pay the last tribute of respect. So in a

train drawn by the "Union," the engine, which had four years before drawn him to Washington, the funeral cortège set out. All the cars and the engine were heavily draped in black and the national colors. Besides the larger casket was a small one which contained the mortal remains of Willie, the son who died at the White House and whose death his father had so deeply mourned.

The route lay through the cities of Baltimore, Harrisburg, Philadelphia, New York, Albany, Buffalo, Cleveland, Columbus, Cincinnati, Indianapolis and Chicago to Springfield. In each city imposing demonstrations had been planned, each striving to outdo the others, not in vulgar rivalry but in the genuine love and sorrow thus expressed. At Baltimore the train was met by thousands of citizens who did all in their power to testify to the sincerity of their grief. In this city but four years before had been formed the first conspiracy against the life of Mr. Lincoln. But now the tragic outcome of the last conspiracy against his life was as sincerely mourned here as anywhere else in the Union. What a revulsion! So marked the change as to seem almost incredible! The downright honesty and the hearty good-will of the man had brought it to pass and nothing less.

From Harrisburg to Philadelphia the railway was thronged, seemingly all the way, with people who gathered to see the black-robed train pass by like some meteor in its flight. At Philadelphia the same scenes were enacted, of long processions and tolling bells, of mourning people and the pomp of black-robed grief. The casket was placed in Independence Hall, which was literally embowered in flowers.

At his head was the old "liberty bell," upon which were engraved the words, "Proclaim liberty throughout the land to all the inhabitants thereof." There was the iron tongue which had first sounded out the sweet notes of liberty and freedom from the tyrant's oppression. There, too, lay the tongue, which almost a century later, had uttered the words which had given freedom to a down-trodden race, and the hands which had knocked off their fetters. It was in this hall four years before that he had made that memorable speech on the anniversary of Washington's birthday, in which he had uttered these prophetic words :

"Now, my friends, can this country be saved on the basis of the Declaration of Independence? If it can, I will consider myself one of the happiest men in the world, if I can help to save it. If it cannot be saved upon that principle, it will be truly awful. But if this country cannot be saved without giving up that principle, I was about to say I would rather be assassinated on this spot than surrender it."

All day Sunday the unending procession swept monotonously by the silent form, and then once more its rest was disturbed and it was taken on to New York, that city where first he had gained for himself a national recognition, and where first, by his Cooper Union speech, his availability for the Presidency had been demonstrated. As New York was the metropolis of the continent, so here the demonstration was most grand and impressive. In the escort were fifteen thousand soldiers, and it was estimated that one hundred and fifty thousand people passed by the coffin one by one, while more than twice that number were disappointed in the attempt to catch a glimpse of the dead face.

As the train approached Albany a most impressive tableau had been arranged. Just as the sun was setting behind the distant Catskills, the train came into view, dark and sombre, like the funeral barge that came to claim the body of ancient Britain's last and greatest king. An open grave was dug on a beautiful green champaign, and a woman, majestic and beautiful, robed to represent the Goddess of Liberty, was observed leaning over the open grave, into which she proceeded to drop the crown of laurel.

The same sad scenes were repeated at Albany, Buffalo, Cleveland, Columbus and Cincinnati, and all the region through which the sad train passed was black with crape and sprinkled with tears, as if in every cottage there was a funeral and in every heart the sting of a personal bereavement. But it was in Chicago that the home-scenes were first reached. Those streets he had walked in his earlier days, there he was known personally to many of the people and much of the activity of his life had been exerted there. While the grief was no more heartfelt and unrestrained than elsewhere, there was the added sentiment of personal affliction, and never had the city by the lake been more profoundly grieved. The demonstration was such as a friend renders to the memory of another whom he has long loved.

Here had been the home of Douglas, and here reposed his body under a majestic monument, reared upon the shores of the lake whose blue waters he loved so well, and here now lay the speechless body of his great and successful rival Well and bravely had

they fought life's battles, each winning by true
native worth and honesty of purpose, and now
the grand old State, their foster mother, received
them back once more to rest in her bosom till the
last great day; the one beneath the green sod
of the prairies, whose spring-tide freshness was
beautified by the many-hued flowers that dyed
the level plain with their brilliant colors; the other
by the side of the great lake, whose waters gently
murmured as they dashed almost against the foot of
his granite monument or roared with mighty
power upon the sands—all alike to him whose ear
could ne'er be soothed again by their musical
cadences.

At last the funeral train set out upon its final trip,
across the two hundred miles of prairies that stretched
between Chicago and the State Capital, scenes all
familiar to the mute occupant of the funeral car. Here
he had ridden in circuit with his brother lawyers
from one county-seat to another, and here were
achieved the first triumphs that paved the way for the
greater ones to follow. Here he had carried the
chain and compass and split the rails which afterwards gave him the name of the " rail-splitter President." Here he knew the people and here they knew
him as a friend and trusted him as a father.

At last the train bore him into the depot from which
he had departed four years before, beseeching his
assembled friends to bear him up and sustain him
with the strength of their prayers.

The casket stood in state in the State House until the
day arrived when the earth should claim its own and
the weary pilgrimage of earth be ended. Some wished

his tomb to be made near the State House, so as to be easy of access, but at the request of Mrs. Lincoln, Oak Ridge, a quiet and peaceful cemetery, was chosen.

At one time, while riding in the country with his wife, Mr. Lincoln had passed by a quiet, country graveyard and, attracted by the peaceful aspect of the place, they had alighted and walked slowly through it. The President seemed to be affected by the melancholy beauty of the place and said, " Mary, I am older than you and you will probably outlive me. When I die I want you to lay me to rest in some quiet, retired spot like this." Taking this to be the expression of his desire, this quiet, suburban cemetery was selected.

Finally, the body was taken from the State House, where it had been viewed by thousands of sorrowing friends, and was placed in the hearse as a choir of two hundred and fifty singers sang the familiar hymn, " Children of the Heavenly King." Followed by a long procession the hearse passed slowly over the mile and a half to the cemetery, where the body was consigned to the grave, and by its side was placed the coffin containing the body of " little Willie." The funeral oration was pronounced by Bishop Simpson and was an eloquent and touching tribute to the dead Chief. But in the whole sermon occurred nothing more touching in the light of recent events, than a quotation from one of Lincoln's speeches, made in 1859, in which, speaking of the slave-power, he said : " Broken by it I too may be, bow to it I never will. The probability that we may fail in the struggle ought not to deter us from the support of a cause which I deem to be just; and it shall not deter me. If ever I feel the soul within me elevate and expand to those dimensions, not wholly unworthy of its Almighty Architect, it is, when I contemplate the cause of my country, deserted by all the world besides, and I, standing up boldly and alone, and hurling defiance at her victorious oppressors. Here, without contemplating consequences, before high Heaven and in the face of the world, I swear eternal fidelity to the just causes as I deem it, of the land of my life, my liberty, and my love."

CHAPTER XXIII.

It has been said that Mr. Lincoln was not an ambitious man, but this is not wholly true. In a broad sense he was ambitious. It is true that his aspirations were not selfish and that he did not desire to obtain honor and renown for their own sake alone. He felt that Providence had placed him in an humble station in life, but had endowed him with gifts which entitled him to occupy a more exalted and honorable position. This he strove to gain by first becoming worthy of it. He hoped to attain distinction, but not until he had earned it.

No man with the ordinary endowments of nature could feel that honor and wide reputation were within his reach without the desiring to secure them. Mr. Lincoln was no exception. He desired office, partly because of the wider and higher sphere of action it would open up to him, and partly to satisfy his honest pride.

He was not ambitious as Napoleon, Cæsar or Alexander, but the exalted ambition of Cromwell and Washington dwelt within his breast, the ambition which would make his own aggrandizement redound to the advantage of his country and of humanity. It is such ambition that has inspired the grandest deeds of the past, and without it the American slaves might yet be in chains.

It is natural that he should be deeply gratified at

the honor conferred upon him by his nomination and election to the Presidency, yet he was never led to magnify his own ability nor the importance of his services. He felt a deep sense of his own unworthiness and did not hesitate to express his sentiments publicly.

In his address at Assembly Hall, Albany, February 18, 1861, he said: "It is true, that while I hold myself, without mock modesty, the humblest of all individuals that have ever been elevated to the Presidency, I have a more difficult task to perform than any one of them."

While his modesty led him to disparage himself no man has ever invested the office, which he was called upon to fill, with a higher dignity. All his personal interests, desires and feelings were sacrificed to the demands of his position. Lincoln, the private citizen, disappeared forever, on the 4th of March, 1861, and Lincoln, the President, the servant of the people, the constitutional head of the Government, took his place.

He was never overbearing and dictatorial, for he felt that he was but the servant whom the nation had deputed to perform certain important duties.

He never exhibited a spirit of undue partisanship nor made unfair distinction between his political friends and foes, for, although he was elected as the standard-bearer of the Republican party, he conceived himself to be the President, not of a party, but of the whole country. From his point of view political sentiments formed no basis for appointment to responsible positions. The only requirements were patriotism and fitness.

The same spirit of humility which he had exhibited in his earlier life followed him throughout his career. The praise and honors that were accorded to him he seldom received as due to himself personally but rather to the high office which he occupied.

At a reception tendered him at Indianapolis he said: "Most heartily do I thank you for this magnificent reception, yet I cannot take to myself any share of the compliment thus paid, more than that which pertains to a mere instrument, an accidental instrument, perhaps I should say, of a great cause."

At Cincinnati he said: "My friends, I am entirely overwhelmed by the magnificence of the reception which has been given, I will not say to me, but to the President-elect of the United States of America."

At Harrisburg he said: "I thank your great commonwealth for the overwhelming support it recently gave, not to me personally, but to the cause which I think a great one, in the recent election."

In his homely phrase he frequently referred to himself as the "lead-horse" of the national team.

If there was ever a time in his career when he might have been expected to indulge in self-gratulation it was when he was informed of his second nomination for the Presidency by the Republican party. The war was in its last stages. The beginning of the end was at hand. The crowning victory could even then be foreseen, and to him more than to any other one person was this result due. Yet his wonted modesty did not forsake him. In his reply to the congratulations of the National Union League, June 9, 1864, he said:

"Gentlemen:—I can only say in response to the

remarks of your Chairman, that I am very grateful
for the renewed confidence which has been accorded
to me, both by the convention and the National
League. I am not insensible at all to the personal
compliment there is in this, yet I do not allow myself
to believe that any but a small portion of it is to be
appropriated as a personal compliment to me. The
Convention and the Nation, I am assured, are alike
animated by a higher view of the interests of
the country, for the present and the great future,
and the part I am entitled to appropriate as a compliment is only that part which I may lay hold of
as being the opinion of the Convention and of the
League that I am not entirely unworthy to be intrusted
with the place I have occupied the past three years.

"I have not permitted myself, gentlemen, to conclude
that I am the best man in the country ; but I am reminded in this connection of an old Dutch farmer,
who once remarked to a companion that ' it was not
best to swap a horse when crossing a stream.' "

His patience and forbearance in the presence of
insult and criticism were remarkable. For the good
of the country he could rise above all personal consideration and become invulnerable to all the shafts
of malice. This quality is most strikingly illustrated
in his relations to General McClellan. The world
will never know just how much he was compelled to
bear from this distinguished General. McClellan not
only disregarded his authority as Commander-in-
Chief, but he even went so far as to violate the cour-
tesy due from one gentleman to another.

Judge Kelly relates the following incident, which
illustrates this fact.

" When the President, impelled by anxiety for the country, waived questions of official etiquette and proceeded to the headquarters of the army, the announcement of his presence was more than once greeted with boisterous and derisive laughter, evidently intended for his ears; and there was one occasion when it was more than whispered by those immediately about the President, that he was made to wait nearly an hour while men who denied the right of the Government to maintain the Union by force of arms engaged McClellan's attention ; and when at his own good time the General concluded to see his Commander-in-Chief, his departing guests visibly sneered at that officer as they passed the door of the cold chamber in which he had been so long imprisoned." [1]

Notwithstanding such treatment, added to absolute insubordination, the President bore with General McClellan and supported him heartily just as long as the public interests seemed to demand it.

Under other circumstances and where less vital interests were concerned such patience would be attributed to meanness of spirit, but here it only serves to confirm more fully the greatness of Lincoln's character.

He never shrunk from taking upon himself the responsibility of any movement or policy which had resulted disastrously, if it had been entered upon by his advice or consent.

When he re-instated General McClellan in the command of the army he was severely criticised on

[1] " Lincoln and Stanton " page 7.

all sides. It was probably the most unpopular move he could have made. When it was announced in the Cabinet meeting, Mr. Stanton expressed his disapproval and stated that no such order had been issued from the War Department.

"No, Mr. Secretary," replied Mr. Lincoln, "the order was mine and I will be responsible for it to the country."

When Mr. Lincoln succeeded to the Presidency, he found the administrative offices filled by Mr. Buchanan's appointees, many of whom were known to be disaffected and others were under grave suspicions. Mr. Lincoln feared to intrust any of them with important Government business and, therefore, called to his assistance several private citizens, who were known to be able, honest and patriotic. This was done largely through the agency of Mr. Cameron, the Secretary of War, to whom the President had given the necessary instructions.

Congress failed to appreciate the situation knowing only that private citizens had been intrusted with large sums of public money without giving any security for its proper application. A resolution was therefore passed censuring the Secretary. Mr. Lincoln was unwilling that his Secretary should rest under a false imputation, and immediately sent the following remarkable communication to Congress."

"May 29, 1862.

" *To the Senate and House of Representatives:*

" The insurrection, which is yet existing in the United States and aims at the overthrow of the Federal Constitution and the Union, was clandestinely prepared during the winter of 1860 and 1861 and assumed an open organization in the form of a treasonable provisional government at Montgomery, in Alabama, on the 18th day of February, 1861. On the 12th day of April, 1861, the insurgents committed the flagrant act of civil war by bombardment and capture of Fort Sumter, which cut off the hope of immediate conciliation. Immediately afterwards all the roads and avenues to this city were obstructed, and the Capital was put into the condition of a siege. The mails in every direction were stopped, and the lines of telegraph cut off by the insurgents; and military and naval forces, which had been called out by the Government for the defense of Washington, were prevented from reaching the city by organized and combined treasonable resistance in the State of Maryland. There was no adequate and effective organization for public defense. Congress had indefinitely adjourned. There was no time to convene them. It became necessary for me to choose whether, using only the existing means, agencies and processes which Congress had provided, I should let the Government fall at once into ruin, or whether availing myself of the broader powers conferred by the Constitution in cases of insurrection, I would make an effort to save it, with all its blessings, for the present age and posterity.

" I thereupon summoned my constitutional advisers, the heads of all the Departments, to meet on Sunday, the 20th day of April, 1861, at the office of the Navy Department, and then and there, with their unanimous concurrence, I directed that an armed revenue cutter should proceed to sea, to afford protection to the commercial marine and especially to the California treasure-ships then on their way to this coast. I also directed the commandant of the navy-yard at Boston to purchase or charter and arm as quickly as possible five steamships for purposes of public defense. I directed the commandant of the navy-yard at Philadelphia to purchase or charter and arm an equal number for the same purpose. I directed the commandant at New York to purchase or charter and arm an equal number for the same purpose. I directed Commander Gillis to purchase or charter and arm, and put to sea, two other vessels. Similar directions were given to Commodore Du Pont, with a view to opening the passages by water to and from the Capital. I directed the several officers to take the advice and obtain the aid and efficient services in the matter of his Excellency, Edwin D. Morgan, the Governor of New York, or, in his absence, George D. Morgan, William M. Evarts, R. M. Blatchford and Moses H. Grinnell, who were, by my directions, especially empowered by the Secretary of the Navy to act for his Department in that crisis, in matters pertaining to the forwarding of the troops and supplies for the public defense.

" On the same occasion I directed that Governor Morgan and Alexander Cummings, of the City of New York, should be authorized by the Secretary of War, Simon Cameron, to make all necessary arrangements for the transportation of troops and munitions of war, in aid and assistance of the officers of the Army of the United States, until communication by mails and telegraph should be completely re-established between the cities of New York and Washington. No security was required to be given by them, and either of them was authorized to act in case of inability to consult with the others.

" On the same occasion I authorized and directed the Secretary of the Treasury to advance, without requiring security, two millions of dollars of public money to John A. Dix, George Opdyke and Richard M. Blatchford, of New York, to be used by them in meeting such requisitions as should be directly consequent upon the military and naval measures necessary for the defense and support of the Government, requiring them only to act without compensation, and to report their transactions when duly called upon. The several Departments of the Government at that time contained so large a number of disloyal persons that it would have been impossible to provide safely, through official agents only, for the performance of the duties thus confided to citizens favorably known for their ability, loyalty and patriotism.

" The several orders issued upon these occurrences were transmitted by private messengers, who pursued a circuitous way to the seaboard cities, inland, across the States of Pennsylvania and Ohio and the northern lakes. I believe that by these and other similar measures taken in that crisis, some of which were without any authority of law, the Government was saved from overthrow. I am not aware that a dollar of the public funds thus confided without authority of law to unofficial persons was either lost or wasted, although apprehension of such misdirection occurred to me as objections to these extraordinary proceedings and were necessarily overruled.

"I recall these transactions now because my attention has been directed to a resolution which was passed by the House of Representatives on the 30th day of last month, which is in these words:

"'RESOLVED, That Simon Cameron, late Secretary of War, by investing Alexander Cummings with the control of large sums of the public money, and authority to purchase military supplies without restriction, without requiring of him any guarantee for the faithful performance of his duties, when the services of competent public officers were available, and by involving the Government in a vast number of contracts with persons not legitimately engaged in the business pertaining to the subject-matter of such contracts, especially in the purchase of arms for future delivery, has adopted a policy highly injurious to the public service and deserves the censure of the House.'

" Congress will see that I should be wanting equally in candor and in justice, if I should leave the censure thus expressed in this resolution to rest exclusively or chiefly on Mr. Cameron. The same sentiment is unanimously entertained by the heads of departments, who participated in the proceedings which the House of Representatives has censured. It is due to Mr. Cameron to say that, although he fully approved the proceedings, they were not moved or suggested by himself, and that not only the President but all the other heads of Departments were, at least, equally responsible with him for whatever error, wrong or fault was committed on the premises.

"A. LINCOLN."

General Palmer tells this story of Lincoln: "I was

once called to Washington to see Mr. Lincoln on a
matter of business. It was in 1865. I was shown
into an ante-room and waited for some time. I saw
Senators and others going in, and finally I was called.
Mr. Lincoln was being shaved. He said I was home
folks and he could shave before me. I said to him :
' Mr. Lincoln, if I had supposed at the Chicago Convention that nominated you that we would have this
terrible war, I would never have thought of going
down to a one-horse town and getting a one-horse lawyer for President.' I did not know how he would take
it, but rather expected an answer I could laugh at. But
he brushed the barber to one side and with a solemn
face turned to me and said : ' Neither would I, Palmer. I don't believe any great man with a policy
could have saved the country. If I have contributed
to the saving of the country it was because I attended
to the duties of each day with the hope that when to-
morrow came I would be equal to the duties of that
day,' and he turned to the barber."

No man could have been more careless of his own
labor and suffering and more careful of that of others.
Bloodshed and suffering on the field and in the camp
caused him the deepest pain. "Oh, when will this
cruel war cease ? " was often the burden of his
thought. The whole weight and responsibility of the
war seemed to fall upon his shoulders and no one will
ever know the anguish of his heart when he felt that
the victory which he hoped to win must be bought
with the price of thousands of precious lives. Well
might one say of him, " truly he was the saddest man
I ever saw."

His nature was exceedingly tender and compassionate and sometimes led him to sacrifice the demands of justice to those of mercy. To maintain the proper degree of discipline in the army it was necessary at times for the officers to inflict the severest punishment upon those who were guilty of cowardice or who had wantonly disobeyed important regulations.

If there were the slightest grounds upon which such a sentence could be commuted or annulled Mr. Lincoln never failed to take advantage of them. The stricken mother or wife was seldom turned away in disappointment. His subordinates accused him of too often mingling mercy with justice and it is more than possible that discipline in the field was less rigid because of the gentle heart of the President.

A personal friend of his says : "I called on him one day in the early part of the war. He had just written a pardon for a young man who had been sentenced to be shot for sleeping at his post as a sentinel. He remarked as he read it to me :

"'I could not think of going into eternity with the blood of the poor young man on my skirts.' Then he added : ' It is not to be wondered at that a boy, raised on a farm, probably in the habit of going to bed at dark, should fall asleep, when required to watch ; and I cannot consent to shoot him for such an act.'"

It is said that this young man was killed at the battle of Fredericksburg and that a photograph of the President was found on his body next to his heart, with these words written upon it, "God bless President Lincoln."

Rev. Newman Hull relates that an officer in the army once said to him :

" The first week of my command, there were twenty-four deserters sentenced by court-martial to be shot, and the warrants for their execution were sent to the President for his signature. He refused to give it. I went to Washington and had an interview with him, I said :

"' Mr. President, unless these men are made an example of, the army itself is in danger. Mercy to the few is cruelty to the many.'

" He replied : ' Mr. General, there are already too many weeping widows in the United States. For God's sake, do not ask me to add to the number, for I won't do it.' "

During the war hundreds of lives were spared, from what now seems a needless sacrifice, by executive clemency.

In this respect Lincoln and Stanton were in striking contrast. The great War Secretary had a kindly heart under his gruff exterior and it caused him deep pain to confirm death sentences, but he felt that the discipline of the army and the welfare and safety of the country demanded it. When applications for mercy were made to him he often assumed the inexorable sternness of a just judge, in order that he might not be influenced by the grief, which appealed so strongly to his heart.

Lincoln could not conceal his feelings and his sympathy showed itself in every word and look and sometimes led him to extend clemency where his reason could not approve.

In an earlier age of the world such merciful interference to mitigate the severity of military law would have been attended with disastrous results to the country and the cause ; at this day it is doubtful if it can even be called a weakness. It is apparent, from the vantage-ground of a quarter of a century that the President's course was the wiser one.

In his personal habits he was abstemious and simple. He wore the plainest and most unpretentious garments and was satisfied with a simple and homely fare. Charges of drunkenness, which were at one time made against him, never had less foundation in fact.

When Mr. Lincoln was visited at Springfield by the committee appointed to notify him of his nomination, he thought, at the close of the ceremony, that custom would require him to treat the committee with something to drink. Opening a door that led into a room in the rear, he called out, "Mary, Mary!" A girl responded to the call to whom Mr. Lincoln spoke a few words in an undertone. In a short time the girl returned bringing a large server, upon which were a pitcher and several glasses, and placed it upon the table. Mr. Lincoln arose and gravely addressing the company, said : "Gentlemen, we must pledge our mutual healths in the most healthy beverage God has given to man. It is the only beverage I have ever used or allowed in my family, and I cannot conscientiously depart from it on the present occasion. It is pure Adam's ale from the spring." Raising his tumbler, he pledged the company in a cup of cold water.

His first printed composition, written when a mere boy was a vigorous denunciation of the evils of intemperance among the settlers in the frontier, and from that time he was a total abstainer. At one time during the war, a number of gentlemen clubbed together and bought a large assortment of the finest wines and liquors and sent them as a gift to the President. The gift was courteously acknowledged and immediately transferred to the city hospitals where it was put to a worthy use.

CHAPTER XXIV.

ABRAHAM LINCOLN stands before the world as one of the most remarkable characters in modern history, such an one as America alone could produce. In no other country could a boy, born in the lowest walks of life, oppressed by seemingly hopeless poverty and without any external advantages save those which nature furnished, aspire to so lofty a career. And even here it is still a marvel that the ragged, ignorant and uncouth backwoods boy may yet become President.

From his earliest boyhood Lincoln's intellectual growth was regular and vigorous. His adverse surroundings only served to stimulate him to increased effort. He had the heart of a pioneer and was not afraid to forsake the paths which had been trodden by his ancestors to strike out into roads which were as dangerous as they were unknown.

His boldness in ignoring precedent, and his confidence in his own ability to overcome the difficulties with which he was surrounded, had their origin in the hardships and privations of his early life. The barren farm and the gloomy woods were hard training schools, but they were thorough and effective, and his whole life showed their influence. Had he been brought up under more favorable surroundings, his

(365)

character could never have developed the peculiar traits which made his career possible. The strength of the oak was in his frame, and the brightness and originality of Nature in her simplicity and purity were in his mind.

In his daily life he frequently showed a lack of culture, but his rudeness was like the rough bark of the oak which proclaims, while it conceals, the solid timber within. The very ruggedness of his character was rendered attractive by the nobility of his nature and kindliness of his disposition.

One remarkable feature of his life is that he was always in advance of his surroundings. His mind was so sensitive and vigorous that, while he did not despise the circumstances by which he was surrounded, he was filled with a discontent which was continually urging him onward to increased exertions. Of this feeling he seldom spoke, but there is abundant evidence of its presence throughout the whole of his earlier life.

The constant tendency of his environment was to bind him down to a dull, plodding life. If he had been content to remain the creature of circumstance his name would have been unknown to the world. Even before he was old enough to recognize the presence of aspirations he had a vague consciousness that the life he was living was not the best attainable. As this consciousness developed into a fixed ambition, evidences of its power and influence multiplied.

In school he was the leading scholar in his classes and easily outranked those whose advantages were far superior to his own.

An illustration of his intellectual superiority over

his associates is given by a lady who was a former schoolmate of his.

"One evening," says she, "Abe and I were sitting on the banks of the Ohio ; I said to him that the sun was going down. He replied: 'That's not so ; it doesn't really go down; it seems so. The earth turns from west to east and the revolution of the earth carries us under ; we do the sinking as you call it. The sun, as to us, is comparatively still ; the sun's sinking is only an appearance.' I replied, ' Abe, what a fool you are !' I know now that I was the fool, not Lincoln. I am now thoroughly satisfied that Abe knew the general laws of astronomy and the movements of the heavenly bodies. He was better read then than the world knows or is likely to know exactly. He was the learned boy among us unlearned folks."

His family and associates were easily content with their humble station and had little ambition to rise in the world. They were satisfied to toil unceasingly if they could thereby win their scanty fare and humble raiment. For more they cared not. But young Lincoln was of different mould. He was not content to live for the present alone, but worked and thought and planned for the future. While others slept he studied.

He was moved by vague and restless aspirations, to what end he hardly knew; but, like a drowning man, he grasped at every straw hoping that in some way he might lift himself a little above the dead level of his surroundings. From boyhood the purpose was strong within him to excel his companions and if possible to make himself distinguished.

This ambition manifested itself, perhaps unconsciously, in his every-day life. He gloried in his physical prowess and never rested until he was recognized as the champion of the neighborhood. But the hand that could fell his rival to the ground with a single blow and bury an ax deeper in a tree-trunk than any one else could also hold the pen. His ambition looked forward to literary distinction, and his rude compositions, which passed for poetry, were the marvel of the neighborhood.

It was not until he came in contact with one of the leading lawyers of the day, that his aspirations took definite shape. Then was placed clearly before him an object which he persistently endeavored to attain. It was a long step from Lincoln the ragged, awkward, backwoods boy to Lincoln the lawyer, yet he was convinced of his ability to take it. Henceforth, he was dominated by a fixed and persistent purpose.

When he had no money to buy books he borrowed them. When he was compelled to labor during the day he studied far into the night by the flickering light of a fire. His purpose never faltered, although oppressed by discouragements and financial failure. At New Salem he was recognized as the most learned man in the community, and when he moved into the more cultured society of Springfield it did not take him long to rise to its level, and even to become an intellectual leader.

As a technical lawyer he did not gain a wide reputation. He recognized the law as the business by which he must support himself, but his tastes ran in other and diverse channels.

In his legal associations he was brought into contact with many bright, keen minds, and from them he gained a stimulus to his own mental powers. The morality of the bar was not irreproachable, but Lincoln never lent himself to those practices which, although of questionable character, were yet common among his fellow-barristers. Others might knowingly defend a guilty man, but he would never do so. It mattered not how large the fee offered, he scorned to do or defend or in any way to countenance a dishonorable deed.

In legal learning he was excelled by many of his associates, but in correctness of judgment, fertility of resources and skill in the conduct of a case he had few equals, perhaps no superiors.

Yet as a lawyer alone he would never have gained an extensive or a lasting reputation.

Much of the success of his after career, however, was due to the training which his legal experiences gave. His quick insight into character and motives, his unerring judgment and the rapidity with which he arrived at right conclusions are all directly traceable to this period of his life.

In politics he was a born leader, standing not only before the rank and file of his party, but far above them as well. He led the advance not as a trained woodsman, who tracks the pathless forests by means of landmarks which others have located, but rather like a mariner, who sets out upon an unknown sea, trusting the unerring compass to guide his course.

In the sparse backwoods settlements in his boyhood the political fever was not wont to run high. His father was a Democrat, but not an ardent one; hence, when a biography of Henry Clay fell into the

boy's hands it is a matter of no surprise that he became an earnest believer in the political principles
which found one of their ablest advocates in Clay,
who for years was the object of Lincoln's ardent
admiration.

But Lincoln's character and disposition would not
permit him to become an old line Whig. As he had
pushed on away from the conservative Democratic
party, so he soon found himself entering new fields
and advancing fresh political doctrines as startling as
they were novel.

He was compelled to labor at his legal practice, but
his heart was in politics and he never was so happy as
when engaged in heated discussions or addressing an
audience with fervid eloquence from stump or platform. Few trained debaters could gain an advantage
over him. By argument and ridicule, by a plain and
convincing presentation of his points or by illustrat-
ing them with apt stories he seldom failed to dis-
comfit his adversary.

He not only excelled in the ability to present, his
thoughts, but also in clear and logical thinking. In
all his mental processes he was careful and painstaking, never sparing the labor necessary to perfect
his knowledge. His habits of thinking, as well as of
speech were moulded by his early life. The Bible
formed his chief text-book and he studied it until he
appropriated many of the characteristics of its sublime style and his mind was shaped by its precepts.

His ability as a speaker established for him a permanent sway over the simple-minded people who
made up the bulk of the population. He never failed
to win and retain the attention of his audience, no

matter what the subject of his discourse might be. He accomplished this by having something to say and being able to say it well.

At the bar, on the platform and in the legislative halls he had but one real rival, and that was Douglas. On whatever field they met their rivalry was ever present, generally amicable, sometimes heated, but always intense.

In politics Lincoln was always in advance of his party, so much so, indeed, that he often appeared as the leader of a forlorn hope, apparently courting certain destruction. Although often called a radical the term could never be properly applied to him; while his political ideal was far higher than that of either great party, he was cautious and conservative when any great step was to be taken, and always counted the cost and planned the way with close attention to the smallest details.

He early determined to take a positive and consistent stand against slavery, for he saw that this institution must continue to be the one paramount question at issue between the North and South until it should be settled either peaceably or by force. He did not often give utterance to his feelings, nor was his opposition of that blind, fanatical sort which chose to destroy the institution, even if at the same time constitutional rights should be violated.

The Abolitionists no doubt did a great work in educating the North in anti-slavery sentiments, yet alone they would never have accomplished their purposes. They would oppose violence to violence, lawlessness to lawlessness. Their actions were heroic and self-sacrificing and ·their names will always be honored by lovers of freedom everywhere ; but their role was agitation. The final blow must be struck by stronger hands guided by cooler heads.

With the radical principles of the Abolitionists Lincoln was never in sympathy, partly from a natural repugnance to their methods, and partly from his association with a class of people who tacitly favored Southern principles.

He believed that the institution was radically wrong ; the sound of the lash upon human flesh stung his sensitive feelings to the quick ; the horrors of the slave pen were utterly repugnant to him ; yet slavery was tacitly recognized by the Constitution, and the Constitution was the organic law of the land, hence the institution could not be attacked without assailing the very rock upon which the nation was founded.

He reverenced the Constitution, and recognized that the safety of Republican institutions could only be maintained by an implicit observance of its provisions. Therefore, he could have no sympathy with those who would destroy the Constitution to attain their end, even if that end should be in itself most desirable. On the other hand, he was an uncompromising foe to all attempts to extend slavery beyond the bounds imposed upon it by the Missouri Compromise. Here, then, was the pith of his political doctrines, the one policy he never deviated from. His position was open to attack on both sides and excited bitter hostility from both friend and foe.

He did not enter actively into the struggle until the repeal of the Missouri Compromise, and from that time he devoted his whole soul to the conflict from which he was destined never to rest until slavery had been eliminated from American institutions. In the very beginning he found himself pitted against his old-time rival, Douglas, and until his election to the Presidency they represented the opposing forces in the great issue.

Mr. Lincoln became the soul of the Republican party in the West and its political censor. It was difficult to impress upon his constituents the truth of his ideas in a time when intense and heated partisanship was the rule, and moderation was not recognized as a virtue. He ran the risk of being repudiated by his party and suffered a temporary defeat rather than modify his principles in the least. "I would rather be defeated on this platform," said he, "than win upon any other."

On this question he was so far in advance of his surroundings that it took his party years to learn the wisdom of his views. When the great Senatorial conflict began he felt that the time and opportunity had arrived to demonstrate the truth of his doctrines to the people. He and Douglas entered into the contest with widely varying motives. Douglas sought vindication and re-election, Lincoln sought to educate and convince the people. He felt that the result immediately in view, the Senatorial election, was trivial in comparison with the uplifting impulse which might be given to the cause of freedom and Republican principles. During the whole debate he stood on a higher level than Douglas and made the more profound and lasting impression.

His views were given greater prominence by the great Cooper Union address, which formulated and

fixed the doctrines that were to define the real issue
between the North and South.

During the dark days that followed between his
election and inauguration he did not fail to appreciate the gravity of the situation and was ready to
make any concession to avoid war up to a certain
limit, beyond that he would not go. In an interview
printed in the New York *Tribune*, January 30, 1861, he
said :

"I will suffer death before I will consent or advise
my friends to consent to any concession or compromise which looks like buying the privilege of taking
possession of the Government to which we have a
Constitutional right; because, whatever I might think
of the merit of the various propositions before Congress, I should regard any concession in the face of
menace as the destruction of the Government itself,
and a consent on all hands that our system shall be
brought down to a level with the existing disorganized state of affairs in Mexico. But this thing will
hereafter be, as it is now, in the hands of the people,
and if they desire to call a convention to remove any
grievances complained of, or to give new guarantees
for the permanence of vested rights, it is not mine to
oppose."

He recognized the fact that the threatened war was
the legitimate outgrowth of a century of strife, and
that the exciting cause was slavery, to preserve which
the Southern people were ready to sever their Constitutional relation with the North, and establish a
separate government. He could not fail to appreciate how disastrous would be the blow to the prosperity of both sections, yet he did not base his actions

upon the plea of expediency, but rather on the fundamental principle of the unity of the nation and the binding power of the Constitution. He impatiently brushed aside the fallacy enunciated by Buchanan, who said that it was no doubt contrary to the Constitution for a State to secede, but when it had once seceded, there was no power in the Constitution to compel it to resume its former relations. In Lincoln's opinion the Constitution was a solemn compact which, as it had been ratified by all the States, could only be dissolved by the consent of all.

He could not at first believe that the better sense of the Southern people would sanction secession, and he was willing to make every reasonable concession to them if he might thereby secure peace. In the light of subsequent history it seems passing strange that the Southern people could so persistently misunderstand him. The truth is that they were taught by their leaders to believe him to be the personification of all the most radical elements which were arrayed against slavery. They believed him to be only waiting his opportunity to coerce them by force of arms and to destroy their pet institution with a malignant hatred which would inflict fiery punishment upon the innocent and helpless. The men, who inspired such beliefs, knew better, but they believed the time to be ripe for their purpose and could find no better way to arouse the common people than by warning them of the terrible results that would follow the election of Lincoln.

Through it all the South had no better nor wiser friend than the President-elect. He had frequently denied that he had any desire to interfere with slavery

while kept within Constitutional bounds; and so decided had been his position on this question that he
had almost alienated the abolition element from his
support. For slavery he would never call out an
army nor declare war. But to preserve the unity of
the country and the authority of the Constitution he
would not hesitate to enter upon the most destructive and desolating war of modern times.

It is marvellous that in this distracting period,
when surrounded by multitudes of counsels, and beset by men of all shades of political belief, each one
determined to win him over to his views, and when
almost overwhelmed by the most complicated political problems which modern civilization has ever
presented, that Mr. Lincoln, an untried man,
should have the sagacity to see his only true course
and the firmness to maintain his position when
opposed by the wisdom and prejudice of his political
friends, as well as by the malignant passions of his
enemies.

At the very time when many believed that he was
demonstrating his unfitness for the position, he was
really giving the best evidence of his superiority over
all the political leaders of the day. History hardly
affords a parallel case and America alone of all countries offers the possibility of its occurrence. A man of
little culture, inexperienced in the details of government, coming from the lowest walks in life, steps forward and solves the difficulties of a situation in the
presence of which the oldest and most astute statesmen
stand helpless. No other evidence than this is needed
of the fact that an all-wise Providence presides over the
destinies of the great Republic and directs its affairs.

Without Lincoln the secession would have become an accomplished fact.

In the general conduct of the war he seldom erred. Where a principle of action was involved he arrived at the right decision by an unerring judgment that amounted almost to intuition. He made many mistakes, but they were largely the results of inexperience, and were mainly in the working out of details.

He tried the patience of many good patriots by not declaring war as soon as hopes of a peaceful solution of the difficulty had passed away, but he saw the immense moral advantage to be gained by compelling the South to become the aggressor, and he did the hardest of all things when he waited while all his surroundings seemed to summon him to action.

The dreadful disasters of the first year of the war are traceable only indirectly to him : they were the legitimate results of the weak, compromising policy of his predecessor and the, as yet, undemonstrated inefficiency of responsible officers.

History shows the surprising fact that no great military movement which was undertaken contrary to his judgment, ever resulted in permanent advantage, while no policy originated and inforced by him, failed to meet with some degree of success. And yet he was an utter stranger to the art of war on the March day when he first assumed the duties of the Presidential office.

His profound sagacity was again shown in the events which preceded and led up to the emancipation proclamation. As a political policy, emancipation never found an advocate in him, for he believed it to be contrary to the provisions of the Constitution.

It was only when the exigencies of the war plainly demanded it that he issued the proclamation, and then only as a military measure.

His delay was ascribed to every possible motive. Many trusted him and were ready to await the opportunity which should be approved by his judgment. Others fretted and bewailed his hesitation and sought to end it by every means in their power. Pressure was brought to bear upon him from all quarters. Delegations of clergymen quoted the words of the Crusaders of old " God wills it." Philanthropists besought him in the name of humanity ; statesmen demanded it as a political necessity; Abolitionists asked it as a consummation of their half century of labor and suffering; military officers told him that it was the only thing that would quell the rising disaffection in the army and unite in the support of the Union all right-minded people. Countless delegations thronged his reception rooms and the mails were flooded with appeals, yet he could not be moved by any of them. Though deeply affected, neither prayers, commands nor threats could induce him to take action until his judgment approved the opportunity.

The will of one man alone stood between the country and incalculable disasters, but that will was strong as adamant.

He made himself not only the civil but military leader of the country. In every department of the Army and Navy, his directing influence was felt. Necessarily the most of the details were intrusted to his subordinates and wherever an official proved himself worthy he gave him the widest latitude.

Had Lincoln been in the field in command of the national forces the war would have been fought more vigorously and more quickly. Strict military tactics might not always have been regarded, and some movements not recognized by the manual, might have been executed, but even if it were unconventionally waged, the war would have lacked nothing of vigor and directness.

It is detracting nothing from the glorious services of officers and men, whether in the Cabinet and Capitol or on the field, to say that the President formed one of the chief elements in the success of the Federal arms.

Mr. Lincoln never had the opportunity to demonstrate his sagacity in the solution of the great problems developed by the successful issue of the war. The reconstruction of the seceded States involved many complicated questions and delicate considerations. There were many theories whose value could only be proven by application, and their application might be disastrous.

He had given a long and careful consideration to the matter, and it is known that he had early formulated a policy by which to guide his actions. This policy was a generous one, more generous than ever a conqueror had dictated to a conquered people before. It was never subjected to a satisfactory test for he was assassinated before the opportunity arrived. There is little reason to doubt, however, that it would have been at least as successful as the one which was afterwards put in force.

The angularities of his character often overshadowed his great merits, but the verdict of history is unaffected by many of the characteristics which were most evident to his associates. His greatness grows as time passes by and his character is better appreciated.

CHAPTER XXV.

IN regard to his religious views he was always extremely reticent. He seldom referred to the subject in conversation, even with his friends, yet it is plain that during the last years of his life he was actuated by high religious principles. Now and then a chance utterance, together with the deep reverence which pervades his proclamations and other public addresses, afford nearly all the authentic testimony we have on the subject.

He cared little for doctrinal beliefs or sectarian differences, but rather grasped the broad principles of religion which are common to all devout people of whatever denomination.

Mr. Fell, an old acquaintance, says of him : "His religious views were eminently practical and are summed up, as I think, in these two propositions : the Fatherhood of God and the brotherhood of man. He fully believed in a superintending and overruling Providence that guides and controls the operations of the world, but maintained that law and order, and not their violation or suspension, are the appointed means by which this Providence is exercised."[1]

Mrs. Lincoln once said to Mr. Herndon : "Mr. Lincoln had no faith and no hope in the usual accept-

---

[1] Herndon's "Life of Lincoln," p. 444.

ation of those words. He never joined a church;
but still, as I believe, he was a religious man by
nature. He first seemed to think about the subject
when our boy Willie died, and then more than ever
about the time he went to Gettysburg; but it was a
kind of poetry in his nature and he was never a technical Christian." [1]

Mr. Herndon, who had exceptional opportunities to
observe his inner life, says "The world has always
insisted on making an orthodox Christian of him, and
to analyze his sayings or sound his beliefs is but to
break the idol. It only remains to say that whether
orthodox or not, he believed in God and immortality;
and even if he questioned the existence of future eternal punishment, he hoped to find a rest from trouble
and a heaven beyond the grave. If at any time in his
life he was skeptical of the Divine origin of the Bible,
he ought not for that reason to be condemned; for
he accepted the practical precepts of the great Book
as binding alike on his head and conscience. The
benevolence of his impulses, the seriousness of his
convictions, and the nobility of his character are evidences unimpeachable that his soul was ever filled
with the exalted purity and sublime faith of natural
religion." [2]

He was particularly impressed with the efficacy of
prayer and more than once bore testimony to his
belief in it.

"I have been driven many times to my knees," he
once remarked, "by the overwhelming conviction
that I had nowhere else to go. My own wisdom, and

[1] Herndon's "Life of Lincoln," p. 445.
[2] The same p. 446.

that of all about me, seemed insufficient for that day."

In speaking of his mother he said to a friend : "I remember her prayers and they have always followed me. They have clung to me all my life."

Upon the death of his son Willie, a Christian lady assured him that many Christians were praying for him, he replied : "I am glad to hear that, I want them to pray for me. I need their prayers."

A clergyman once said in his presence that he hoped "the Lord was on our side."

"I am not at all concerned about that," replied Mr. Lincoln, "for I know that the Lord is always on the side of the right. But it is my constant anxiety and prayer that I and this nation should be on the Lord's side."

It is but just to say that many of his early friends affirm that in his younger days he was not only irreligious but that he was a positive atheist. It is said that he delighted to deny the inspiration of the Bible, the divinity of Jesus Christ and the existence of God, and, furthermore, that he once wrote a bold, atheistical treatise which he intended to have printed but which a wise friend secured and destroyed. These allegations are so at variance with his character in after life that it is difficult to believe them. It is certain that, if they are true, he gained wisdom with advancing years and abandoned his atheistical belief.

It is pleasant to turn from these statements to his proclamations aud public addresses during the war. No President has ever evinced a more exalted piety or deeper reverence for the Supreme Being in his public utterances than did Lincoln, and no one who knows the native sincerity and honesty of the man, can believe they were assumed.

In a letter to Rev. Alexander Reed, the General Superintendent of the Christian Commission, dated February 22, 1863, he said :

"Whatever shall be, sincerely and in God's name, devised for the good of the soldiers and seamen in their hard spheres of duty, can scarcely fail to be blessed; and whatever shall tend to turn our thoughts from the unreasoning and uncharitable passions, prejudices and jealousies incident to a great national trouble, such as ours, and to fix them on the vast and long enduring consequences, for weal or woe, which are to result from the struggle, and especially to strengthen our reliance upon the Supreme Being for the final triumph of the right, cannot but be well for us all."

During the summer of 1863 the feelings of the people were wrought up to the highest pitch. The air was full of the rumors of a Northern invasion. It was known that Lee was making extensive preparations for an expedition into Pennsylvania with the intention of carrying the war into the hitherto peaceful regions of the North. The siege of Vicksburg was dragging along with little apparent prospect of ultimate success. When the news came of the fall of the Southern stronghold and, almost at the same time, of the great victory at Gettysburg, the rejoicing of the people was unrestrained. It was during this period of jubilation that Mr. Lincoln issued a proclamation,

"To set apart a time in the near future, to be observed as a day for national thanksgiving, praise and

prayer to Almighty God, for the wonderful things he
had done in the nation's behalf, and to invoke the
influence of his Holy Spirit to subdue the anger
which has produced and so long sustained a needless
and cruel rebellion, to change the hearts of the insurgents, to guide the councils of the Government
with wisdom adequate to so great a national emergency, and to visit with tender care and consolation
throughout the length and breadth of our land, all
those who, through the vicissitudes and marches,
voyages, battles and sieges, had been brought to suffer
in mind, body or estate, and finally to lead the whole
nation through paths of repentance and submission
to the Divine will, back to the perfect enjoyment of
Union and fraternal peace."

.   .   .   .

"It has pleased Almightly God to hearken to the
supplications and prayers of an afflicted people, and to
vouchsafe to the Army and Navy of the United States,
on the land and on the sea, victories so signal and so
effective as to furnish reasonable grounds for augmented confidence that the Union of these States will
be maintained, their Constitution preserved, and their
peace and prosperity permanently secured ; but these
victories have been accorded, not without sacrifice of
life, limb and liberty incurred by brave, patriotic and
loyal citizens.   Domestic affliction in every part of
the country follows in the train of these fearful
bereavements.

"It is meet and right to recognize and confess the
presence of the Almighty Father and the power of His
hand equally in these triumphs and these sorrows."

His proclamation, issued at the close of the event-

ful summer of 1863, setting apart a day for national
thanksgiving, has rarely been excelled in beauty of
language and exalted sentiment. It is not possible
that the man who penned these lines cherished any
doubts as to the existence of God or that he believed
Him to be only a beneficent first principle pervading
the universe.

"The year that is drawing towards its close has
been filled with the blessings of fruitful fields and
healthful skies.

"To these bounties, which are so constantly enjoyed
that we are prone to forget the source from which
they come, others have been added which are of
so extraordinary a nature that they cannot fail to
penetrate and soften even the heart which is habitually insensible to the ever-watchful Providence of
Almighty God.

"In the midst of a civil war of unparalleled magnitude and severity, which has sometimes seemed to
invite and provoke the aggressions of foreign States,
peace has been preserved with all nations, order has
been maintained, the laws have been respected and
obeyed, and harmony has prevailed everywhere
except in the theatre of military conflict, while that
theatre has been greatly contracted by the advancing
armies and navies of the Union.

"The needful diversion of wealth and strength from
the fields of peaceful industry to the national defense
has not arrested the plow, the shuttle, or the ship.

"The ax has enlarged the borders of our settlements, and the mines, as well of iron and coal as of
the precious metals, have yielded even more abun-
dantly than heretofore.

"Population has steadily increased, notwithstanding the waste that has been made in the camp, the siege and the battlefield ; and the country, rejoicing in the consciousness of augmented strength and vigor, is permitted to expect a continuance of years, with large increase of freedom.

"No human council hath devised, nor hath any mortal hand worked out these great things. They are the gracious gifts of the most high God, who, while dealing with us in anger for our sins, hath, nevertheless, remembered mercy.

"It has seemed to me fit and proper that they should be solemnly, reverently and gratefully acknowledged, as with one heart and voice, by the whole American people. I do therefore invite my fellow-citizens in every part of the United States, and also those who are at sea, and those who are sojourning in foreign lands, to set apart and observe the last Thursday of November next as a day of thanksgiving and prayer to our beneficent Father, who dwells in the heavens ; and I recommend to them that while offering up the ascriptions, justly due to Him for such singular deliverances and blessings, they do also, with humble penitence for our national perverseness and disobedience, commend to His tender care all those who have become widows, orphans, mourners, or sufferers in the lamentable civil strife in which we are unavoidably engaged, and fervently implore the interposition of the Almighty hand to heal the wounds of the Nation, and restore it, as soon as may be consistent with the Divine purposes, to the full enjoyment of peace, harmony, tranquility and union."

In a letter written to Mrs. Eliza P. Gurney, dated September 30, 1864, the following passage occurs: " I am much indebted to the good Christian people of the country for their constant prayers and consolations, and to no one of them more than yourself. The purposes of the Almighty are perfect and must prevail, though we erring mortals may fail to accurately perceive them in advance. We hoped for a happy termination of this terrible war long before this; but God knows best and has ruled otherwise. We shall yet acknowledge His wisdom and our own errors therein; meanwhile, we must work earnestly in the best light He gives us, trusting that so working conduces to the great end He so ordains. Surely He intends some great good to follow this mighty convulsion which no mortal could make, and no mortal could stay. Your people, the Friends, have had, and are having, very great trials on principles and faith opposed to both war and oppression. They can only practically oppose oppression by war. In this hard dilemma some have chosen one horn and some the other.

" For those appealing to me on conscientious grounds I have done and shall do the best I could and can, in my own conscience, under my oath to the land. That you believe this I doubt not and, believing it, I shall still receive for my country and myself your earnest prayers to our Father in heaven."

A few words of his illustrate a different aspect of the same question, and give more than a hint at the practical, every-day character of his religion.

Late in 1864, two ladies from Tennessee came to the President to beg for the release of their husbands,

who were held as prisoners of war at Johnson's
Island. They were accorded several interviews before their request was granted, and at each visit one
of the ladies urged, as additional grounds for her
husband's release that he was a religious man. Finally their request was granted, and the order was
given for their release. Mr. Lincoln said to the lady,
who had reminded him so persistently of her husband's religious character :

"You say your husband is a religious man ; tell
him when you meet him that I say I am not much of
a judge of religion, but that, in my opinion the
religion that sets men to rebel and fight against this
Government, because, as they think, that Government doesn't sufficiently help some men to eat their
bread on the sweat of other men's faces, is not the
sort of religion upon which people can get to
heaven."

These illustrations show that his thoughts were
not wholly centred on the things of this world, but
that he had pondered deeply upon the higher problems of life, that he had felt the need of light, and
had sought until he found it.

He was not a constant attendant upon church services, but this is far from proving that he was heed-
less of religious influences. The seeds of true religion
are not necessarily planted within the walls of a
sanctuary.

That religion is truest and best whose profession is
made in a pure life and a self-sacrificing love for
humanity. The spirit of Christ may manifest itself
more perfectly in deeds than in words.

If ever a man lived a religious life that man was

Abraham Lincoln.   Love to God and love to man
was his creed.   The world was his church.   His sermons were preached in kindly words and merciful
deeds.   His loving benediction still rests upon the
heads of millions of his fellow-men, whom he raised
up from the humiliation of bondage to the level of
manhood and womanhood.

> "O, slow to smite and swift to spare,
>   Gentle and merciful and just !
> Who, in the fear of God, didst bear
>   The sword of power—a nation's trust !
>
> "Thy task is done ; the bond are free ;
>   We bear thee to an honored grave,
> Whose proudest monument shall be
>   The broken fetters of the slave.
>
> "Pure was thy life ; its bloody close
>   Has placed thee with the sons of light,
> Among the noble host of those
>   Who perished in the cause of Right."

INDEX.